Wildflowers of Terezin

WILDFLOWERS OF TEREZIN

Robert Elmer

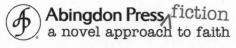

Abingdon Press fiction
a novel approach to faith
Nashville, Tennessee

Published by Abingdon Press, P.O. Box 801, Nashville, TN 37202
www.abingdonpress.com
All rights reserved.

Published in association with the literary agency of Alive Communications, Inc.,
7680 Goddard Street, Suite 200, Colorado Springs, Colorado, 80920,
www.alivecommunications.com.

Cover design by Anderson Design Group, Nashville, TN

This book is printed on acid-free paper.

Library of Congress Cataloging-in-Publication Data

Elmer, Robert.
Wildflowers of Terezin / Robert Elmer.
   p. cm.
ISBN 978-1-4267-0192-4 (pbk. : alk. paper)
1. Clergy—Denmark—Fiction. 2. Jews—Denmark—Fiction. 3. World War, 1939-
1945—Underground movements—Denmark—Fiction. 4. Jews—Persecutions—
Denmark—Fiction. 5. World War, 1939-1945—Jews—Rescue—Denmark—Fiction.
6. Theresienstadt (Concentration camp)—Fiction. I. Title.
PS3555.L44W56 2010
813'.54—dc22

                                    2009046457

Printed in the United States of America

1 2 3 4 5 6 7 8 9 10 / 15 14 13 12 11 10

To Mogens Maagaard

Mange tak, min ven.
Many thanks, my friend.

1

I live in a crazy time.

— ANNE FRANK

H anne Abrahamsen awoke with a start in the middle of a bad dream, something about being in nursing school once again and a man who looked like Adolf Hitler (but with the face of a codfish) announcing at her graduation that she was a Jew, and didn't everyone already know that? The graduation had stopped, and she remembered wanting desperately to escape but not being able to move.

Hanne had never thought much about dreams, or cared. Until now.

Somewhere outside her window she heard what had awakened her: a line of cars and trucks roaring through the narrow streets of *København*, on their way to the devil's business. And even louder at this time of the morning, when the only ones awake were the *skrallemænd*, emptying garbage.

She shivered and pulled up the covers to her chin, but couldn't put away the feeling that something was not right. It was not the first time she'd heard German vehicles at odd hours, so maybe it was just the dream. Still, she slipped out of bed to check the window that faced *Tuborgvej*. Of all the nurses' apartments on the *Bispebjerg* Hospital campus, hers commanded the best, and sometimes the noisiest, view of the city. She shivered at the September predawn chill, reaching the window in time to peek through the heavy blackout shade and see a pair of brake lights flash as a vehicle careened around the corner.

"Well, they're in a hurry, aren't they?" she mumbled, pushing at the upper pane of her window to keep out the draft.

A Dane? Not likely. No *dansker* would dare make so much noise at this time of the morning—especially not after all the troubles and tension they'd seen here in København over the past several months. After the strikes and all the troubles this past summer, no one wanted to make themselves a target.

No, she'd heard German vehicles—and then another truck screeching around the corner confirmed what she'd feared. This one carried armed soldiers in back, holding on for dear life. This could only mean that the Germans had stepped up their campaigns against the Danish Underground—and that they were flexing their muscle in an early morning raid somewhere in the city.

Hanne drew back as the little cuckoo on the wall of her kitchen sounded four . . . five . . . six times.

"Too early, my cuckoo friend," she told the clock with a sigh. "Though I suppose I needed to get up for the morning shift, anyway."

But she stood there, shivering in her nightgown and bare feet, unable to move and unable to forget her dream—or the nightmare outside her window.

———⊗∞∞⊗———

ON THE STREETS OF KØBENHAVN
FRIDAY MORNING, 17 SEPTEMBER 1943

"We're late."

Wolfschmidt frowned and checked his watch once more as he squeezed the backdoor handle. Was he the only one in this operation who cared about being punctual? It would take a Gestapo man's attention to detail to make this work.

His young driver from the *schutzpolizei*, the German Security Police, mumbled a weak apology and wiped a bead of sweat from his forehead as they squealed past the famous Round Tower, then careened around the corner and approached the Jewish synagogue on *Krystalgade*.

Ahead and to the right, he could make out the large, blond-bricked building, rather square and squat despite a row of stained-glass windows running the length of the second floor level and a stepped roof even higher to the rear. Wolfschmidt thought it rather base looking and nowhere near as grand as a proper German cathedral, though that did not surprise him. A place of worship, indeed!

"Do you see it?" Wolfschmidt sat on the edge of his seat and pointed to a clear spot on the curb, directly in front of a gate in the street-level fence. "Stop there."

"Yes, *Herr Sturmbannführer*," replied the driver, using Wolfschmidt's proper Gestapo title. At least he could do that correctly. But now Wolfschmidt grabbed the young man's shoulder to get his attention and to go over their instructions yet one more time. Despite the utter routine of their action this morning, Wolfschmidt couldn't help feeling his heart pounding in his ears. He was made for this work.

———⊗∞∞⊗———

"Listen carefully, *Anwärter*," he told the young recruit. "You will accompany me into the building. I will be two steps behind you. If any doors are locked you will break them down. If anyone tries to stop you or question you, step aside and I will deal with it. Keep your weapon holstered but loaded and ready."

"I understand." The driver shut off the car's ignition and waited. The good news was that if they needed to, Wolfschmidt was confident this large young man had the required beef to make his way through any door they needed, locked or otherwise. Much more so than Wolfschmidt himself, who was slight of build and might break his shoulder if he attempted such heroics.

"Good. We will locate this librarian and escort him back to the car, so he will assist us in our task."

Again the driver nodded. How hard could this be? But by now they were almost five minutes off schedule, and Wolfschmidt could feel his anxiety rising as he pushed open his door and stepped out into the cool September air. No more delays. No more foolishness.

"All right, then," hissed Wolfschmidt. "Let's be about our business."

He straightened his high-peaked gray hat where it perched on his precisely short-cropped blond hair, then checked to be sure his matching gray trousers still held a crease after his short ride. Why was it so hard to find anyone in *København* who knew how to properly clean and press his uniform? Soon that would change, however, once this war was won and a more full measure of the Reich's efficiency found its way to this city.

Or they could simply flatten it and start over. In his opinion that might prove to be the more efficient solution. Frankly, he didn't care either way.

"After you." Wolfschmidt waved for the young man to lead the way through the gate.

Happily it swung open with hardly a complaint, though he had to say that didn't surprise him, either. These Danes had no sense of how to secure their buildings. They would be content, he imagined, to remain fat and protected by Germany, enjoying their cheese and beer and sending the best of their own produce to help keep the German army well-fed. In this way they could at least be useful, even if too many of them did not appreciate the advantage such an arrangement posed to their wealth and security. What did the Danes know of that?

Three steps up from the outer gate, the building's large oak outer door swung open just as easily. This was going to be too simple. Checking his own pistol, Wolfschmidt stepped in behind the driver as they entered a high-ceilinged foyer. It smelled of ancient, institutional dust in the way of most such buildings, which gave him even more reason to despise the place. He stepped on the driver's heel to hurry him along.

Beyond the red-carpeted foyer a set of double doors with small glass windows opened into the synagogue's main auditorium, an expansive room with lofty ceilings and a horseshoe-shaped balcony level all around the back.

This could make a fine movie theater, he thought, and made a mental note of it.

But right now he focused on the task at hand, which would lead the way for a more sensible use of the building. Up in front, a cluster of twenty or thirty men had gathered for their Friday morning prayer service, dressed in the peculiar head garb that left no doubt of their religion.

Wolfschmidt had not come to pray. Despite his revulsion at being found in such a place, he straightened his back and coolly strode to where a robed, bearded man stood before the group. This would be the rabbi. And by this time they had stopped their prayer, or whatever Jewish thing they were doing, and all stared wide-eyed at the remarkable impertinence of Wolfschmidt and his assistant.

"Pardon me, sir," began the rabbi, visibly shaken as he should be, "but—"

"Josef Fischer will accompany us immediately." Wolfschmidt interrupted the rabbi. He naturally had no time for nonsense or small talk, even if he had been so inclined. To emphasize his commands he made a point of moving a hand to his holster, making certain they all noticed. They would understand his meaning, if not his German.

He needn't have worried. A pink-faced little man in the front row stepped out after an uncomfortable silence, gently pushing aside the hand of a friend who halfheartedly tried to hold him back.

"Ich bin Fischer," said the man, who adjusted a pair of round spectacles and stepped up to face them. He ignored the whispered warnings of his nearby friends, which Wolfschmidt counted for blind stupidity. So this was the man they'd gone to all this trouble to apprehend?

He might have respected a little more defiance, just for sport, even though this man stood a full foot shorter than himself. But never mind. They would all face the same fate, sooner rather than later. This Josef Fischer could appear brave as much as he wanted to, for all the *sturmbannführer* cared.

He signaled with a nod so that his assistant grabbed Fischer by the back of the collar and guided him roughly back up the aisle toward the exit. The man's tasseled prayer shawl fell at Wolfschmidt's feet, but when the Jew bent to pick it up Wolfschmidt couldn't resist holding it to the floor with the toe of his boot.

"Keep walking!" ordered Wolfschmidt.

"Wait!" objected the rabbi. "What has he done? You can't just come in here like this, disrupt our prayer meeting, and abduct our people!"

Wolfschmidt would have gladly taken on this man, here and now, had it not been for his specific orders and the even more specific task at hand. But with a deliberate motion he picked up the shawl and quite deliberately tore it in two. The ripping sound pleased him, even more as he watched the expressions on the men's faces turn from fright to horror.

Without another word of explanation he turned on his heel to follow his assistant and their charge out to the waiting car.

———

Fifteen minutes later Sturmbannführer Wolfschmidt stood with arms crossed in the middle of the Jewish Community Center offices on *Ny Kongensgade*, New King's Street. Surely it didn't need to take this long to find a simple file of addresses?

And this librarian—Fischer—worse than useless. They could have easily broken down the front door, and never mind the keys which the little man now held in his trembling hands as he watched five uniformed schutzpolizei taking apart his office, file by useless file.

"It's not in this one, either," reported one of the polizei, tossing another file drawer into the middle of the room. Still the librarian trembled.

"You're wasting our time!" cried Wolfschmidt. "Or would you rather we simply torch this place and be done with it? We're going to find it, whether we destroy your office or not."

———

Fischer looked to be in pain as he closed his eyes and mouthed . . . what, a prayer? Little good it did him now, because a moment later one of the schutzpolizei let out a cry as he pried open a locked metal file cabinet with a crowbar.

"I think I found something!" said the young man. Fischer winced but said nothing as they poured out the contents of the drawer, and then another—hundreds upon hundreds of cards, each one neatly printed with a name and address. Wolfschmidt smiled and stepped over to pick one up.

"Davidsen, Noah." He smiled as he fingered the card. "You don't imagine this could be a Jewish name, by chance?"

By this time the schutzpolizei had dumped the contents of several drawers on the floor. Which was all very well, but now they would just have to gather them all up and cart them away.

"In a box," he said with a wave. "All of them."

All of them, yes. The name and address of every Jew in this little country—and that would constitute close to seven thousand names. Perhaps that didn't amount to much, compared to populations in other countries they had liberated. But it was enough to make their job much easier when the time came.

And that, he knew, would be very soon.

2

*The matter is very simple. The Bible is very easy to understand.
But . . . we pretend to be unable to understand it because
we know very well the minute we understand, we are obliged
to act accordingly.*
—SØREN KIERKEGAARD

*P*astor Steffen Arne Petersen never cared much for broken glass. Neither the sound nor the feel of it, even less the sensation of having Hans Larsen's bakery window rain down in crystal slivers atop his head. But having left the parsonage in such a hurry, he had not taken the time this cool September evening to find his hat, which in hindsight he now wished he might have done.

It might have shielded his head a bit more as he skidded out of control and tumbled off his sensible, black, Danish-built gentleman's bicycle—a gift from the congregation for five years' of service since his graduation from seminary in 1938.

But all he could think of now was rescuing the small communion set he carried in his inside coat pocket, the tiny bottle of wine and package of cross-stamped wafers he should have left in their velvet-lined case but had simply grabbed so his favorite eighty-four-year-old parishioner might enjoy the Lord's Supper from her sick bed at Bispebjerg Hospital.

Under the circumstances, he thought, *Fru Kanstrup might forgive me for arriving a few minutes late.* That, and he wondered how much trouble it might be to repair his only means of transportation.

He did not think of himself yet, even as he plowed the pavement with his chin and came to rest on the sidewalk just past the bakery. The little handbag he'd strapped to the back of the bicycle tumbled along beside him, although his robe and pleated clerical collar would be all right.

In contrast, his head buzzed in shock at the impact, and the cuff of his black trousers tangled in the bicycle chain, but nothing hurt as he might have expected.

Yet.

Three more muffled explosions echoed down the street and off the five-story graystone buildings fronting *Nørrebrogade*, North Bridge Street, the wide *København* boulevard. Gunshots. He'd heard such before, unfortunately, and more often of late. As he did his best to shield himself while gasping for breath, a rough shout echoed from down the street.

"Head down, fool!"

"Yes, of course." Steffen ignored the rudeness but did his best to crouch closer against the bakery building, where even the bricks smelled of generations of fresh rolls. Yet he felt something wet against his side, imagined he was bleeding, and whispered to himself. "But how am I going to get another bike tire?"

At the moment no one had an answer for him. After a bit more shouting, shooting, and general unpleasantness had shattered the muggy evening air (not to mention several more windows), he dared look around to see if anyone found themselves in a similar predicament. It wouldn't do to have passersby see the pastor of *Sankt Stefan's Kirke*, Saint Steven's Church, lying in an undignified heap on the pavement.

Two more shots made him duck again.

Troublemakers, he told himself. *They shouldn't rush their own funerals.*

Funerals he would likely be called upon to conduct. Since he could at the moment do nothing about it, he thought it best to at least get inside—though pulling free of his wrecked bicycle and standing up would not prove as easy as he'd hoped. Not when much of his body remained backwards and improbably twisted.

Then he saw the blood on the pavement and on his hand when he touched his chin, wet and warm. He could smell the vague, salty dampness even before tasting it.

"Not so good, I'm afraid," he whispered. He was used to seeing a bit of blood at the butcher's shop, but not his own. It appeared just as red.

This time when he tried to twist himself free from the wreckage, he felt a bite in his right side, just above the belt. A few moments later his starched white shirt had soaked crimson like a red-and-white Danish flag.

Pretty, almost.

At once fascinated and horrified, he couldn't decide whether to hold his side or cradle his chin. In any case, he knew he had to get up, despite all the terrible noise. So he yanked his legs back as hard as he could, ignoring the pain that shot through his twisted knee. Now his head was too dizzy, and a woman scurried by with her dog and disappeared into the shelter of a nearby alleyway.

Please, Lord, don't let it be someone from my church.

Even if it was, his light head overruled, he would politely ask her for a helping hand, *if you please?*

"*Være så venlig?*"

But no one stopped as his rattled mind loosened its moorings, slipping away from what he knew of Holy Communion, twisted bicycles, and broken bodies. When he finally touched his hand to his shirt he realized what kind of glass had actually punctured his side.

The little bottle of communion wine. That was it! The blood of Christ, symbolic or not, mingled with his own blood, very real indeed. There might be a sermon illustration in there, somewhere. Right now, though, he couldn't think of it.

"Fru Kanstrup will forgive my being detained," he whispered.

She must. He heard another popping sound, no, two, and then a pair of shoes running on the pavement past his head. But by that time he wasn't at all certain if his eyes were open or closed, or why it had grown so dark so quickly. And he heard that rough voice again, only this time much closer.

"Let's get you out of here."

Steffen looked up to see a young man with flaming red hair crouching next to him, grabbing him by the collar and hauling him like a sack of potatoes across the pavement and into an alleyway. Well, was that necessary?

He might have objected, but yet another shot echoed in his ears as the young fellow with the red hair pulled him to safety. Or perhaps it was thunder he heard this time, or another warning.

"Nikolai! Let him go!"

And that was all he remembered.

"Oh, dear!" The other young nurse looked up from the shattered glass on the hospital floor with a big-eyed expression of terror. "Your flowers, Hanne! I'm so sorry. I didn't mean to—"

"Don't worry about it, Ann-Grete." Floor supervisor Hanne Abrahamsen didn't have time today to worry about dropped vases, no matter who the expensive flowers came from. She patted her friend on the shoulder as she sidestepped the mess. "Just let's be sure to sweep it up before Dr. Jørgensen sees. You know how he gets after . . ."

No need to finish the sentence. Her voice trailed off as she rubbed her eyes and checked her wristwatch.

After working the past fifteen hours straight.

"You won't tell your boyfriend, I hope." Ann-Grete bent to pick out the roses from the glass mess. "See? I'll put them back in water right away. He won't know the difference."

"Ann-Grete, he's not my—oh, forget it. Thanks." Hanne nodded and checked her clipboard, forcing her addled brain to make mental notes as she hurried down the hallway and past the survivors of this latest riot. This past summer København had been heating up in more ways than one, as street demonstrations grew more and more violent. Flowers were the least of her worries.

In 39A, gunshot wounds to the shoulder. He'd been lucky the shooter's aim was a bit off. In 40B, multiple fractures after a run-in with a German guard swinging a half-empty bottle of Tuborg. She wondered how the poor man had made it home. And then there was Room 41, the priest. She paused at the door, wondering if she should bother him.

"Awake yet, Father?"

He blinked, and again. Looked up at her with the same weak, puzzled expression most people wore when waking up in a strange hospital bed.

"I was on my way to Bispebjerg Hospital . . ." His voice cracked. Likely he still didn't know where he was.

"You made it."

"In a manner of speaking." Now he tried to straighten up, which, given the tubes he wore pinned to his arm, might not have been the best of plans. "I was going there to visit one of my parishioners and found myself in the middle of a street battle. Poor timing, I'm afraid. And now—"

"Here, don't move." She stepped in and took his hand. "You've lost some blood."

"Blood . . . *ja*." He looked up at her peaked nurse's cap and understanding finally flooded his eyes. "Oh! Well, as long as I can borrow some more, I'll be happy to return it in a few weeks."

At least he still owned a sense of humor. That had to be a good sign.

"That won't be necessary, Father." She popped a glass thermometer into his mouth and located his pulse as he mumbled and gestured with his free hand. But when he tried to reach for the instrument she beat him to it, pulling it back out enough for him to tell her.

"Just 'Pastor' is fine." He smiled, and even behind the bandages on his chin and forehead she noticed the nice row of teeth and a very pleasant twinkle in his blue Scandinavian eyes. "I'm not a Catholic priest, you know."

"I see." She popped the thermometer back in. Priest or pastor, it was all the same to her—though she had to admit the man was charming, in a different sort of way. "You've had a concussion. And you were just lucky all that broken glass didn't put your eye out."

This time he rolled the thermometer to the side of his mouth like a cigarette.

"Ah, luck. Now there's an interesting concept. You believe in it?"

She smiled and adjusted it so he couldn't talk.

"You may call it whatever you like, *Pastor*. My job at the moment is simply to keep you quiet long enough to take your pulse and temperature. And if you don't stop talking, I have another way to find out if you're running a fever. Whichever you prefer."

That settled him down just fine, until Hanne finally extracted the thermometer from between his lips with a brief, professional smile. Except now Ann-Grete burst in, her face flushed with excitement.

"There's a German officer out in the hall!" hissed the other nurse, eyes bulging. "I told him to wait, but he's asking all about—"

Uninvited, the black-eyed man in a matching black Gestapo uniform stepped into the room.

"I'm sorry." Almost without thinking Hanne stepped up to block his entry, like a mother hen protecting chicks. "The patients in this room are not able to see any visitors. You'll have to wait out—"

"I'm here to speak with a man who was involved in an incident on Nørrebrogade." He tried to slip by her as he checked a small notebook, but she sidestepped and gave no ground. "A man on a bicycle, wearing a pastor's collar? We just need to ask him a few questions. A routine matter."

Routine? Hanne knew that with the German occupiers nothing was routine. And this fellow spoke with the kind of heavily accented Danish that blended an unseemly gargle of German phrases, just as unwelcome as the sputum of a highly contagious bronchitis patient. Still she refused to flinch, crossing her arms and resisting the temptation to shield her face. Sweat trickled down the back of her neck and she clamped her fingers tightly so no one would notice their trembling.

"As you can see," she spat back, speeding up her diction out of spite, "he's heavily sedated for the moment. He couldn't speak with anyone if he wanted to. Not to the doctor, even. And most certainly not to you."

She hoped the pastor would catch her meaning as she turned to see him lying with his eyes closed and his hands folded on his chest, the picture of serenity. Good boy.

"Hmm." The German frowned and finally backed up a step. If he peered around Hanne's squared shoulder he would surely not miss the black coat jacket still hanging beside the bed. "I'll ignore your rudeness for now. But I *will* be back in the morning, then, when he *will* be awake and able to answer my queries."

Without another word he swiveled on his polished black boots and strutted out the door, leaving a trail of black scuff-marks behind him on the newly polished tile floor.

No introduction, no names, and no one said a word until several long moments later. That's when Hanne finally breathed.

"Wow, Hanne." Ann-Grete checked down the hallway, still white-knuckling the doorframe. "You were a bulldog. I never knew."

And speaking of not knowing . . . Hanne turned to their "heavily sedated" patient with a frown. She didn't want to imagine the trouble he could have brought on them—or might still.

"You didn't tell me you were in the Resistance, Pastor."

He opened his eyes and looked around, eyes wide this time.

"Is it safe to talk?" he wondered aloud. "Because I don't know why you're doing this, but—"

"It's all right." She raised her hand. "You don't have to explain anything to me. In fact, I'd rather you didn't. It's much better that way."

"No, you don't understand."

"Did you see his beady little eyes?" Ann-Grete kept watch at the door. "I saw a snake like that at the zoo in Frederiksberg, once. Gave me nightmares when I was a little girl."

"I know what you mean." Inwardly, Hanne shivered the same way she had when the German trucks had awakened her out of her Adolf Hitler nightmare. But outwardly she made very sure her voice carried enough gravity so there would be no mistaking her intent. "But as soon as the Gestapo fellow is out of the building, we're moving our pastor out of here."

"Moving? Where?" If Ann-Grete's eyes got any bigger . . .

"He will be checked out of this ward immediately. Paperwork will indicate he was well enough to return home."

"But I thought the doctor said he wanted to observe him overnight."

Hanne sighed.

"Then we'll move him down to the psychiatric ward for now, just for a short time. If anyone asks we'll say he's confused and we don't know his name. You understand?"

"He's not the only one who's confused." But now Ann-Grete nodded seriously as Hanne finished her instructions. Ann-Grete was a good first-year nurse, even if it took her a little longer to catch on.

"And I don't have to tell you—"

This time Ann-Grete nodded gravely.

"I understand. No more paperwork. Just a note that he's been discharged."

Good. But just to be sure, Hanne glanced at her patient once more. He stared back at her, his mouth slightly agape, his hand on his cheek in wonder, or so it seemed.

Quite the actor.

3

*Our form of heroism is cheerful defiance with the
least possible show. We shall never learn to be ceremonious, and
this was our strength in these years. The German chains were
broken by Danish laughter.*

—Ernst Mentze

*L*isten, nurse, uh, none of this is actually necessary. Is it?"
"Here we go. One, two—"

Nurse Hanne helped him slide out of bed and into a
wheelchair by the side of his bed. From the cool draft on his
legs, he wondered how much his skimpy hospital gown actually covered. Unfortunately, at the moment he could do very
little to change the situation.

"As I told you, I'm not a member of the Underground," he
went on, trying to sound as authoritative as when he mounted
the steps to his elevated pulpit on Sunday morning. "I was
just on my way here to visit a parishioner, an elderly woman
who had fallen and broken her hip. Nothing more."

"So you said." The lovely raven-haired nurse checked the
wheels on his chair and offered him a blanket, which he
gratefully accepted. "But please don't worry. If we are asked,
that's exactly what we will say, as well."

"No, you don't understand. I am most certainly *not* who
you think I am."

"And who do I think you are?"

"Look, this is getting very confusing and existential, so unless you want to discuss the finer points of Kierkegaard's philosophy, then perhaps—"

"I did a paper on Kierkegaard in school." When she interrupted him her hazel eyes seemed to twinkle with purpose. He'd never seen such brilliant color; she could not know how they drew him in.

Or perhaps she just enjoyed being petulant. She checked her clipboard once again. "Patient displays obvious confusion about his identity. Recommend relocation to E Ward."

"That's not what it says."

She concealed an amused look.

"So you feel as if you were a piece in a game of chess, when your opponent says of it: That piece cannot be moved. Is that it?"

"You're quoting Kierkegaard, again."

Steffen looked up at her and sighed in resignation. By now he knew without a doubt this was a person who was used to getting her way, and nothing he could say would change her mind about who he was. The Germans had been shooting at him for a reason, she believed, so that was that. And the Gestapo man's visit to his room? Quite proof enough for her. Perhaps he could try another angle.

"You haven't heard of any clergy working with the Underground before," he asked, "have you?"

"There's always a first time." And this time she kept her eyes on her wristwatch as she tucked his arm against her and counted his pulse. He feared it might be racing a bit at her touch, though he would never admit it. He certainly would not admit the tinge of disappointment he felt when she let his arm go to jot another note on her clipboard.

"I'm going to live?" he asked. She lifted her eyebrows.

"Not such a safe bet, these days, especially for those of us traveling through gun battles. I suppose how long you want to live, well, that's up to you, then."

He opened his mouth to argue the point, then thought better of it as she began to wheel his gurney out of his room and into the hallway.

"Wait." He pointed back at the room. "My bomb-making supplies?"

"Of course." She paused their parade and fetched the small handbag with his robe and collar. When she handed it to him he clutched it protectively, like a pillow. Certainly she must have known what was in the bag (it had obviously been opened and examined), and still she seemed to think he was implicated in the incident? Yet she probably had no idea how hard his ceremonial collar was to starch and press.

"All right, then." She tucked the pen into the clipboard and hung it from a hook on the end of his bed. "So here we go."

Despite the soreness, he was sure he could have walked just fine. No need for this. But he decided he might as well enjoy the ride and appreciate Nurse Hanne's overprotective initiative. So he gripped the sides of the gurney as they shuttled down the polished hospital hallway, and kept an eye on her as they wove in and around examination carts and other staff. This nurse was obviously on a mission, one in which he found himself quite the center, perhaps.

At the same time, he couldn't help admiring this young nurse, several years his junior and pretty in a way he hadn't noticed at first. Though not all Danes were fair-haired and blue-eyed in the way that outsiders expected of Scandinavians, Hanne's features held just a hint of the Mediterranean, if one was looking closely for it. Her smooth skin and features reminded him of a late-summer tan, with a hint of gold. And her eyes—but he had already noticed that part of her.

Eventually they made their way down a ramp and through one of the hallway-like tunnels connecting the stately, attractive brick buildings scattered about the Bispebjerg campus. Along this route they would see none of the landscaped acres, some of the prettiest in København. And they would miss seeing how Bispebjerg, or "Bishop's Mount," was so aptly named—though the "mount" was little more than a gentle rise in the city landscape. Instead they would slip underneath it all, through Nurse Hanne's shortcut.

But he didn't ask questions this time. She knew where she was going; he obviously did not.

"I don't want you to be alarmed at some of the patients you might encounter in the psychiatric ward," she finally told him as they wheeled through another set of doors, then up another ramp. She didn't even seem to labor behind his weight. "As a pastor, though, naturally you've seen these kinds of cases many times before."

"*Naturligt.*" He nodded.

Unfortunately, he had.

"I actually don't get out to this part of the hospital very often," she admitted, pushing him carefully into another hallway. "I don't have a problem with injured bodies. It's the injured minds that are difficult. I don't know how you deal with it."

"Sometimes I wonder, myself. But it's funny. I guess I've always looked at it the other way around—admired the way people like you can patch up bodies. Seems like a very . . . like something Christ would do, if he were here. Me, I'm not very useful when it comes to blood. A little queasy, I'm afraid."

"No one's ever accused me of being like Christ." She laughed for the first time—a soft, warm sound that he could almost feel rather than just hear as it lit up her face. He wanted to ask her to laugh once more, just for the experience.

"No?" He looked up at her as they wheeled down the hall, seeing her face upside down but no less attractive. She visibly stiffened when a voice called her from down the hall.

"Hanne! There you are!" A man hurried up behind them; fortunately he was Danish. "I've been looking for you all over."

She didn't slow down as they pulled into a shadowy patient room, which—from what Steffen could see—looked very much like the one he had stayed in before. He guessed the windows didn't open to the outside world, though.

"I'll be right back." Hanne excused herself before turning on the lights. It wasn't hard to hear her hushed whispers echo in from the hall.

"How did you get in here, Aron?" she asked, and now Steffen couldn't miss an unmistakable edge to her voice.

"Saw you from down the hall," he replied. "Ann-Grete said you'd be here. New patient?"

She paused. "Something like that. Look, Aron, I'm sorry. I really need to get back to work. And, uh . . . thank you for the flowers."

"You'll call me soon?" The man sounded rather pushy to Steffen—though he couldn't say why it mattered to him. "The rabbi asked for you at Sabbath services."

"Rabbi Melchior, you mean?"

"He's still filling in since Rabbi Friediger was arrested. But people were asking about you."

"I've been busy here at the hospital."

"And I'm hearing that more and more often, lately. Hanne, I'm concerned."

Another pause. Steffen almost wished he could see what was happening out in the hallway, instead of having to guess.

"Nothing to be concerned about," she finally answered, and her voice had changed to something softer, perhaps more defensive. "We can talk when I get off my shift. But right now I'd better walk you to the door. I still don't know how you got in here without someone questioning you. After all, you don't look like a doctor."

This time he laughed as the voices faded down the hall.

"What?" he said, "You think the stockbroker's suit gave it away?"

Steffen still listened closely, but he could not hear her laugh at the lighthearted remark. Only the man, the stock-broker. But now the room grew quiet once more, save the low, husky voice from the corner.

"What are you here for?"

Steffen nearly jumped out from under his blanket.

4

Being born in a duck yard does not matter,
if only you are hatched from a swan's egg.

—HANS CHRISTIAN ANDERSEN

S teffen could not remember a longer night, trying to pretend he was asleep after he had exhausted his store of
encouraging words for the man who saw all kinds of people
hiding under his bed and German soldiers just outside the
door. Fortunately, this time he was mistaken, but Steffen
couldn't convince him of that.

And Steffen must have finally dozed off, as it turned out,
when the next thing he remembered was someone shaking
him awake.

"Steffen, what are you doing here?"

Steffen woke to see his younger brother Henning's face,
only centimeters away. In some ways it was like peering too
closely into a mirror: Henning had been given the same large
ears, deep blue eyes and long nose, only his hair had turned
lighter and wavier. That, and he looked much younger than
the four years between them.

"Henning!" gasped Steffen, shaking off a drowsy headache.
"You startled me!"

"Not as much as you startled me, when I heard."

Steffen's mind spun. "But how? How did you hear?"

"One of my friends told me there was a shootout yesterday on Nørrebrogade, and that that they carried two German soldiers and a pastor away. He thought he recognized you, but he wasn't sure if you were alive."

"Well, I was, last time I checked. Did you hear what happened to my bicycle?"

"Look at you!" Henning pointed at the bandages on Steffen's chin and forehead. "You're nearly left for dead in the street and the only thing you're worried about is your bicycle."

"Not true. I'm worried about getting out of here, too. But I do like the bike."

Steffen tried to point with his eyes at his roommate, who looked very much asleep, but one could never be sure. Henning studied the man a moment before turning back to his brother and lowering his voice.

"Listen, you weren't . . ." He hesitated, as if searching for words. "You weren't actually part of that action, were you? Because if you were, I need to know."

"I thought you Resistance guys kept that sort of thing secret from each other."

Henning frowned. "Stop messing around. Were you, or were you not, part of what happened there on Nørrebrogade?"

Henning looked so expectant, it almost reminded Steffen of the days after their mother died, when his little brother was just eighteen and their father was in Venezuela, or Siam, or wherever in the world his ship had taken him, and between the two of them Steffen was all the father they had. Not that it would have mattered much if *Far* had been home. But that was a long time ago, and he needed to not think about it so much anymore.

Still, for a brief moment, Steffen was almost tempted to tell his younger brother that he had been injured in the line of duty, so to speak. That he was . . . doing something for the Resistance, smuggling weapons, taking part in a street demonstration . . . or whatever else Henning and his Underground friends were doing. Instead he sighed and explained what had really happened, and watched as Henning's expression deflated, word by word.

"That's what I thought," Henning told him after Steffen had spilled all the details he could remember. "For a minute, there—"

"You needn't worry about me, little brother." Steffen reassured him, pointing to his bandaged forehead. "This is the worst kind of trouble I've gotten myself into. But you of all people know it wasn't my fault."

"Of course it wasn't." Henning frowned and straightened back up. "And that's precisely the trouble."

"I don't see how that's a problem." Steffen felt his temperature rising despite all his efforts to keep his voice level and his expression cool.

"Well, it is. You're too cautious. You're always too cautious. With women you're too cautious. Why else are you not married, yet? With politics you're too cautious. With life in general you're too cautious."

"Interesting. I don't recall inviting you to come here and insult me."

Steffen glanced over at his roommate, who had finally stirred a bit as Henning raised his voice. Or perhaps they had both raised their voices. Henning didn't seem to care.

"I'm not insulting you," he fired back. "It's true. When other people are out in the streets, putting their lives on the line, you're safe inside, preparing your next sermon."

"Oh, yes. It's quite obvious how safe I've been." Steffen showed off the bandages on his hands to contradict his brother's charges.

"As you said, it wasn't your fault."

"And it wasn't my fault the Gestapo fellow came looking for me."

"Wait a minute, what?" Henning nearly choked. "You didn't tell me anything about Gestapo."

"You didn't ask." Steffen shrugged. "But he came to the other room I was in, wanting to question me."

"And?"

"And the nurse turned him away. Said I was sedated or sleeping and couldn't be disturbed."

"I take it you weren't."

"I could hear what was going on. But as soon as he left she wheeled me over here."

"Smart girl. I'm going to have to thank her, next time I see her."

"But you don't know who I'm talking about."

"You mean Nurse Hanne?" Henning smiled. "She's the one who told me where to find you."

By this time Steffen's roommate was sitting up in bed, fully awake. As the brothers spoke he pointed to the hallway.

"They're here!" he shouted at the top of his lungs. If that didn't bring a nurse running, nothing would. They looked at each other, then out at the empty hall.

"Who's here?" Henning finally asked. But the poor man cowered in his bed, breathless and still pointing.

"Hitler and his bodyguards! Don't you see? Right out in the hallway. They're looking for us. Get out of here while you still can!"

Steffen lowered his voice once again and leaned toward his brother.

"He's been saying that kind of thing all night. He sleeps and then he wakes up and shouts something absurd."

"You don't believe me?" asked his roommate. "Look for yourself!"

Well, yes, someone had arrived at their door, all right— probably in response to the man shouting. Fortunately it wasn't Hitler or his men, but Nurse Hanne Abrahamsen, holding a bulging paper sack. She didn't smile.

"He's back, already," she told them. And by now Henning would probably have a good idea who she was talking about. "He might not find you in this ward, but—"

"I'll take that." Henning took the bag of Steffen's clothes. "We'll be out of here in just a couple of minutes."

"I'm very sorry, Pastor." She looked straight at Steffen. "I know it's very much too soon for you to leave. But I don't know if the German is going to believe our story."

"Well, but . . . thanks for everything you're doing. You have no idea how much I appreciate—"

"I'll take care of him." Henning took charge. "Thanks, Hanne. You know we always appreciate what you all do here at Bispebjerg. Especially when it's my brother. But you'd better go."

Steffen didn't know what to say as the nurse gave him a knowing look as she nodded and slipped back out of the room. What had she heard of their conversation?

Meanwhile Henning passed his brother the bag of clothes, helping him first with his ripped white shirt, then his trousers.

"Better wear your coat over that shirt," said Henning. "Looks like you've been in a battle."

True. The front of the shirt carried blood stains and several holes from the glass and the street. But when he shrugged on his black jacket a stabbing pain in his side reminded him of where he'd been injured by the glass.

"Ow!" He winced. "But . . . wouldn't there be some kind of paperwork to complete? I would have to check out."

"From where, Steffen? You're not even checked in."

"Right." Steffen had to think it through. No sense in doing something illegal, or anything that would cast him in a less than positive light.

"No time for that, now," said Henning. "We'll leave by the side entrance."

"How do you know your way around here so well?" wondered Steffen. Henning didn't answer, so he paused by the door and turned to his roommate.

"Get out while you can!" cried the man. Steffen smiled and nodded his goodbye.

"Come on." Henning took him by the arm, and it was all Steffen could do to keep up with him as they practically sprinted through the hallway and pushed through a side entrance. The strange thing was, none of the nurses seemed to give them a second glance.

Even more strange was the waiting ambulance outside the back door, unlocked and unmanned. It resembled one of the Falck—Danish rescue and fire service—station cars, only older, like a large van with the long hood, painted bright red on the lower half and black on the upper. Henning glanced quickly around the courtyard, then climbed into the driver's seat and motioned for his brother to get in the other side. Steffen shook his head in disbelief.

"What are you doing?"

"What does it look like I'm doing?" Henning reached under the mat for a set of keys, then started up the engine. "Now hurry up and get in before somebody sees us."

"This is crazy!" Steffen stood his ground. "I'm thinking maybe you belong back there in the psychiatric ward, too. And I will not have any part in this."

"Would you shut up and quit complaining?" Henning jumped out and guided Steffen by the elbow around to the passenger side and nearly shoved him inside. And in his condition, Steffen could hardly resist. But in the process he couldn't help noticing the handle of a small pistol tucked into Henning's belt, hidden only partially by his shirttail. Steffen pointed at the weapon.

"Do you want to tell me what that's all about?"

Henning didn't explain as he slammed the passenger door, ran back around and climbed in the driver's side, and put the car in gear.

"Henning!"

"What? I didn't steal it, if that's what you're worried about. In fact, I use this thing all the time. It's a 1934 Buick. I like the American cars, don't you? We picked it up for not so much when the Falck rescue people were getting new ones just before the war. So all you have to do is sit still and stay quiet."

"I'm not talking about the ambulance, Henning, although I have to say it worries me a little. But the gun. I'm talking about the gun. You can't be serious about this. What if we're stopped?"

"Oh. Well, actually, we won't be stopping for anybody—especially not Germans."

"But . . . you really wouldn't use it, would you? I've never seen you with a gun, before."

But now Henning wasn't answering any more questions as he grit his teeth and they wound through the narrow streets of København. And true to his word, Henning almost didn't stop for pedestrians or bicyclists making their way home from work. He followed *Lygtenvej* along the rail line, then turned underneath the line and weaved through a sea of bicyclists on busy Nørrebro Street and past the park to Sankt Stefan's Kirke—most surely not named for its current pastor.

Steffen had come this way a thousand times on his bicycle, only never like this. He tried to ignore the pain in his side and the stitches that threatened to burst. And Henning grinned as they turned into the back entrance, screened by several trees.

"By the way," said Henning, "I'd watch out for that nurse, if I were you."

"Pardon?" Steffen tried his best to sound confused.

"Don't play dumb; you know what I mean, Steffen. Anybody could see the way you were keeping an eye on her. And I have to say, it looked mutual to me."

"You're seeing things."

"I sure was. But tell me. You know I'm not a theologian or anything like you, but isn't there some kind of church law against pastors dating Jewish nurses?"

"Oh, brother." Steffen shook his head. "Look, I don't know what you think you saw, but you're way ahead of yourself, or way off. There's nothing to worry about. Nothing at all."

"Whatever you say, big brother." The grin never left his face as they pulled up in the back alley behind the church with a squealing of tires. "But I'd still be careful. And here we are."

Henning kept the motor running and the lights off while Steffen actually wondered what his brother had seen. Had it really been that obvious? Henning stepped around outside and opened the passenger door.

"So for now you just need to get back into your church and lay low," he told Steffen in a low voice. "Take it easy, all right? Don't tell anyone about the shooting thing, if you can help it. Just say you had a bike wreck."

Steffen could only nod dumbly. What else could he say now?

"I didn't want to pull up in front of your apartment building and attract a lot of attention," Henning went on. "Are you going to be okay getting home?"

Steffen nodded through the throbbing pain in his side as he pulled himself out. The early afternoon had not yet warmed up that day, and a hint of fog seemed to hang around the rooftops and towers of the city, waiting to strangle its life. Maybe that's what would happen now, and he looked up at the mist that swirled about the sturdy bell tower of Sankt Stefan's. He had always admired the imposing red brick building, ever since he was a young boy and he'd craned his neck to take it all in.

"Steffen?" Henning roused him from his dark thoughts.

"Right." Steffen shivered and stepped away from the ambulance. "I guess I know who to call now, if I ever need a ride."

"I told you to forget it," replied Henning, placing the ambulance back into gear. "Go back to your sermons. Take the people's minds off the war. Stay inside your church. That's where you belong."

Steffen didn't answer and he didn't even have a chance to thank his brother before the ambulance sped off again and disappeared around a corner, leaving him standing there alone.

"You really know where I belong?" Steffen asked the quiet street. "I don't even know that."

At the moment he didn't care to discuss the matter, however. Not even with God and certainly not with his brother. So after unlocking the back entry he slipped into the cool, comfortable embrace of the church building. Maybe Henning was right. Here it smelled of Scriptures and dust, communion wafers and the faintest hint of candle wax. Here he didn't even need to find a light switch; he knew every passage, hall-way, and stairway by heart, and if he ever went blind that might be a useful skill. And though he didn't need to, he closed his eyes briefly as he ambled slowly down one hallway, then the next, and painfully mounted the twelve steps up to the next level and the small room he called his office.

Strange, he thought, noticing for the first time a weak glow spilling out from under the solid oak door. Who would have left the light on?

He found out in a moment, when Margrethe the janitor scrambled from behind his desk as she saw him opening the door.

"Margrethe! I wasn't expecting to see you!" He had jumped nearly as much as she had—though with her portly build she would have a more difficult time gaining altitude. He some-times wondered how she managed to maintain her weight despite food rationing for the past four years of German occupation, and on her salary. Perhaps it was just that way with some women.

"Oh! Pastor! Nor I you. I mean . . . I was just doing some dusting. I didn't hear you coming." Margrethe stumbled over her feather duster and her words.

He looked around his comfortable little world to see that everything appeared undisturbed. Bookcases loaded down with Bible commentaries and the occasional murder mystery filled one wall. These were his friends.

A glass display case housed several souvenirs from his com-petitive rowing days with the D.S.R., the *Danske Studenters Roklub*, or Danish Students Rowing Club. His favorite, an inscribed bronze rowlock, took its place next to all the little rocks he'd collected from different places around Danmark: a small jet-black stone from the northern tip of *Skagen*, chalk from the white cliffs of Møen, a round gray rock from the remote island of Bornholm. These were his memories.

His large walnut desk—the only piece of furniture to come with the study—took up most of the remaining space.

On the wall, a framed photo of his parents with him and his younger brother could probably have used dusting. So could the ledge below his only window, which looked out over a lovely copse of elms planted along the north side of the church building. Their leaves were just beginning to reveal traces of autumn gold, and their branches supported the little bird feeder he'd hung in front of his window a couple of years ago.

Piles of sermon notes lay scattered on his desktop. But now Margrethe had noticed something else that needed straightening.

"Your face, Pastor! Are you all right?"

"Quite well. Just a little, er, bicycle incident. Accident."

She looked a little more closely as he pulled the front of his coat a little more tightly to hide his shirt.

"I hope I don't have a bicycle accident like that," she finally told him.

"Ja, well, I'm a little banged up, but none worse for wear. Still ready for Sunday."

"That's good to hear." She gathered up her things. "Actually I was just finishing up. A couple more pews out in the sanctuary to clean. And the floor. I'd better go."

He didn't ask what might be so dusty that she'd had to open his desk drawer, he just stepped aside as she shuffled past him and out the door. Well, Margrethe was always thorough. His stomach rumbled as he checked his watch.

Two-thirty? To Steffen it felt like dinnertime, and all the more when he remembered how little food he had at home in his tiny, cold apartment, just across the street on

Nørrebrogade. He thought he had a couple cans of green beans, perhaps. He could heat up one of them on his little single-burner Primus kerosene stove, along with a dry piece of pumpernickel and a mystery sausage. Or maybe a bit of pickled herring, again?

No, he'd eaten the last of it three days ago.

All right, then. Since eating out had become far too expensive, lately, perhaps a little diet wouldn't hurt him. If only he had something for the throbbing pain in his side where they'd stitched him up. He straightened up his open Bible and sermon notes from the corner of his desk, snapped off the light, and turned to go.

Go back to your sermons, then.

His brother's words had cut deeper than the glass that dug into his side.

Stay inside your church.

He held a hand to his forehead but the headache—like the words—would not leave him.

That's probably where you belong, after all.

For the first time since he'd accepted the call at Sankt Stefan's, Steffen wasn't entirely sure just where he belonged.

5

I know what I have to do.
—Georg Duckwitz,
in a journal entry

G eorg hunted and pecked as well as could be expected, though if pressed he would have to admit he was as unfamiliar with the typewriter keyboard as he was with the reasoning behind Hitler's newest directive. He mumbled to himself as he composed yet another draft to his letter.

"I fear that should the current course of action be carried out as proposed, we may find . . ."

He paused, fingers suspended. We may find . . . what? That we have betrayed whatever shred of conscience remains in the German soul? He feared it was too late to be talking of morals now.

"As Nietzsche would say . . ."

He paused again. Nietzsche was a fool, in his humble opinion, but quoting him might add value to his argument with a military bureaucracy where fools and foolish dogma seemed to have taken control at every level. If they wanted Nietzsche, then, Nietzsche they would have. So he continued his letter, futile as it seemed.

"As Nietzsche would say, that this is a matter beyond good or evil, one of pragmatism alone. My pragmatic view then is that after this past summer of strikes and troubles, I sense the Danish people require just one flimsy excuse, a spark to set this country ablaze. This action is that spark."

He looked out his office window at the København harbor beyond. His eyes followed the waterfront, where he and his wife had enjoyed strolls before this wretched war. There the Little Mermaid stood watch over her harbor, though unfortunately this was no fairy tale. In less than two weeks, two German transport ships would take up station there, ready to transport Danmark's 7,500 Jews to a camp just north of Prague.

Theresienstadt.

And now nothing he wrote or said would make any difference, of that he was certain. He could quote every wretched philosopher, past or present. But why did he now bother with yet another hopeless letter of protest—especially after what he had already done to jeopardize his career? He whipped the latest sheet of onionskin paper out of the typewriter, crumpled it, and tossed it in the overflowing wastebasket at his feet. Better that he should burn the lot—and he seriously considered how he might accomplish that without drawing the attention of the København fire department.

"Is it worth it?" he wondered aloud. And when he took off his horn-rimmed glasses to rub his tired eyes, the harbor scene blurred before him. He heard a soft knock at the door just before his secretary poked her head just inside.

"Pardon me again, Herr Duckwitz, but are you certain you would not like me to type that letter for you? Because Herr Best—"

"Nein, nein." He cut her off as he rolled yet another piece of paper into the typewriter with a flourish. "I'm nearly finished."

"But sir—"

He held up his hand. No, the last thing he wanted was for his gray-haired secretary to know what had been on his mind for the past week, ever since Werner Best had briefed him on what was to happen to Danmark's Jews.

"This is one I'd rather do myself, Anna. I'm still thinking it through, and it would waste your time to have me stumbling about with my words. But thank you for your concern."

"Sir, I mean to say that Herr Best is waiting on the telephone for you."

"Oh! Why didn't you say so? Well, tell him I'm not . . ." Duckwitz paused for a moment before changing his mind. "All right, then. I'll take it."

He stared at the telephone on his desk for as long as he dared, then sighed and picked it up, as if he had no idea who was on the other end of the line.

"Shipping Agent Duckwitz here."

"Georg!" Werner Best's voice boomed over the telephone, causing Duckwitz to hold the receiver away from his ear several centimeters. "Glad to hear your voice. You are here in the city, are you not?"

"Of course, Herr *Reichsbevollmächtigter*." He nearly choked on the pretentiously overlong title, which seemed quite overweight even in the language so used to lengthy compound names. Plenipotentiary of the Reich. The man who ruled Danmark's affairs with the gravity and certainty of a Roman emperor, reporting only to Hitler himself. "I'm right here in my office, as always."

"Glad to hear it." It could have been a friendly challenge, nothing more. Georg couldn't quite tell from the tone of the other man's voice. "It's just that you've been gone quite a bit, lately. How was Berlin, by the way?"

"Berlin?" Duckwitz did his best to hold his voice steady. Perhaps everyone knew he had been to Berlin. He just hoped not everyone knew why. "Yes, Berlin was . . . busy as always."

"But they didn't listen to you."

"Listen to me? I'm afraid I don't—"

"Georg, Georg. It's no secret you've opposed the evacuation plan. I know that you went there to lobby for a change."

Duckwitz swallowed hard. If Best knew that much, perhaps he'd also found out about his recent trip to Stockholm and the secret agreement he'd brokered with the Swedes to accept thousands of Jewish refugees, should the need arise. That trip, however, had not been on his official docket.

"Georg?" For a moment Best sounded far away. "Are you there?"

"I'm here, *ja*. Perhaps the connection is not so good."

If only it wasn't.

"Ah, well, as I was saying, frankly I was concerned to hear that you'd taken it upon yourself to go to Berlin. Some people said that in so doing you displayed a certain degree of . . . disloyalty."

If he knew where else I'd been this past week. Surely he would not have to impose upon the goodwill of the Swedes for his own safety and that of his wife. But he knew the worst could happen, and the thought of escape did cross his mind. Duckwitz swallowed hard as the other man continued.

"Me? The thought never crossed my mind. You're a loyal party member. But, you know, in a way I'm glad you were able to hear all the facts straight from the Führer. That puts your mind at rest, does it not?"

Duckwitz didn't pause long enough to let the other man wonder about his muddied allegiance, though he felt his stomach turning at how much Werner Best knew about his trip, about its purpose . . . even with whom he had spoken.

"Absolutely it does." He hoped he'd added the appropriate dose of enthusiasm.

"I'm gratified to hear you say that. Then you needn't worry anymore about whether this is the best course of action. I mean to say, the *only* course of action, *ja?*"

The man was so obviously probing for weakness, for a white flag. He would receive it.

"Ja," replied Duckwitz, "the Führer was very clear to say that the idea of Jews walking around Danmark free was reprehensible and must be stopped. So Danmark shall be *judenrein*, cleared of every last Jew, very shortly. We are all committed to that."

"Wonderful, wonderful. We'll discuss more details tomorrow. But this success will be a highlight in your service to the Reich."

Or the most shameful thing I would ever accomplish. Duckwitz remained silent and kept his thoughts to himself.

"Oh, and Georg, I needn't mention the critical and confidential nature of these plans?"

"Of course, Herr Reichsbevollmächtigter. I understand completely."

Duckwitz wondered if there was technically a difference between understanding confidentiality and actually protecting it.

"Excellent, then, Georg. I have every confidence in you. Always have."

"And I in you, sir."

Naturally Werner Best would not know they still held two entirely divergent views as to how Danmark's Jews might be evacuated, or to where they might be taken.

Georg Duckwitz prayed Best would never find out.

6

In Jewish history there are no coincidences.
                                            —Elie Wiesel

anne finally retreated to her apartment at the end of her shift plus two long hours of overtime. Once inside, she leaned back on the front door with sigh, clicked the deadbolt shut, and kicked off her sensible nurse's shoes.

A glance at her watch told her she'd missed the nightly news program, but she was too exhausted for bad news. Instead she located one of her favorite records, slipped it onto the player, and collapsed onto her small couch to the sound of Artie Shaw's "Begin the Beguine."

Ja, that's better, she told herself, allowing a small sigh. As she rubbed her throbbing feet she looked up at the window and did her best to avoid the pang of guilt as the music continued. Yes, but with the mandatory blackout shade drawn, what good would it do to light the two traditional Sabbath candles, anyway? At least she kept them on the windowsill— a symbol of her tattered allegiance to the religious customs that had framed her childhood.

In her mind's eye she imagined her mother standing before four candles at home, faithfully lighting them no later than eighteen minutes before sundown every Friday evening. As Mor had reminded Hanne and her younger sister, Marianne, so many times when they were young, the first signified *zakhor*, remembering the Sabbath, as they had been commanded in Exodus 20.

"What do the Scriptures command us?" their mother had asked, and Marianne was always the first to eagerly recite the verse:

"But the seventh day is a Sabbath to the Lord. . . . On it you shall not do any work, you or your son, or your daughter, your male servant, your female servant."

"How about your female nurse?" Hanne asked the darkness.

Meanwhile the phonograph's needle swept in a dizzy arc through the center of the record, back and forth, popping and hissing past the end of "Begin the Beguine." She flipped through her sizable record collection in the wooden crate on the floor, added to since she was a young teen. Perhaps "It Ain't Necessarily So" or "Jeepers, Creepers" might put her in a better mood. She liked the Americans, Benny Goodman and Duke Ellington. But in the end she sighed, lifted the arm back to its cradle, and snapped off the phonograph.

If only Marianne could have joined her here, Hanne would have gladly lit a candle for her sister's sake. She looked back across the shadows to the small framed photograph on her bookshelf, next to the phonograph. Two young girls in pinafore dresses smiled at the camera for the occasion of Hanne's eleventh birthday, just days before Marianne had died.

"And what about this candle?" The memory of Hanne's mother thankfully interrupted, after all these years, still probing the young sisters for a better answer to the weekly Sabbath quiz. Marianne would answer first, as always, once more.

"The second reminds us of *shamor*," she would say in her bright little voice. "To keep. To guard."

That was the right answer, yes, week after week. But who had kept and guarded her little sister, after all? Who had guarded her against what had happened?

Even after all these years Hanne fought back tears as she closed her eyes. She wished she could not see her mother carefully lighting each candle, waving her hands across their rising heat three times as if to welcome the Sabbath, then covering her face with her hands to hide from the light before reciting the blessing:

Barukh atah Adonai eloheinu melekh ha-olam . . .

Blessed are You, Lord our God, King of the universe, who sanctified us with His commandments and commanded us to kindle the Sabbath candles.

Perhaps yes, this King of the universe had commanded them to observe the seventh day. And she might have, if Adonai had kept His end of the bargain. Now she found herself standing once again and looking down at the cold candles, mindful of just how far she had come since her growing-up years on *Schacksgade*, when she and her parents and Marianne would bundle up against cold December rains and walk together through *Ørsteds* park and across busy *Nørre Voldgade* to the Friday evening service at the synagogue on *Krystalgade*. Summers were much better. The only thing she didn't like back then was how long she had to wait before they returned home to the Sabbath meal, when her father recited a brief *Kiddush* prayer and they were finally free to eat.

"Well, I'm starving." She dismissed the memories with a wave of her hand, mindful of just how much it looked like her mother's, over the candles. She paused to wonder. Perhaps it wouldn't hurt to light just one, just to bring a little cheer to her small studio apartment. No one would see it from the outside. So she struck a single match to light one of her candles. Just one. Anything more, and it might appear she was giving in once again to the lopsided bargain of a God who seemed to demand everything and yet gave so little in return.

Just for the warmth, she assured herself. For the atmosphere. *Hygge*, they called it, and the concept applied to everything from the knit cushion covers for the older upholstered chair in the corner of her tiny den, to the lovely lace curtains she'd received from her grandmother. Everything should add to the atmosphere. That was the Danish way.

The roses, however, were an entirely different matter. She had no idea how Aron had even come upon them during these days of ration cards, riots, and food shortages. How much had it cost him, with scarce *kroner* that would better be spent on something a little more practical?

Even so, with a pair of scissors she trimmed their stems and replaced them in the vase, granting another day or two of life. Funny how they smelled of nothing, though. Not of spring, or summer, or distant golden fields out of reach of this embattled city, occupied by foreign troops with ugly gray uniforms and grim, hard expressions.

Barukh atah Adonai . . .

Her mother's words still echoed as Hanne's lone Sabbath candle sputtered for a moment before catching its full flame, as if considering whether it actually wanted to remember, or not. Hanne would remember, though on her terms.

She stood alone in the chilly apartment, waiting for the clang of the radiators to warm the evening. Meanwhile she kept her knit sweater on and huddled in the lone light of her single Sabbath candle, unorthodox as it was and not lit with the necessary prayer. And despite it all, her mind drifted to the thought of the pastor, Steffen, wondering how he was doing and if all his injuries were healing.

———

"Hanne! Phone call!"

She jumped when Kirsten knocked on the door, but didn't answer right away. She and her neighbor often traded nursing shifts, but Kirsten spent most of her time with a boyfriend in town. Despite the eight p.m. curfew, Hanne thought it funny that she would be in tonight and here to answer the single phone down the hall. Maybe she'd been waiting for a call herself.

"Hanne! You in there? I think it's your boyfriend."

Still Hanne didn't answer, just watched the glow of the candle as Kirsten knocked one more time.

"I'm going to tell him you're out with Dr. Kielsgaard tonight."

Hanne had to smile. Was that the best Kirsten could come up with? Dr. Kielsgaard had to be the shortest doctor on staff, with a mousy little voice and a crooked smile that only a mother could love. Or a wife. As it happened, Dr. Kielsgaard was also happily married with three young children.

Fortunately that was Kirsten's last effort, as Hanne heard her neighbor mumble something else and pad back down the hallway. So Aron was probably wondering why Hanne hadn't showed up at Sabbath services once again. This time her well-used excuse that she wasn't feeling well might not hold up as much as it had before. But she simply could not

———

bear the thought of going through the motions with Aron and her family, once again. Please, no.

Instead she would put on another record, perhaps, and if she still had enough kerosene she might even heat up a can of ham she'd been saving for a special occasion. Talk about guilty pleasures for this lapsed Jewish girl! A warm sponge bath might be nice, as well.

She would explain to Aron that she'd had to work late, and he would have to accept it. There. Was there anything else to decide?

Out in the hallway, she heard the phone ringing once more, and again. Only this time, no one was answering.

"Come on," she whispered through the door, "someone pick up the phone, out there."

Still it rang, until Hanne finally had to unbolt her door and peek out to make sure no one else had heard. Surely? But whoever was calling this time wasn't giving up.

Against her better judgment she tiptoed out onto the cold wood floor in her stockings, past the silent doors of three other nurses, and hovered above the single black phone on its spindly little stand at the end of the hallway. For a moment she wondered if it could be Aron again. She could always pretend it was a faulty connection and hang up.

"Hello?" She finally answered. And speaking of Dr. Kielsgaard—

"Hanne! I'm glad I reached you. Where is everyone?"

"I, ah. . . ."

She would truthfully have told the attending emergency room physician that she had no idea what happened to the other girls on a Friday evening, but he didn't give her a chance.

"Never mind. I need you back in here right away. Several more . . . incidents."

Hanne caught her breath but knew better than to question the doctor. *Incidents* would mean more young men from the Resistance had just been brought in, perhaps with gunshot wounds or worse. She simply bit her lip and nodded.

"I'll be right there."

She was about to hang up the phone, but he had one more request.

"And see if there's anyone else on the hall who can come with you."

"Right away."

This time Hanne set down the receiver and hurried down the hall, knocking on doors. Was she a good Jew? Maybe and maybe not, depending. She would save the canned ham for another time. But if she was a good nurse—well, that question seemed much easier to answer.

7

One act of obedience is better than one hundred sermons.
—DIETRICH BONHOEFFER

ime of death, five minutes to half-eight." Dr. Kielsgaard
stripped off his rubber gloves and flung them in the general direction of a trash bin. Naturally, Hanne didn't want to stare, so she pretended not to notice as she turned away and did her best to fill in the details on her clipboard.

Seven twenty-five in the morning. She squeezed her eyes together to focus. Name, Nikolai Nielsen, if the identity card they'd found in his ripped trousers could be believed. Age, sixteen, with flaming red hair. Still a boy. Cause of death—

She didn't have to ask the doctor, who now leaned up against the corner of the exam room in sheer exhaustion. Gunshot wound to the side, she noted in her best handwriting. On the form she found no space to indicate that the bullet came from a German gun, fired by a German soldier, under German occupation. No space to explain the total stupidity and waste of what had just happened. Finally, Dr. Kielsgaard took a deep breath and cleared his throat, as if steeling himself for what surely came next.

"We did all we could," whispered Hanne, as if that would make any difference. Of course they had. But the doctor just shook his head.

"Just like we did yesterday, Hanne, and the day before. And where does that leave us?" He brushed by her on the way to the door. "Are his parents still out in the waiting room?"

She nodded, knowing he wasn't waiting for her answer. "They've been there since his friends brought him in last night."

So the parents had obviously defied curfew, and they'd prayed, and they'd paced the waiting room for the past six hours. But all the prayers in the world hadn't brought their son back to life. And now Dr. Kielsgaard had to bring them the news they did not want to hear. He frowned with his hand against the swinging door, obviously composing himself.

Hanne would much rather run in the opposite direction, away from the body that now lay cooling on the operating table, and away from his two friends, all seriously wounded in some kind of midnight sabotage attempt gone wrong. Yes, and neither of them had fared much better than Nikolai Nielsen—except for the fact that they still breathed. Barely.

Perhaps she should have run, while she still had the chance. That, or collapse on the floor in exhaustion from the extra shift she had just survived. Instead her eyes focused on the doctor and she mindlessly followed him into the waiting room, where he faced the unenviable task of telling the parents their son had died.

Actually, Dr. Kielsgaard needn't have worried about eloquence or words to say, if that's what concerned him. His dark expression must have told them all they needed to know, even before he opened his mouth. And just moments after he entered the small room with the uncomfortable wood chairs lined up against the wall, a couple in the corner looked up at him with a mixture of disbelief and horror splashed across their tired faces. Without a word the woman buried her face in her husband's shoulder and sobbed, while his eyes widened in pain and he pressed his quivering lips together.

"We told him not to get involved," said the father, arching his head back and talking to the ceiling. "He wouldn't listen."

"We did everything we could," replied Dr. Kielsgaard, echoing Hanne's helpless words as he stood awkwardly in the middle of the small room, his face mask dangling by a string around his neck. "And I'm terribly sorry, you understand. But by the time he was brought in, he'd already lost too much blood. We could not save him. There was nothing more to be done."

Hanne knew the truth of his words all too well, though that surely must not have made it any easier for the parents to hear. Fortunately, the only other person in the room, a large woman stuffed into one of the waiting chairs, slept with her head back and her mouth wide open. She punctuated the sound of this couple's mourning with her snores.

Strange, though, how resigned this couple seemed to be, despite their obvious grief. They didn't shout *"Nej!"* or accuse the doctor of being somehow mistaken. Now they just stood in the corner, holding each other up. Perhaps they had already known what would happen when they brought their son in.

And now Hanne genuinely wished she had not followed the doctor here to see this horrible, heavy sadness that filled the room, though it was not the first time and would most certainly not be the last.

"He was only sixteen," sobbed the mother. "He was going to take his exams this year. He was such a good boy."

Now the mother looked up and her tortured gaze locked on Hanne. And for the longest moment neither could pull away, as the full weight of pain nearly brought Hanne to her knees.

"If you'll follow me, please." Now the doctor had regained a measure of his professional composure, as Hanne would have expected. "We'll have some paperwork for you to fill out."

The father nodded numbly, as if giving in to the maelstrom from which none of them could escape. The mother had returned to her helpless sobbing but still held to her husband. And so the bereaved parents followed Dr. Kielsgaard past Hanne without another word, for they had also died and this paperwork was their unavoidable duty as members of the otherworld.

I should never have answered the phone last night, thought Hanne, her tired mind retreating into its protective bunker of "what if." *I should have shut the door, locked it, and not opened for anyone. Not for Dr. Kielsgaard. Not for Aron. Not for the Nazis. I should have hidden myself in the closet.*

If she could just lock the door and keep it locked until this was all over, she reasoned, perhaps she could better survive the nightmare that had darkened København streets for the past several months. And in her twisted state of fatigue, such a silly proposition almost seemed to make sense. Hide. She glanced up at the clock once more, trying to remember if seven thirty-five was morning or evening. She still clutched her clipboard with the notes of how this brave young man's life had ended, and when.

Time of death, seven twenty-five. Cause of death, murder.

She set the clipboard on the nearest counter, dropped the pencil, and walked away.

———⊗⊗⊗———

Steffen leaned back in his comfortable leather chair and tidied his sermon notes again on his wide oak office desk, next to his open Bible. Still the words stuck in his throat as he rehearsed them from his notes.

"Were there not ten that were healed?" he read aloud, raising a hand to the bandage on his side, still good and sore but now well-hidden beneath his cleaned and pressed shirt. The scars on his chin and on the back of his hand, hopefully no one would notice. "Where are the other nine?"

He'd given the same sermon two years ago, according to the every-other-year church reading calendar and with the calm precision and orderliness that defined his world.

For the most part.

Perhaps he just needed a little more rest, especially after all the excitement with the bicycle incident and his short stay at Bispebjerg Hospital. So he rested his chin in his hands, listening to the quiet ticking of the gold mantle clock on the corner of his desk, and tried to shake the persistent image of that nurse, Hanne.

She was just doing her job, he told himself. *I'm sure she's equally as pleasant to all her patients. That's what she's called on to do, just as I'm called on to deliver this sermon.*

Yes, if he could. He caught himself smiling and still unable to forget her face, her voice, or the touch of her hand as she took his pulse.

"Your heart rate seems a little high, again," she had told him. If only she'd known why. He actually tried to forget about the dark-eyed nurse as he stared out his office window at the elms that lined *Stefansgade*. A motorcycle roared past with a German soldier in a sidecar. Why were they always so loud, and always in such a hurry? This time Steffen granted

———⊗⊗⊗———

himself a private frown for the way the war had strained and pushed at the borders of his ministry. But they had not broken through, he added with a touch of pride. Services commenced promptly at ten o'clock every Sunday morning, even as they had before the war began. The work continued. So too did burials and baptisms, weddings and confirmations. He'd confirmed eleven young people in the last confirmation class, only last month. Everything continued as it always had.

What's more, Steffen was certain that if they—that is, the people of his parish—would simply continue to exercise restraint and caution, this storm would blow over and the invaders would return home, just as the motorcycle had turned the corner of and disappeared down Nørrebrogade. Hadn't King Christian himself ordered them not to resist, but to keep calm and cooperate? This he could do, and he could advise his congregation to do the same.

If only his own brother would follow that advice.

Because the . . . *unpleasantness* could hardly last forever, and resistance—particularly the violent sort Henning advocated—could only make things worse, in his humble opinion.

For a moment he thought he could smell the motorcycle's exhaust, drifting up from the street below, until he realized it was a smoke of another sort—an amber cigar smoke, pungent and nose-tickling. This early? Now at least he had an excuse to step away from his desk, notes in hand, and to stretch his own legs.

Moments later he made his way out of the back door to join Pastor Viggo Jensen. Lost in thought and a cloud of home-rolled cigar smoke, the retired pastor looked up with a start from his spot by the garbage cans, almost as if Steffen had just caught a schoolboy sneaking a forbidden cigarette.

"Ah, Steffen! Didn't expect to see you here so early." Pastor Viggo peered out through his smoke screen and from under a pair of gray eyebrows made even more impressive by the near-lack of hair on the man's head. And like a matching bookend, his well-polished shoes reflected a smile as he glanced at the papers in Steffen's hand. "Working on your sermon? The story of the ten lepers?"

None other.

"Actually, yes. I was thinking how they received their healing after obedience. One of my commentaries has a bit about that. In the Greek, *hupakouo*, 'I obey.'"

The other man smiled. "I actually do know a few words of Greek."

"Of course you do. But the point is, perhaps that's our situation here: If we obey King Christian's word, we may be healed as a nation. If not . . ."

"Hmm." Now Pastor Viggo wrinkled his forehead in concentration. Steffen could hear it coming.

"It's all a matter of obedience, don't you think?" continued Steffen, hoping to make a good enough impression to gain the elder pastor's approval this time. If he did, though, that would probably be a first.

"Perhaps," he continued, "but then the question would be, to whom?"

Steffen hadn't considered that way of looking at it. Pastor Viggo went on, as if he wasn't expecting an answer.

"And don't you have any personal experiences you might relate to that passage? Some practical application? How's your health these days? Anything you can be thankful for, after that accident of yours?"

"Oh, you don't mean after my little bicycle wreck?" Steffen shrugged away the experience. "I'm certain no one would want to hear about that."

"Really? Why not? Your brother seemed quite interested, when he came to check on you. Speaking of which, he's, ah, quite active these days, is he not?"

"Yes, his work at the bookstore keeps him busy."

Pastor Viggo paused again, as if waiting for more, then nodded his head.

"In any case," he said, "wasn't there something in this passage about how the fellow's faith made him well? You're well, are you not? I wonder if you couldn't tie in your experience that way?"

"Actually . . ." Steffen backed away from Pastor Viggo. He should have known the elder pastor would suggest a personal angle. And the personal angles, it seemed, would always make him look . . . well, foolish. "There's very little to explain. I lost my balance. They stitched me up quite well. That's about all there is to the story."

"Well, but I'm sure you'll think of something from one of your books, then," said Pastor Viggo. Now he seemed unflappable, as if this little exchange bothered him not the least. "And I'll very much look forward to hearing it tomorrow. You always come up with something appropriate."

Yes, appropriate, thought Steffen. Safe. Unlike his brother. He thanked Pastor Viggo, wondering if he should not have stayed in his office with his friends the commentaries—where it was quiet.

8

Life can only be understood backwards;
but it must be lived forwards.

—SØREN KIERKEGAARD

"You never told me where you got that gun, you know."
Steffen didn't mean to sound like their mother when he
spoke to his younger brother, Henning. It just came out that
way, even when he lowered his voice to a whisper. And it
wasn't hard to decipher Henning's reaction by the way he
frowned as he leaned against a weighed-down shelf of dusty
books.

"Why do you ask?" Henning lowered an upside-down copy
of H. C. Andersen's *Collected Fairy Tales*. He looked more
like a soccer player than a bookstore clerk. "You want to borrow it?"

"Borrow it? *Nej*. One of us getting arrested would be quite
enough."

Henning fidgeted as he glanced around the cluttered little
store, piled high with used books of all kinds in floor-to-
ceiling shelves that groaned under the weight. None of the
other three customers looked up from their books, and in
fact seemed to making a good show of ignoring the entire
exchange.

"Look," said Steffen. "I just thought we needed to talk about . . . you know, what happened the other day. I don't want you getting in more trouble."

"Who said I was in trouble?" Henning pushed aside a lock of blonde hair with an irritated puff of air. He had always worn his hair too long, even when they were both in Gymnasium, before Steffen went on to the School of Theology at the University of København and Henning dropped out.

"I'm not saying you are, Henning. But listen to me. Have you already forgotten what they did to that *Times* editor last month . . . what was his name?"

"Clemmensen."

"Right. Clemmensen. And what they did to him is exactly what they do to anybody else who sticks his neck out."

"I'm surprised you knew anything about him."

"Clemmensen was an editor for the biggest paper in København, for goodness sake!"

"A shame too. I hear he was a good man."

"*Was*, Henning. Past tense. They killed him, don't you see?"

"Oh, I see, all right." Henning didn't back away. "But he's not the only one, you know. A kid named Nicolai Nielsen was shot and killed last night. Two of our other people were badly hurt. And do you know how old he was?"

Obviously Steffen had no idea, so Henning went on.

"Sixteen. The kid was just sixteen! And the thing was, even at that age he was willing to give his life for what he believed."

"Sixteen." Steffen shook his head in disbelief. "This is starting to get really dangerous. I think you need to be more careful."

"Me? You're just getting out of the hospital, and you're telling me to be careful? That's a good one."

"Yes, I'm well aware of how it sounds. The difference is, you're directly involved, and I'm not. I'm just saying that you ought to consider getting out of this while you still can."

"Not this conversation again." This time Henning's face flushed as he ran his fingers through his hair, and turned back again. "But you're right about one thing. Things *are* getting worse. I've heard the Nazis are making plans to round up every Jew in Danmark."

"No, they wouldn't dare." Steffen crossed his arms. "This isn't Poland. This is their model protectorate. They've promised not to do that sort of thing here."

"You are so naïve." Henning slapped his own forehead with the palm of his hand.

"Now, wait just a minute. You—"

"No, you listen. You think you're being safe and neutral, and you don't even see what's happening. You think you see it, but you don't. And you know what? One of these days you're going to be riding your bicycle down the street again, and they're not going to miss."

"Who are we talking about, now? Who exactly is *they?*"

"The Nazis. The sympathizers. Doesn't matter. Meanwhile you just go ahead, keep telling your people to 'Let every soul be subject unto the higher powers,' and you say they need to keep their heads inside their shells. Right? Isn't that what you say? The Nazis won't hurt us. They'll get tired of little Danmark and eventually they'll go home. Listen to yourself! Well, it's not working out that way. The only way these Nazis are going home is if we show them the door and push them out."

Steffen paced in a circle as he tried to make sense of it all.

"All right," he finally said, "so now I'm confused."

"You got that part right."

"*Nej.* I'm confused because just the other day you said I should stay in my church. Stick to my sermons. Isn't that what you said?"

"Did I say that? Well, after what just happened to that boy, I think maybe I'm changing my mind. Maybe I was wrong."

"My little brother, wrong? I've never heard those two words in the same sentence before."

Henning only smiled for a moment, then returned to his serious self.

"*Ja,* well, lately the Nazis are shooting first, asking questions later. Everyone can see they're getting desperate. Our people have to respond."

"But not like this. Not with violence."

"Well, if you don't choose a side, if you just stand in the middle of the tracks, you're going to get run over by this train, brother."

"Henning, you really don't understand my position. You—"

"*Nej,* this time you're the one who doesn't understand, Pastor. If you keep playing the middle, next time whoever's shooting in the street might think you're a *stikker.* And you know what they do to them."

"That's ridiculous. How could anyone possibly think I'm collaborating with the Germans?"

"I'm just saying, 'He who is not with me is against me,' right? Isn't there something in your Bible like that?"

Steffen didn't like the way his brother said *your* Bible. And that was about all of a lecture he cared to hear, for now. This wasn't what he came here for. In fact, what did he come here for? To look up a book, the way he often did? To convince his brother that working in the Resistance was getting too dangerous? He stepped over to the window and pulled out a volume of Kierkegaard's *Enten/Eller* from the display.

Either/Or. Funny that it would have a place in the window next to a collection of fiction, like Jensen's *The Long Journey* or Dinesen's *Out of Afrika.* Perhaps a customer had replaced it there without thinking.

"Hey, don't touch that!" Henning stepped out from behind his counter and grabbed the book from Steffen's hand before replacing it carefully in the stand where it had been propped up.

"My apologies. I thought you sold books, here."

That would be more than enough arguing for one day. Steffen started for the door, but his brother held him back by the arm.

"Look, Steffen, I'm sorry. But the book has to stay right there in the window." He paused and sighed, a hand on his hip. "It's a signal, okay? When Kierkegaard is in the window, it's clear for my contacts to come inside."

And do what? Steffen paused to let his brother's words sink in, and he wondered what else was going on right there in the shop, right under his nose. What about the other customers, who still seemed absorbed in their reading? Maybe they all worked for the Resistance, as well.

"What if it's not clear?" he asked, wishing instantly that he had not.

"H. C. Andersen."

"Kierkegaard clear, Andersen away. Come in for theology, stay away from fairy tales."

"Something like that." But Henning's expression darkened and he pressed his lips together the way he always did when he was in trouble. All right, then. Steffen didn't need to know any more. He didn't *want* to know.

"I shouldn't have come, Henning," he finally said. "I was just wanting to talk some sense into you. But after our conversation, and what happened the other day, I can see I've made a mistake."

"You said what you had to say, big brother. I appreciate that, believe it or not. And look, I . . . I shouldn't have said what I did. I was out of line. It's just that when you start talking at me the way *Far* used to do . . . you know how that is."

Unfortunately, Steffen did know. And he would take that as an apology, though he wasn't sure how much he liked the reference to their father. By that time he noticed a man stopping by the window outside, tugging the brim of his hat a little more tightly over his eyes before glancing toward the Kierkegaard book, the briefest of glances and nothing more.

"I really should be going," Steffen told his brother. "Take care."

"I hope you do too, Steffen."

This time Steffen tried not to look at the man as they slipped past each other in the doorway, one coming and the other going as the little bell on the front door jangled with a cheer that seemed so clearly out of place.

So each brother clearly thought the other was in greater danger, did they? Steffen could see that now. He just couldn't quite see who was right this time.

9

*Duckwitz is not a well-known name, though it deserves to be.
It is the name of a good and true-hearted man.*

—EMILIE ROI

Anna, would you please look again for a telegram before you leave for the day?"

Georg Duckwitz checked his Swiss watch as he paused from his pacing. Only two minutes to five. If any special instructions were going to arrive from Berlin, they would have been here long before now.

"Still nothing, sir." His office manager looked in from the reception area. "Do you want me to—"

"That's all right." He tried to smile as if nothing were wrong. "Why don't you just go home for the day? You've been working hard."

She seemed to think about it for just a moment before nodding politely and retrieving her purse out of her desk by the door.

"Thank you, sir. I'll be on my way, then. And . . . I'm sure your message from Berlin will arrive tomorrow."

"I'm sure it will." Again Duckwitz did his best to appear casual, as if it was just another Tuesday evening, at the end of just another day. But he knew better. As soon as Anna had shut the door behind her he reached for a cigarette to calm his nerves. But his right hand shook as he flicked his lighter, and he managed to pace only to his window and back before snuffing his smoke in the ashtray on the corner of the desk. He jumped at the sound of the telephone and ran out to grab the call at Anna's desk. Perhaps—

"Office of the Shipping Agent," he said, clearing his throat. "Duckwitz speaking."

"Georg!" His wife's voice sounded more distant than he would have thought, for just a cross-city connection.

"Oh!" He sighed. Without a telegram and without a phone call to the contrary, now his decision loomed that much closer. He stared up at the portrait of Adolph Hitler on the wall above the reception desk, and he had to force himself to believe that *der Führer* would not now be listening in, or watching. Hopefully, neither would anyone else—including his wife.

"Georg? You sound disappointed it was me."

"*Nein*, of course not. I was just expecting . . . ah, well. I was hoping for a call from Berlin."

"I see. You're always expecting a call from Berlin."

Not like this one, he thought as his wife went on.

"So what happened to Anna? Was she not working today?"

"I told her to go home early."

"On a Tuesday? Well, that's all very nice of you, but how about letting the shipping agent come home, for a change? Tell him his wife is cooking his favorite tonight for his birthday."

That kind of talk was almost enough to soothe his jangled nerves. Almost.

"*Schnitzel und spätzle?*" he asked, his mouth watering at the thought of how his wife used to prepare a tasty breaded pork tenderloin. But with all the rationing, how long had it been since she'd been able to prepare his *lieblingsessen?* He would not ask where she had been able to find such a delicacy. And spätzle! These Danes had nothing like it—doughy noodles cooked in boiling bouillon. He could almost taste it now.

"Of course, schnitzel und spätzle, silly. But I'm not going to bring it to the office, or I'd probably be robbed on the street. You'll have to come home if you want some. Dinner, I mean! You are coming home soon, aren't you?"

"Ja, of course. Very soon." He bit his lip and glanced at his watch once again, calculating how quickly he could complete his errand—if he was to carry it out. "But Liesl, I have to—"

"What? You give me one good reason not to throw this schnitzel out the back window for the local cats to carry off."

"No, please. It's an important meeting I need to attend first. It won't take long at all. I should be home by . . . perhaps seven o'clock at the latest."

"Seven." His wife groaned on the other end of the phone. "You're always working late, these days. Can't it wait until tomorrow?"

"I'm sorry, *schatzi,* just not this time."

He tried to apologize once more, but still his vague excuses didn't seem to appease his wife. He didn't blame her. But as he hung up he couldn't help staring at the portrait of Hitler, and his forehead throbbed with pain.

Am I sure about this? he asked himself, wondering what would happen if he simply went home to his wife to enjoy a good meal, well-deserved. What would happen if he simply remembered his civil service oath? Herr Hitler's eyes seemed to follow him around the office, as did the words:

"I swear I shall be loyal and obedient to Adolf Hitler, the Führer of the German Reich and people, respect the laws, and fulfill my official duties conscientiously, so help me God."

So help me . . . Back at his desk his heart pounded in his chest as he fingered the confidential report from Werner Best and pulled on an overcoat from the coat tree. Of all people, Best must never know. The problem was, Duckwitz had already told his wife too much. What if she was questioned?

Nein. It was too late and he knew what he had to do, no matter the cost. He felt his face flush as he thought of what would happen if he did nothing.

Nein! So he snapped off his desk lamp, breaking the little knob in the process. And he hesitated for only a moment, the broken knob in his hand, before tossing it aside and heading for the door.

And I cannot tell her, he reminded himself. *Not ever.*

By that time he also decided it best to leave behind his documents, his proof of what was to come. They would have to take his word for it. But he couldn't help rehearsing what he would say as he hurried out of his office and around the corner to catch the streetcar that would take him as close as he could get to 22 *Rømersgade*. He hopped on and found a seat near the back, out of the way.

If he didn't meet anyone's eyes, and if he didn't open his mouth, he thought perhaps he might be mistaken for a businessman or a banker on his way home after another day at the office. Perhaps. He hunched behind yesterday's copy of the *Times*, scanning the bland headlines that revealed little truth, not reading a word and doing all that he could to slow the racing of his heart. But he could not. An older woman looked at him curiously from across the aisle as he produced a monogrammed handkerchief and mopped his forehead. Yes, it was a bit warm in the streetcar, was it not? She would not know what "GFD" stood for, even if she could make out the initials.

"Oh, here!" Duckwitz didn't mean to call out, and he needn't have worried as the distracted conductor brought their coach to a jerky stop. Duckwitz wasted no more time but pushed outside and gulped the cool evening air to calm himself down. It didn't work. He checked his watch and hurried toward the Labour Library building where he was certain his contact would be talking politics.

Hans Hedtoft, a leading member of the powerful Social Democrat party, would still be here, huddled with other Danish politicians in one of the meeting rooms surrounding the Labour Library. Yes, even at this hour. Because ever since the Danish government had resigned in protest last month, Hedtoft practically lived in the smoky huddles of emergency meetings and crisis councils. So Duckwitz pushed through an outer lobby as if he belonged there. Only now he ran the risk of someone recognizing him. Never mind.

"May I help you, sir?" A young woman, perhaps a receptionist of some kind, intercepted him as he approached one of the closed meeting room doors. She obviously didn't know who he was, which was just as well.

"Yes, actually, you may. I assume Herr Hedtoft is in that meeting." He made his best guess and nodded toward the nearest closed door. "Will you please inform him I'll be waiting for him over there?"

He pointed toward a far corner where he hoped they might attract a minimum of attention.

"Er . . . yes, of course, sir. Whom shall I say will be waiting?"

But Duckwitz had already set off to find a discreet place to sit in the far corner of the library, beyond several meeting tables and on the other side of a bank of shelves. He pulled up pair of small armchairs and told himself over and over to calm down. And he waited. Two minutes later the Secretary of the Social Democrats stood over him with a puzzled frown.

"They said you wanted to see me, Georg?"

"Sit down, please." Duckwitz tried to contain himself, though he still felt as if he was hyperventilating. Hedtoft must have noticed.

"You look pale." Hedtoft looked closer as he slipped into the other seat. "Is everything all right?"

"Not exactly." He shook his head but managed to keep his voice down. Still, he could not look the other man in the eyes. Instead he stared off into the darkening window, and he gripped his hands to keep them from trembling. Surely Hans Hedtoft would be able to tell.

"You're not well. Here, perhaps something to drink?"

"No, no." Duckwitz finally turned back to the conversation and cleared his throat. "Listen to me. The disaster is going to take place."

"The disaster," echoed Hedtoft, obviously not following. He would in a moment. Meanwhile he rubbed his high temples in confusion as Duckwitz continued.

"That's right," he said. "All the details have been planned. Two ships will be in the harbor to transport five thousand. Trains for the remaining twenty-five hundred. Unless you do something in the next forty-eight hours, your poor fellow citizens are going to be deported to an unknown destination. All the names and addresses are known."

Now Hedtoft nodded slowly as his eyes widened. By this time he had to understand. Did Duckwitz have to spell it out for him even more explicitly?

"I'd always suspected something like this would happen," said the Dane. "But when?"

"October first, starting at ten o'clock in the evening. It's calculated precisely so they'll all be in their homes for their holiday. Apparently, it's one of the major Jewish celebrations, whatever they call it."

"Just three days . . ." Hedtoft spoke as if his head was spinning. "How will we—"

"I've already spoken with the Swedish government. They've agreed to take in as many refugees as you can transport across the Sound."

"I see. But over seven thousand! I assume no one else knows? What about Best?

"No one else." Duckwitz shook his head no, which left Hedtoft to marvel at the sheer lunacy of what they were discussing in a corner of the comfortable Labour Library.

But there, now he'd gone and said everything. What else was there to be spilled? Or how much more treason could there be? Yet Duckwitz now felt a strange lightness, as if a load had been lifted and he could walk out of the library without ducking his head in shame. He accepted Hedtoft's strong handshake, and he could already sense the Danish politician's mind moving ahead.

"I'll pass the word along immediately," said Hedtoft, still pumping his hand. "Henriques will want to know; he's the head of their community. And Dr. Marcus Melchior, the acting chief rabbi at the Krystalgade Synagogue."

"Whatever is appropriate. I leave it up to you."

Duckwitz nodded as his mind drifted to schnitzel und spätzle.

"I can't tell you how much we appreciate what you've done."

Hedtoft understood what the information might cost.

"I'd best be going," Duckwitz answered, finally turning away. "My wife is holding dinner for me."

"Yes, of course." As they parted ways Hedtoft flashed one of the warm smiles that helped make him one of the most popular Danish leaders in the city. "But if anyone asks . . ."

He paused as Duckwitz looked back over his shoulder.

"I will have absolutely no recollection of this conversation."

10

There may be times when we are powerless to prevent injustice,
but there must never be a time when we fail to protest.
—ELIE WIESEL

S o you're feeling a little guilty, are you?"
Hanne's mother held on to her arm as they walked down
Krystalgade toward the synagogue for the Wednesday morn-
ing service. But what kind of a question was that?

"*Mor!* I'm not coming to the service because I'm feeling
guilty. I'm coming to the service because I have today off,
and because you asked me."

"Anything else? What about the start of Rosh Hashanah
tonight?"

"Well, sure. And I want to be here with you."

"Of course you do." Mrs. Abrahamsen clutched a small
black leather purse in her left hand. "You haven't been to
Sabbath services in two months, and now on the Day of
Judgment, when the destiny of all mankind is recorded on
the Maker's Book of Life, now you come."

"Mor, you are far too dramatic." Hanne tried to keep it
light as she smiled. "And it's only been a few weeks."

"You think blowing the shofar is too dramatic? You think
the New Year's meal is too dramatic? I think you could use

a little more drama in your life, maybe. A child or two, perhaps."

There. Hanne knew her mother would be slipping it in, sooner or later. And she tried not to roll her eyes.

"Please don't start with the children thing again."

"Why not? A mother has a right to express her opinion, does she not?"

"Not if it makes you sound like . . ." Hanne searched for words.

"Watch your tongue."

"I am, believe me. But you should hear yourself. The typical Jewish mother, pressuring her daughter to have children. Sometimes it's just too much for me to believe."

"I say the same thing. Sometimes it's just too much for me to believe."

"All right, fine." Hanne waved her free hand for emphasis as they neared the synagogue, less than a block away. "How about this: How about if I go out and get pregnant next month. Tell me if you want a boy or a girl. I'll have both. Then will you be satisfied?"

Hanne's mother stopped dead in the middle of the sidewalk, looking up at her taller daughter, and waved a warning finger.

"I don't like the way you joke," she told her.

But Hanne couldn't help smiling back.

"I'm sorry, Mor. It's just that you're always bringing it up, and I don't know what else to say."

They started walking again.

"Don't say anything, just do. You know that Aron would marry you in a minute."

Hanne sighed and pressed her lips together. Her mother was right about that much. Problem was . . . she didn't know what the problem was. Or if there was one. Who would be a better match than the son of her deceased father's best friend? And in a moment her mother would begin reminding her all over again why she should marry Aron Overgaard, and as soon as possible.

"He has money, you know, and plenty of it. So he needs a little fattening up? That's not hard to do. What's the problem? I thought you always liked him."

"I *do* like him, most of the time. He's very sweet. He brought me flowers at the hospital the other day."

"There, see? And?"

"And he's very sensible. Men like him are very sensible."

Yes, and everything about him looked the part—from his serious brown eyes and his dimpled chin to the prominent nose. Sensible.

"Well, then. What else can you ask for? You told me once that you thought he was the one."

"I was only fourteen at the time." She counted cracks in the narrow sidewalk as they neared the synagogue. He would be there today. She couldn't avoid him. But she certainly didn't want to hurt him, either. She could imagine the hurt puppy dog look on his face if she ever did.

"So just tell me this." Her mother wasn't giving up that easily. "What if he did ask you to marry him? What would you say?"

"Actually, Mor, he already did."

"What?" Her mother nearly exploded. "You never told me this. You never tell me anything! Should I not have known about this? What did you say?"

"Relax. That was ten years ago."

"Oh. You give me a heart attack with that kind of talk, and for what? Sometimes I wish your father was still alive just so he could discipline you. Here you are, twenty-five years old, and you still need someone to discipline you. You need a husband."

"I know. I miss him, too."

Hanne's mother let the answer slip by, perhaps not realizing.

"So what did you tell him?"

"Who? You mean Aron?" Hanne thought they'd better agree on terms, here. "I think we're talking about two different 'hims,' here."

"Aron, of course I mean Aron. The man who asked you to marry him. I was married when I was eighteen, you know. Fifteen's not that much younger than eighteen."

"You can't be serious. I told him I was going to be a doctor and that I wouldn't have time for men."

"You said that? Why am I not surprised?" This time Hanne's mother nearly dragged her black pumps across the sidewalk, looking more dejected with every step. "And look at her today. My daughter the prophetess. My daughter the nurse. The still-single nurse."

"Mor," Hanne said with a smile as she squeezed her mother's hand, "you're incredible."

"Your father would have been proud to hear you say that. Now if only you meant it in a nice way."

"You know I did."

Hanne would have been happy to keep the verbal sparring match going if not for the somber greeter standing between the familiar iron outer gate and the blond brick building's main entry. The Hebrew inscription above the outer door read "Welcome in the name of God." Tobias Simonsen, a young man who worked at the Tuborg brewery, must not have read the inscription.

"Please hurry inside and find a seat," he told them with an urgency that seemed quite out of place for the holidays.

Tobias, in a hurry? He looked up and down the street for any other stragglers before following them inside the lobby and slamming the door shut behind them. The sound reverberated throughout the building, sending a shiver up Hanne's spine as she helped her mother climb the stairs to the women's balcony, lofted high above the pews below.

"Strange how they're celebrating the high holy days this year," Hanne's mother wondered aloud as they found a seat by Gitte Lewenstein next to the railing, looking down some eight meters or so to where the men sat. At the front of the synagogue, the ornate platform enclosed with a railing held the eight-armed menorah as well as a podium for the rabbi and the ceremonial scrolls of the Torah.

"Do you have any idea what's going on?" Hanne wondered aloud as she searched the crowd.

Fru Lewenstein shook her head and knit her crooked fingers together on her lap; she looked as confused as anyone else.

"All they've been doing is rushing around and whispering to each other down there." She leaned across to speak to Hanne's mother. "No telling what they're up to, but I'll tell you one thing: It's not the service we're expecting."

Still Hanne looked out across the sea of men's dark hats and the occasional yarmulke. The ornate prayer hall normally seated around 650, with standing room for another 100. This morning plenty of open seats remained, but the nervous buzz told Hanne that Fru Lewenstein was right about one thing: Something was surely not as it should have been.

"I think they're going to make some kind of announcement." Fru Lewenstein pointed toward the front. By that time Aron had found his usual place near the platform, but only nodded nervously when he looked up and picked them out of the crowd peering down at him from the balcony. Hanne raised a tentative hand in greeting.

Finally Rabbi Melchior stood up in front, dressed not in his customary dark robes, sash, and tall pillbox cap, but in a rumpled black suit and tie that looked less pressed than slept in. And though he did at least wear a fedora, his hair stuck out to each side as if he had thrown it on in quite a hurry.

What could be so wrong that he would not have dressed for the occasion? Hanne still could not guess.

For a moment he stood fidgeting with his round-lens eyeglasses, pulling them off and then placing them back on his nose, then pulling them off once again. Eventually he got his glasses adjusted, so when he raised his hand the hall fell instantly silent.

"Thank you all for coming," he said, his baritone ringing throughout the hall. It sounded more like a greeting at a funeral, rather than the prelude to a two-day high holy days celebration. He paused for a deep breath before continuing. "But there will be no service this morning."

A soft gasp of surprise spread through the congregation until he held up his hand once more to continue.

"Instead, I have very important news to tell you. Last night I received word that Friday evening the Germans plan to raid Jewish homes throughout København to arrest all Danish Jews for shipment to work camps."

Again he paused, as if gathering strength to continue. Fru Lewenstein winced in pain at the announcement, bringing her hands to her cheeks in shock. Others around her looked as if they had been slapped. Hanne couldn't bring herself to look at Aron's reaction, only kept her focus on the rabbi as he stood before the congregation and bravely went on with his announcement.

"They know . . . they know that at the close of Rosh Hashanah our families would normally all be home. The situation is very serious. We must take action immediately. You must leave the synagogue now and contact all relatives, friends, and neighbors who are Jewish and tell them what I have told you. You must tell them to pass the word on to everyone they know who is Jewish. You must also speak to all your Christian friends, anyone you can think of, and tell them to warn the Jews. You must do this immediately, within the next few minutes, so that two or three hours from now everyone will know what is happening. By nightfall tonight we must all be in hiding."

"In hiding?" asked one of the men up front. "But where? And for how long?"

Several others added their agreement as the rabbi nodded.

"Arrangements are being made right now for evacuations to Sweden. I am informed by . . . by sympathetic sources in the government that the Swedes are prepared to take in as many as are willing to come. So my recommendation is to find a secure hiding place near the coast, among people you can trust. We will all pray for a safe passage, and that we will be able to return home soon."

Once again the men lobbed questions at one another, prompting the rabbi to raise his hands for silence. He straightened up his shoulders as if he'd found some measure of courage, and without warning began singing the words of the *Shehecheyanu* blessing.

> *Barukh atah Adonai, Eloheinu, melekh ha'olam . . .*
> Blessed are you, Lord, our God, sovereign of the universe . . .

For a moment his voice wavered, as if he remembered how this blessing would otherwise have been part of a mealtime celebration, now abruptly cancelled. There would be no apples dipped in honey this year, no hearty *challah* bread or candle lightings. Still he gave them what he could.

> . . . *shehecheyanu v'kiyimanu v'higi'anu laz'man hazeh.*
> who has kept us alive, sustained us, and enabled us
> to reach this season.

By this time Hanne could not imagine a dry eye in the congregation as they all echoed a teary "amen." She searched her purse for a handkerchief as the rabbi stepped down from the platform. His knees seemed to buckle, but he had one last thing to tell them.

"Go now. Quickly. *Hurtigt.* Please do not delay."

Visibly shaken, he collected a prayer book and shawl from a seat on the front row and accepted a hand from a couple of the closest men, then made his way to the exit.

The rest of the congregation now sat in stunned silence, while the only sound Hanne could hear was soft weeping and sniffling all around—and not just from the women's section. On one side, Hanne's mother stared blankly at the far wall, obviously in shock. On the other, Fru Lewenstein had burst into tears and sobbed uncontrollably. Hanne would have to move first, so she stood up between them.

"Come on, please, ladies," she told them, tugging gently at her mother's elbow. "You heard what the rabbi said. We need to go now."

By that time others around them had taken Rabbi Melchior's admonition to heart, as well, and were pressing toward the exits. The good news was that Fru Lewenstein's little husband had pushed up through the retreating crowd to collect his wife. When he found them he slipped a protective arm around her shoulder, mentioning something about taking a train to a relative's summer beach house in *Gilleleje*, up the coast, to hide there. But then they were gone.

"Actually, that sounded like a good idea," Hanne told her mother, who still said nothing. But by that time Aron had found them, and he waved over several heads for them to follow him to a side entry.

"I'm going to be staying with my cousin in *Roskilde*," he told them, as soon as they'd joined him. "You will come, too. And your mother, of course."

Under normal circumstances her mother would surely have appreciated Aron's invitation. But even now she just followed the crowd with her wide eyes as they hurried toward the exits, flowing past on all sides. Hanne wasn't even sure if she heard what Aron was saying.

"Roskilde?" Hanne quizzed him. "No. That's too far away, and the wrong direction. You heard what Rabbi Melchior said about making arrangements for Swed—"

"Of course it's far away," Aron interrupted her, his dark eyes blazing. "That's the point. But listen, there's no time right now to discuss it. We're getting as far away as we can, as quickly as we can. I'm certainly not going to wait here in the city for the Germans to pick us up. As soon as you can pack your bags, we'll leave immediately."

"Wait. *We?*" Hanne tried desperately to think, to make sense amidst the noisy panic that swirled all around them. "Aron, please. I just don't think that's a good idea. Listen, I have contacts at the hospital. I think they would help us. There are a lot of good people there."

"Absolutely not." Aron shook his head again, as if her ideas weren't worth discussing, and he, the final arbiter, had made an executive decision. "I just need to ask Tobias a few things, and then we'll go."

How could he say that? And how could he even think of going all the way to Roskilde, some thirty-five or forty kilometers to the west? Hanne could not say that she liked seeing this side of Aron, though she wasn't at all sure how to react.

But now, where to hide? How to hide? Who would help them? Hanne couldn't yet answer. In fact, nothing seemed clear, except one thing: Going to Roskilde would be a fatal mistake, no matter what Aron said. This she knew beyond a doubt. She looked to her mother who ran a hand along the rich walnut trim of a nearby exit door, as if seeing it for the first time. After what they had heard, perhaps it would be the last. Either way, her mother didn't seem to hear the exchange. And Hanne had a sinking feeling that their lives might depend on what she decided right here, right now. She pressed her lips together and held Aron's arm before he turned to go.

"We can't go with you, Aron." Her voice came out as a squeak, she thought, and he looked at her as if he hadn't heard.

"What are you saying?" His eyes clouded even more. "You can't be serious."

"We're going to the hospital. I know there's going to be help there. You should come, too."

He opened his mouth to say something, but the hurt look in his eyes told Hanne more than she wanted to know. How easy it was to hurt someone, without even trying.

"Aron!" Tobias Simonsen came up through the crowd, in a hurry like everyone else. "Are you coming?"

Now it was Aron's turn to choose, and he looked from his friend to Hanne, and back again. Finally, he turned back to Hanne.

"I won't leave the country without you, Hanne. Wait for me?"

"Aron, I can't—"

"Aron, honestly." Tobias wasn't about to wait any longer. "We need to go."

So Aron turned to go, but not before squeezing Hanne's hand in his.

"*Shana tovah*, Hanne," he told her, and the traditional holiday greeting could not have sounded more out of place. "I'll see you again."

"A good year to you, too," she replied, as someone in the back of the synagogue sounded the shofar. The echoing sound of the ram's horn always gave Hanne goose bumps, even more this time as she watched Aron disappear through the crowd.

But she knew where to go, now, and she knew what she had to do. She took her mother's cold hand and headed for the door.

"Let's hurry," she said, as they left the synagogue and headed back out to Krystalgade. They just had two days now to hide—and escape the only home Hanne had ever known.

11

To save one life is like saving the whole world.
—JEWISH PROVERB

O nly a few hours after the announcement in the synagogue, Hanne found herself back at the hospital on her
normal shift, feeling anything but. She studied the clipboard
by a patient's bed, forcing her eyes to focus, seeing nothing
but panic.

Settle down, she told herself. *Everything's going to be all right.
People here at the hospital will help.*

"The glass of water, nurse?" The woman in the bed looked
up at her with weak puzzlement. "You said you'd bring it?"

Hanne breathed again, tried to bring her thoughts back as
she replaced the clipboard into its holder at the foot of the
bed.

"Yes, of course. I'm sorry." She turned and nearly ran into
Ann-Grete, one of the morning shift nurses, who must have
just stepped into the room. Ann-Grete held her by the arm
as they stepped out into the hallway.

"It's all arranged," Ann-Grete told her in a quiet voice as
her eyes scanned the hallway first one way, then the next.
"You're taking my apartment, and I'm taking yours. We'll

trade personal things but leave the furniture in place, so we don't attract too much attention."

"But Ann-Grete, this is more than an inconvenience to you. This is—"

"This is just what we do. If the Germans think they know where to find you, they'll find me instead."

"But then what would you tell them?"

"How about, 'Look at me! Do I look Jewish to you? Hanne doesn't live here anymore!' "

Hanne sighed. "Oh, but they'll know. They're very good at that. All they'll have to do is check the personnel records."

"Which are being modified right now. From what I understand, you quit your job without warning three weeks ago. And you left no forwarding address. Everyone will say the same thing, and they'll have no idea what's become of you. See? There's one more missing Jew."

"Ann-Grete, I don't know what to say."

"Don't say anything. It's only temporary, you know. I hear they're already getting fishing boats together to ferry people across to Sweden. Besides, I might not like your furniture. Say, you do have furniture in your place, don't you?"

"Of course I do." Hanne smiled for the first time since all the trouble had started. "Bought the sofa just last year at Juhl Hansen. A nice floral print. You'll like it just fine."

"Ah, she even has good taste in fine furniture stores. On second thought, maybe I'll just stay in your place for a while."

"Yes, and I can just go on being a ghost here in the hospital."

When they laughed Hanne forgot for just a moment that her identity at the hospital—everything that once had her name on it—was being erased to save her life. And when she checked her wristwatch her heart jumped.

"Oh, no! I told my mother I'd meet her at the front doors in ten minutes. Would you bring the woman in 43 her glass of water, please?"

Ann-Grete nodded as Hanne hurried off down the hall, her mind spinning. What more could she be doing? Perhaps *Mor* could stay with her for a few nights, here at the hospital—if it was safe. But she wasn't sure about that, or how it would look if someone came searching. Perhaps it would be better someplace else. She hurried down the stairs to the ground floor, not noticing that someone else was laboring up.

"Oh!" She stopped short. "Pardon me. *Undskyld.* I didn't mean to . . . Pastor?"

When he took off his hat he didn't look like the patient she had helped stitch up just the other day. This time he looked far more, well, not so disheveled. And very nice, really. He smiled when he recognized her.

"Nurse Hanne. Very good to see you again." He patted his side. "And thanks again for all your good work."

"I hadn't expected to see you back here so soon."

"Well, better to be walking in than carried in, right?"

"You're right about that." She laughed in spite of herself. "I'm glad you're feeling better."

"Much better, thanks to you. Actually, though, I'm here on official business, visiting one of our older parishioners again. Teglgaard?"

"Ah, ja. Broken hip. She would be in room 24, if I recall. Um . . ." She nodded her head politely before taking another step and continuing down the stairs. "I hope you'll continue to feel better, as well."

He thanked her as she continued down the stairs, until a thought crossed her mind and she had to stop once more.

"Actually, Pastor," she called out, and her words echoed in the stairwell. Fortunately they were the only ones there, as far as Hanne could tell. And she blurted out the words before she changed her mind. "I wonder if I might ask you something else."

"Steffen," he answered, turning quickly. "Please call me Steffen."

"Er . . . okay. Steffen. But I was wondering." She looked up and down the stairwell again, just to be sure. No telling who might be listening. "When you were here previously, and your brother came to take you home, I couldn't help overhearing . . ."

Hanne paused, wondering what she was getting herself into. Well, but if she didn't ask, who would? He raised his eyebrows but did not interrupt, so she took a breath and went on—but this time in a guarded whisper.

"I couldn't help overhearing him talk about the Resistance. And I know it's not common knowledge, or public, but people here at the hospital know about the ambulance. He often parks it here, I think perhaps to make it look more legitimate. I hadn't known it was your brother, though."

"He surprises us both, eh?" He smiled at her, and she enjoyed the warmth of it. "But you probably know more about that ambulance than I do. He doesn't tell me a lot of those kinds of things, if you know what I mean. He tells me to stay in the church and preach my sermons, and then he gets upset with me for not doing more."

"More?"

He lowered his voice to match hers. "In the Resistance, I mean. But I'm sorry. You meant to ask me something?"

By this time Hanne was pretty sure Pastor Steffen—Steffen, that is—was telling her the truth about what he did or didn't know of the Resistance movement. How could those eyes lie to her, or to anyone? Maybe it was even better that he was not involved, yet. But she couldn't help asking him.

"I was going to ask you about putting up some friends—my mother included—perhaps at your church. I've never been inside, but I'm thinking perhaps there might be a basement, or some rooms that might be safe for them to stay in. For just a few days, that is, until we can find a way to get them to safety."

"Wait. Your mother? You want your mother to stay in our basement?"

When Steffen wrinkled his nose she couldn't help thinking of him like a cute little boy, puzzled at a school assignment he didn't quite understand. And she couldn't help smiling.

"I'm sorry. I didn't explain." Now she would tell him everything. What else could she do? It's what Rabbi Melchior had asked of them. "This morning at the synagogue Rabbi Melchior told us that the Nazis are finally coming for us. It's been decided."

"He knows this for certain?" Steffen's eyes widened in disbelief as she tried to reassure him.

"He would not have told us if it were not true. Everyone is going into hiding immediately, and we're letting as many Jewish people know as we can."

"But how would your rabbi know? I can't imagine the Germans would have advertised such a thing."

"Nonetheless it's true. They say it will happen on the night of the Rosh Hashanah celebration."

"Friday night. *I morgen aften.*"

"You knew that?"

"It's in my Bible too."

He shrugged, as if every Christian person in Danmark might be just as aware of the High Holy days. She knew better. But now he nodded slowly, as if he's just figured something out.

"I understand. So you're—"

"Jewish? Yes." She practically whispered the words. "But I'm okay for now."

She thought it over for a moment. She could go with her mother, or help to get her and the others to safety. Given her job, though, was there really any choice? Standing here in the hospital, her next step seemed a little clearer.

"I think I'm going to try to stay here for just a little longer," she explained. "With everything going on, there's so much to do here."

"You wouldn't leave with the others?"

"Actually, it's my mother I'm worried about, and several of our friends from the synagogue. I'm not sure any of them know where to go."

Steffen didn't appear to have any answers, either, though he did know how to listen well. He nodded as she went on.

"The only thing I've heard is that we're going to get fishing boats to take everyone across to Sweden, but it may be several days. In the meantime, they still need a place to hide."

She stood on the step beside Pastor Steffen, holding her breath as he rubbed his forehead in obvious thought. Finally he struggled to his feet as Hanne helped steady him. He straightened and looked directly at her.

"But so many," he whispered, as if still considering the task. "Five thousand? Six?"

"We're over seven thousand. But who's counting?"

"The Nazis, I expect. And I wonder what happens when they come knocking at your doors to find you not home?"

This time it was Hanne's turn to shrug. "I'm not sure of that, Pastor. I hope no one is punished or gets in trouble over this matter. But what would you do if they were coming after the Christians instead?"

She rather liked the way his eyes seemed to twinkle as he pondered her question. And Pastor Steffen seemed to do a lot of pondering, besides. Finally he allowed the hint of a smile to lift the corners of his mouth.

"Just the same as you're doing now." He nodded, the decision obviously made. "I just hope the church cellar won't be too damp and dreary for them."

Hanne smiled. "Better than the inside of a German prison camp, I imagine."

"I suppose you're right. So just tell your mother to knock on the back door of the church, on the side facing *Vedbækgade*. We should wait until after dark, should we not?"

Hanne wasn't sure about that, either, but it seemed like a good idea.

"I've never done this sort of thing, before," she told him as he made his way up the stairs again.

"Doesn't matter. Tell her to come after dark but before curfew. Eight o'clock? Two knocks on the back door like this . . ." He demonstrated on the inside of the door leading to the second floor hallway. "Then three more. Can she remember that?"

Hanne nodded.

"She'll remember."

12

May God keep you all. May God keep Danmark.
—KING CHRISTIAN X, 9 APRIL 1940

I still can't believe you told them they could hide here,"
Henning told Steffen that evening as they rolled a couple
of blankets out on the floor of a lower level storage room.

"We're going to make it *hyggeligt,* as cozy as we can. And if
they're cold, they can keep their coats on. They'll be fine."

A lone bare lightbulb hanging from the ceiling would help
just a bit, though it cast harsh shadows on boxes of assorted
cleaning supplies lining the far wall. He just hoped no one
minded a little dust.

Best of all, Steffen imagined they might not be found here,
secluded under a stairway and with an entry door with no
handle that seemed to very much blend into the shadows
and cracks of a lower level wall. One would have to possess
very sharp eyes or know the door was there to open it.

"Cozy? No, that's not quite what I meant." Henning waved
his hand around the tiny room—barely large enough to turn
around in. "I meant, I can't believe *you* agreed to all this. I'm
surprised at *you.*"

"Oh, is that it? After all the times you've been lecturing me, *lillebror,* I thought you would be happy we were actually doing something constructive."

"You can call me little brother all you want. But this is impulsive. This is a little dangerous, compared to your normal, er, way of life. This is definitely not you."

"Well, perhaps I'm just doing my patriotic duty for our country?"

That, and a little more. But no one said Steffen had to tell his brother *everything.* Especially not if he—that is, Steffen—wasn't even sure of his own motivations. He couldn't escape the feeling that he himself was a bystander, looking on, while another personality had hijacked his own life. In that way, Henning was entirely correct. What was happening here was definitely out of character for Steffen.

"Hmm." Henning stroked his chin, obviously still trying to sort things out. "And just a few days ago, you were telling me how foolish the Underground movement was, how King Christian said not to resist, et cetera. Come on. What's different now?"

"You're so suspicious. The need presents itself. Things have changed." Which was mostly true.

"Then how much are they paying you?"

"Shame on you for even suggesting such a thing. I'm a pastor."

"I was joking, all right? But come on! I still don't believe you just woke up this morning and suddenly decided to open up your church storage room to hide Jewish refugees."

"Why not?"

"It's just not . . . I mean, it just doesn't make any sense. Unless it's all about the girl . . . that's it!"

"Would you stop?" Steffen clapped his hands of dust and reached into his jacket pocket for a letter, which he handed over to Henning. "Here, read this. It might help you understand."

"Oh?" Henning squinted as he held the letter up to the light. "On behalf of all Danish bishops, eh? Sounds auspicious. Or suspicious. Where did you get this?"

"The Bishop. It went to the Germans today. They want us to read it from the pulpit this Sunday."

Henning read a few lines to himself, then out loud.

"All Danish citizens enjoy equal rights and responsibilities before the law, and full religious freedom," he read, then paused. "Very nice. That sounds just like something you would have written, to be sure."

"I didn't, though." Steffen pointed at the bottom of the page. "See the signature?"

"Hmm, okay." Henning pulled the letter away and kept reading. "Perhaps I should visit the service to hear it for myself."

If Henning knew they'd broached a sensitive topic, he made no sign of it as he handed the letter back.

"Perhaps you should," Steffen answered, stooping to straighten up a blanket that did not need straightening. "It would be nice to see you more than once a year."

Yes, and it would certainly prove to be cold and hard in this cramped space beneath the staircase. He would not like to consider sleeping there, himself. But he could think of no better place for anyone to hide, if that is what they had to do.

"Did I make it last Christmas?" wondered Henning.

Steffen didn't answer this time. He and his brother had more than enough to argue about, already, without getting into his brother's indifference about faith, and church, and other things Steffen held most dearly. They'd covered that ground before. Now Henning looked as if he was about to say something when someone knocked on the storage room door. They both stiffened and looked at each other.

"I thought no one else was supposed to know about the room down here," whispered Henning.

"Ja," replied Steffen, "no one but—"

"Steffen?" A rusty hinge squealed as Pastor Viggo pulled open the small door and poked his head inside. "Ah, there you are. I thought I heard familiar voices down here. Wasn't sure what was going on."

"Didn't realize we were making so much noise," said Henning, bumping his head on the slanted ceiling as he straightened out. "Ow!"

"Henning. Good to see you again. Although I can't recall the last time I've seen you in this building. Perhaps when I confirmed you?"

Henning laughed at the joke. He'd certainly been here since he was twelve, once or twice. Hadn't he?

"Henning was just helping me, er, straighten things out." Steffen wasn't sure they needed to go into too many details, and now he wished they'd kept their voices down. Because now Pastor Viggo looked curiously at the blankets and hand towels they'd set up next to a couple of wash basins and a pitcher of water.

"I see. Well. Sort of like the Hunchback of Notre Dame, is it? Only in this case, I don't imagine you'll be ringing the bells."

He looked expectantly from Steffen to Henning, a hint of a smile playing at his lips. Perhaps he thought this was amusing. But what else could they say, now? Henning looked at his brother and shrugged.

"It's your call this time, big brother."

As a matter of fact, yes it was. Steffen drew the older man inside and the door creaked shut behind them.

"It's not what it looks like."

Two hours later Steffen did his best not to be startled by the next gentle knock at the door—this time the back service entrance of the church.

"Did you hear that?" he whispered to Henning, who had already snapped off the inside light.

"I heard it. They're late. Open the door."

"No, wait." For a moment Steffen considered blowing out the flickering flame at the end of the brass candlelighter rod he held in one hand. He sniffed and sneezed as it smoked in his face.

But there it was again, this time two knocks and then three, and Steffen swallowed hard despite his dry mouth. Keeping the back light turned off, they swung the door slowly open, and Steffen shivered at a draft of cool outside air. Before he could catch a glimpse of who had been knocking, the candlelighter flame immediately blew out.

"Anyone there?" His voice cracked and he strained to see anything in the darkness. Naturally the rest of København lay muted and dark behind blackout shades, as it did every night. Only a shuffling sound on the cobblestone pavement told him someone was there.

"Pastor Steffen?"

Steffen recognized the nurse's voice close by, almost next to him, and felt a hand on his arm. Steffen's or Hanne's, he wasn't sure.

"Let's not be chatting out here," snapped Henning, sparking his own lighter. A golden pool of light revealed four frightened faces huddled just outside.

"Please come inside," Steffen told them, keeping his voice steady. He set aside the candlelighter and helped an older woman over the single step, while others followed. Once they were all inside, Henning pushed the door shut, and they snapped on the hall light.

Steffen blinked his eyes to see five frightened people, not just the four he'd been expecting. Still lovely in a dark overcoat and scarf, Hanne Abrahamsen made brief introductions.

"This is my mother, Elsebeth." She pointed at an older woman, perhaps seventy, but wearing a wide-eyed expression of fear that added years and made her resemble a frightened animal. Even so, the stooped woman nodded politely even as she kept the scarf over her head in place. Next Hanne indicated a couple standing just inside the door, every bit as reluctant to remove their coats.

"Mr. and Mrs. Levin," said Hanne, "and their friend Elias."

Elias seemed to force a tiny smile.

"We're imposing on your kindness," said Mr. Levin, in thickly accented Danish. He could have been Austrian, perhaps German. His guttural accent reminded Steffen of the way German soldiers sometimes butchered their Danish, often mixing in foreign words or confusing matters by imposing that peculiar German word order. "But we have no relatives here, and no other place to go. Only Elsebeth was kind enough to tell us of her daughter, that's Hanne, and Hanne said—"

"Pardon me for interrupting." Henning cleared his throat. "But we should probably show them to their room, shouldn't we, Steffen?"

The newcomers looked at Steffen, then at Henning, before addressing Hanne.

"*Wer ist das?*" he asked in German, but his wife just poked him in the side and would not tell who it was.

"Danish, only Danish," she scolded him. "No more German. I'm never speaking that language again, and neither will you."

Her husband frowned but listened.

"This is my brother, Henning." Steffen answered the question, which his high school German had helped him understand. "He's the one with contacts in the Underground, and he's going to be helping arrange your passage to Sweden as soon as he can. Meanwhile, you're going to need to stay here, as quietly as possible, and without showing yourselves in the main or upper portions of the building. Certainly not in the sanctuary. Never in the sanctuary."

"And not here," Henning told them. "Your room's down this hall."

Even with his words of encouragement they didn't move as they looked around the dimly lit back room, as if they still didn't understand. Hanne's mother clung to her daughter's arm, tears welling up in her eyes. Henning looked at them with a puzzled expression.

"They've never been inside this kind of building," Hanne finally explained. "They weren't so sure it was a good idea to come here. I had to convince them."

"Oh, I see." This time Steffen tried to sound reassuring as he led them toward their hiding place. "Well, we've tried to make it as comfortable as possible for you down here. Henning has even helped me prepare some blankets and things for you. Nice and *hyggeligt*. Cozy, you know? It won't be long before we'll get you a boat and away to Sweden, where you'll be safe. Henning's friends are working at it. Meanwhile, you can be reassured that no one will find you here."

"Absolutely," added Henning, taking a couple of their frayed carpetbags in tow. "And my brother won't make you take communion, either."

Henning was the only one who chuckled at the joke, which seemed so obviously out of place. The refugees looked at one another with worried glances. Still they followed him down the hall toward the hiding place under the stairs.

"I apologize for my brother," Steffen whispered to Hanne as they followed the others down the hall. "He means well. But you'll be comfortable here for the time being."

Hanne shook her head.

"Actually, I'm not going to be staying here," she told him in a low voice.

"What? I thought you—"

"I only came to help my mother and her friends."

"But . . . you're in just as much danger as your mother. Surely you know that. In fact, you must stay here. They'll find you."

Still she shook her head, obviously determined.

"My place is in the hospital. I'm staying in another nurse's apartment, where they won't find me. We've switched identities, as a matter of fact. But I am glad of your help. And your concern."

Steffen felt his mouth gaping, unsure of what else to tell her, or how to convince her to go. The truth was, at the moment he felt a glimmer of something new—something he had not felt before and could perhaps not name. As if he had something to protect.

"We just want to be sure you're all safe," he said.

Perhaps she was right, and the Germans would not catch up to her at the hospital. And if she stayed there a while longer, surely he would see her again. That would be worth looking forward to.

Out of the corner of his eye, though, he thought he noticed a movement in the shadows.

"Fru Husted?" he said. "Margrethe?"

A door slammed at the end of the hallway and Hanne stopped as well.

"Something wrong?" she asked, and of course he didn't want to concern her.

"No, nothing. Just the janitor, I'm sure. She's always puttering around the building." He laughed. "I'm just a little jumpy. Never done this sort of thing, after all. Hiding Jewish refugees, I mean."

She looked at him with understanding in her eyes.

"We're all learning this as we go." She paused. "Thank you."

But as they hurried to catch up to Henning and the others, Steffen couldn't help looking back over his shoulder one more time. An acolyte's robe hanging from a rack in the hallway still swayed in the draft.

13
SANKT STEFAN'S KIRKE, KØBENHAVN
FRIDAY EVENING, 1 OKTOBER 1943

A winter long and dark and hard, for five cursed years,
has squeezed the land in its embrace of cold and hunger and want.
—FROM "DANMARK'S FREEDOM SONG"

Sturmbannführer Karl Wolfschmidt checked his watch yet again. Eight minutes to ten. The broad-shouldered young truck driver beside him stretched his well-muscled wrestler's neck, looking straight ahead, waiting for the next command.

"Seven minutes," said Wolfschmidt, now tapping his fingertips on the metal dashboard and looking out into the darkness. Just ahead and to the right, the familiar Jewish synagogue's façade showed brightly enough to be seen even at this time of night. Adjacent to the synagogue stood the Jewish home for the aged. They would have no problem finding their way.

And yes, this operation would go smoothly, there could be no doubt. This time, the catch would be better than just an outdated Jewish community membership roster. He would see to that. What's more, Berlin would be sure to hear how well they carried out their duties tonight. They would hear how well the Sturmbannführer had led his men. He would see to that, as well.

In the darkness he couldn't read the wrinkled piece of paper folded in the breast pocket of his tunic, his orders and instructions for the operation. But he didn't need to. Instead he pulled it out and turned away from the young driver, then held the paper out the open window and up to the end of his cigarette. He blew on the orange spark. A moment later the paper burst into flames as he held it gingerly by his fingertips, watching it burn. The driver watched out of the corner of his eye but said nothing. He obviously couldn't know that Wolfschmidt had his own ideas on how to get results tonight—and that they would be better ideas than these weak "suggestions" from Berlin.

"Let's go," said Wolfschmidt, dropping the last of his burning paper to the street. Enough time waiting. Enough time talking. Time to act. He popped open his door and slapped the side of the truck three times, his signal to alert the squad of soldiers waiting inside the covered back end. He raised his voice, now that his timeline had begun. It would not matter now if anyone else heard them. It was too late for anyone to whimper for help.

"Raus!" he shouted, strutting toward the open tailgate. "Out! What are you boys waiting for? A written invitation? We have work to do, and not much time to do it!"

With that his troops bounded from the back of the truck, one of them slipping and nearly falling. Clumsy. They would need to perform better than this if they were ever going to bring credit to the Reich and the Führer. And where were all the others? Wolfschmidt berated the clumsy soldier and pointed him to the building next to the synagogue, a similar-looking blond brick structure facing Krystalgade. Idiots.

By that time perhaps a dozen other trucks had also pulled up in front of the old-age home, and not a moment too soon. He caught a beam of a headlight to check his time once again. Six minutes before the hour. Better a little early, he always thought. This war could be won or lost by punctuality, efficiency, and attention to detail.

———✎———

Steffen grabbed the phone on his desk off the hook before it had a chance to ring twice. Never mind the late hour.

"How are your guests?" asked Henning, not even waiting for Steffen to say hello, and certainly not identifying himself.

"Godt. They're quite well, thank you." Steffen rubbed the sleep from his eyes and the drool from the corner of his mouth, all the time wondering how long he'd been sitting here with his face planted on his desk. "Ready to leave, but well."

"All right, good." Henning lowered his voice, as if that would make a difference. "We're going to be ready for them within twenty-four hours, I think. I've almost got it arranged."

"Good. I'm already running out of food for them, and none of it kosh—"

He bit his tongue and could almost feel the heat from Henning's end of the call. They both knew of the very real possibility that someone could be listening in to the conversation.

"All right, forget it. Stop by tomorrow morning. Look for *The Little Match Girl.*"

That would be the signal book this time in the window of the *Ibsen Boghandel.* All right then. But now that Steffen's mind had cleared just a little more, he had to know something else.

"Wait; don't hang up. I just thought of something. The, the . . ." He struggled to veil his thoughts to anyone who might

———✎———

be listening in, if that were possible. Honestly, though, how could the Nazis have enough ears to hear so many conversations? Finally he gave up. "The old people, Henning! Next to the . . . you know. Has anyone warned them? Do you know?"

The other end of the line hung silent for a long moment, seasoned only by a ubiquitous background hiss. Henning would have no answer, until finally:

"We're doing what we can, okay? You can't help everybody. Sit tight until I—"

The rest of Henning's sentence was cut off, leaving the telephone deathly silent.

"Henning?" asked Steffen, pressing the receiver to his ear, wondering what had happened and realizing he had just repeated his brother's name once more. All this secretive business. "Are you there?"

But Henning had obviously been cut off, along with all telephone service. While that could happen occasionally in wartime København, the timing seemed odd, indeed. Had someone been listening in, after all? He looked at his watch. Ten o'clock exactly.

So Steffen hung up the phone, praying he had not compromised his brother's efforts. Surely not. But the thought of several dozen old Jewish people sitting helplessly in their rooms, while soldiers came to drag them away. . . . Surely the Nazis would not consider them a threat. He couldn't picture such a thing, but there was much about this war he could not picture.

Instead, he made his way to the church's front entry, stepping out into the night for a breath of fresh air and a way to clear his thoughts.

This can't be happening, he told himself. But his words fell short of convincing as a large gray truck careened around the corner and skidded to a stop with a squealing of brakes, directly in front of an apartment block across the street and only a couple of doors down. Steffen gasped quietly and drew back inside, ready to bolt the door against any intruders who would come for his "guests." He needn't have worried, as a squad of five or six German soldiers jumped from the back of the truck and, ignoring the church, hurried inside the apartment building. An officer in a distinctive peaked hat followed them at a slower pace, his hands knit behind his back.

Within seconds Steffen heard the crashing of what sounded like splintering wood—doors being smashed in, perhaps—and then shouting. None of them sounded pleased, particularly not when they reappeared outside a few short minutes later.

"I promise you, sir," one of the soldiers told the officer, now pacing the sidewalk in front of the building. "We looked everywhere. We looked in the right apartments."

"Then why aren't you out here with sixteen Jews, *obergefreiter?*"

By this time the lance corporal's voice trembled.

"Just like the last place, sir. There was just no one home. They must have known we were coming."

The officer leaned in so closely to the other man's face that Steffen could barely make out the words. Even so, there was no mistaking the venom they contained.

"And how could something like that have happened, do you suppose?"

Fortunately for the lance corporal, his officer didn't wait for the answer. Instead he backhanded the lance corporal's chest in obvious frustration and marched back to the truck.

"We'll be on our way, obergefreiter. We still have several more addresses on our list. They couldn't have just disappeared, every last stinking one of them!"

"No, sir, they couldn't have. We'll find them, wherever they're hiding. Just like we find rats, hiding in the kitchen."

The lance corporal scrambled to pull the others in line and jump once more into the back of the truck. Meanwhile the officer paused to look around the dark neighborhood, focusing on the steeple at Sankt Stefan's while Steffen stiffened in his hiding place.

Hanne lay in the darkness, heart pounding, unable to sleep. With every sound she held her breath, listening. Here, a steam pipe rumbled and creaked as the heat came on in the hospital building, with its peculiar ping, ping, ping—as if it might explode at any moment.

That much sounded familiar, though the strange apartment she had moved into offered none of the same comfort, except a thin promise of safety. Despite the warmth of her wool blanket, she shivered and burrowed deeper into her hiding place, playing and replaying what most certainly could be happening outside in the city and beyond. She imagined soldiers knocking down doors all around her little country, doors identified by brass plates engraved with names like Rubenstein or Levin. Not the usual Danish names, certainly, but still no less Danish.

A breeze rustled her blackout shade, reminding her that the draft came from a window cracked wider than she had intended. She turned over, burying her face in the thin pillow, which carried the faint scent of powdered cleaning soap. She didn't want to listen, just couldn't help it. The window shade rustled even more, and she imagined someone crawling in from the courtyard outside. Only this was the third floor. Still her mind raced.

Would the soldiers see past their scam and find their way back to this apartment, a floor above and half a building away? Would they believe Ann-Grete if she told them that Hanne Abrahamsen no longer worked at Bispebjerg Hospital, no longer lived here in the nurses' apartments? Or would she change her mind and perhaps lead them back to her old apartment? Under threat of violence, Hanne would not blame her friend if she betrayed this fragile trust. Honestly, Hanne could not say what she herself might do, if roles were reversed and it was she who faced the barrel of a German rifle. She might herself crumble, too.

"It's okay, Ann-Grete," she whispered into the pillow. "I won't hold it against you."

A door slammed somewhere below, and she dug her fingernails into the edge of her blanket. This could be it. She imagined where she had left her clothes in this unfamiliar space, and wondered how long it would take her to dress if someone suddenly pounded at her door. She would not, she decided, come to the door in only a nightgown and robe. No. She would open the door fully dressed and hair combed, or they would simply have to break down the door. If that's what they wanted to do, she could do nothing to stop it.

She turned over again and sat up straight.

Breathe, she told herself. *Slow down.*

But she could not, as voices and shouts below told her that something was going on. And if they found her here in this strange apartment, would they not find the other Jews hiding in the tunnels below the hospital campus? Or worse yet, in the basement of Steffen Petersen's church? Surely someone would tell them.

She whispered a desperate prayer, and found herself repeating the words of the Hebrew traveler's prayer. She thought it strange how it came back so easily, the words, so long after the train ride she had taken with her mother, when she was twelve, and Mor had recited it aloud right there in the train station:

> V'tatzilenu mi-kaf kol oyev . . .
> May You rescue us from the hand of every foe, ambush along the way, and from all manner of punishments that assemble to come to earth.

She heard more shouting, sharp men's voices, obviously in German. Then heavy footsteps in a hurry, growing louder.

> Barukh atah Adonai sho'me'a t'fila.
> Blessed are You, Adonai, Who hears prayer.

Did He? Now Hanne heard a woman's voice, muffled but pleading, repeating words Hanne couldn't make out. And for a moment Hanne considered getting up and stepping outside to give herself up. Others should not suffer on her behalf.

Instead she found herself praying that she could disappear completely under the covers. She knew she should slip out and get dressed, but that meant she would have to turn on a light. And a light might attract attention. She could not make her legs move. She shivered uncontrollably.

And now she pulled the covers well over her head, pulling herself into a fetal position, listening and shivering. And she decided it was even worse knowing what danger approached—much worse than not knowing and simply being surprised once. She decided she would rather be ignorant of the danger, than recognize it coming closer and closer. Either way, she could do nothing to change what was happening outside her door.

"The door!" Sturmbannführer Wolfschmidt shouted to his men, then pointed at two other trucks. "You and you, take up positions around the alleyway and the back of the building. Hurry! You're late. I want no one leaving this place unless it's in front of your weapon, and then into the back of your truck."

So it would be. Wolfschmidt promised himself that he would see to every detail, no matter how insignificant it might seem to someone else. That was their problem. No one ever cared about the details the way he did. But this time, nothing would be overlooked, and no opportunity missed. As he headed for the entry he nodded back at his driver, who pulled out the thick metal bar they'd stowed behind the seats. Now he brought it with him towards the door. Details.

"They're not answering the doorbell, Herr Sturmbann-führer!" A panicked *schütze* looked back at Wolfschmidt as he stepped up to the street entrance. "And our orders say to avoid—"

"Shut up and step aside, private. Your orders are what I tell you." Wolfschmidt wore the gray ashes of their orders on the soles of his boots. Didn't they know? He waved for his assistant to proceed, while the cluster of gray-suited troops hovered in position, ready to spring. They'd brought 150 troops to secure this position, which under normal circumstances would prove more than adequate.

With a hearty swing and a satisfying grinding sound of metal-upon-metal, the bar easily took out the door's lock. Wolfschmidt stepped up beside his driver before the other man could complete the break-in, kicking the door open with his own boot. Unfortunately that would leave a scuff, but that could be shined out in the morning, when this oper-ation was all over and he'd collected enough commendations for the day. The door exploded open, slamming something inside with a satisfying crash.

"I want everyone in this building assembled in the syna-gogue next door," he shouted, making certain everyone around him heard him well. "Everyone, do you hear me? Immediately! You have ten minutes."

And they seemed to require all of those ten minutes, despite the fact that none of the residents of this old-age home could have put up any resistance. Nine minutes later, Wolfschmidt paced in front of the ornate podium inside the synagogue, waiting for the last of his elderly captives. None looked younger than about sixty, and the latest arrival—bound with leather straps and dragged to the front of the auditorium— might have been in her eighties or perhaps nineties. Many of these Danes seemed to live to a ripe old age. But really they were Jews, all of them, and he reminded himself of the fact. No, to him it certainly didn't matter how old they were, how weak, or how infirm. To Wolfschmidt, a Jew was a Jew, no matter which country they found themselves in.

"Why are you doing this?" The wizened old woman looked up at him with a pitiful expression, tears in her rheumy eyes. Her gnarled hands trembled as she lay on the hard tile floor, and her silver hair unfolded in a fan around her shoulders. "We've done nothing to deserve such treatment."

"What is your name?" he demanded, hands on his hips. And as soon as he had asked the question, though, he regret-ted it—as if hearing her name spoken aloud might lend her more personality than he cared to acknowledge. He should not have asked, and it was not in their instructions or their orders to do so. But there; he'd asked her. And now she would answer, or suffer for her insubordination.

"Paikin," she whispered back, still daring to look him straight in the eye. Such an attitude would easily be modified. "My name is Fru Paikin."

"Well then, Fru Paikin, you're an enemy of the Reich," he reminded her with a smirk. "Or didn't you know?"

Given her age, perhaps she was only a symbolic enemy. He would grant her that. But an enemy nonetheless. And certainly she could not refute the facts, as Wolfschmidt understood them. This time she did not try, only pressed her thin lips together and remained mute. Just as well.

On the other side of the room, an eager young *scharführer* had a Jewish man backed up to the wall, pushing him for information about this or that saboteur. Thus the sergeant had been instructed in their orders, naturally. But what those orders did not detail was that he would certainly find out nothing of value here in this place. Wolfschmidt knew this without a doubt, but still he conceded it might be prudent to make the effort—or rather, to allow the scharführer to make the effort. Let him try. But before long the old man crumpled in obvious fear beneath the *scharführer*'s blows to the face and head, while Wolfschmidt looked on with approval. Yes, he decided, this might be a useful exercise for the men.

Up in the front of the auditorium, on the platform, several of Wolfschmidt's more enterprising young soldiers had improvised a new location for an impromptu indoor urinal. They looked back with a laugh while he signaled for them to continue.

Too bad there aren't more valuables here, he thought. *We'll just have to do the best we can with what we find. If nothing else, these boys deserve a souvenir.*

Meanwhile, the rest of the old people seemed to have taken offense at the interrogations, and after several minutes several had simply dissolved in tears or started mumbling in that peculiar language of theirs. At this, Wolfschmidt decided their efforts had gone far enough.

"Enough, already!" He waved his hand for attention. "We have several more addresses to visit before we're done for the evening. Let's get these hauled out to the truck."

Over on the side, the scharführer had finished his interrogation and stood with a boot planted firmly on his subject, the way he had been trained to do. Wolfschmidt motioned him over, so a moment later the scharführer joined him with a satisfied grin.

"I suppose they'll have enough time for prayers where they're going, won't they, Herr Sturmbannführer?"

"Absolutely." Wolfschmidt nodded and checked the time. Even with the extra effort they'd finished well ahead of schedule here. Time to deliver these Jews to the waiting ship in København's harbor, and move on. They had many more Jews to transport before they could reach the Führer's goal of making this protectorate, like all the rest of Europe, *judenrein*.

Free of Jews.

14

*Our task today is recklessness. For what we Christians lack is not
psychology or literature . . . we lack a holy rage—the ability to
rage when justice lies prostrate on the streets, and . . . a holy anger
about the things that are wrong in the world.*
—PASTOR KAJ MUNK

*L*ock the door behind you!" Henning made his meaning
clear. And Steffen, barely inside the door of the shop,
reacted just as quickly. Closing time, already? He turned the
deadbolt and flipped the sign in the window from *aaben* to
lukket.

Meanwhile Henning pulled down a large blackout shade
on the window, not so much to follow regulations—though
by five o'clock it was certainly dark—but almost certainly to
ensure no one out on Nørrebrogade would see what he was
about to do.

"I don't think they're going to last much longer," Steffen
told him. "They know what's happened, and they're ready to
bolt."

"They're staying where we hid them?"

"For now. But like I said, they're—"

"They just have to hold on a little while longer." Henning
held up his hand as he pulled a few books out of a shelf.
Behind them he'd hidden a radio receiver. Steffen whistled
in admiration.

"Short wave? I've never seen this before."

Henning shrugged as if it was nothing.

"You never asked. Now keep it down; I want to hear what they have to say. It's amusing, sometimes."

This time Henning fiddled with the dial a bit, tuning out the static and keeping it tuned to a local bandwidth. Tonight they would listen to the German-approved propaganda, rather than an illegal foreign broadcast like the BBC. Finally Henning cocked his head to the side, listening.

"I usually can't stand to listen to these stikker," he said. "Traitors. They'll do anything the Nazis ask."

Steffen kept still and listened just as intently as his brother. Finally the announcer's voice came in more clearly.

"As a result of measures taken by the German authorities," the announcer told them in a monotone, "the Jews have been removed from public life and prevented from continuing to poison the atmosphere, for it is they who have to a considerable degree been responsible for the deterioration of the situation in Danmark through anti-German incitement and more and material support for acts of terror and sabotage."

"Poison, eh?" At that Henning actually laughed. "If only they knew who was really behind the sabotage."

Ja, thought Steffen, studying his saboteur brother's face. *If they only knew.*

Still the announcer droned on. Steffen couldn't be sure if it was actually a German sympathizer, but he seemed to be doing a good job of putting listeners to sleep.

"In the next few days, in response to the inquiries of large sections of the Danish population, release of interned Danish soldiers will begin and will continue at a rate corresponding to the technical possibilities."

"In other words," Henning interpreted for them as he snapped off his radio, "they're going to release our boys to keep people off their backs while they deport Jewish families to death camps. Danish families."

They looked at each other, fire matching fire, and for the first time in a long while Steffen didn't feel as if they were about to lapse into an argument.

"It's not going to work," said Steffen, before pausing. "Is it?"

"Of course it's not going to work." Henning slammed his secret cabinet shut, then put his shoulder to the bookshelf and rolled it shut. "Do you know how many Jews they've found so far, out of the seven or eight thousand in the entire country?"

He seemed a little too well-informed about the matter, but Steffen wasn't going to ask too many questions.

"I have no idea. But last night I saw a truckload of soldiers enter the apartment block right across from the church, and they left without having found a single one."

"Exactly! I heard some of the old folks didn't find a hiding place soon enough. A few others didn't get the word. But it's a big failure, Steffen. A wonderful flop!"

Perhaps so far. But Steffen wasn't forgetting the people hiding in the basement of his church. And he assumed thousands more still found themselves in the same situation.

"So what do we do now?" asked Steffen, choosing his words carefully—and well aware that he had just stepped over a line he'd never crossed before.

"That depends." Henning looked him over seriously.

"On?"

"On whether you're involved." He rubbed his chin, as if sizing up his brother. "Are you?"

Steffen didn't answer right away as he walked through the familiar, comfortable shelves of books. Always he'd felt a sanctuary here, in this world of ideas and theories that only demanded his attention and nothing more. He could offer it or not.

This time, however, he knew the people in his church basement needed more than a sermon. He fingered the spine of a volume of Ibsen's poems to keep his hand from trembling, then finally nodded.

"I suppose I'm already involved," he found himself saying. "We have to get these people to safety, don't we?"

Henning didn't answer, but Steffen jumped as someone pounded on the door.

"We're closed! Lukket!" Henning shouted over his shoulder without looking to see who it was. Still the pounding continued. "I said—"

"Please!" A familiar voice brought Steffen to attention. "It's Hanne Abrahamsen."

Henning raised his eyebrows at his brother and flashed a smile. Steffen didn't react but simply unbolted the door and let Hanne inside. She quickly looked from one brother to the next, then around at the empty shop.

"Nobody here but us," Henning reassured her as she stepped inside. Her eyes looked red and puffy and her hair windblown, as if she had not slept well or had been crying.

"You're all right, then?" Steffen asked as he locked the door once more. "You heard what happened last night."

"I heard." She hugged her shoulders and kept her long coat buttoned all the way up. Perhaps it was colder out there than Steffen remembered. "And I'm very sorry to have come here, but—"

"You really shouldn't have," Steffen told her, feeling like a big brother all over again. "It's not safe for you to be out on the street. But how did you know to come here?"

Henning filled in the blank. "You followed my brother here to the store, didn't you?"

"Well, yes, but . . ." She opened her mouth to explain, then frowned. "Look, I know it's not particularly safe out on the street, but my identity card doesn't have any sort of Jewish designation on it."

"Not yet," countered Henning. "On the other hand, they must know who you are. And pretty soon you know they're going to have a watchlist."

"So can you help me with . . ." She paused to take a breath, "with another identity card?"

Henning looked as if he was thinking it over, but nodded his head slowly.

"That's not easy to do," he finally told her with a sigh. "But I'll ask around. I assume you'd want a nice Danish name like Olsen or Nielsen or Hansen, am I right? Meanwhile, you have to avoid getting stopped on the street."

She nodded her agreement, though Steffen could tell she hadn't just come to inquire about getting a fake identity card.

"Something else?" asked Henning.

"Ja." Now it was Hanne's turn to sigh. "Look, we've taken in a good number of refugees at the hospital. More than my directors are comfortable with, actually. And already many of them are being moved up the coast to find a boat across from Gilleleje. But the people in your church. My mother. They're still safe, are they not? And how soon can we get them to safety?"

"They're safe." Henning crossed his arms in a way that signaled confidence. Or in Henning's case, perhaps a little arrogance as well. "And we're getting them out tonight."

Relief flooded Hanne's features as her shoulders slumped and she appeared to breathe easier.

"Good. But you're taking them out from our harbor here? Really? Not from up the coast, where it's closer to Sweden?"

Henning's firm expression never changed.

"You wanted us to get them out? So that's what we're going to do. They'll be transported at midnight in a rowboat, meeting the fishing boat just outside the inner harbor. So they'll be past the German patrols in just a few hours, and eating breakfast in Sweden by daybreak. Does that meet your approval?"

Hanne's face clouded as she backed away a half step. This was starting to sound like serious business, and Steffen didn't especially care for the tone of these negotiations. He started to interject a word of compromise, but with a raised hand Hanne wouldn't allow it.

"I didn't come here to offer my approval," she said, "and I'm not trying to tell you how to do your job. I was just wondering—"

"No offense taken." Now Henning managed a smile, while Steffen could only look on helplessly. "You'll be interested to know, however, that your pastor friend here is going to be rowing your refugee friends himself."

"He is?" Hanne's face showed at least as much surprise as Steffen felt. What in the world?

"I am?" Steffen gulped, while Henning gave them both a mock expression of confidence. Surely he was kidding, now. When had he come up with such a plan, and not even told Steffen the details?

"Of course he is. You're looking at the man who took fourth place in the 1928 Olympic trials. Have you seen the medals in his office? He missed making the Danish team by just a half second. I'll bet you didn't know that."

"No, I didn't." She furrowed her brow at Steffen with a look that brought color to his cheeks. She needn't have looked quite so surprised, even if Henning didn't remember his facts so well.

"So we need to see your first person at eleven forty-five, not a second before or later. Steffen will be waiting in his boat under the east side of the *Nyhavn* Bridge. You know the place?"

"Did you say Nyhavn?" Hanne's eyes widened in surprise. "That's crazy."

"Yes, I know." Henning smiled at his audacious plan. "Right in front of the Germans' noses. But that's exactly the point. And that's why it's going to work."

"Right there in the busiest part of the harbor," said Hanne, still looking as if she didn't quite believe it.

"And nearly two sea-miles out to the Sound," he went on. "But to Steffen, that's nothing."

Steffen wasn't sure whether to thank his brother for the vote of confidence, or refuse immediately, before it was too late. Nyhavn. New Harbor. Though it had changed some in recent years, this narrow canal was still one of the most, well, *questionable* collections of colorful waterfront pubs and worse. And getting through that venerable waterfront neighborhood after curfew would surely pose a challenge in itself. But Hanne nodded gravely and Henning went on.

"So I want the second person two minutes after the first one, and the last two at two-minute intervals. Two, four, six, eight. No one will say a word or make a noise, they'll just crawl under the tarp in the back of the boat, and stay there until the boat is clear of the inner harbor and we're ready to make the transfer. Understand?"

"I'll tell them," she agreed. "And I'll let them know an Olympic rower will be taking them to freedom."

"Only out of the harbor, and then you transfer to another boat, one with a permit to be out there. It will be waiting."

By this time Steffen could only watch the conversation work its way back and forth, like a table tennis match.

Neither Henning nor Hanne asked for his opinion; perhaps they had forgotten he still stood there. And most notably, no one acknowledged the fact that he had a sermon to deliver tomorrow morning, and that staying out all night rowing Jewish refugees past German guards and out into the Øresund sounded like the wildest form of insanity. No one mentioned that part. Instead, Hanne discussed details with the detached manner of someone negotiating the sale of a fresh cod from the apron-clad fishwives on *Gammel Strand* in the old water-front quarter.

"I see," Hanne replied, shifting to look at Steffen this time. "And where again will you be waiting?"

"As I said." Henning didn't let his brother offer a word of his own, which in this case was all well enough. What would Steffen have said, anyway? "Under the bridge. And mind you're on time. If you're not all there by eleven-fifty, he's going to be leaving with whoever is on board. Any questions?"

Hanne looked from one brother to the other, and shook her head no. He wished she might have asked about how they planned to avoid German soldiers on the street, how they hoped to steer clear of German patrol boats on the water, and exactly where they intended to meet up with the fishing boat, somewhere beyond the inner harbor. She asked none of that.

"Actually," Steffen put in, "I took fifth place, not fourth. I was at least a half minute off the pace. And I haven't been able to get out and row for months."

Henning rolled his eyes and steered Hanne back toward the door.

"Don't mind him," he told her. "I think his bicycle accident might have affected his head. But believe me, he still knows how to row. You should see him, sometime."

Steffen took that as a compliment, and Hanne looked over her shoulder with a polite smile. But then he could think of nothing appropriate to say. He could not tell her this was the very first he'd heard of his brother's scheme. Nor could he explain how he'd gone from a respectable pastor to a law-breaker who illicitly harbored refugees in his church basement, to an active participant in his brother's illegal activities. He dared not even think of the potential consequences, if they were caught. Even more than that, he dared not quote Paul's letter to the Romans anymore—despite the fact that the bish-ops themselves had quoted it in their protest letter. Because this was different. This was real, except for the fact that Hanne Abrahamsen had stepped into his life in an odd sort of way.

But Henning could have been right about one thing. It had all started with the bicycle accident. And now?

Perhaps it really had affected his head.

"Well, Steffen?" As they walked down Nørrebrogade a few moments later, Henning was obviously waiting for an answer, but Steffen remained silent as his brother continued.

"I admit I presumed quite a bit back there in the shop."

Yes, Henning had presumed, and quite a bit at that. But Steffen flexed his arms and remembered the satisfaction of competitive rowing, back before his seminary days. And he had won a few races, had he not?

"You said you wanted to help," added Henning. "But if you can't do it, tell me now and we'll find someone else. I know it sounds crazy. But are you in? I need to know."

Perhaps it was the kind of thing best prayed over and con-templated. The kind of thing about which he should seek God, making sure he did the right thing. But he also knew that they had to act tonight, and act quickly. And if he didn't agree?

"I'll do it," he said, before he could change his mind. "All right? I'll do it."

15

*For God does not create a longing or a hope without having a ful-
filling reality ready for them. But our longing is our pledge,
and blessed are the homesick, for they shall come home.*
—ISAK DINESEN, IN *THE DIVER*

S teffen didn't think anyone could see him as he bobbed in
the inky cold water under the Nyhavn bridge. Probably
not. Maybe not. But he held his breath when two German
soldiers walked past on the cobblestone street above, obviously enjoying their evening a bit too much. One of them
lit a cigarette, fumbling with a match as the other sang a
German drinking song, off-key. These Germans seemed quite
happy to spend the war taking in the comforts of occupied
Danmark.

So Steffen burrowed a little deeper under the canvas and
covered his head so that only his eyes could see out. Here it
smelled of tar, seawater, and old fish—a combination that
made his stomach squirm. He tried to breathe through his
mouth while not making a sound.

The good news was that no one seemed to notice the long,
narrow rowboat as it tugged on its mooring line and occasionally scraped against the stone embankment. Not the passing
German soldiers—who eventually moved on—and not anyone else. The bad news was that he'd begun to shiver after

seawater in the bottom of the boat sloshed up high enough to soak his knees and ankles.

"You could have at least gotten me a boat that didn't leak, Henning," he mumbled and shifted his weight. A tin cup washed against his foot, and he used it to bail out a few more scoops. The water made his fingers needle-numb. How had he gotten himself into this mess?

To pass the time, he chewed on a small piece of salty black *salmiak* licorice and did his best to run through the sermon outline for the next morning, the one he'd deliver if he actually came back alive. But all he could think of was the opening verse of their reading for tomorrow, the fifteenth week after Trinity Sunday.

> *Therefore do not be anxious about tomorrow, for tomorrow will be anxious for itself. Sufficient for the day is its own trouble.*

"Easy for someone else to say," mumbled Steffen as he tried to crouch above the cold waters. His shoes leaked and his socks felt wet when he wiggled his toes. He worried what his shoes might look like tomorrow when he stepped into the pulpit. Don't be anxious for tomorrow? What about being anxious for the next hour? He hunched down a little more under the tarp and dared to snap on the flashlight he'd brought, just to check the time on his wristwatch.

Eleven-forty. Almost *midnat*. If he was lucky, perhaps no one would show up, and then he would just have to worry about making it home again to his own warm bed, dry and safe and nowhere near the harbor that assaulted his nostrils with pungent odors of beer and low tide.

Except if they didn't show, that meant he would still have to care for them in the church basement, unless they could find another, more reasonable way of getting to safety. No one had ever explained to him why they hadn't just been put on the train to Gilleleje with everyone else.

Don't be anxious for tomorrow? He wondered how four normal-sized people might even fit under the tarp here without tipping the boat over backward. And then he heard footsteps up on the cobblestones again, this time much softer than the heavy thud of German boots—a shuffle and then a stumble, a pause and then a sprint—and then two people stood awkwardly next to the boat, each holding a large suitcase.

Oh, no. Herr and Fru Levin. Standing out in the open, looking for all the world as if they were ready to take a cruise together.

"Under here!" Steffen hissed, motioning for them to come closer. He jumped out of the boat and pulled them in under the shelter of the bridge. "You were supposed to come one at a time."

"It's my fault," said Fru Levin. "I didn't want to come alone."

"No, it's not." Her husband set up his argument. "I wouldn't let you."

"Shh." Steffen managed to clamp a hand over the man's mouth. "Never mind."

The bigger question was, how did they manage to come all this way with their suitcases! And not attract attention? Steffen craned his neck to see if anyone had followed, or if any soldiers approached. He saw none. Good. But they still had a problem.

"Those suitcases," he began. "There's no way we can take them with us. You'll hide them up there, under the bridge."

Through the darkness he could hear the despair creep into Fru Levin's voice.

"But my wedding dress is in there."

"All right, then. You decide: your wedding dress, or your husband. Because trust me, there's not room on this little boat for both."

They looked at each other for a moment before Herr Levin grabbed his wife's suitcase and shoved it into the deeper shadows, farther underneath the span.

"I told you not to bring all that stuff," he grumbled, far too loudly. "We'll never get it across, I said. And now look what's happening."

Steffen felt a pair of desperate hands grip his shoulders.

"You'll take it back to your church, will you not?" Fru Levin's voice trembled. "You don't know how much it means to me. Then when we come back—"

She dissolved again into tears and Steffen honestly wished he could have promised her, or lied to her. All he could do was turn away to pull the tarp into place, helping them step into the back of the small boat.

"Keep your weight down," he ordered. "Find a place in the bottom of the boat and stay there."

"But . . ." Fru Levin objected once more. "It's wet down here!"

This time her husband shushed her as they found their places. And by this time Steffen knew it would take a miracle for them not to be discovered even before they left the shelter of the bridge.

"Is this the right place?" Now the couple's friend, Elias, tapped Steffen on the shoulder. Where had he come from? At least he kept his voice down, but when he signaled to the darkness Hanne's mother emerged to join them, and Steffen hurried her along. Tonight the darkness might be their best friend, but it would not also swallow all the noise they had to be making. At least these two weren't carrying suitcases.

"Into the back of the boat," Steffen told them, aware that the stern had already dipped dangerously. "Hurry."

But he wasted no time giving instructions or redistributing the weight; he simply tossed the tarp over the four of them and prayed they wouldn't immediately capsize. And then, once he'd untied the last rope holding them fast, he pushed out from their shelter and into the dark but open canal.

It had been a few years. But the oars felt snug in his grip, and he braced his feet against one of his passengers. Despite the danger of the open water, he smiled as he reached for his first stroke, deep and slow as they turned and made way for the inner harbor.

"It's still wet," he heard Fru Levin whimper in the darkness. Her husband told her to stay quiet, and Steffen fell into a rhythm as they glided silently past the dark ghosts of fishing cutters and empty freighters. Reach, pull, pause. Water gurgled under the bow as they avoided the outlines of cranes and piers on the shore. Feather the oars so they won't catch. He remembered his last race, when a stitch in his side had slowed him down and cost him the race.

This time he fell into deep, regular breaths, keeping his eye only on the tiny wake that sparkled in the moonlight that had just ventured out from behind a cloud. A glance over his shoulder every few strokes helped keep them from veering too far off course, and then he pulled in earnest, digging in and arching his back with each stroke, faster and faster. Perhaps he could do this, after all. A ripple of a breeze sent tiny waves across the inner harbor, scudding under the bow with a comforting rhythm and the occasional slap against the hull. He could almost have forgotten the danger all around them until his cargo began to move and the boat listed dangerously to the side without warning.

"Stay down!" Steffen almost shouted as he missed a stroke and toppled backward into the bow of the boat, arms and legs flying. The oar slipped out of his right hand with a splash, leaving him on his back with just the left one.

"What are you doing?" he demanded, hoping his voice didn't carry across the waters. Fru Levin's head popped out from underneath the tarp.

"I'm going to be ill," she announced, and Steffen thought it was probably a good thing she was so close to the edge of the boat. But as the boat rocked even more her husband grabbed her around the shoulders in obvious panic while cold water washed in over the side.

Without thinking Steffen leaned out the other side, doing all he could to balance the panic. But instead of steadying the boat he tumbled over the side into the icy harbor.

"Pastor!" he heard someone shout his name, while the shock of icy water closed all around him with a thousand needles, sucking the air from his lungs. He flailed his arms and swallowed a mouthful of bitter seawater until he connected with something hard—the oar!

Meanwhile a dark shape approached from the direction of the sound, and he heard a low, distinct chugging coming closer, directly at them. If he could have scrambled back up into the boat and steered away, he would have. Instead, all he could do was slip the oar back into their boat and cling to the rail as a fishing cutter pulled up alongside, nearly sandwiching him in the process. He looked up to see strong hands grab him by the shoulders and lift him clear.

"Trying to swim all the way, are you?" A man in dark coveralls looked him over from the deck of the fishing boat, hands on his hips. A scale-encrusted pile of net lay on the deck beside him as Steffen gasped for breath, still on his knees on the rough wood deck.

"Should we throw him back, Neils?" The man who had rescued Steffen seemed to think he was quite funny. "He's pretty small."

"Shut up and get the others on board," answered a man behind the wheel. Their engine popped as they idled in a gentle swell. "German patrol should be coming back this way any time, and they all need to be down in the hold."

"What about the boat they came in?" asked the fisherman.

"Let it sink, Mogens. We don't have time to fool with it."

"Nej, wait. I'm not going." By that time Steffen had regained some of his breath, and he was able to struggle to his feet with a raised hand. He'd left a large puddle of dark seawater on deck, and his wet clothes clung to his body. He couldn't keep from shivering.

"Can't change your mind now." Mogens the fisherman appraised him even as he lifted the other four refugees over the side of the larger boat. "You heard him, get below."

"You don't understand. I'm not Jewish. I just rowed these others out here for you to pick up. I have to get back. In fact, I have a sermon to preach in the morning."

Mogens looked at him a little longer, then broke out laughing.

"Did you hear that, Neils? This one says he has a sermon to preach. What's it going to be about, walking on the water? Because if you think you're going back in that thing . . ." He pointed at the rowboat, nearly awash. "You're going to need some divine intervention."

"Perhaps. But we got here in that boat, and I am going back in it."

"Let's go!" Neils leaned out of the pilothouse in the stern as he revved up the engine and pointed toward a distant light on the water, moving quickly their direction. "In or out, I don't care. But the Germans are coming this way, and we're not going to have passengers out on deck when they pass by."

"I'm going. Thank you. *Tak*." Steffen straddled the knee-high railing and prepared to jump. The little boat would have to hold him, one way or another. But before he could make his move, Hanne's mother grabbed him around the neck and landed a kiss on his cheek.

"You didn't have to do this," she told him as the lights from the patrol boat drew nearer. "But please, my Hanne, she . . ."

Her voice faltered as Mogens tossed a bucket into the little boat with a wave. Steffen thought she said something about "was going to be married," but that made no sense.

"What did you say?" he asked. But the others had pulled Hanne's mother way from the side of the boat.

"Lay low," Mogens told Steffen. "They won't see you if we get their attention. But if they spot you, well, you seem to know how to swim pretty well."

Which didn't sound encouraging, but Steffen did know how to lay low. He'd been getting plenty of practice in that. So he crouched in the bottom of the boat, trying to ignore the cold water that washed around his feet and over his ankles. He looked back up at the fishing boat as it powered up and turned away toward the distant Swedish coast, here only about twenty-five kilometers across the Sound. Lights winked just north of distant *Malmö*, neutral in the conflict and a safe haven for the Jews he had delivered this far. He imagined Hanne's mother huddled now in the safety of the fishing cutter as they faded from sight.

"Don't worry," he whispered, and the words surprised him. "I'll take care of her. I promise."

Which seemed rather audacious, especially given the circumstances. Right now, he wasn't at all certain he could take care of himself, much less Hanne Abrahamsen. He wasn't even sure he could get himself back into Nyhavn without being seen, and before dawn. He imagined a half-drowned man rowing a small boat in from the Sound might not go unnoticed.

For now he could only remain low in the drunken little boat as it rocked in the waves, sluggish and drifting before a freshening wind that carried traces of distant mown hay and golden leaves in neat piles, the scent of green things in gardens, laying down for an autumn nap of freedom.

Was that the scent of freedom?

Steffen found himself wondering how a breakfast in Sweden might taste as he listened to the chug-chug of the fishing boat, this time growing fainter in the distance. Perhaps those wonderful pancakes, topped with sweet lingonberry sauce. Meanwhile the lights from the German patrol boat grew larger as they powered by with a throaty buzz, powerful and throbbing, and to be avoided at all cost.

Steffen watched, never taking his eyes off the lights. He even wondered if he might actually jump into the water and try to hide if it came toward him, the way Mogens the fisherman had suggested. Probably it would do no good. They would find him, and if they did, they would connect his presence there in the Sound with the departing fishing boat, headed toward Sweden.

Father, let them be blind, he prayed for the men on the boat, and as he prayed he forgot to shiver. *Blind and deaf. Show them nothing but a dark, empty sea.*

He waited, bucket in hand. And the German patrol did not seem to change course, but remained a kilometer or two off shore as it continued south. Another wave sloshed over the side of his boat, waking Steffen once more to the very real danger of completely swamping. And who would come to his aid if he did?

Still he felt cheered as he laid to the task of bailing as much water as he could from the boat. Good thing Mogens from the fishing boat had thrown him the bucket. Bailing with a tin cup might not have worked as well. Ten minutes later, he had the water back down to the floorboards, and the exertion helped him almost forget how wet he still was, except that now his clothes rubbed under his arms and across his chest, painful and like cold sandpaper.

Never mind.

Finally he shipped both oars back into place and pointed directly away from the scent of farms, directly away from the lights of Malmö and back to the darkness of his home—a fearful city guarded by a silent, cold mermaid. He pulled with a steady rhythm once more, quickening the pace and ignoring the chapped pain of his wet clothes. He rowed faster now, and his breathing matched each stroke, regular and strong, as he headed for home.

Did I really say I'd take care of her? he asked himself, not allowing the caution that had always framed his life to blot out the picture of Hanne Abrahamsen, who he knew was the real reason he had just done this crazy, insane thing.

He kept pulling at his oars, moving backward toward the familiar threat of curfews and ugly hooked crosses, backward toward the deadly occupation where Hanne and so many others still hid in closets and barns. For his beloved Danmark was not yet, as the Germans supposed, judenrein. He strained at the oars, now harder than ever, ignoring the blisters forming on his palms and fingers. He rowed away from the scent of freedom and back to the terror, before he could change his mind.

16

*I swore never to be silent whenever and wherever human beings
endure suffering and humiliation. We must always take sides.
Neutrality helps the oppressor, never the victim.
Silence encourages the tormentor, never the tormented.*

—Elie Wiesel

Steffen cleared his throat and looked out over the small sea of faces in Sankt Stefan's congregation, waiting expectantly for him to begin the liturgy and read his prepared sermon on *Mattæus*, the sixth chapter. The one about serving two masters and not worrying about tomorrow.

He looked down again at his shoes, wiggling his toes to feel how soggy they remained after his dip in the Sound. Holding them over candles when he arrived home hadn't helped much. He cleared his throat again and pulled out the crumpled paper, the letter he'd shown to Henning. This would not be a usual Sunday, particularly since he'd not slept all night. This would be a first, in more ways than one.

"Before we begin this morning," he began, "I've been asked to read you the following letter on behalf of all Danish bishops."

He looked up once more to see every eye on him. Pastor Viggo nodded from his usual seat in the third row from the rear. He already knew what the letter said.

"It says that the Danish bishops have on September twenty-ninth, this year, forwarded the following communication to the leading German authorities."

Steffen tugged at his earlobe and worked his jaw up and down, trying to set the last bit of seawater free, then flattened the letter out in front of him and resumed reading.

"Wherever Jews are persecuted as such on racial or religious grounds, the Christian Church is duty bound to protest against this action . . ."

Duty bound. As he continued reading he could not escape those words, even as they pummeled him so hard he felt beaten and bruised. And the worst part was, he used to think he understood that phrase, and even how to live his life by it. Now he only knew that he knew nothing of the sort. Because whatever had once been duty to him, something else entirely had taken its place. So as he kept reading, his voice began to shake.

"Number one: Because we can never forget that the Lord of the Christian Church, Jesus Christ, was born in Bethlehem . . ."

The letter went on about God's promise and His chosen people, the call to love others, and the Danish concept of justice. "Despite differences of religious opinion," he read, "we will struggle for the right of our Jewish brothers and sisters to preserve the same liberty that we prize more highly than life itself."

Even if it meant rowing out into the choppy cold waters of the Sound with a boatload of illegal Jewish refugees. Steffen did his best to maintain his composure as he read the letter's final paragraph, but he found his voice rising with emotion.

"The leaders of the Danish church are fully aware of our duty to be law-abiding citizens who do not set themselves up against those exercising authority over us."

This part sounded like the old Steffen, the Steffen he once understood. What came next did not, and the truth dug in its teeth and shook him like a dog would shake a knotted rope. He took a deep breath, certain that no one would understand why their pastor was disintegrating right in front of them.

"But at the same time we are in conscience bound to assert the law and protest any violation of it. Therefore we shall, if occasion should rise, unequivocally acknowledge the words that we should obey God rather than man. Signed on behalf of all Danish bishops, H. Fuglsang Damgaard."

There. That most certainly got their attention. In fact, Steffen could only dream of such focus from his congregation when he delivered his sermons. And the thought did cross his mind that perhaps he should read this kind of letter from the pulpit more often. When he looked down at his letter, he noticed a drop of water, which startled him until he realized it was a tear.

His tear. And it shamelessly threatened to dissolve his practiced Lutheran demeanor. Because Lutheran pastors— and especially this Lutheran pastor—did not deviate from the script, nor did they entertain uninvited emotions. See now what had happened.

"Please pardon me for a moment." He turned away with a handkerchief, well aware that every eye still rested on him, and blew his nose as if a minor touch of a cold might have caught up to him in an unguarded moment. And it certainly might have, given what he'd been doing all night.

When he turned back, he'd reclaimed most of his composure, setting aside the wrinkled letter in favor of his sermon notes. He took a deep breath and shook it off.

"Well, then. Let us rise for the reading of the lesson, found today in the first book of Moses, the eighth chapter, beginning at the twenty-second verse."

He waited for the congregation to respond as they always did, in the words they had all recited since they were old enough to see over a pew:

"Praise be to thee, oh Christ."

The words soothed him, for the most part: the familiar Scripture, the antiphonal readings, back and forth between himself, the congregation, and perhaps even the Lord himself. On the best of Sundays, Steffen could easily lose himself in the service, rising on his toes in worship. Even though that would be as demonstrative as a Lutheran could expect to get, it was enough, and he assumed even God did not expect any more of him.

Now, as he read flawlessly through this Sunday's Epistle (Paul's letter to the Galatians, *Galaterne,* starting with verse twenty-five of chapter five) and the Gospel (his preaching text from Mattæus the Evangelist, beginning at verse twenty-four of chapter six), he could hear his own voice echoing from the lofted beams high overhead. He had once liked the sound of that voice, as it seemed to fill the sanctuary so easily, and in such a way that even old Pastor Viggo in the third-from-the-last row had no trouble hearing him. He knew just by looking, as the older man nodded with approval at all the right places. He could count on that much.

But this morning he could see his own words fall short of the ceiling and return clattering in broken pieces, back upon their heads. Inadequate and powerless, all of them. He wondered why his people didn't duck for shelter.

No one else seemed to notice, however, how he'd left out one line in the reading from Mattæus. One line that screamed his name. And when he reached that line, he simply paused and left it out, skipping over as if he'd never even noticed:

Oh you of little faith.

Worse yet, after the service Steffen had to smile and shake people's hands with appropriate enthusiasm as they complimented him on his empty words. One or two of them even seemed to mean what they said as they stepped out large oak double doors into the midday sun, trying its best to make an appearance.

"Very nice sermon, as always," said Fru Vestergaard, extending her white gloved hand. "Well said. *Vel sagt.*"

But then she said that every Sunday, didn't she? "Will we be seeing you at the get-together this afternoon? We've invited a few friends, just a casual early dinner."

He cringed inwardly and scolded himself for not having a legitimate excuse on hand. Something. Anything. But his mind went blank, and he smiled back, helpless to refuse.

Someone, it seemed, had not informed Fru Vestergaard and her husband, Ernst, that there was a war on, that most people hardly had enough rationed potatoes to eat (certainly not enough meat), and that people were actually being gunned down in the streets. No, to Herr and Fru Vestergaard in their spacious flat in the fashionable *Charlottenlund* district, life went on as always, one gala after the other. Her "casual" early dinner would include many of the city's most wealthy couples and politicians, some of them dropping in just to make a brief appearance.

And if all went according to plan, Pastor Petersen would again be seated next to the Vestergaard's single daughter who possessed the most annoying laugh Steffen had ever heard, and who knew all the latest American band leaders, but very little else. Despite their wide age difference, Fru Vestergaard thought her daughter the perfect catch for a young pastor and made little effort to hide her opinions in that regard.

"Jytte will be there," said Fru Vestergaard with a sly smile. "She's taking a break from her studies. Of course you would be welcome to bring a guest, as well."

Fru Vestergaard knew that Steffen would have no guest to bring, though she would mention the possibility for protocol's sake. And if there was one thing Eva Vestergaard knew, it was protocol.

"That's very kind of you. I'll . . ." His mind still raced for a gracious way out. And all this time, Fru Vestergaard never released Steffen's hand. "I'll of course be very glad to stop by. The usual time?"

"A little earlier today. Say, three? It's been getting dark so early, these days. We don't want to keep people out late."

Did she even know about the citywide curfew? Steffen doubted it. At least she finally released his hand, apparently satisfied she had set her daughter up for one more shot at the pastor. Steffen, however, now puzzled over how he could avoid another vapid, awkward conversation with the twenty-one-year-old Jytte. What would they talk about this time?

But Fru Vestergaard had one more thing to give him—a 50-kroner note pressed quietly into his hand, and with a wink. She leaned into his face, as if revealing a secret.

"It's for the poor Jews the bishop mentioned in his letter," she whispered. "Perhaps you can buy something for them."

Steffen tried not to look too shocked at her gift, but he thanked her and stuffed the bill through a slit in his robe and into a pocket before the rest of the congregation passed by.

"Don't forget," she called back. "Three o'clock."

17

We have to go into the despair and go beyond it,
by working and doing for somebody else,
by using it for something else.
—ELIE WIESEL

Three o'clock, right. That would give Steffen a couple of hours for a quick nap before he had to report for duty at the Vestergaard home. The question was, if he fell asleep that afternoon, would he ever be able to wake up again? He wasn't entirely sure as he stepped outside the church to Nørrebrogade, kneading his forehead. His temples pounded, and his eyelids felt like lead.

"Are you all right?"

He hadn't noticed anyone coming up behind him, least of all Hanne Abrahamsen on a bicycle. She stepped off her bike and laughed softly when he jerked around.

"I'm sorry." She looked rather nice in a hand-knit white sweater and a dark skirt, with her dark hair pulled back beneath a red scarf and her cheeks rosy in the fresh breeze. "I didn't mean to startle you."

"Quite all right, but what brings you here? You missed the service. Er, that was a joke."

She smiled again in that easy way of hers. No offense taken.

"Ja, I suppose I did. Actually, I just wanted to find out about my—"

"Your mother. Of course. She's fine, as far as I know." He looked around to be sure no one on the street was close enough to overhear their conversation. "I saw her onboard the fishing boat myself. Everything went . . . as planned. Pretty much."

She looked at him sideways and nodded, and he was glad she didn't ask anymore about the "pretty much."

"I'm so relieved," she said. "And I'm very grateful for what you've done. You surprised me."

"What, you mean you didn't think I'd help? It was nothing, really." He pressed his lips tightly together, still wondering if anyone might notice them talking. A quick look back at the church only showed Margrethe, scurrying about with a small trash bucket, the way she sometimes did after a Sunday service. Nothing out of the ordinary.

"Nothing?" Hanne shook her head and touched his arm, which he liked. "No, you're wrong about that. You opened up your church, and you rowed people to safety, my mother included. I'll always be grateful for that. You placed yourself in a lot of danger for the sake of people you'd never met before."

"The bishop said we should obey God rather than man." Now he followed a crack in the pavement with the toe of his black shoe. "It appears that's what we're doing, these days."

"I heard about that letter. But you've saved lives. You know that, don't you?"

"I hadn't really thought about it that way." He rubbed his chin, trying to decide if what she'd said about him was true. "It just needed to be done, and I wasn't sure who else would do it. You know what I mean. You save lives at the hospital all the time."

"Not like this. Not while I'm risking my own."

"But you are risking your own life now, just by staying at the hospital. Just by riding your bicycle. You really shouldn't still be here, you know. You should have left with your mother."

Judging by the way she looked at him, it might have been better had he not reminded her. "The Germans don't know who I am or where I live," she protested, her voice softening to a whisper. "I'm safe for now."

"Until they track you down, perhaps, and then you're not safe at all. But what about all those other Jews hiding at the hospital? They're still here, are they not?"

"We're getting them out as fast as we can," she said. "The boats are moving, as you know. Right now the problem is money. It's expensive to move so many across to Sweden, and some of the fishermen are pretty nervous about it. We can't expect them to do it all for free."

"So what happens if you don't raise the funds quickly enough?"

"Then everything moves that much more slowly. There's more chance of being discovered. It endangers more lives."

She gripped the handlebars of her modest black bicycle. Down at her feet, the front tire had nearly gone flat, but she didn't seem to notice.

"Look here." He crouched down to inspect the bald tire, which had been patched several times already in the spots where the rubber had worn down entirely. "It appears you might be walking the rest of the way, wherever you're going."

She sighed, a hand on her hip. And she still hadn't explained what had brought her here. But an idea occurred to him as he remembered the bill from Fru Vestergaard.

"Do you…" He paused before going on. "Do you have a plan for raising the money you're going to need?"

"We're doing the best we can," she explained. "Several of the doctors have given a few kroner. We're asking around. But as I said, it's not coming in quickly enough."

"All right." He straightened up and fished the bill from his pocket before holding it out to her. "Here's a start. But I'm going to need your help for the rest."

"The rest?" She took the money and turned it over in her hands. "Where did this come from?"

"From Eva Vestergaard, just a few minutes ago. She must have been moved by the bishop's letter."

"And you think she'll give more?"

"Maybe. I wonder if you would come with me to Ernst and Eva Vestergaard's home in Charlottenlund this afternoon."

"Charlottenlund?" Her eyebrows lifted. "That's—"

"I know. The Vestergaards are quite well off. Herr Vestergaard, you'll hardly ever see him. He sits in his library and smokes his cigar. She drags him to church on Christmas and whenever else she can. But Fru Vestergaard—Eva—is a faithful attender. She means well."

"I see. And you want me to . . . ?"

"Well, they're having some of their friends over for what she calls an 'informal gathering,' at their place. I was speaking with Eva just before you came along, and she always invites me to these galas. Every time, she asks me to bring someone along, and I know she's just being polite, but this time perhaps I will. I mean, if you'd come along."

There. Steffen could feel his heart beating a little more quickly, now that he'd said it.

"In fact," he added, "you'll be doing me a great favor by coming along. Eva has this daughter she's always trying to pair me up with. I don't really—"

"Oh, now I understand," Hanne interrupted, but Steffen couldn't tell if she was serious or if she really understood. "You just need some protection, is that it?"

"That's just part of it." He smiled. "But if you're up for it, we're also going to be doing some outrageous fundraising."

"Outrageous fundraising?" Hanne repeated the words, apparently considering, and her forehead wrinkled in con-centration. "What time did you say?"

Five minutes until three Hanne stood out in front of the address Steffen had given her, trying to look inconspicuous and wondering why she had agreed to something like this. She could not think of anywhere she would feel more out of place, especially as another well-dressed older couple passed her on their way up the stairs to Number 201. She'd very seldom passed through this neighborhood, much less entered into one of its most well-to-do flats. Perhaps King Christian might pay a visit as well?

Another couple made their way up from the street, car-rying flowers and a bottle of wine, but Hanne looked away before they could stare and wonder. Did she really look as out of place as she felt? Would her tiny box of *chokolade*, saved from three years ago for a special occasion, measure up? Finally Steffen came hurrying down the sidewalk, consulting his watch as he stepped up to greet her.

"Sorry," he told her, forcing a smile. "Have you been wait-ing long?"

"Just got here. Well, not long, anyway." She held him back before they reached the stairwell that would lead up to the second floor. "But look, Steffen, I'm not sure if this is such a good idea. Just going to a fancy party like this is one thing, but going in and asking people for money. . . . Really, I don't know."

"It's not what you think." He looked a lot more confident than she remembered seeing him. "I've spoken with Eva, again—Fru Vestergaard—and she not only likes the idea, but she's going to make her own announcement. She doesn't mind being bold. As I suspected, she's very keen on helping out."

"Oh. Well, if that's the case."

"I promise no one's going to bite. But if they do, you be sure to tell me. And by the way . . ." He paused on the way up the stairs. "You look very nice."

She felt her cheeks flush a bit. It wasn't her newest dress but one of her favorites from before the war—navy blue with a white belt. And she had to admit, she didn't have much occasion to wear it, lately.

"Tak." Her words were drowned out as someone opened the door up ahead and a tuxedo-clad butler ushered them into a large formal room filled with older people. She left her box of chocolates inconspicuously on a side table, where the hostess might not see it.

The place might have passed for a ballroom in one of Danmark's finer manor houses, with ceilings easily three meters high, supported by gilded colonnades. The floor was a fine marbled Italian tile, and around the large room were placed tables laden with drinks and fancy appetizers Hanne couldn't even identify. And this wasn't even the dining room. She had not seen so much fine food since before the war.

"Don't ask where it all comes from," Steffen told her. "These people have probably never seen a ration card."

"They leave that kind of thing to the servants, do they?" she whispered back.

A few of "these people" she recognized from the newspapers—business executives and government leaders, perhaps a member of the royal family? But as Hanne gaped at the sights, a sprightly gray-haired woman in a lovely black formal dress spotted them from across the room and made her way over to them.

"Pastor! I'm so happy you could make it. And this is—"

"My friend Hanne," said Steffen. "The one I mentioned over the phone?"

The woman's expression flickered for just a moment as she glanced behind her, then turned back with a full smile.

"Of course, dear, I'm so pleased to meet you. Please call me Eva." She gave Steffen a conspiratorial wink. "Pastor, you didn't tell me she was so lovely. I should have known."

Hanne smiled and shook the woman's hand. She could not help but instantly like Eva, especially the playful sparkle in her eyes as she took Hanne by the hand, leading her from one couple to the next, making introductions as if they had always been best friends. Here was Herr and Fru Christensen. Steffen whispered in her ear that he was high up in the Tuborg Beer fortune. There was C. Jens Hedtoft, who set aside his cigar to shake her hand. According to Steffen, an executive with A. P. Møller, so he made a lot of money in the shipping business. And so on. They even met Eva's daughter, who looked like a sweet young thing though perhaps not as glad to meet Hanne as the others had been. By that time Eva was tapping on a wine glass with a spoon to get everyone's attention.

"Ernst and I are so glad everyone could make it this afternoon," she told them, smiling all around. "But before we go in to dinner I wanted to introduce a special young lady. Her name is Hanne and she is currently working at Bispebjerg with many of the . . . shall we say, refugees. I think you all know to whom I'm referring."

As if on cue, a rumble from out on the street told them a convoy of some sort was passing by. And from where Hanne stood she could just make out the tops of several ugly gray trucks, each marked with the army cross of the German forces. She held her breath and looked away.

By this time the hall had grown deathly still, and every eye focused on Hanne. Even the men standing at the far end of the room around the fireplace with their sherry and cigars craned their necks to see. Their hostess ignored the rumbling outside, which eventually passed.

"Because I feel confident in your trust and patriotism, I just wanted you to know that this brave young woman, along with our very own Pastor Steffen Petersen from Sankt Stefan's Kirke—and ja, he is also a saint, if you ask me—they are making it possible for these poor people to travel to their temporary accommodations in Sweden. Please forgive my even mentioning such a delicate matter, but in these times such things must be said. So may I please be so bold as to suggest that perhaps some of you might be able to help underwrite the efforts? I can vouch for them, certainly. And we all know what's happening out there. So if you are able to speak with her or the pastor, I know they will deeply appreciate it."

So bold! Hanne certainly didn't expect the applause, nor what happened next. Herr Christensen was first in line with 5,000 kroner, which he peeled inconspicuously from his bulging leather wallet.

"If there's one way to stick it to those Nazis," he told her, lowering his voice and placing the bills in her hand, "this is the least I can do."

She looked down at the bills, not quite knowing what to do with so much money. But she managed to smile and thank him as she stuffed the contribution into her purse.

Moments later Hedtoft the shipping executive guided Hanne by the arm to the corner of the room, where he placed even more money into her hand. She was afraid to count or even look at it.

"Personally I think the Jews are a little odd," he told her, leaning a little close and spilling his sherry on his pants leg. "But they're still Danes. And you know we're not going to let any Danes be shipped off to some concentration camp, like so many cattle. Not if we can help it. It's just not right."

No, it wasn't, and Hanne could only nod and thank him, as well. But that wasn't the end of it. One after another, sometimes just the men but often the wives as well—each came up to Hanne with cash and a similar story of outrage.

This can't be happening to our people.

We'll show those Nazis.

This has gone too far.

Soon Hanne's little purse couldn't hold any more and she looked across the room to where Steffen had been cornered by men with cigars and serious looks. At one point she caught Steffen's eye; he smiled and winked at her before they moved into the dining room for the main course, as one more guest pressed a wad of bills into his hand.

By six that evening Hanne and Steffen were both headed home on the S-train into the city. Huddled in the corner of the train, Hanne could hardly contain her excitement.

"Did you talk with the big round fellow?" she asked. "The one with the huge moustache?"

"You mean Parslov." Steffen shook his head. "No, actually, I think he wanted to speak with a lady."

"I don't know anything about that." She felt her cheeks color a bit, but by this time it didn't matter. "But first he gave me five thousand kroner, and then after dinner he added . . . I don't know how much."

She looked down at her bulging purse. "In fact, I have no idea how much we collected tonight. How much do you think? This was incredible!"

"I'm thinking perhaps a hundred thousand kroner," he told her in a low voice, breaking out in a smile. "Enough for at least a hundred tickets across the Sound, maybe more. I'm not sure. All I know is that we're not counting anything until we get back to the church."

Hanne sat quietly in the train next to Steffen, enjoying the warmth of his closeness and the almost giddy realization of what had just happened. Outrageous fundraising, indeed. And though the tingle she felt inside could have come from the glass of sherry after an amazing dinner, she wasn't so sure. She didn't mind slipping her hand through the crook of his elbow.

18

*We must forget the nightmares, but remember the lessons and how
they made us aware that we're part of a people that just wanted to
live our lives in peace.*
—POUL OVERGAARD NIELSEN

B ack for another visit, Pastor? You're early today."
Steffen did his best to look surprised when he noticed
Hanne hurrying down the hospital hallway, headed in his
direction. He couldn't quite remember which of his people
might be expecting a pastoral visit first thing Monday morning,
but he was hoping there might be one or two. And while he
was there, it certainly wouldn't hurt to stop by the emergency
ward.

"Early?" He smiled and slowed, checking his watch again.
"If half-ten is early, you're early, yourself."

"Every Monday the same." She held her clipboard close.
"But actually I do have a question for you. Perhaps you'll give
me a short head start, and then follow me down the hall?"

The request set him back just a bit. Even so, Steffen did
his best to appear nonchalant.

"Of course." He kept his voice loud enough so an orderly
rolling past with a wheelchair could hear. "I'm just here visiting my people, as always. See you again sometime."

Hanne smiled back at him and continued on down the hall, while Steffen watched her out of the corner of his eye as she ducked into a stairwell.

"Pastor?" An older woman he did not recognize motioned to him from one of the adjacent patient areas. For a moment he considered pretending he had not heard her, but she'd already caught his eye and waved once more. He sighed and stepped inside her small room, stopping by her bed.

"Are you the one who's arranging for my funeral?" she asked as she reached out and grabbed his arm.

"Pardon?"

"My funeral. The casket. I want to know if it's all ready. I arranged to have it delivered here, but no one is helping me."

"Actually, nej, I'm not on staff here, as you presume." Steffen tried to pull gently away, but the woman only tightened her hold. She looked old, yes, well into her eighties. But her grip told him she might not be as near death as she seemed to think. "I'm the pastor at Sankt Stefan's. I just visit my people. I mean, not *just*, but that's why I come here. You don't live in my parish, do you?"

Well, she certainly could have, though Steffen had never seen the woman before.

"I've been to Sankt Stefan's a time or two," she replied. "For my sister's wedding."

"Oh? Recently?" He imagined she sounded slightly out of touch with reality, but couldn't help asking.

"Well, it would have been in . . . oh-three, if I remember correctly. You wouldn't have been the pastor then, I suppose?"

"No, ah, that was a few years before my time, I'm afraid."

Steffen tried to back away as he spoke. He just needed to break free, now, and he hoped she wouldn't try to grab him by the wide, old-style clerical collar that identified him and his office. But that might be a problem, since the collar flared out all around his neck in the traditional style worn by Danish pastors for hundreds of years.

"Well, I want you to check on my funeral," she told him. "I've told my son how it should be, but he keeps saying I'm not going to die, yet."

"And you don't think he's right?" Finally Steffen ducked from her vise-like grip. If this woman was dying, so was he. "You look quite healthy to me."

"Ak, ja." Now she waved him off in obvious disgust. "You're just like my son. Nobody believes me."

"Well, you just let me know if there's any way we can pray for you." Steffen stepped toward the door with a smile. "And you're always welcome at Sankt Stefan's Kirke."

Without waiting for an answer he slipped out the door and made for the exit where he'd last seen Hanne. He avoided looking into any other patient rooms, then slipped through the exit door and into the stairwell before pausing. Up or down?

"What took you so long?" Hanne asked from the landing below. He stepped down to meet her.

"Sorry. I was roped into a conversation with an older lady who was convinced she was terminal. She didn't seem that way to me."

Hanne smiled and casually adjusted her white nurses cap.

"Oh, Fru Ibsen! Isn't she a sweetheart? She comes in every few months with what she believes is a life-threatening illness. We really ought to admit her to the psych ward, but she's usually quite entertaining. It seems easier just to let her rest in a room for a day or two, and then we call her son to take her home again."

"Ah. Well, this time she seemed to have her funeral all planned out."

"Again? Oh, dear. She did that two months ago. And that means she's probably having another casket delivered here to the hospital. We'll take care of it." A door slammed a couple of floors above, and she waited until it was obvious no one was coming. "But look, that's not what I need to ask you."

"No?" Steffen wasn't sure what she was talking about now.

"I mentioned we're full of Jewish refugees here at Bispebjerg. But it's getting critical. They're in the tunnels, they've been admitted as patients, we've appropriated entire wards for them. We couldn't take one more if we wanted to. And I would like to. There's just no place to put them."

Steffen raised his eyebrows in interest.

"You have all the money we collected yesterday."

"Yes, yes. It's safe. And that's not the problem."

"So the problem is?"

"The problem is we have Germans in here fairly often. Even Gestapo, sometimes. I believe you've seen that Wolfschmidt fellow. He's keeping an eye on us."

"So why don't you get the people out of here, out to the coast? We need to move them out now, don't we?"

Steffen wasn't sure if she noticed how he said "we," either. But there. He'd said it.

"That's just it. They can't just walk out there with their suitcases."

Steffen let her continue.

"They're stopping cars now, searching everything. It's much more aggressive. They're stopping people getting onto the trains—especially trains going north, up the coast. We don't know how to get these poor people out of here without endangering their lives."

By this time Hanne was pacing from one end of the landing to the other, her arms crossed.

"I don't know why I'm telling you this," she continued, and looked out a small window to the outside. "It's just that we need to do something soon. Maybe your brother would have some ideas."

"My brother?" Steffen thought about it for a moment, wondering if this was why she had confided in him. Because of Henning? His younger brother certainly didn't have all the answers, and Hanne couldn't really know how headstrong Henning might be. But he couldn't just come out and say so. Actually, he had a better idea. A little crazy, perhaps, but one never knew about this sort of thing.

"How many people do we need to move?" he finally asked. "And to where, exactly?"

She looked at him curiously.

"Right now we have sixty-eight. No, sixty-nine. Mothers, fathers, kids, babies, old people. As far as where they're going, well, there's only a couple of escape routes out of København, because of all the Germans here. You took one already. And frankly, I don't know why you weren't spotted. I told my mother she should have taken a different route."

"You did what? I thought you wanted her to get to safety."

Now Hanne turned away and didn't look Steffen in the eye as her voice lowered.

"I thought it was too risky, what you were doing. But she insisted. She said she trusted you."

"And you don't?"

"I didn't say that." Hanne turned back to face him. "But it's my mother we're talking about, you know."

Steffen thought he could feel some of the pain and concern in her eyes, but he didn't know how to tell her that without sounding too familiar. He imagined though, that if they traded places, he might be saying the same thing.

"What about you?" she asked. "Are your parents . . . ?"

"My mother died when I was younger. Henning was eighteen. I kept an eye on him."

"I'm sorry." She didn't ask about their father, which was just as well. Instead she looked at him with the biggest brown eyes he had ever seen, and for a moment he knew why she was a nurse. Neither said a word until he realized that he was staring and shook his head.

"Well. About getting these people out of here. What are you being told?"

"Right." Hanne snapped back to business, as well. "We're hearing that most of the fishing boats are meeting people up the coast from as close as *Tårbæk*, maybe, but then up toward Rungsted and Humlebæk, all the way up to Gilleleje."

"Then that's where we need to take them, correct?"

"Ja. But as I said—"

"I know." He held up his hand. This could work. "Listen, could you meet me back here in two hours? I think I know how we can get a few people out. Let's start with . . . three?"

"Three? Are you sure?"

"We have the money to pay their way now, do we not?"

"Well, yes, but—"

"Just let me try something. Where did you say Fru Ibsen's coffin was delivered?"

"Probably at the service entry, but what does that—"

"Good. That's where I want to meet you at—" he looked at his watch—"nine-thirty."

He didn't wait for her answer, just hurried outside. Once out in the cold mid-morning sun, however, he had to stop and ask himself.

What am I thinking?

19

Where words fail, music speaks.
—HANS CHRISTIAN ANDERSEN

Half an hour later Steffen burst into the Ibsen Boghandel, forgetting to check if Hans Christian Andersen was in the front widow. Never mind. He had no time for that kind of nonsense. He waited until a spindly older woman finished buying a used romance, then stepped up to the counter.

"I need the keys to your vehicle, Henning," he whispered.

His brother turned to face him, and Steffen stopped short. Henning's face looked badly bruised, with dark welts on his face and around his right eye. A gash on his chin had been taped together, and his right hand wrapped in bandages.

"What happened to you? You look . . ."

"Don't say it. I'll be fine."

"You look like you were run over by a truck."

"That's not far from the truth. It's a long story. But what are you doing here?"

Steffen wasn't sure if he should press his brother harder to find out what had happened to him. Henning didn't look eager to share details. But now there wasn't time.

"Actually, we're going to have a funeral, and we're going to get some of those people out of Bispebjerg. I just need the vehicle, and I was going to ask you to help me, but . . . where are the keys?"

"You don't know what you're asking, Steffen." Henning looked around to be sure no one overheard. "First of all, I can't just be driving that thing around in the middle of the day. Especially now with my hand. I can't hardly work the cash register, much less drive. And second of all, what are you talking about, a funeral?"

"You know, a funeral. It's where you put bodies in a casket—in this case, three bodies—and, yes, I know that's going to be a tight fit. But we need to transport them from the hospital to the coast, where they'll be transferred to a fishing boat. Do you understand now what I'm saying?"

Henning didn't have to ponder very long before he motioned for a single customer to follow him to the front of the store.

"Sorry, sir, but we're closing for lunch," he explained, opening the front door. The confused-looking older man set down his book but followed him outside. Henning wasted no time locking up. "We eat lunch a little early around here. Be back in just a little while."

They left the customer standing on the narrow sidewalk, while Henning led the way around the building and back around to the garage in the adjoining back alley. Steffen didn't bother telling him that this would probably end up being a long lunch hour.

"By the way," Steffen asked, "you don't happen to have a suit, do you?"

Henning gave him a stern look. "Do I look like I have a suit?"

"Just thought I'd ask. I thought it would look better if the pallbearer was a little more, you know, dressed for the occasion."

"Oh, so now I'm a one-handed pallbearer?"

"You've never been one before, have you?"

"Can't say that I have." After a quick look up and down the alley, he pulled open the garage door with his good hand and stepped inside. When Steffen followed, Henning paused a moment, and with a frown tossed the keys at him.

"You're driving the ambulance."

A moment later they were speeding through the narrow streets of København on their way to the hospital. Steffen had to admit he was a little rusty in his driving skills, but it wasn't his first time.

"You drive like an old lady." Henning told him, cross-armed. "Where are we going?"

"Sorry about that," Steffen steered the ambulance into the hospital campus, barely missing a curb. "The service entry. Hanne will be waiting for us."

And she was, just inside the large double doors through which hospital supplies and such were loaded and unloaded, where trucks routinely backed up. Only this time it was Henning's ambulance. They hopped out, the pastor and his assistant. Once inside, Steffen looked around the storage area to find not one casket, but two. Both looked ornate in carved rosewood and brass handles, certainly not cheap. Steffen turned to see Hanne enter the loading area.

"Fru Ibsen has good taste, has she?" he asked.

Hanne shrugged. "Her husband owned one of the larger department stores downtown before he died. And of course she is, as you've seen, a little . . . eccentric."

"Then she won't mind if we borrow her casket for a few hours?" Steffen walked over to the caskets, checking inside to make sure. He thought he heard Hanne gasp, and he looked over to see that she had noticed his brother's injuries.

"You need someone to look at that," she said, examining his head. He pulled away like a little boy from his mother.

"It's nothing," he said, "and it's not why I'm here."

"What about your hand?" She persisted.

"What about it? Listen, nurse. We came here to help you, and I happen to still have one good hand at the moment. Let's just get it done, all right?"

She appeared to bite her tongue but finally nodded and backed away.

"All right, then. But I wish you'd stop by the emergency ward a little later to have a doctor get a better look."

"We'll see."

By the way he said it, Steffen knew Henning had no intention of having a doctor—or anyone else—get a better look. And there was nothing Steffen could do about it.

"Maybe we should get these people loaded up?" Steffen suggested. "Three people only."

"You're not saying what I think you're saying?" Hanne turned her attention to him.

"Don't tell them what you're doing. Just bring them here any way you can. If there are any very small children, I think you'd better sedate them. We may be stopped, you know."

By that time Hanne's eyes had widened, but she caught on quickly and nodded. And while she left to fetch their first passengers, the two men wrestled the nearest casket closer to the door.

"This thing is heavy enough," mumbled Henning, beads of sweat rising on his forehead, "even without the people inside."

Sure enough it was. And it didn't help that Henning could only use his one hand. But just a few minutes later Hanne returned, pushing a gurney covered by a large sheet. Behind her a young orderly pushed a young woman holding what looked like a rag doll, limp and lifeless. The orderly looked at the open casket in confusion, then back at the woman she'd been pushing.

"I don't understand," she told Hanne.

"You don't have to." Hanne patted the girl on the shoulder and led her back to the door through which they'd come. "Now just go back to what you were doing, and keep this to yourself. Do you understand?"

The young girl nodded solemnly and hurried away. For their sakes Steffen hoped she would do as Hanne had told her, but there wasn't time to worry about that now. Hanne pulled away the sheet from her gurney, revealing a young man whose face looked as white as the sheet he had been hidden under. But he seemed more worried about the other woman, who by now was sobbing.

"Who would hurt my baby?" asked the young woman, holding the limp child close. "Who would think of hurting my child? Why would they—"

Hanne came up beside the distraught woman and slipped an arm around her.

"No one's going to hurt her, I promise." She led her slowly toward the casket. "But you know that if she cried, someone might hear her, right? That's why we had to sedate her."

The mother, who couldn't have been more than nineteen or twenty, nodded silently. Meanwhile Hanne continued to calm her with a soothing voice.

"Now she'll wake up in three or four hours. But those pills you have—give her one more as soon as she wakes, understand? Just one." She looked at the young man. "Dad, can you make sure that happens? Make sure she swallows it, even if she doesn't want to. That way she'll still be relaxed on the way over to Sweden. Do you understand?"

This time the young man nodded but they could not console the weeping mother.

"Please." Steffen tried his best. "You'll need to settle down a bit so we can get you into the . . . box. But don't worry about anything. You'll have plenty of air to breathe—we'll make sure of that. And we'll get you out just as soon as we've reached a safe waiting place on the coast. All right?"

His voice must have calmed them, because now the couple looked a little less likely to break down completely as they stepped gingerly into the padded casket and curled up inside with their sleeping child. But the young mother held up her hand and looked first at Henning, then at Steffen.

"Please. I don't suppose either of you know the *Tefilat HaDerech*."

She looked so desperate that Steffen honestly wished he did. Instead Henning looked to his brother for help.

"Do you have any idea what she's talking about?"

Steffen nodded. "The Traveler's Prayer. I'm . . . I'm sorry. I know what it is, but I don't know the words. Perhaps you'd allow me—"

"Excuse me." Hanne interrupted softly. "But I know it."

Perhaps the couple wasn't used to having a Danish nurse lead them in such a prayer, but in the absence of a rabbi, well. The young mother nodded as Hanne recited the Hebrew words in her soft, musical voice:

Y'hi ratzon milfanekha Adonai Eloheinu . . .

She went on like that for a few sentences more. Though Steffen wasn't sure of the words, he could sense their meaning and warmth as he prayed along with these precious souls.

And he was able to pick out a word or two, here and there. *Shalom*, of course. Peace. *Barukh atah Adonai.* Blessed are you, Adonai. He knew Adonai was another word for Lord, but the rest escaped him until Hanne volunteered a brief translation.

"Guide our footsteps toward peace," she whispered, "and make us reach our desired destination for life, gladness, and peace. May You rescue us from the hand of every foe."

After that she resumed in Hebrew, apparently picking up where she'd left off. And as they finally said their amens Steffen gently closed the lid, leaving an inconspicuous piece of folded cardboard in place to make a crack for fresh air. He added a silent prayer of his own for their safety, this one in Danish, for their God was multilingual.

"You look like an old pro at this kind of thing," Henning told him as he went around to test the handles.

"I've done it a couple of times before," answered Steffen. "Only under slightly different circumstances."

"Yeah. The people weren't alive, were they?"

"Something like that. Let's get this loaded into the back of the ambulance and get out of here."

Easier said than done. He looked over at Hanne, who now stood off to the side as if not quite sure how to help. She nodded before heading to open the outside doors for them.

"Thank you," he told her, bending to take his handle. "You could have been a rabbi."

That brought him a shy smile. Steffen wasn't certain, but he was pretty sure the synagogue didn't allow such a thing.

"Thought you said no more jokes," Henning reminded him. They both grunted as they lifted their heavy load, which despite the small stature of the occupants, felt almost impossibly heavy.

"So that's why they put these things on rollers?" Henning grunted with the effort as the veins on his neck stood out.

Yes, they could have used some kind of mechanical advantage. Lacking that, they had no choice but to manhandle it into place. Henning staggered backward as Hanne opened the doors and they moved unsteadily toward the back of the ambulance, fortunately just a few meters away.

Not so fortunately, Steffen had neglected to look both ways before they stepped outside. And that would be the time a German soldier on a motorcycle decided to come by on his rounds, obviously policing the area. Henning must have seen the look on his brother's face, as he turned around and in the process nearly lost his grip on the casket.

"Oh, no." Steffen groaned under his breath, though the motorcycle's noise would mask their conversation. "Just what we need."

The rider looked over just in time to notice them as he pulled past, though Steffen averted his eyes and tried his best to look very dull, doing one of his dull daily duties. It didn't work.

"Don't look!" he told Henning, "but the German is turning around!"

He was, but by that time Steffen and Henning had nearly lost their grip on their casket, and both wavered where they stood. They actually tried to move the last step and lift it up into the back of the ambulance, but missed by a few centimeters. As the soldier pulled up alongside them they could only balance the end of the casket on the rear bumper, trying desperately not to drop their precious cargo.

"Help, you need?" the soldier asked them in a broken blend of Danish and German.

"Nej, no. Nein." How many languages did it take to stop this fellow? Steffen smiled and shook his head violently as Henning turned his face to busy himself with the casket. "We're doing just fine."

Unfortunately the young soldier could see as well as anyone that they were not. Ignoring Steffen's protests, he dismounted his motorcycle and jumped to their aid. With the help of his young muscles they easily lifted the end into the ambulance and slipped it in the rest of the way.

"Heavy, ja?" The tall young soldier held his hands out in sign language. "Large person?"

"Ja, ja." Steffen stood back awkwardly, his heart thumping both from the exercise and the fact that this soldier didn't seem to be in any hurry. "Funeral. We're headed to the funeral. Better go. Thank you."

But this young soldier was too polite for his own good. He stood smiling, extending his hand in introduction.

"Obergefreiter Max Kaufmann," he said, pointing back at himself with his left hand as he bowed slightly. Steffen would be expected to do the same, and he hesitated only slightly before accepting the man's hand.

"Er . . ."

But by that time Henning slammed the back door shut and ran around to the passenger's side.

"Got to get going, Pastor," he said. "Or we'll be late for the funeral!"

"Yes, right." Steffen smiled at the soldier and moved away to join Henning. "Don't want to be late. Thank you again, corporal. You have no idea how helpful you've been. And may God bless you."

He looked back over his shoulder, unsure if the young man understood all his words. But he couldn't miss Hanne's face following them through a small window in the hospital's double doors, before she pulled back inside.

Steffen hit the gas, sending the casket sliding and Henning scrambling for a handhold.

"May God bless you?" Henning asked through clenched teeth as they powered through the hospital campus toward the main road. A couple of white-coated doctors scurried out of the way. "I think I would have said something else."

Steffen shrugged in self-defense.

"That's why you're the saboteur and I'm the pastor."

"Even so," replied Henning, never taking his eyes off the road ahead. "You'd still better be careful who you ask God to bless. He might finally listen to you, one of these days."

God might finally listen to him? Steffen thought about that as they drove the back way to Tårbæk, some ten kilometers up the coast but more than twice as far when they avoided the main highways and kept to winding narrow lanes and through golden beech woods flaming in gold. As Henning explained, they'd best keep to these roads to stay away from any Germans, helpful or otherwise.

But, God might finally listen to him? Steffen thought about a comeback, but honestly couldn't say anything. Henning was right, after all. Which left the question: Did God listen to him at all? As they bumped along somehow he doubted it—despite his years in seminary and his degree, despite his pulpit and his clerical collar. A flurry of golden leaves swirled around and behind them as he and Henning pushed toward the coast a bit faster than allowed, though a speeding ambulance might be overlooked in that regard.

And now? He tried to pray, but the words all seemed to fall short. All he could hear was Hanne, back on the loading dock, as she prayed over the frightened little family in the casket.

"Guide our footsteps toward peace," she had prayed. And with the gray German army trucks parked up ahead, they would need that kind of guidance very soon.

20

Do not wait for leaders; do it alone, person to person.
—MOTHER TERESA

Y ou're pulling my leg now, aren't you?"
Hanne couldn't keep from laughing when the pastor told her his story as they walked toward the main hospital exit after her shift. He held up his hand in a promise.

"Honestly, that's what the soldier said. 'Please accept my sympathy. Please go ahead.' And then he waved us through. Waved us through! But that's after he sees Henning with tears streaming down his cheeks, and after Henning tells him his sad story about how his aunt, his beloved *tante*, died in an auto accident, and he was almost killed as well, and we're transporting her to her family grave."

"Well, at least he had the injuries to prove it. I'm still worried about his hand, by the way. Have you seen it?"

"He wouldn't show it to me, either. All I can tell you is that it has to hurt, and badly. He can't hardly move it, much less grip anything."

"It could be broken, or worse. He needs to let us look at it."

"Sure he does." Steffen chuckled. "But you think he's going to listen to me? He has a high pain threshold. He actually made me poke him in the eye, just for effect, so it might water a little more easily."

"Hmm. Then did he explain to the soldiers why a pastor was driving the ambulance?"

"I think so. But by that time I was so nervous about Henning overdoing it, I don't think I heard a word of what he said. In fact, I was ready to confess everything, and I think I just might have if the soldier had said anything else to me directly."

"Good thing you didn't." By that time they had reached the front door. "We need you in this work."

Pastor Steffen stiffened noticeably at her words, and she bit her tongue. She hadn't meant to be so direct. Still she meant what she'd said. Because Steffen—that is, *Pastor Steffen*—brought a sort of innocent authority to the rescues that his reckless brother could not.

"Henning did say he had five more people waiting in the back of his bookstore." Steffen lowered his voice. "And after that, we should pick up more from the ones waiting here at Bispebjerg."

"What time?" she asked. Her mind spun as she considered which people should be evacuated next.

"Six o'clock tonight," he replied, his hand on the door. "And actually, Henning's injury gave me an idea. I have some stage makeup. You know, blood and that sort of thing. We'd like to dress up the people we're carrying, just in case."

Hanne thought about it for a moment. Perhaps it could work.

"Henning liked that idea?"

"I'm not sure how much he actually liked it. But that hand is hurting him so much, he just told me to go ahead."

"That sounds convenient. Perhaps you should ask him some other favors, while you can."

Steffen smiled at the joke. "And we'll need a doctor or a nurse to ride along. I hate to ask you, but do you know anyone who you think we could trust?"

Hanne caught her breath. Hiding Jewish refuges in the basement was one thing. But riding along among Germans was quite something else. But if she didn't, who would? Finally she nodded.

"Me."

"No, no, that's not what I meant. It's too dangerous for you. I was thinking of someone else you might know. It won't take long."

"I can't think of anyone else. I told you I'll do it."

He looked at her and frowned, as if trying to figure out how to win this argument. But he could not.

"So, I'll see you at six?" she asked, steeling her voice once again to keep it from sounding as shaky as she felt.

He sighed and shook his head.

"You are one determined woman."

"What exactly do you want me to do?" she asked.

He frowned again. "You would just be riding along, the way a nurse would do. If anyone stops us, we can just be having an emergency, and you can do all the things an emergency calls for. I'll make sure that you're safe."

"And how exactly would you do that?" she wanted to know.

"Well, ah . . ."

As he spoke another nurse hurried down the hall toward them, looking flustered with her peaked white nurse's cap falling off to one side.

"Hanne!" Ann-Grete panted for breath as she caught up with them. "Hanne, I'm so glad you didn't leave, yet. He called from Roskilde."

For a moment Hanne wasn't sure who "he" might be. But really there could be no doubt. She just wished Steffen wasn't standing so close by, and looking curious at that.

"So Aron hasn't left for Sweden, yet." Hanne put on her best professional voice and hoped for the best. She wasn't sure how advisable it was for him to call from anywhere in Danmark, though. Ann-Grete leaned close enough to almost whisper.

"Apparently he's still hiding in someone's basement in Roskilde, and he really needs to get out."

"Yes, don't they all. Did he say why he was calling here? Does he think we can help him?"

"He asked for you, Hanne." Ann-Grete glanced at Steffen with a nervous smile. "I didn't know what to tell him."

"But you told him I was still here?"

"I couldn't lie. I told him I would pass along the message."

"So you did." Hanne groaned quietly and scratched her head, not sure what to say next. Yes, she wanted Aron to be safe, the same way she wanted all the people in the hospital basement to be safe. And yes, she couldn't deny she'd had feelings for Aron—once. But after their last minutes together in the synagogue, she just wasn't sure. Her time with Pastor Steffen had only confused the issue even more.

Even if she had the chance, could she and Aron once again be the couple her mother had always wanted, with all the grandchildren that went along with such an arrangement? Hanne couldn't say.

"He said he's going to get here as soon as he can," added Ann-Grete. "That he's going crazy in hiding."

"As soon as he can?" Hanne couldn't believe it, and tried not to raise her voice. "Did he say when that might be? Why would he come here?"

Ann-Grete shook her hand and held up her hands, as if she was scared of being scolded. "All he said was that if you're still here, he has to see you. Oh, and he said that you need to go with him to Sweden."

"Has to, need to. This is crazy. He really told you all this?"

By this time Steffen had drifted away a few steps, looking as if he was politely avoiding a conversation obviously not intended for his ears. But by the way he glanced over every now and again, she could tell he was listening.

What to say? Her stomach tightened into a knot. At least she'd missed the call. Or maybe it would have been better if she had spoken with Aron, after all. Then she could have told him not to come.

"What are you going to do?" asked Ann-Grete, looking from Hanne to Steffen as if she recognized the dilemma hanging over her head. Hanne wrung her hands and turned in a circle.

"I don't know," she finally answered. "All I know is that I'm not going to Sweden. Not yet. He doesn't understand there's too much for me to do here."

"But other people can do what you're doing," argued Ann-Grete. "You don't have to be the only one to stick your neck out."

"She's right." Steffen cut in, though it was not his place to do so. "You shouldn't be the one to put yourself in danger. I shouldn't have asked you to help. I'm sorry."

"Please don't apologize. I'm in a safe apartment with a safe ID card, and I'm not in danger, all right?" Hanne held up a finger for emphasis and looked at them both. "And even if I was somehow in danger, how about if you both give me the courtesy of letting me decide when I should go—or even if I should? I don't need other people telling me that. Not Aron, and certainly not either of you."

Ann-Grete looked as if she had been slapped, and it hurt Hanne to see. Still she turned to go, then stopped and turned one more time.

"But thank you for telling me, Ann-Grete. I'm sorry. I don't mean to yell. It's not your fault, all this, after all. Pastor, I will see you at six."

She hoped her extra-firm tone of voice might leave no doubt about her intentions to remain here at Bispebjerg. She would care for the sick and injured, and she would continue to work until every last Jewish person had been taken safely across the Sound to Sweden. Even then, she might not leave.

Besides, she meant every word of what she said about not having others tell her what to do. She was a big girl, after all. She could take care of herself. And why should she allow the Germans—or anyone else—to decide her life this way? This would be her personal form of protest—staying alive and staying put, doing her job and not running for safety. Not that she faulted anyone else for doing what they needed to do. She simply knew that she had been placed here for such a time as this. Why couldn't everyone else understand what she knew most deeply in her heart?

As she stalked away, heels clicking on the hall's polished tiles, she heard Steffen ask Ann-Grete "Who's Aron?"

She didn't wait to hear Ann-Grete's answer, though perhaps she should have told him before this. Perhaps she still would. Either way, she wasn't eager to have Aron Overgaard show up uninvited at Bispebjerg, especially not if he was still intent on having her accompany him to Sweden. No, that certainly would not do.

On the other hand, she almost had to laugh at the idea of seeing Aron hiding under a hold of fish, as some of their refugees had already been forced to do. Aron, who hated the thought of getting his hands dirty or his ties wrinkled. Aron, who always had to be in control of his own agenda, as well as the agendas of everyone around him. For a moment she wondered how he might be holding up under the stress of these past days. It would certainly not be good for his high blood pressure.

I'm sorry, Mor, she thought as she turned off toward one of the tunnel entrances. *It's not going to happen.*

And under no circumstances would she entertain the idea of escaping to Sweden with Aron Overgaard. Not while she had anything to say about it.

Among other things, right now she needed to check on the medication of one of the little girls down there who was suffering from asthma. Who else cared about these people the way she did? Living and sleeping in a damp basement did nothing to help the poor little girl's condition, and she should be moved as soon as possible.

But now came the hard part: deciding who would stay, and who would be able to escape today. She hoped it might not be a permanent decision, and she assumed everyone would eventually be allowed a chance. At least the money she and Steffen had gathered would help.

But still Hanne sighed and leaned against the metal stair railing, gathering strength to go downstairs with the kind of cheery face and attitude the refusees needed. So Steffen thought she was determined, did he? He had no idea how much she quivered inside and would not recognize her bleak doubt if it hit him in the face.

Determined? Maybe. But she wondered how the unenviable job of playing God had fallen on her shoulders.

21

If one is forever cautious, can one remain a human being?
—Aleksandr I. Solzhenitsyn

A ll right, now!" Hanne held up her hands and tried not to bump her head on the ambulance ceiling. "I need everyone's attention, please."

Six frightened refugees huddled in back behind the curtain separating the driver from the rest of the ambulance. They'd arranged for a grandmother and her son, his wife, and three young teens—a boy and two girls. If they could have fit more, they would have.

Steffen kept the vehicle idling, and a wary eye out for any approaching traffic. While still in the Bispebjerg parking area, however, she assumed they were safe. Perhaps. For now. She turned to the driver. "Steffen?"

"Yes, right." Steffen cleared his throat. "Hanne is going to dress you kids up a bit for the trip."

Hanne held up her jar of theatrical blood as he continued explaining.

"This is the same thing that actors paint on their faces or limbs. Dramatic, like Herod and Cleopatra in *The Idealist.*"

No one reacted.

"You know, Kaj Munk?" Steffen softened his voice a bit. "You've heard of his plays, haven't you?"

Their blank looks betrayed the fact that this audience might never have heard of the Danish pastor and dramatist.

"Oh, well." He shrugged. "Doesn't matter. All you need to know is that if we're stopped, you adults under the blanket need to keep completely still, and you three with the makeup just need to groan a bit and look injured. Got it?"

This time the young actors nodded seriously, because their lives depended on it. Hanne dipped a wooden tongue depressor into the jar of sticky, oozing red and nodded to her first victim.

"You've got a head injury from an accident with a delivery truck," she told the boy, who looked perhaps thirteen or fourteen. "Or how about with a bus? Can you do this? Let me hear you groan."

The boy looked around at the others, as if embarrassed.

"Come on." Hanne dabbed a little more blood on the boy's forehead. "A little louder. You're in pain!"

So he finally complied, but didn't seem nearly as enthusiastic as his sister. If anything, she carried the groaning thing a little too far.

"All right, perfect." Hanne ripped the collar of his shirt a bit for good measure. His mother would thank her, later. "You're going to get a job in the movies when this is all over."

Hanne finished painting the faces and arms of her three patients—the boy who winced whenever she applied another dab of red, and his two sisters. "Two of you lie down, and one try to sit up. Remember, you're seriously injured."

She looked up at Steffen, hoping this idea didn't turn out to be as crazy as it seemed. All they needed was for one thing to go wrong.

He nodded back at them. "Let's go?"

He placed the ambulance in gear, jerking only a little, and eased them away from the loading area and out to the wide *Tuborgvej*, Tuborg Road. Their only problem was obvious. Because instead of heading toward the hospital, now they headed away, toward another rendezvous on the coast. Steffen looked nervously in his mirrors as he steered north and east.

"What am I going to say if we do get stopped?" he wondered aloud. Hanne couldn't think of a good answer.

So they drove on in silence, tension in the air. No one made a sound except the occasional nervous cough. With six Jewish refugees in the back of their ambulance, anything could happen. And as they sped down Tuborgvej in the direction of the coast, Hanne almost wasn't surprised when they slowed to a stop on the outskirts of Gentofte, on the northern outskirts.

"What's going on?" asked one of the sisters. "Why are we stopping?"

Hanne turned to them again.

"I see a couple of soldiers up ahead, checking traffic. Remember, you're in pain. But don't overdo it."

A little voice came from the teenage boy, propped up next to the two who lay across a single stretcher.

"I think we should sound the siren," he said. "Maybe we'll get away more quickly."

Hanne looked over at Steffen, who clenched his teeth.

"Or maybe we'll get noticed a little more quickly," he added.

They needn't have worried about being noticed. A moment later, two German guards marched up and demanded to see their identification.

"*Papieren, bitte,*" barked the first soldier, holding out his hand and snapping a finger with impatience. He couldn't have been more than twenty years old.

"We're transporting these people," Steffen told them, sounding rather panicked. "It's an emergency!"

So it was. A second guard came up from the other side and shined his flashlight at them. Hanne did her best to appear frantic as she wrapped the boy's arm in a gauze bandage. She was careful to squeeze a large puddle of the costume blood out at just the right time.

"We've got to get them to this hospital, quickly!" Hanne told them, adding as much urgency as she dared. "It looks like they're losing too much blood!"

She nudged the boy, who gave an appropriately soft groan. Good. Even so, the guard seemed to take his time examining their identification papers, each folded into a small pouch, like a passport. He held up Steffen's to the light of his flashlight, comparing the real face from his passport.

"I didn't know pastors drove ambulances," said the young German. "This is not Falck?"

Of course the German would know about Falck, the Danish rescue and fire service. Maybe he'd never seen any other kind of ambulance.

"No," Steffen replied with a straight face. "It's a private service for the hospital. You know what I mean, of course."

Of course. Perhaps the guard would not know there was no such thing. And as he next turned to Hanne's I.D. and frowned at it in the light from his torch.

"You are a nurse at Bispebjerg, Miss Hansen?"

Hanne almost had to force herself to respond to her new "Danish" name, but managed to nod as she held to her patient's wrist and counted the pulse. The boy's heart was racing, by the way, but for the same reason as was her own.

"Really, this is an emergency," insisted Steffen, his voice agitated. "Surely you can see. We must be on our way."

"To the hospital?" asked the guard.

"Yes, yes." Steffen made a show of placing the car back into gear with a terrible grinding noise, then stalled the ambulance.

"Then you are heading the wrong direction." The German pointed back at the way they had come.

"What?" When Steffen gasped, Hanne knew he didn't know what to say next. So Hanne turned back and made a show of desperation, waving her hands angrily and slapping Steffen on the shoulder.

"You idiot!" She raised her voice to a yell. "I told you to turn left, but you said you knew where you were going! I knew we shouldn't have listened to you! And now look what's happened! Someone's going to die back here because of your stubbornness."

Hanne wasn't completely sure if the Germans followed every word of her rapid-fire Danish, but she knew they would understand her tone. And sure enough, the nearest guard stared at the exchange and burst out laughing. A moment later he motioned for two more guards to come join in the joke.

"Very funny," whispered Steffen, under his breath. "Now can we get out of here, please?"

Still the Germans seemed in no particular hurry. But after some discussion and chuckling the other two finally backed away, returning to their posts by the side of the road, while the first guard slowly handed back their cards, and Steffen restarted the stalled ambulance.

"Well," he told the German, "we'll just be going, then."

"Nein!" The guard grabbed Steffen's steering wheel before they could get away, then pointed to himself and his nearby motorcycle. "I know where is the hospital. You will follow me now. Verstehen sie? Understand?"

What else could Steffen do but nod? Still laughing, the guard stepped over to his cycle, started it up, and waved through a cloud of exhaust for them to follow. Steffen quickly rolled up his window while their passengers groaned. But Hanne patted her patient.

"You can stop groaning, for now," she told him. But she wanted to groan herself as Steffen turned the ambulance in the middle of the road and obeyed the guard's directive, heading back the way they came.

"What are we going to do now?" she wondered, trying to make out the time on her watch. "We can't go back to the hospital. We need to have these people to the beach at Tårbæk in less than an hour. They may not get another chance."

"I know all that." Now Steffen set his jaw as they followed the helpful soldier through the outskirts of the city, back the wrong way. He pressed his lips together as they passed through Skovshoved toward a major roundabout.

And then without warning he yanked the wheel over, sending them spinning through the roundabout, around a corner, and into an unmarked alley.

"Hold on!" he told them, though it might have been more useful if he'd said so a moment earlier. As it was, Hanne flew out of her front seat, nearly ending up on Steffen's lap. Everyone in back tumbled at least as much as they cried out. But Steffen accelerated through the darkness, screeching around yet another corner, and flying out into the clear.

"Please!" cried the older woman, but now they sped through empty lanes and back roads on their way back to the coast, avoiding, of course, the place where they had encountered the German roadblock.

"Are you sure we should have done this?" wondered Hanne, looking over at their driver. "Now they know our names."

He almost smiled, but kept his eyes on the road.

"Maybe so. But what did we do? If they go to the trouble to look us up, we just explain how easy it is to get lost out here."

Hanne shook her head as she looked back to check on their passengers. And she wondered about the man who now drove six more Jews to safety, risking his own life in the process. Why? Even just a few days ago, she would never have expected this of him. Serious? Yes. Conservative? Definitely. But something else now drew her to him—until he broke into her thoughts like a tour guide.

"Next stop, Tårbæk," he announced. They passed the turn-off to the Tårbæk beach that she remembered from earlier day trips here with friends from school. "Where you'll board your luxurious cruise ship for your final destination, the beautiful city of Malmö, Sweden, home of—"

Hanne interrupted him with a hand on his arm.

"Pastor, I think they're going to Landskrona."

"As I said, the beautiful city of Landskrona. Home of . . . what is it the home of?"

"These days" she said, "it's the home of a lot more Danish Jews."

He looked at her out of the corner of his eye and smiled as they pulled up behind a small waterfront warehouse. In the ambulance's shielded headlights, it appeared weathered and rust-streaked. As if on cue, a shadowy figure in a dark coat and tall rubber boots stepped out from behind the shelter of the building and approached as Steffen rolled down the window.

"Six," said Steffen, without introduction, "as you agreed with my brother?"

He pulled a bulging envelope out of his shirt pocket and extended it to the man.

"Tak," said the man—a brief thank-you that sounded almost like a grunt. And without another word he disappeared the way he'd come as a garage door swung open from the inside, just wide enough for them to pass through. Once inside Steffen cut the engine and the door closed behind them, like the jaws of a great fish.

"Here we are," Steffen told them as someone pulled open the ambulance's back doors. "May God bless you, and . . . *shalom*."

According to plan, their passengers left the ambulance at this transfer point. They all reached out a hand with a whisper of thanks, and Hanne gave the mother a hug. But moments later they were all gone, leaving Hanne and Steffen alone and waiting for the warehouse doors to reopen.

Hanne listened to soft voices outside, perhaps the voice of the fisherman who had taken their money, and the distant but distinct wheeze and pop of a fishing boat's engine. The smell of salted fish drifted in through the ambulance window. Steffen broke the silence.

"A little like being left inside a jar of pickled herring, eh? Makes me ill."

She couldn't help smiling, even if he couldn't see her.

"Really? I sort of like the smell. I'm just not used to all this, this . . . you know, secret agent kind of thing. But, Pastor—"

"Just Steffen. Please. If you risk your life with someone, at least you ought to be on a first-name basis, don't you think?"

"Well, yes, but I just wanted to apologize for speaking so harshly back there. For calling you an idiot."

"Oh, that's right." He sounded surprised, as if he'd forgotten. "You did, didn't you? Well, if it makes you feel any better, I know you didn't mean it. Or did you?"

They both laughed at that, as Hanne explained herself.

"It's just that my father would never let me use that word, when I was a little girl. I tried it once, when I was six. I think I was playing outside. My *Far* overheard and gave me quite a spanking, let me tell you."

"Sounds like a traumatic memory."

"You know what I mean. So tonight I honestly almost choked on the word, but I thought perhaps it might help convince the Germans."

He chuckled. "I think you did a very adequate job of convincing them, all right. You were wonderful, in fact. You nearly had me convinced."

"Well, as I said, I am sorry about that."

"No, you're not. You enjoyed it."

They laughed again, leaning their faces together, until he added another question.

"But . . . your father? You've never mentioned him before."

"Oh, I . . . ah—"

She paused, wishing she hadn't mentioned him at all.

"I didn't mean to be nosey," said Steffen, but she shook her head.

"No, it's not that. You're not being nosey at all. *Far* was—is an engineer. His company sent him to work on a bridge project in Holland before the war."

"Holland?" Steffen sounded alarmed, as well he should have.

"We begged him not to go, of course, for obvious reasons. You know. But he was always convinced nothing could happen to him. And now we haven't heard from him in over three years."

"I'm sorry to hear that. Perhaps . . ."

Thankfully he didn't finish the sentence with a platitude she'd long ago rejected. But even in her weaker moments, did she really not hold some glimmer of hope that she might see her father again?

"Actually, I keep expecting him to show up on my doorstep, acting as if nothing had ever happened and apologizing for making us worry. But I know . . ."

She did her best to mask her voice with lighthearted banter, knowing very well that Steffen wasn't fooled. When she looked over, a flicker of light from outside lit up his sad face as he stared out his window into the dark warehouse.

"Well, I pray that he does." Finally he straightened in his seat. "And I'm sure your father would be proud of his daughter today. Just as I am. Six more to safety. How many left?"

She didn't even want to guess. But among them would be Aron Overgaard, which reminded her that she had not explained that part of her life to Steffen, either. Not that she owed him any explanation. Or even if she tried, she might not be able to make sense of it all anymore.

So she leaned out her window, took a deep breath of briny air, and waited.

22
SANKT STEFAN'S KIRKE, KØBENHAVN
SUNDAY MORNING, 10 OCTOBER 1943

Every man's life is a fairy tale written by God's fingers.
—HANS CHRISTIAN ANDERSEN

A word, Pastor?"

Pastor Viggo stood in the shadows of the narthex, obviously waiting for Steffen to step back inside after greeting everyone as they filed out from that morning's service. Steffen paused as his eyes adjusted once again to the shadows. But the elderly pastor made no move, so Steffen joined him. He couldn't help but feel a little spooked, the same way as when a professor had called him to his desk to reprimand him for a failed test or a missed assignment.

"Something wrong?" asked Steffen, his mind racing. Still he could think of nothing that might have upset of the genial older pastor.

Viggo looked him over closely, not allowing him enough personal space to breathe well, and Steffen couldn't help but back up several inches.

"Not yet," Viggo told him, his voice steady and low. "But I think there's about to be."

"I don't understand." Steffen shook his head. "Did I miss something in my sermon? Something I could have explained better? You heard the whole thing, didn't you?"

From Luke chapter seven, beginning at the eleventh verse.

Og Gud har besøgt sit folk.
And God has visited His people.

Perhaps he'd turned a phrase incorrectly, or Pastor Viggo didn't like the way he'd compared the people in the crowd—the ones who had witnessed Jesus raising the dead young boy to life—to the Danish people witnessing new life in their streets and towns, in the narrow alleys of København and the fishing villages that dotted their coast. Surely, Steffen had told them, God was visiting His people in a new way.

"I heard every word, Steffen. It was by far the best you've ever preached. Even the joke about the fisherman. In fact, I've never seen you speak like this. Something's gotten into you."

"Oh." Steffen breathed a little more easily. "I'm glad you think so. But then . . . what is the problem? Not with the sermon?"

"Yes, that's exactly the problem. Look . . ." Now the elder pastor turned, his arms crossed. Perhaps he needed his cigar to settle down a bit, but Steffen had seldom seen him this agitated. Finally he turned back to Steffen, and tears rimmed his eyes.

"When you were assigned to this parish, Steffen, I had a difficult time biting my tongue at first. In fact, I probably should have attended somewhere else in my retirement, just to stay out of your way."

"No. I have always valued your wisdom. I have never felt as if you've interfered. Whose idea was it to keep your office here, even when the bishop wasn't so enthusiastic?"

Pastor Viggo gave him a little smile.

"You're right about that."

"And if someone comes to you with a problem or a suggestion, the way they might have done when you were in the pulpit, you always turn them straight over to me, don't you?"

Again a little smile from the older pastor.

"Most of the time. Yes."

"And you always sit way in the back, as if you don't want people to notice."

"Exactly." Now he turned serious once more. "And that's just it. Listen, I know what you've been doing these past several days. And I have to say that personally I admire you for it. I never expected it of you, but I admire what you're doing."

This time Steffen wasn't sure how to answer, or how to acknowledge. So he just nodded as Viggo went on—this time wagging a finger at Steffen.

"But when I sit in the back, I see things you don't. There was a Gestapo man here today, trying to blend in. He was watching you, Steffen, and I don't think he liked what he heard."

"What? You're mistaken. I usually see everyone."

"Obviously not everyone."

"But how would you know he's Gestapo? Did you ask him?"

By this time they were getting into things Pastor Viggo obviously was not comfortable sharing. He pulled at his collar and mopped his shiny forehead with a handkerchief.

"This is where it gets complicated, Steffen."

"Complicated?" Steffen tried to keep his voice from rising an octave as Viggo raised his hand to settle him down. "But what are you saying?"

"I didn't think it made any difference. Margrethe's been here a long time, you know. Since before I even came to this parish. Her family's always attended. I went to school with her brothers."

"Now you've really lost me. What does Margrethe have to do with anything?"

"All right." Viggo's shoulders slumped. "A week before they tried to round up the Jews, I noticed Margrethe speaking with a German officer out in the alley. They didn't see me, and at the time I didn't fault her for it."

"We've all been stopped at one time or another."

"Exactly. And that still might be the case. I'm not accusing her of collaboration, you understand. But the man she was speaking to was the same one who slipped into the back of the church this morning, listening."

"You're sure of that?"

He frowned at Steffen in a way that required no answer. Of course he was sure.

"Then . . ." Steffen's throat suddenly felt dry, even more than when he'd been driving the ambulance, nearly every day this past week. "What are you suggesting?"

"I'm suggesting that you need to be much more careful of what you say in public, here in the church office, and especially in the pulpit. Come on, son. Was it really so hard to miss your meaning, this morning? Men have been shot for less. And how long do you think it will take them to put together the pieces? Pastor Steffen who preaches against the German occupiers. Pastor Steffen who drives his brother's ambulance, rescuing Jews. Pastor Steffen, who spends nearly all his free time with a Jewish nurse from Bispebjerg."

"Wait a minute." Steffen held his forehead in his hand. "How do you know all this?"

"I keep my eyes open." Viggo shrugged. "I promised God that as long as he kept me here, I would keep an eye open for you."

Steffen felt his cheeks flush—mainly in knowing that Pastor Viggo could see so many of these things so plainly. And if Viggo could see, who else could?

"I don't want to cause you any trouble," mumbled Steffen.

"Trouble? Ha. Not me. You just worry a little more about yourself. Because you know who else was here this morning?"

This time Steffen was ready for anything. Perhaps King Christian had dropped by on his horse, unannounced. And Steffen had been so taken up in his own preaching, he'd missed it all. Pastor Viggo looked at him with a mixture of amazement and amusement.

"You really don't know? Well, that proves how oblivious you were today. I used to be like that on a good Sunday, when my head was full of my preaching. Fortunately I'm not that way anymore."

He chuckled again, but Steffen couldn't stand it.

"All very good, but who are we talking about?"

"Oh, you mean this morning. Yes, of course. The young lady friend? Dark eyes? Dark hair? Very striking? Works at Bispebjerg, I believe?"

Steffen groaned and closed his eyes. He must have looked toward the back row a hundred times in the course of the morning and never noticed. But then, as Viggo had said, perhaps his head *was* a bit full of his preaching.

"How long was she here?" he finally whispered. And when he opened his eyes, Viggo was smiling at him all over again.

"Nearly the entire service. She slipped in about fifteen minutes late, left about five minutes early. She has an eye for you. And you made her cry, by the way. Now whether that's good or bad, I'm not sure, but—"

"I had no idea." Steffen couldn't stop shaking his head now. Hanne? Here at Sankt Stefan's? "I had no idea."

"Obviously not. But maybe that's a good thing. I have a feeling you might have embarrassed her, if you had noticed her. She looked to me as if she wanted to remain anonymous."

Then it occurred to Steffen, and he gripped Viggo's shoulders in his hands.

"The Gestapo man! Do you think—?"

"Oh, he saw her, all right. That's what caught my eye in the first place. He saw her come in, and he kept track of her the entire time. Because as soon as she slipped out the back—and this was before the end of the service—he went right after her."

"I have to go tell her." Steffen broke away and started for the door, only not before Viggo caught him by the arm.

"Let me tell you something, Steffen. I never give you advice unless you ask for it. But this time I must. I don't know what your Jewish friend has done to hide her identity. I can only guess. But whatever she's done, the Gestapo is still watching her. And now they're making the connection between you and her. So you have to be careful about what you say, and about what you do. And don't forget about Margrethe."

Steffen nodded, understanding. But that didn't change what he would need to do next.

"And if this girl is your friend," Viggo continued, "you'd better tell her to get out of the country while she still can. I will be praying every day for both of you. Only you have to be much more careful, do you understand? Careful like you've never been before."

"I understand."

"I hope you do. Oh, and one more thing, Steffen."

Steffen paused halfway to the front doors, unsure how to thank the older man.

"That was still the best sermon I've ever heard."

"Tak," Steffen answered back softly. "Even if it kills me, right?"

23

It is so hard to believe because it is so hard to obey.
—SØREN KIERKEGAARD

*H*anne put her head down against the wind and pulled her scarf around a little more tightly. She still couldn't believe she'd been so foolish, visiting Steffen's church. Foolish! She had just wanted to see him again, to understand his heart and what drove him to do the things he did.

But what had she expected, for him to read from the Torah?

Instead, she'd been struck by a strange story about a prophet who raised a young man from the dead and hit full force by a kind of passion she'd never before seen in Steffen.

She was, however, fairly certain he had not seen her slip into the back of the Lutheran sanctuary. That at least was a relief. The other relief was the familiar smell of candles. If she closed her eyes and didn't listen to any of the strange back-and-forth singing between the pastor and his congregation, she might almost have imagined herself in the synagogue.

But that was a lot of ifs. And more than anything she was quite certain Rabbi Melchior would not have approved, had he known where she had spent this Sunday morning.

Mor would not have approved. Aron would've had a heart attack.

Call it simple curiosity. But this felt more like a moth drawn to the candle's flame, and she could not avoid the heart of the words Steffen had read from his strange but Jewish-sounding Scriptures:

"Fear seized them all," he'd read from his big Christian Bible, from up on his podium, at the end of the story where the young man had been raised back to life. "Fear seized them all, and they glorified God, saying, 'A great prophet has arisen among us!' and 'God has visited his people!'"

She was not so naïve as to not recognize many of the names in the reading. *Lukas* they called the evangelist. And before that *Paulus*, the apostle. And of course the reading from Job, the one she knew already. But she wondered at the words of the Greek *Lukas* and those two Jews, as they were recorded in the Christian Bible. How could God himself have visited his people?

If only such a thing could happen, she thought. The idea actually made her shiver. Or perhaps it was the cold breeze, laden with a hint of drizzle. She hurried her steps to outrun the oncoming weather.

She still couldn't imagine how the Lord had actually visited his people. But just supposing he had, as those Jews in Steffen's scriptures seemed to believe, then Hanne imagined there would then be no Hitler and no deportations, no death camps, and no German troops in the streets of København. Such a visitor would not allow these things, would he? Therefore it could not have happened the way he'd read.

So why did the story keep reverberating in her head, like truth or a jazz melody that played over and over and over?

Even more than that, how in the world had it moved her to tears, as if she were standing suddenly in her mother's kitchen as they sliced onions for dinner? That part baffled her completely. She would have to think on it some more, and she turned the story around and around in her head as she approached the familiar brick buildings of the Bispebjerg campus.

Years and years ago they'd built the hospital at the city outskirts, beyond narrow København streets, shoulder-to-shoulder shops, and four-story apartment blocks presided over by dozens of church spires. How strange that she had grown up here in the shadow of all these ornate old churches, yet had never dared to enter one until this morning.

As the pavement grew slick with drizzle, she paused once again to adjust her scarf, and out of the corner of her eye caught sight of a tall man in a dark coat, pausing at just the same time. Familiar? She wasn't sure. But she supposed anyone else had the same right to be walking down *Tagensgade* as well. A woman pushing a stroller with a young boy hanging on her coat crossed by on the other side, along with several young girls and an old man. Nothing out of the ordinary there. Except that when she began walking again, she casually stopped at a shoe repair window to notice a collection of sturdy leather walking shoes, men's shoes at that. Again out of the corner of her eye she noted the man behind her, staring in his own window, and she could see the sign over his head.

Jensen: Tøj til Kvinder.

Jensen's Clothing for Women.

If Hanne hadn't been a Jew in a country where all other Jews were either in hiding or being deported to death camps, she might have thought nothing of it. Or if she didn't hold a forged identity card with another woman's non-Jewish name, she might have shrugged it off. But her mouth went dry as she turned away, knowing that something here was not right.

Without waiting she turned and hurried toward the safety of the hospital, and it was all she could manage not to run in panic.

I'll get there, she told herself, because now she could see the hospital buildings looming larger. *I'll get there, and there won't be anything they can do to stop me.*

Now she didn't dare turn around, but she felt the man's eyes on her, closer and closer. Yet even as her heart beat wildly she kept up a normal Sunday stroll, forcing herself to deliberately slow down.

Breathe. Relax. Don't panic. It's nothing.

She didn't believe a word of the lies she told herself. And now she almost wished she had stayed back in the church, perhaps even spoke with Steffen. At the hospital she could lock her borrowed apartment door and hide, but then what?

Finally she entered the comforting embrace of the Bispebjerg campus, where that familiar cluster of buildings told her she was almost home. She ducked under an archway and down a covered walk, her footsteps echoing, then into a service entry where linens from the hospitals were taken. She knew this way better than most. Surely he would not follow her here?

Against her better judgment Hanne casually glanced back around and down the breezeway, waiting for . . . nothing out of the ordinary.

Silly, she told herself. *He was just out for a walk, the same as you. You're making a lot out of nothing. Why would anyone follow you, anyway?*

Still, she waited in the service alcove for just a few more minutes, just to be sure. And when she gingerly stepped out into the breezeway again she kept a wary eye on the path through the campus from the street where she had seen the man. A doctor in a white frock bustled along the path, clipboard in hand. A maintenance man in coveralls pushed a cart laden with tools and towels. Just what she would have expected.

There, see? You were just being paranoid. Everything is under control.

Now she stepped out with even more confidence, back out into the breezeway and the open courtyard. The afternoon drizzle had lightened into a mist, not even enough to justify an umbrella. In this case, a smile of relief would do the job, and Hanne lifted her face to the mist as she took the long way through the gardens to her apartment.

Her little celebration was cut short, however, when she noticed Ann-Grete headed her direction, arms crossed across her chest and a stormy look on her face, as if someone had just died. That, and Ann-Grete wore no coat, even in the chill of the afternoon.

"What's wrong?" Hanne asked the obvious question, but Ann-Grete only shook her head stiffly, grabbed Hanne by the arm, and dragged her away from the center of the plaza.

"Don't ask questions," said Ann-Grete, barely moving her lips. The expression of terror on her face sent a chill up Hanne's spine. "Just walk with me."

"Where?" Hanne was afraid she didn't want to know what had shaken up her friend this badly. "And what in the world is going on?"

Again Ann-Grete shook her head. And her grip on Hanne's arm nearly cut off the circulation.

"They're here, and they're searching your apartment."

"They. You mean—"

"The Gestapo. That awful man who's been in and out of the hospital, asking questions all the time?"

"Wolfschmidt?"

"Him, yes, and four soldiers. They looked like they were determined to find you."

"But how?" Hanne still couldn't believe it.

"I have no idea how they found out. I don't know. All I know is you can't go back to that apartment. Not now."

As numb as she was, it crossed Hanne's mind that the man who had been following her might still be waiting now, perhaps out on the street or at the edge of the Bispebjerg campus, behind a car or a tree. Her legs stiffened.

"Didn't you hear me?" hissed Ann-Grete. "Go wherever your Jewish friends have been going, but you've got to get out of here. You can't pack your bags. I mean now! Nu!"

"But what about you?"

"Forget about me. I can work my way out of this. I can just tell them I was reassigned to your apartment when you escaped, and that I didn't know what was going on. They can't prove anything."

"I don't want you to get in trouble for my sake."

"Believe me, I'm not, all right? Now just don't worry about anything except getting out of here. I'll take care of your stuff, as much as I can. I'll listen to your records. But do you have somewhere to go?"

Hanne thought for a moment. The only option that crossed her mind now was the church basement, where she'd taken her mother. She nodded.

"I know a place."

"All right, then." Ann-Grete gave her a quick hug, squeezing Hanne breathless and then letting go just as abruptly. "You'd better go there before they see us together. Get out of here!"

Hanne paused a moment longer than she probably should have, trying not to think of what she so suddenly had to leave behind. Her work and her friends. Her apartment. Her life.

Even her new identity and all that had come with it. There had to be some mistake—but she knew there was not.

By that time they'd reached the edge of the campus. And though Hanne looked all around, she still couldn't see the man who'd followed her. Maybe she'd lost him.

"I just thought I'd have more time to prepare," she managed.

"I thought so, too. But there's no time to prepare, Hanne. I'm sorry. I'll see you when . . . when this is all over."

Without another word Ann-Grete turned and hurried back to face her own danger. Hanne thought of calling out, but no more words would come, and neither would tears. Only a shock that hit her so hard in the stomach that she could hardly breathe. That, and a brief but blinding wave of anger for the men who would do this.

Ann-Grete was right, though. Even without a suitcase— not even a toothbrush!—now Hanne could only hurry away to find whatever sanctuary she could.

If she still could.

24

*Remember the signs of the Christian Church have been the Lion,
the Lamb, the Dove, and the Fish . . . but never the chameleon.*

—KAJ MUNK

H anne paused before knocking on the back entry to Sankt Stefan's Kirke, her hand in mid-air. Had it really come to this? She thought she detected the faint odor of cigar smoke in the air, though perhaps that came from the murky refuse cans lined up along the tall stone wall of the church. Unpleasant or not, the alley looked clear and she could not delay, so she knocked and waited.

No one came.

She knocked again, now wondering if it would be safe to walk around to the front, in plain sight of anyone passing along Nørrebrogade. Probably not. Though she had not noticed the man who had followed her to the hospital less than an hour ago, she could not now risk both her own safety and the safety of Pastor Steffen.

Perhaps she should try somewhere else to hide. But where? She hunched her shoulders against the drizzle, wishing she had an umbrella or at least a scarf to keep her hair from getting soaked. But it was far too late for that. She shivered, feeling colder than ever, and knocked on the door again.

"Come on!" she pleaded with the large wooden door, hitting it harder now with her closed fist. "Someone answer!"

Finally she heard a shuffling sound from somewhere inside, then a deadbolt unlatching and the creak of hinges. Finally!

"I'm so sorry to bother you," Hanne began, even before seeing who now peered out at her from the shadowy interior of the church. "But I have a very large favor to ask, and—oh!"

It had not occurred to her that anyone other than Steffen might answer the door on a Sunday afternoon. But she did recognize the silver-haired former pastor. He peered out at her with a curious expression, nodded once, and signaled for her to come in.

"Hurry, now," he said, stepping aside and then bolting the door shut after she stepped inside. "Did you see anyone out there?"

She wasn't sure who he might mean by "anyone." But she shook her head no.

"I don't think so. But actually I came to see Pastor Steffen. He's here, I hope?"

Now the older man guided her down the hall to the little safe room under the stairway. Perhaps he didn't realize she had been in the building before.

"He and his brother are out looking for you, as a matter of fact. But you're welcome to wait here for them, if you like. I'll get you a towel to dry yourself. Would you like some coffee?"

"Coffee?" She perked up at the word. "You really have coffee here?"

Perhaps this was a better hiding place than she thought. He chuckled softly, and she liked the sound.

"Oh, you know. I call it coffee, just to be charitable. Perhaps you're as good at pretending as I am. But chicory root and a few other things, once you get used to them, well . . ." He made a funny face. "Yes, it's still awful. But we drink it anyway, don't we?"

He left to retrieve his wartime coffee, but Hanne still had to know.

"Wait." She stopped him. "What did you mean, they're looking for me?"

Again he studied her with a bit of a sideways glance, as if sizing up whether she was to be trusted, or not.

"Steffen's brother, Henning, showed up just after the service this morning, terribly agitated. You have to understand that it takes something quite out of the ordinary to bring Henning to this place. He's not normally a churchgoing man."

Hanne nodded politely, not letting on that yes, she knew this about Steffen's brother. The older pastor looked as if he enjoyed telling his story.

"So Henning comes running up to the church, all red in the face, and I hear him say something about how the Gestapo knows everything, how they're going to her apartment, and how another refugee just showed up at his bookstore without warning. How the Gestapo knows everything is another question, you see. But before I can say anything else they're both running out the door. Off to find you, they said."

"I see. Well, I do appreciate you opening your door to me."

"Of course, of course. But it looks like you barely escaped, isn't that correct?"

"Pardon?" Hanne still wasn't sure how this man knew so much.

"You're not carrying a suitcase." He pointed at her empty hands. "So I assume you had to leave wherever you were in a terrible hurry. That can't be the best of circumstances. Nevertheless, God is taking good care of you. You're still well, and we'll have coffee together, just as if nothing evil was going on outside."

Hanne had to admit she had not looked at it from quite that perspective. But yes, she was still well, even without her luggage and her things.

"And we're very glad you're here," he added, as his expression turned serious and his voice lowered. "But let me just give you one word of caution."

"Of course." Hanne replied, unsure what to expect.

"I have to tell you there's a cleaning woman here in the building. Sometimes she comes in after the morning service, other times not until Monday. I can't go into too much detail, but it would be best if she did not see you, for the time being."

"I'll do my best to stay out of her way." Hanne nodded, fearing the worst about this woman. "But one other thing. Did you say Henning had another refugee in his store?"

"I think so, yes. Apparently told to go there by an Underground contact. But I can tell you Henning wasn't happy about it."

"No? Why not?"

"I'm not entirely sure." Pastor Viggo shrugged his shoulders. "Perhaps you'll find out for yourself, before long."

———

For Hanne the next two hours of waiting seemed so much longer. She couldn't rest in the dreary little safe room under the stairs, and she couldn't think of anything except what might happen to Ann-Grete at Bispebjerg. Every sound or creak in the ancient building made her think German soldiers had finally caught up with her. What would happen to the pastors, then?

Finally she heard the alley entrance slam shut, then footsteps and familiar voices coming closer.

———

"I told you, we're taking you here because the shop is just a way station, all right?" Henning obviously made no attempt to disguise his irritation. "You're just lucky I happened to be there when you arrived. You should have called ahead. I'm not usually there on the weekend."

"I'm sure we'll find her," added Pastor Steffen. His voice sounded on edge, almost pleading. "We're pretty sure they haven't caught up to her yet. I spoke briefly with her friend at the hospital."

"And she couldn't tell you where Hanne had run to?"

Hanne froze at the sound of Aron's voice, though it seemed hoarse and raspy, hardly recognizable. So he was the one Pastor Viggo was talking about!

"All she could tell me was that Hanne said she had a place to go to." Steffen pulled at the hidden door as he spoke. "I can't imagine where that would be, except—"

"Except here?" Hanne finished his sentence as the door opened. And she enjoyed for a moment the warm glow in Steffen's eyes as he realized she was safe. She couldn't help but return the quick smile.

On the other hand, Henning and Aron wore looks of frozen astonishment.

"Hanne!" croaked Aron, stepping forward. He hardly looked like the same man she'd left in the synagogue, the morning of the announcement. His beard looked wild and unkempt, his bloodshot eyes framed with dark circles. Clearly the hiding had not been an easy time for him.

But still he stood staring, as if not quite believing he'd actually found her. He reached out his hands but quickly pulled them back again. Finally she broke the awkward silence.

"How did you get here, Aron?"

He shrugged. "Back of a delivery truck, all the way from Roskilde. Long ride. Long story."

"Well, I'm glad you're well."

And she did mean it. But just then Pastor Viggo came scurrying down the hallway.

"Oh, there you are! See?" His cheeks looked rosy and his smile genuine as he patted Steffen on the shoulder. "And you were so worried the Nazis might have caught up to her."

Steffen looked at the floor, the light in his expression turning to embarrassment. Meanwhile, Aron stood awkwardly by the entry to the safe room, smelling as if he hadn't had a bath since the last time she'd seen him.

"Well, this reunion is all very nice." Henning had a way of getting to the point. "But we're making arrangements for you both to leave Danmark."

Hanne looked at him, and he must have recognized the pleading in her eyes. She thought desperately how she might argue her case, and of ways she might convince them that she should stay. But after what had happened this afternoon, nothing made sense any longer.

"There's absolutely no argument this time," Henning told her. "I learned just this morning the Gestapo knows who you are and they know what you look like. Someone must have tipped them off."

"Is it true?" she asked Steffen, but he could only nod glum agreement. "Who would do that?"

Henning didn't seem particularly moved.

"Someone at your hospital? I don't know. But you just can't stay here anymore. You must understand. In fact you can't stay anywhere in Danmark. We have a boat that will take the two of you to Sweden."

"That's right." Steffen forced a smile. "In fact, we've arranged to have you wait in a beach house just a few kilometers up the coast, close to Tårbæk. The fishing boat will pick you up just before midnight."

Hanne let the words sink in as she repeated the word.

"Midnight?" she wondered aloud.

"Yes," said Henning, nodding. "Tonight. And no rowboat adventures."

Tonight! Hanne caught her breath at the suddenness and sat down on one of the cots Steffen had set up in the safe room. Aron sat down next to her, but she wasn't sure she heard any of what he said. Instead she looked up at Steffen to see the saddest, most helpless expression. And finally her own tears let loose—for herself and for everything that had happened to her that day. For her country and her people. Even for Aron, who now slipped a tentative arm around her shoulder.

Steffen pressed his lips together and said nothing as he turned away. If she could have said anything to him, she would have. But she could not, and the lump in her throat only grew as she buried her face in her hands and sobbed.

25

It is a kingly act to assist the fallen.
—MOTHER TERESA

What's taking them so long?" Aron grumbled as he paced the bare wood floor in the tiny beach cottage. Hanne thought his voice carried much too far in the dark night. Surely the German guards who patrolled this beach would be able to hear them.

"I told you it's not time yet," came Henning's voice from where he crouched just under a picture window facing the sea. To his credit, he only whispered. "Not for at least another half hour, and then we make contact with the boat."

A glimmer of moonlight trickled inside when Henning peeked out through the shade, enough for Hanne to make out the dark forms of Aron pacing and Steffen sitting by the door, as if guarding against any intruders.

Hanne didn't move, just sat with arms wrapped around her knees in one of the tiny room's lumpy, mismatched chairs that smelled of a cottage locked tightly for far too long. She sneezed again as the dust tickled her nose.

"Hmmph." Aron apparently wasn't satisfied with the time, as if they could push ahead the hands of their watches and make it so. "I thought you said they'd be here by midnight."

"That's exactly what I said," replied Henning, not disguising his own impatience as he let the shade slip back into place. "It's only half-twelve. Eleven-thirty."

"You're certain your watch is correct?" asked Aron.

Henning only harrumphed in reply. It had been like this all evening, and Hanne's head buzzed with tension while the rest of her body rebelled with a fatigue that had hit her the moment she'd sat down, over two hours ago. Perhaps she would be able to rest when they got on the boat. But in the back of her mind she knew that would only be the start.

"There go the guards again," whispered Henning, peeking out at the beach. "Every twenty-six minutes, just like clockwork."

"I like predictable Nazis," said Steffen, but then his voice caught. "I mean, no, I don't like Nazis. I just like them more when they're predictable. Ak, you know what I mean."

Henning peeked out once more. In a shaft of moonlight Hanne saw Steffen gazing in her direction, and she felt her own heart beat more quickly. But of course that would only be from the tension of the moment and the thought of sneaking through the night past the watchful eye of the beach patrols, and nothing more. Aron moved to the door.

"I need to go out for a moment," he announced. In response Henning stepped over to block the door, as well.

"I told you to take care of that kind of thing before," he said.

"Listen, I can't help it. And I'll just be a moment, all right?" Aron wasn't taking no for an answer. "Those guards are headed down the beach, anyway. You said so yourself. No one is going to see a thing."

"We're still not sure of their pattern," replied Henning.

"You said they were clockwork."

"Fine." Finally Henning sighed and apparently gave way. "But don't blame me if they catch you in the outhouse."

A moment later Aron had slipped outside.

"Anyone else want to announce the fact that we're smuggling a dozen more Jews out of Danmark tonight?" asked Henning in a sarcastic whisper. "Perhaps we could all go out on the beach and light a bonfire, sing some farewell songs, invite the guards to join in. Then we can take them around to each of the four beach cottages where people are hiding, and make introductions?"

No one answered. Hanne certainly didn't dare. But Henning slipped outside as well, mumbling something about having to check on the other cabins, and that Steffen should keep watching the door and out the window. After several moments of quiet, in which the only sounds were the waves lapping outside and Steffen's nervous foot shuffling, Hanne spoke up.

"Are they still out there?" she wondered aloud, instantly regretting the silly question.

"I saw Henning a moment ago," he replied, sounding more patient than she might have. "But I don't see your . . . I mean, Aron."

At last Hanne could not sit there any longer, waiting, so she unfolded her legs and quietly stood up.

I'll never see Steffen again, she told herself. *What does it matter now?*

"We were never engaged," she told him, and surprised herself for even opening her mouth.

"You mean to Aron? I—"

"My mother wanted us to be, and everyone in the synagogue assumed we would be. But we weren't."

"It's . . . none of my business."

"Maybe not. I just thought I should tell you. Aron is a good man. He deserves a good Jewish wife. I'm just not sure I'm that person."

This time he chuckled softly, and she couldn't help smiling along with him.

"What?" she asked. "I don't mean to get personal. I just—"

"No, no. I don't mind. Although maybe I should set up a confessional booth in my church. What do you think of that?"

"I don't know about confessions, Steffen. All I know is you've been very kind to me. Risked your life, even. I don't know how to thank you for what you've done, because I just didn't expect what happened."

"I'm just sorry I couldn't do more for you, and for all the others. And the little travel bag we put together for you, well, it's not much."

"Better than what I had, thank you."

She looked at her feet, avoiding his direct gaze. The waves continued to wash ashore, adding their soft, soothing background to the conversation. And in the dim moonlight she could see him turn to face her.

"I guess I didn't expect things to turn out like this, either." Now his voice wavered. "And we haven't known each other for a long time, but—"

"But it seems much longer, doesn't it?"

"It does." He laughed nervously. "And I like the way you finish my sentences. But look, we'll see each other—"

"Again, of course. As soon as all this is over."

"Meanwhile, I'm so sorry for the way things have turned out. I wish they could have been different."

He took another step closer.

"I wish they could have been different, too," she replied, and she felt his breath on her cheek as he reached out to hold her. She returned his embrace, felt his soft kiss brush by her lips and land on her cheek.

"Please be careful," he finally whispered. "And if there's a way to send letters, you know the address of the church. Or you could just address them to my apartment on Nørrebrogade. Perhaps that would be safer. Nørrebrogade 225."

"Nørrebrogade 225. I'll remember." She felt herself choking up as he pressed a small book into her hand.

"In case you need something to read. It's by a Christian pastor, not a rabbi, but even so. His poems make me think. Kaj Munk? Perhaps you'd like them as well."

"Thank you. I know of him." She accepted the little volume and slipped it into the top of the small overnight bag Steffen had given her.

"And I, I'll be praying for you. Maybe, when you get back . . ."

Then what? She waited for him to finish his thought, but he obviously could not. They would still live in different worlds. And right now, if she was honest with herself, she wasn't entirely sure she *would* get back. She wasn't even entirely sure she'd make it across the stretch of water separating them from Sweden.

But she might have thanked him once more, except that Henning pushed in through the door just then and they both stepped back from each other. Henning didn't act as if he noticed anything, just slipped in with Aron in tow.

"Five minutes," said Henning, all business. "Do you have the flashlight, Steffen?"

"Right here." Steffen replied, taking up his station by the door once more. "Is everyone else ready out there?"

"There isn't anybody else," he replied, his voice steady. "Not as far as I can tell."

"What?" Steffen raised his voice. "I thought there were supposed to be at least ten others, waiting in the other cabins."

"We checked every one," replied Henning, and Aron added his nervous explanation.

"There must be some mix-up," Aron told them. "This isn't good. They didn't show."

Steffen groaned. "Does this mean—"

"Means nothing." Henning obviously wasn't giving up. "We're still going ahead. The boat's still going to take these two."

———⊗⊗⊙———

Steffen clutched the flashlight as if his life depended on it. Actually, perhaps Hanne's did. And Aron's, too, naturally. He tried to settle his wildly beating heart, telling himself that the boat would still take these two to safety and that nothing had changed.

But things *had* changed. Everything had changed, now that Hanne was leaving. And as much as he wanted the best for her, as much as he wanted her safety, a part of him just wanted to hide her away in the church a little longer. Just a few more days.

But he knew he couldn't think like that. Now he needed to concentrate on doing his job. So he pulled the shade aside slightly, as Henning had instructed, and pointed his flashlight straight out toward the water. Now would be the time.

"Four blinks," Henning whispered.

"I know, I know." Steffen counted one, two, three, four.

And they waited. Steffen strained his eyes to see a return signal.

Nothing.

"Did they see you?" asked Aron.

———⊗⊗⊙———

"Keep still," Henning told him.

"I was just—"

"Nej, Aron. From now on you keep your mouth shut, and you just do what I tell you. Understand?"

"I understand." Hanne answered for them, her quiet voice soothing the tension. And Aron must have left it at that. Well, if he was smart, he would—and Steffen wasn't at all certain of that. But Henning ordered his brother to try again.

"They'd better be there," Steffen whispered between clenched teeth, just as a faint return blink told him they had caught the attention of their offshore contact. There!

"All right, good." Henning obviously noticed the signal, as well. "Now we give them four minutes to beach their boat, and then out you go, Aron. After that Hanne, you count to ten and follow. Don't run. Just hurry."

In the moonlight he pointed to Hanne, and she nodded as Steffen silently counted the seconds, waiting. With the door slightly ajar, he thought he heard a crunch of a boat on the beach.

"Go!" whispered Henning, and without another word Aron bolted.

"I said, don't run!" Henning tried to warn him, but Aron tripped off the cottage's front step and landed with a thud and a grunt in the low beach grass.

"That guy's single-handedly going to get us killed," said Henning.

"Three, four, five . . ." Now Steffen counted, and he squeezed Hanne's hand as she stood by the front door, waiting for her chance at freedom. She returned the squeeze, as if she might hold on.

"Eight, nine, ten," Steffen whispered as she released his hand and quietly stepped out the door into the darkness. "Now!"

What happened next must have taken just a matter of seconds, though it seemed to Steffen an eternity, and slower: First the sound of the dogs, before they even saw the bright flashlights from behind a nearby cottage. Henning swore when he realized what was happening, because suddenly this was not going according to plan.

"Where did they come from?" asked Henning, but his reaction was swift as he backed away from the door and headed for the window on the far side of their cabin.

"Steffen!" he hissed as he tumbled across the room. "It's too late. We've got to get out of here!"

Steffen could not make his feet move, even if he had wanted to. He could only stare in horror as gruff German voices shouted and their flashlights caught first Aron, then Hanne as they ran. And they looked more close together than Steffen had realized, with Hanne only a step or two behind Aron. She reached out to him with a cry, stumbling in the sand, but he only sprinted even more quickly, leaving her behind without a backward glance.

A staccato burst of shots filled the air, flashing from the muzzle of the guard's gun. Hanne fell to her face.

"Halt!" the German yelled over the wild sound of barking and growling. "You can't escape!"

From the back of the cabin Henning called Steffen's name once more, and Steffen turned to see his brother halfway out the window, waving wildly.

"You can't do anything to help her, now, Steffen. Please!"

Steffen wasn't so sure. But he knew he couldn't just run away as dogs were loosed on Hanne, or worse. Even from a distance he could see the stricken look on her face as she rose to her knees in the sand. She glanced first to the ocean, where Aron had disappeared into the darkness, then back at the cottage. And for a moment she looked straight at him, shaking her head and mouthing the word.

"Nej!"

Steffen did the only thing he could imagine doing. He stepped out the front door, hands in the air, shouting at the top of his lungs.

"Hey, there! Over here! Call them off!"

Perhaps it was the unexpected shout or the tone of his voice, but the two large German shepherds did pause for a moment, several yards from where they would have come upon Hanne on the sandy beach. By that time, their two handlers had caught up to them. Steffen kept his arms raised as he marched in their direction, like a fool to his death. But if this was the way he was going to die, Steffen thought, then so be it.

"Leave her alone!" he roared, with a voice that sounded many times bolder than he felt. "I say, leave her alone!"

Now the Germans would have to decide which of the three they would capture first. The girl didn't seem to be running, and by now Aron must have waded through the gentle surf to the waiting small fishing boat. If he had not already been shot in the process, but they would find that out soon enough. Steffen thought he heard the sound of a small boat's engine over all the chaos of barking and shouting. But now he himself approached with his hands in the air. He would make the choice simple for these two soldiers, he thought.

Strangely enough, the two young Germans decided to hold their snarling dogs in check, as one of them circled around to prevent Hanne's escape and the other trained his light directly on Steffen's face. Although it made Steffen blink in pain, he could still clearly make out the ugly snub end of a machine pistol pointed directly at him.

"Face down on the ground!" yelled the soldier. For a moment Steffen considered pretending he didn't understand, and he paused.

"Listen to me," he blurted out, doing his best to keep his voice soft and reassuring. "I'm a pastor. See my collar? A pastor. And look, we have money. Lots of money. Just a little now. But I can get you more. Perhaps that will make it easier to forget this ever happened. See? Buy something nice for your girlfriend. How much do you want? Five hundred kroner? Think of it as a gift."

Unaccustomed to the art of bribery, Steffen started to reach for his pocket, but that was his mistake.

"I said, don't move!" yelled the young soldier, suddenly stepping forward with his gun drawn.

"No, no, see? I'm just getting my wallet. For you. Understand? *Verstehen sie?* A gift." Steffen tried to hold his hands out at his sides, but it was too late, as the soldier used his weapon like a club to the back of Steffen's head.

Steffen did try to duck, but could not avoid the worst of the blow. And as he crumpled to the sand the last thing he heard was Hanne's painful scream.

"Steffen!"

After that he remembered nothing else.

26
Vestre Prison, København
Monday morning, 11 Oktober 1943

A prison cell, in which one waits, hopes, and is completely depen-
dent on the fact that the door of freedom has to be opened from the
outside, is not a bad picture of Advent.
—Dietrich Bonhoeffer

For the second time in recent weeks, Steffen awoke with a burning, throbbing pain. Only this time it wasn't from a bicycle accident but from a run-in with the handle of that young German soldier's gun. He groaned as he rolled over in a stiff, unyielding cot, the back of his head throbbing from a goose egg.

"Oh, that's the worst," he moaned, barely able to form the words. His mouth felt as if it had been stuffed with cotton and his arms as if they had been pulled from their sockets. Perhaps he had been tossed around after what had happened the night before.

"Hanne?" he sat up straight, which only made his head pound even more. Stars danced in front of his eyes, until he finally opened them just enough to see where he was. She was the last thing he remembered, though he could not put his finger on the exact time or place.

"Sorry, friend." A soft, low voice greeted him from the other side of a small room, dark like a closet and smelling much worse. "But if she's the one who sold you out, you're probably better off without her."

"Pardon?" Steffen blinked and did his best to focus in the dim light.

"You heard me. Nobody gets in here unless the Gestapo wants to know what you know, and then usually not unless someone else sold you out. But don't worry. It happens to the best of us."

"I don't know anything," whispered Steffen, gingerly testing to see how large the bump on the back of his head really was. "And I'm sure no one did such a thing. It wasn't like that at all."

"Oh, really? Here's a new one. What was it like, then?"

Even as his cellmate chuckled Steffen couldn't help wondering about Margrethe and how well the cleaning woman had kept track of what took place at the church over the past several days. Surely she could have had nothing to do with his capture or Hanne's capture on the beach. No. He had brought it all upon himself.

"It's a long story," he finally mumbled. "I wouldn't want to bore you."

Again the other man laughed.

"In this place? Bored? You're proving to be entertaining."

Steffen wasn't so sure about that. But at length he understood he'd been locked in a windowless cell with a high, rounded ceiling. Its pale yellow paint had been mostly chipped away by previous occupants, who had also carved their initials or defiant statements wherever they could.

On the plus side, a narrow shaft of light filtered in through a sort of mail slot cut into the formidable entry door, though it gave no real clue as to what time it was or how much time had passed. He noticed his watch and his wallet were missing, but that's what surprised him least about all this. What surprised him most was that he still lived and breathed, despite the hammering of his head.

It also took that long for the other man's words to register:

You're better off without her.

No. He clenched his fist. Not now, he wasn't. And he surely was not better off in this place, compared to anywhere else he could think of.

He examined the cell. Two wide wooden benches ran the length of each side, each covered with a threadbare gray blanket that would barely cover a man's shoulders in the draft. A foul-smelling bucket had been stowed at the far end, under the other bench, its purpose all too clear. And on the other bench, a bearded man in a ripped T-shirt and dirty gray trousers sat up against the wall, studying him the way a visitor to the zoo might watch a caged monkey.

"So how do you like your accommodations?" asked his cellmate. "Was she worth it?"

Steffen swallowed his pain and straightened up, determined not to answer questions, especially not cheeky ones. Instead he would ask a few questions of his own. He pretended he had not heard.

"How long have I been out?" he asked. "Do you know?"

The other man shrugged. "They brought you in last night."

That wasn't much of an answer, but the man went on.

"You're just in time for breakfast, though. Although I don't think it rates being called 'breakfast.' That's far too dignified a name for the slop they serve us."

"Hmm." Steffen's stomach didn't feel as if it had missed anything, only ached with the vague uncertainty that might come after trauma—such as having been hit head on by a fast-moving freight train. "So what is this place?"

When the man grinned he revealed a gap in his front teeth, even in the shadows. A badge of honor in the Resistance struggle perhaps. Or perhaps he just needed to visit a dentist.

"You really don't know? Either that, or you're a better actor than the last poor fool they put in here with me."

"I'm no actor."

"So you say. But if you want to survive in this place for more than twenty-four hours, you'd better develop a few acting skills. The last fellow never did."

"What do you mean? What happened to him?"

"They took him out and shot him. And that's what's going to happen to you, unless you learn."

"You're not serious."

"You don't think so? Then you're just as foolish as he was."

Nothing seemed to bother the man. Except that now when Steffen had a closer look, he could make out a disturbing collection of cuts and bruises on this man's face, the black eyes and the jagged cuts on his cheeks. One eye, in fact, appeared nearly swollen shut. And still he grinned.

"So why haven't they killed you?" asked Steffen, suddenly feeling bold—or more foolish than he should have been. The other man shrugged.

"Oh, I suppose they'd very much like to. Maybe they just haven't found out the information they're looking for, yet. Not that I have it, you understand."

Steffen shook his head, marveling at the composure—or the insanity—of this man.

"You never told me where we are," Steffen told him.

"Forgive me." The man spread out his arms in a grand, sarcastic gesture. "Welcome to Vestre Prison, located right here in beautiful København and operated by the ever-efficient *Geheime Staatspolizei,* or for you whose German is a little rusty, the Gestapo."

"Thanks for the clarification."

"Lars Hansen." He extended his hand without getting up. "Of course, that's not my real name. If I told you my real name I'd have to kill you. And judging by the size of your skinny little neck, that would be a simple task."

Steffen shuddered and blinked back his first reaction to run away from the man, any way possible. Given where he now found himself, however, perhaps he should not have been so surprised at the company.

"Pastor Steffen Petersen." He reached across the narrow aisle that separated the two sleeping benches, barely enough for a man to walk. "That's my real name."

The man nearly crushed his hand.

"So are they actually rounding up pastors these days?" asked Lars.

"No, I, ah . . ." Steffen was about to explain what had happened to him the night before, when a dark thought occurred to him. Who was this man, really? He could just as easily be a German sympathizer, planted here to collect incriminating information from new, unsuspecting prisoners. Couldn't he?

And if that were possible, Steffen decided he should probably not mention his brother Henning's name, for fear of implicating him.

"You . . . what?" asked the other man.

"Actually, I'd rather not say."

"You'd rather not say?" Lars Hansen laughed bitterly before collapsing into a spasm of dry, evil-sounding coughs. "Now there's a bold statement, considering who you are and where you're at."

"I'm sorry," Steffen told him. "Undskyld. It's nothing personal. Perhaps you'd like to talk about something a little more . . . well, you know, safe?"

"You catch on quickly. I don't know you, and you don't know me. You don't tell who you know, and I don't mention my friends, either. We keep it that way. And in a God-forsaken place like this, we both stay alive. For now."

Steffen was about to correct his new cellmate about his use of "God-forsaken" when the man rolled off the bed with surprising speed, grabbing Steffen's collar and pinning him to the bench. Startled, Steffen gasped for breath.

Was this how it would all end?

"But if you're a stikker," he told Steffen, "and they put you here to get information out of a decent, law-abiding citizen like me, then I'd be afraid for my life, if I were you. *Forstår du?*"

"Ja, I understand." Steffen gasped like a herring out of water, gripping the other man's wrists and kicking his feet helplessly. Finally Lars Hansen—or whatever his name was—eased up enough for Steffen to catch his breath.

"But I'm not a stikker," Steffen gasped. "I'm not the bad guy here. I'm the pastor at Sankt Stefan's Kirke, believe me."

Lars spit on the floor as he released Steffen with a shove.

"Believe you? Ha! That's how I got here, by believing people who would have sold their own mothers to the Nazis, if there was any profit in it. I don't believe anybody anymore."

"I see. Then I'll try to stay out of your way."

Which, given the confines of this tiny cell, might not be easy. But Steffen thought he still might clear the air.

"But look, ask me something theological, or something about the Bible. I'll prove to you I am who I say I am."

"I don't ask theological questions." Lars squinted at him warily. "And it doesn't matter who you are, anyway."

All friendliness aside, Lars Hansen turned away in his cot and acted asleep. What else was there to do in this place? A cold draft whipped though the cell, making Steffen shiver as he closed his own eyes and tried to piece together the events that had brought him here. His mind would only stumble here and there. So he wrapped the blanket around his shoulders and rocked back and forth, ignoring his headache until a jangle of keys in the lock outside their door brought him awake once more.

Two guards stood at the entry, silhouetted in the light from a single lightbulb hanging from the hallway ceiling. While the second guard covered his partner with a drawn Luger pistol, the first one drew out a pair of handcuffs, pointed directly at Steffen and motioned for him to put his hands out.

"You!" he grunted the way Steffen might have expected a prison guard to grunt. "Come with us. Now."

Guard one snapped a pair of cold metal handcuffs on Steffen's left wrist, then in one movement briskly twirled him around and attached the right wrist behind Steffen's back. Steffen had to wonder how this fellow had become so adept at inflicting that kind of pain.

"Nice knowing you, Pastor," said Lars, sounding almost as cold as the guards that marched Steffen down the hallway. "I'd be doing some praying now, if I were you. Which I'm not, fortunately."

Steffen had no answer, not the way he always had when he'd visited people at Bispebjerg Hospital. He just stumbled ahead of the guards down a long hallway lined with cell doors. At nearly every door a waste bucket waited to be emptied.

"Where are you taking me?" he asked, fighting to keep his balance. The guards would not answer as they prodded him on. Perhaps, he thought, they intended to take him out and shoot him, like the other roommate. He found himself reciting, over and over, the words to a psalm they often read aloud together in church.

"Cast me not away from thy presence; and take not thy Holy Spirit from me."

Yet despite the reassuring words, it seemed to Steffen that God had never felt quite so far away. Someone groaned from the other side of a locked door, and without thinking Steffen slowed to listen. A guard jabbed him in the back with the end of his pistol.

"Keep walking and don't slow down," said the guard. Two steps later and halfway down the hall, Steffen couldn't help but cry out in pain at a particularly vicious jab.

But before falling to his face he noticed what the guards did not see: a lone hand, extending through the tiny access door, silently blessing him with its reach. Even so, Steffen couldn't help tripping and planting his face on the cold stone floor. He grunted in pain.

"Up!" yelled the guard. "Get up!"

Steffen would have been glad to comply, but with two hands clamped behind his back, his sense of balance had abandoned him. So other cruel hands yanked him by the collar to his feet.

"Please, where are you taking me?" he asked, taking care not to fall again. The guards didn't answer, but at the end of the hallway they shoved him through a doorway to a staircase and then down a flight of stairs to another level and finally to a plain but large corner office.

From behind a large gray steel desk a gray-suited German officer pivoted in his chair and looked them over with a stony glare that nearly matched the one of Hitler from the portrait on the far wall. Just inside the door the lead guard stopped short and clicked his heels.

"We've brought the prisoner you requested, Herr Sturmbannführer."

"Very well." The officer nodded at the two guards and waved them off as if they had just flown into his picnic. "Leave us for now."

The two guards clicked their heels once more and about-faced out of the office, closing the door behind them and leaving Steffen to stand alone before the *Sturmbannführer*. As with every other German he'd met, the man obviously took his position quite seriously. His officer's jacket was decorated with a number of impressive-looking blood-red ribbons and such, as ostentatious as the glint in his steely gray eyes and the military cut of his trim blond hair.

"Pastor Petersen." He folded his hands in front of him on the desk, where everything appeared arranged and just so. "How good of you to come on such short notice. Of course, it's an unpleasant surprise to see you here. But please, won't you sit down?"

The officer pointed to a nearby wood chair but Steffen shook his head and turned slightly to reveal his cuffed wrists.

"Ah, did they really do that to you?" The officer sounded surprised. "My apologies. I'm sure they were just following standard procedure. In any case, perhaps it's good that you're here, so we can work out a few issues. Face-to-face."

Steffen had no idea what issues he had to work out with a Nazi officer, but he stood silently and waited as the man continued.

"Forgive me, Pastor. My name is Wolfschmidt, and I've been told you were detained last night. Is that correct?"

Steffen decided he could nod his agreement to an obvious question whose answer everyone would already know, as Wolfschmidt continued.

"I'm also told you interfered with the lawful apprehension of a fugitive? Now, I'm confused about that, how a person such as you could find yourself in such an awkward position. Perhaps you could enlighten me, if you would."

Despite the practiced civility of the man's question, Steffen knew this wolf would bare his teeth at any moment. So he braced himself and kept silent.

"Well?" The man with the piercing eyes stared at him for a moment and tented his fingertips as his jaws worked and strained. But then he seemed to pull back from the brink with a dismissive smile.

"I can understand your reluctance. You hardly know me, after all. But as a matter of fact, you and I are in the same line of business, are we not? We are both in the business of cleansing this bland little country of Jews. We just need to coordinate our efforts a bit more closely."

Still Steffen kept silent. His gaze shifted to the view out the window, where red-tiled roofs and church towers spread out across his city. If he knew which way to look, he might be able to make out the spire of his church, perhaps five kilometers to the north. Still Wolfschmidt wasn't giving up his attempt to cajole his victim into talking.

"We influence people, do we not? Help them make the right decisions. Up until just a few weeks ago, I understand you did an outstanding job of that. What happened?"

Steffen felt the confusion growing.

"Ah, you're wondering how I know." Wolfschmidt smiled and leaned back in his chair. "But actually, that's not the question at hand. The real question is, how can we restore your good reputation and help you do what's right in the sight of God and the Führer? Or, pardon me, God and the King? That's what I'd like to help you with."

Steffen couldn't help it, any longer. "I'm not sure I understand."

"Really? Think about it for a moment. Up until a few weeks ago, you consistently advised your parish to cooperate fully with the authorities. This is as it should be. You used your position of influence to help others come to the same conclusion. Am I right so far?"

Steffen pressed his lips together, and the other man smiled as he went on.

"I see that I am. But more recently, through some unfortunate series of events, you've stumbled into the wrong side of a criminal operation. Perhaps you weren't fully aware of the danger; I'll give you credit for being naïve. It could very well be that you've been used. So now I'd like to help you recover your former influence and good sense, Pastor. Is that not clear enough? The only thing is, I will need your cooperation to get this unfortunate mess sorted out."

"I see." It seemed to Steffen that keeping silent wouldn't help him any longer.

"Do you?" Now Wolfschmidt's voice rose and his cheeks reddened as he leaned forward. "Do you really? No, I don't think you yet understand the gravity of your situation. Because normally I would simply have a person in your situation shot and be done with it. I still might. Perhaps you're aware; we do a lot of that at this facility. Are you understanding this a little better, now?"

Steffen tried to swallow but could not.

"I think so," he squeaked.

"You think so? You think so?" Now his face boiled in rage. "What is it about being shot that you don't understand?"

He reached into the top drawer of his desk, pulled out an evil-looking Luger pistol, and pointed it at Steffen's head.

"Would you like for me to demonstrate to you what it means? I think in many respects it might be simpler if—"

"No, I understand."

Steffen fought the urge to close his eyes and duck. In a way, though, he was glad his hands were still cuffed behind him, shaking but out of sight. Wolfschmidt seemed to consider his options for a moment before frowning and carefully setting his weapon back down.

"I knew you would. But I'll tell you this: We need to know everyone you worked with or had contact with."

By this time Steffen's heart beat out of his chest. He could not imagine what would happen if he revealed Henning's name.

"Everyone!" shouted Wolfschmidt.

"I . . ." Steffen fumbled for words. "They came to my door. The Jews. I didn't know them, and I didn't ask their names. They asked for help." He kept as close to the truth as he dared, hoping his embellishments would not show. But though he also knew how inexperienced he was at deception, he pressed on. "So I arranged to drive them, and we found a fisherman."

"The name?"

"He never told me his name. They all said that names would only get someone in trouble."

"Yes, of course. Convenient, for the time being. Perhaps we can work out an arrangement where you'll introduce us—in the near future?"

"Well . . ." For a moment Steffen wondered what would happen if he simply went along—if he made Wolfschmidt believe he would cooperate. "I felt sorry for them, but I see now . . ."

"What?" Wolfschmidt snarled. "What do you see now?"

Steffen paused a moment before answering, considering his options. What else could he say?

"I see now what a mistake it was."

"You do? Excellent. I'm pleased to hear that."

Wolfschmidt had the uncanny ability to switch from a polite gentleman to a boiling rage—and back—at will. By this time the officer grinned as he got up from his chair and stepped around to the front of his desk. "And with that understanding in mind, what would you like to tell your congregation about the Resistance movement?"

"I'd like to tell them that . . ." Steffen swallowed hard, working past the huge lump in his throat. ". . . that it's a mistake. That Scripture requires us to obey the king and the authorities."

"Ah, I hear a sermon coming on, don't you? A good one. Perhaps I'll even visit your church sometime to hear how you're going to express this conviction. But just for clarification, who are those authorities?"

"You are, Herr Sturmbannführer."

"How kind of you to say so."

Steffen shivered as he spoke the words, cold in the realization that he had just stepped off a cliff. His head spun, dizzy with the feeling of betrayal—to save his own life, perhaps, and to save Henning's. But betrayal, nonetheless.

And he knew from the empty feeling where his heart used to be that he'd just lost a large piece of his soul.

By this time Wolfschmidt had strolled around behind Steffen, and Steffen could feel the warm breath on the back of his neck. It smelled of stale cigarettes. He didn't dare turn, but stood straight and still as the officer leaned in closer.

"But do you know what, Pastor?" He rested a hand on Steffen's shoulder. Wolfschmidt's hand felt like a talon, digging into his flesh. "I don't believe a word of what you're trying to sell me. Not a word. At least not until you demonstrate your good faith."

As Wolfschmidt continued Steffen did his best not to flinch or cry out in pain.

"Ah, but even so you're a very lucky man. Did you know that? God must be smiling down on you right now. Because here's what's going to happen. You're going to walk out of this building a changed man. In your sermons you're going to tell your people to obey the proper authority, just as you said. Because we'll be listening very carefully, you know. We'll also arrange for those introductions. Just keep in mind, you're so much more useful to your people alive than . . . well, you understand the alternative, don't you?"

Steffen nodded and Wolfschmidt finally loosed his grip, then stepped to the door and barked for the guards to rejoin them. They'd apparently been standing just outside the door, waiting.

"The cuffs!" he said, gesturing toward Steffen's wrists. "Remove them now, and escort him outside. I want this man released immediately."

The soldiers obeyed, snapping open the cuffs. As Steffen rubbed his wrists Wolfschmidt took something else from the corner of his desk and tossed it at Steffen. His wallet!

"We're not thieves," Wolfschmidt told him. "And my men don't accept bribes."

Steffen didn't dare mention what else he might call the guards who then pulled him out of the office—but not before Wolfschmidt asked one last question.

"Pastor!" He commanded them to pause. Steffen couldn't bring himself to turn, but waited stiffly at the doorway. "I'm surprised you didn't ask."

"Pardon?"

"The girl, of course." He laughed. "You didn't ask what happened to her. I assume that the size of the risk you took for her means something?"

Steffen still didn't answer, and Wolfschmidt laughed once more.

"Never mind. Just remember that her fate may now be determined by the degree to which you cooperate. You understand my meaning."

Steffen closed his eyes and sighed. Oh, he understood the threat, all right. But was it genuine? He didn't want to find out.

The guards shoved him down the hall on their way to the multiple checkpoints and the one way through the wall that surrounded the dull gray prison building. He ignored the chill of walking through so many soldiers, wondering if he would actually make it out, or if he would still be shot in the process. But without further ceremony he found himself outside just a few moments later, blinking at the sudden freedom, and shivering at how close he'd come to death.

Lord, did you not notice? Did you not see?

He looked back at the surrounding wall, which he had only ever seen from the outside before. Up on the third floor he imagined the prisoners left behind, and Lars Hansen, still waiting in his cell, waiting to be beaten once more, waiting to die. A Mercedes with blood-red swastika flags on the front bumpers whisked past him, stirring up dead leaves and leaving Steffen coughing at the exhaust. But no one noticed him now, and no one came running through the checkpoint to drag him back inside.

So he hurried away, along *Vigerslev Allé* in the general direction of Sankt Stefan's, feeling now as filthy on the inside as he did on the outside. He crossed the rail line to the nearby *Enghave* station, while his head still throbbed in pain, now worse than ever. He tried to forget what he had just done, knowing that he could not. And still he wondered.

What had they really done to Hanne?

27

Never shall I forget that night, the first night in camp,
which turned my life into one long night.
—ELIE WIESEL, IN *NIGHT*

F or the first few hours Hanne could have pretended she
was on holiday, taking the train south—despite the black
cloud of despair that threatened to envelop her with every
passing hour. And when the little dark-eyed girl sitting next
to her in the train's second-class seating began crying once
more, Hanne wanted nothing more than to join her. Instead,
she swallowed back her own tears and tried to smile.

"I'm Hanne," she said. "What's your name?"

At first the girl wouldn't look up, but she finally admitted
her name was Bela.

"Well then, Bela, wouldn't it be fun if we could go to Paris?
Or how about Rome, or even Jerusalem? I'll bet you've never
been to Jerusalem before, have you?"

The little girl stopped sniffling long enough to shake her
head.

"My papa told me about Jerusalem," the girl finally replied.
"It's far away, isn't it?"

"Yes, it is. But I'd very much like to see it, someday. It's a
city for Jews. King David's city! We could walk through the

streets together on the way to the grand Hurva synagogue. Can you imagine? We'd pass shops filled with spices from all over the world, like mustard and cinnamon and paprika." She sniffed at the gritty coal fumes drifting in from the cracked window. "Can you smell it?"

The little girl smiled for the first time since they'd been herded into this car at København's train station, even as she coughed.

"I smell it," replied the girl. She hugged a worn little knit doll to her chest as she listened. "Tell me what else we see."

"And here's an old Arab man with a donkey, selling olive-wood, and there an ancient oil lantern from the court of King David himself! Oh, and look! Do you see the ancient wall from King Solomon's temple? We think we have old buildings here in our little country, but just think how old is the Western Wall! This is where Jews come to remember—and to pray."

By this time the girl had closed her eyes as the train rocked on, and Hanne thought she could see the trace of a smile on her lips. The girl's mother nodded her tired thanks and tried to quiet a baby in her arms who had been fussing most of the way. Hanne had seen no sign of the father, and was reluctant to ask. She sighed as she closed her own eyes for a moment, allowing her mind to drift to thoughts of how Steffen had bravely made a place for refugees in his church basement, and how she and Steffen had driven to the coast together in the ambulance. She held fast to the memory and kept a hand on her little travel bag—all she now truly owned in this world. Fortunately, that included the book of poems Steffen had given her.

But the peace lasted only another five minutes or so, when the train jerked to a stop and the mother held her two little ones close. Bela woke with a start, looking wide-eyed and puzzled.

"Don't worry," Hanne whispered to her. "You just stay close to us, and we'll all take care of each other, yes?"

German guards at either end of the closely packed passenger car came to attention, as if they knew what was coming next.

"Everybody out!" yelled the guard at the front of the car. "Bring all your things. Hurry! *Schnell!*"

"Here," Hanne grabbed one of woman's suitcases. "Let me take that for you."

"Oh, no," replied the woman. "We can handle it. You have your own bag. We can handle it."

"I'm sure you can. But mine is of no consequence. A man packed it, so it weighs next to nothing."

Well, perhaps she should have explained that. But the little bag contained little in the way of truly useful items, aside from the book Steffen had given her. No clothes or food, for example, just two bars of soap, a couple of hand towels, a comb, two men's shirts... Fortunately her gray hand-knitted sweater kept her warm enough—for now.

"Where are we?" wondered the young mother, probably not expecting an answer. By this time the little girl was clinging to her mother's arm, looking more terrified than ever, and Hanne could not blame her. Hanne checked outside to see only a darkened train yard crowded with the hulking shadows of freight cars and flat cars, engines and tracks. In the distance a ring of thin men in tattered overalls huddled around a tiny flicker of a fire.

"I'm not sure where we are," she answered, "but my guess is we're not in Danmark anymore."

A chill ran down Hanne's neck when she saw a sign— *Flensburg*—and she knew then they had crossed over Danmark's southern border into Germany. She could have expected to come this far south eventually. She just wished someone could give them a better answer about what was happening. No one had spoken to them since København, many hours ago.

The carload shuddered and threw several of the older people to the floor with a screech. Hanne reached down to help one old woman to her feet again, and the prisoners milled toward the exit as the guards yelled and prodded them. Why such a hurry?

"Pardon me," Bela's mother asked the guard standing at their exit. "But could you please tell us where we're going? I need to find a place for my children to get something to eat, and then a place to sleep."

The broad shouldered young man only grunted and kept the crowd moving with a baton.

"Did you hear me?" The woman tried again, motioning with a hand to her mouth. Perhaps her grammar school German wasn't understandable. "Something to eat?"

Outside, a wide path had been cleared between two rows of guards, several of which held back snarling, snapping German shepherds—not the kind of dog anyone would want to pet. Bela gripped her doll even more tightly and walked between the uncertain protection of her mother on one side and Hanne on the other.

Steffen, thought Hanne, *if only you knew what was happening to us. Are you praying for me, the way you said you would?*

She hoped so. At the same time, she wondered what had happened to him—what the Germans had done to him when he'd come out of the cottage to save her, to buy her freedom, even. Had he really thought the Germans would agree? Poor brave, foolish Steffen! She was not at all sure he would be able to talk his way out of trouble this time, especially not after the brutal blow to the head he'd received from the German soldiers who had surprised them on the beach.

Oh, Steffen. It was all my fault. If you hadn't tried to help me.

Above them, bright floodlights lit the way, giving the damp, rancid-smelling train yard an unearthly glow. The confusing part was, their path seemed to end at the open side of a cattle car, its doors slid open wide like the mouth of a giant fish ready to inhale Jonah.

"Everyone inside!" yelled the guards. They allowed their dogs to lunge at the cringing people on the sides of the crowd, sometimes tearing clothes and occasionally tearing flesh. Most of the women now cried in fright, and the children along with them. The men tried to shield their families with suitcases and outstretched arms, while the dogs and their soldiers kept this little stream of Danish Jews moving toward the gaping maw of the cattle car. Hanne held on to the woman's suitcase in her left hand and little Bela with her right, with her own small bag under her arm, until they had reached the car and clambered inside.

The stench that greeted them revealed the fact that this car had obviously not been cleaned since its previous occupants had been transported, probably from the farm to the slaughterhouse. Hanne wondered if theirs was the same destination.

"Why are they doing this to us?" sobbed Bela's mother, and no one could give an answer. She couldn't sit down, either, even if she had wanted to, as more and more people packed in behind and around them.

"Mor!" cried Bela. Hanne wanted to cry out to her mother, too. Instead she held on as the doors were unceremoniously slammed shut, plunging them into a darkness broken only by cruel, bright needles of light broken off from spotlights outside and left to shatter on the huddled heartbreak inside. Hanne still tried to understand the brutal outpouring of hatred that had swept them to this place, but could not. Crying subsided into low moans and unending sobs, while a group of the men recited the kadish prayer.

"Yit'gadal v'yit'kadash sh'mei raba," began the oldest man in their group, his gray beard bobbing with the ancient words of mourning.

May His great Name grow exalted and sanctified in the world that He created as He willed.

Hanne followed along silently as she had at the funeral of one of her mother's friends the year before. The words gave way to numb exhaustion as Hanne hummed some of her favorite Tommy Dorsey tunes, passing away the next several hours until the train finally jerked and they were on their way once more.

"Here, you sit on the suitcase." Hanne eventually carved out a space for Bela. "Your mother and I will keep you from falling."

Which was no easy task, with all the rocking and jerking as they headed south. They held on, through stopping and starting and unending hours and hours that no longer resembled anyone's holiday—pretend or otherwise. They had not even a bucket or a hole in the floor, and so the relentless press of people soon grew unbearable. Only one young man by the doors, one of the last to be forced aboard, had found a small knothole in the siding, and so announced the cities and towns as they continued their hellish journey southward, through the night and all through the next day.

Schleswig and *Neumünster*, *Hamburg* and *Hannover*, *Magdeburg* and *Leipzig*. They saw the signs flash by in a blur. And finally, by misty sundown of the following night, when all the words had been long ago spent and Hanne could no longer swallow from thirst and bitter exhaustion, the boy at the door raised his weak, hoarse voice.

"I don't think we're in Germany any longer."

"What? How do you know? Let me see." Another young man pushed him aside to look for himself. The others only stood with glazed expressions as they heard the news that they had crossed over into Czechoslovakia, for now the signs in passing train stations no longer bore German names, but even more strange, unpronounceable ones like *Krásny Les* and *Ústí nad Labem*. By that time Hanne had fallen to her knees, as they took turns standing or leaning against one another, as they were able. Many were not, and Hanne feared the weak and the old would not survive such a trip. But then their transport jerked to a stop once more, and after a moment they watched the doors slide open to a scene much like the one they had left behind.

They stood and stared, still clinging to one another, afraid to move, unable to move. Hanne blinked at the light, wishing for blindness so she might not see what awaited them. They had passed through to another country, but they had not escaped the familiar shouting of German soldiers and the barking of their dogs.

Only this time Hanne could not move as quickly as she had before, and she would not leave Bela and her mother behind, despite yells and prods.

"Out! Out! Out!" The soldier would not understand how faint his screams now seemed as Hanne helped Bela clamber down to the muddy rail yard at *Bogosovice*, marked by a crooked sign on a dingy shed with broken windows that passed for a train station. Never mind; Hanne avoided looking at the guards and hurried to follow the others away from the station and down a dark trail, perhaps as wide as a country lane and just as rugged.

A cold drizzle had filled puddles and quickly soaked everyone to the skin as they paraded into the night, but this time

Hanne did not waste the energy to ask where they were going. Despite the cold and the rain she tilted her head back in the autumn night for just a moment, knowing that stars still shone somewhere above the low, pregnant clouds. And if they did, perhaps so did hope.

"Move on!" yelled another guard, proving to Hanne that they did not possess the ability to speak in a normal voice. So they moved on, shoulders slumped against the rain.

"Don't let your doll get wet," Hanne told Bela. "We want to keep her nice and clean, don't we?"

Poor little Bela was so far beyond answering, or even walking. So Hanne summoned more strength than she knew and hoisted the little girl to her back as they walked down a muddy lane lit only by the flashlights of their guards. A young boy just ahead of her stumbled and fell with a cry, face-first, into the mud. Without hesitating, a guard (not a German soldier, this time) snatched him up by the collar like a sack of potatoes and shouted at him in Czech. Despite not understanding a word he said, no one seemed to have the strength to argue—or even to think of escaping into the night. They simply shuffled through mud toward a distant walled city lit by the occasional trash fire belching foul smoke into the night. Hanne's legs would surely not move unless she commanded each step, and as the soles of her shoes grew more and more caked with mud, a Czech gendarme motioned for them to hurry along.

After all they'd been through? But he looked right through her as they were herded through a dimly lit gate in the castle-like walls, past a double checkpoint of barbed wire fencing and grim-faced gendarmes wearing old-fashioned rounded helmets with visors and double-breasted coats with rows of brass buttons and shoulder pads that looked like something out of the last war. One of them, a barrel-chested man with a stony expression and a gray moustache, motioned for them to set down their luggage and continue on to several tables set up in the shadow of an empty city street, where it was darker and even more desolate than Hanne had expected. Portable spotlights hanging from wires stretched overhead gave the area the look of a deserted carnival, and they cast ghostly shadows as they swung in the cold wind.

But Hanne and the others were not the only ones in this strange, haunted village. From somewhere the music of a string quartet broke the eerie silence, making Hanne wonder if it might be a recording somewhere.

But no—in the shadows of a covered entryway four musicians huddled with their instruments, swaying slightly as they played a dark, intricate melody. Beethoven, perhaps. Hanne could never be sure with this kind of music, only that the four played as one, that they played with great talent and without looking at any printed music in front of them.

"What a nice welcome," said Bela's mother, as they walked by. But these street musicians didn't seem to know anyone else was there, which gave Hanne a strange, dislocated feeling. She looked up at a second story window and saw a hollow-faced ghost of a child staring until he was pulled back into the shadows and disappeared once again.

"Look!" Bela saw the face as well and pointed. "Who's that, Mor?"

Of course her mother didn't know.

"Come, then," Hanne told her two friends, turning her attention back to where they stood. "I smell food, don't you? Aren't you hungry? Let's listen to the music as we eat."

She didn't need to ask, as she led little Bela and her mother to the line where a thin potato soup was being ladled into small cups and passed around to the newcomers.

"Thank you," Hanne told the older woman who handed her the cup of greasy, lukewarm liquid, along with a chunk of suspiciously green-tinged French bread. But just like the musicians, the woman didn't look up, just held out the cup to the next person in line.

What kind of nightmare village could this be, inhabited by apparitions? Since there was nowhere to sit in the middle of a cobblestone lane, Hanne stood among her traveling companions and sipped at her lukewarm soup, smiling and calling it delicious even as she tried not to gag at the rancid taste. Bela seemed to go along with the charade and didn't complain as she emptied her cup as well. Strange what hunger could do.

While they remained standing and before most had finished eating, a shiny black German staff car with the familiar swastika flags on the front fenders was admitted through the same gate they'd just passed through. The gendarmes obviously recognized an authority and straightened up as the car screeched to a halt on the far side of the road, a safe distance beyond the newcomers and the makeshift feeding station.

The driver jumped from the front and hurried around to open the back door, opening an umbrella as he did. The rain had paused by this time, though. Presently a ramrod-straight Gestapo officer made his appearance at the edge of the light, under his umbrella. The musicians halted in mid-note, making an awkward end of their little concert. Even the soup servers paused what they were doing when he stepped up to make his announcement on the hushed street.

"Welcome to Theresienstadt," he told them in a booming baritone. "I am *Kommandant* Burger. After you have finished your meal, you will be shown to your barracks, which you will find most comfortable. Then in the morning, you will complete your processing and receive a work assignment. But first, you will have a chance to write home to your friends and loved ones, telling them of the fine reception you've received here. We trust your stay here will be a pleasant one."

His galling words hung in the air as he turned on his heel and returned to his idling car. A moment later one of the older women cried out in fear when it nearly ran her over on its way out of the city. The kommandant's car didn't even slow down. But Bela's mother looked at Hanne with a spark of hope in her eyes.

"At least we'll have a place for the kids to sleep," she whispered. "A place for *us* to sleep."

But there would be no rest just yet. For now they were herded to another series of tables, where they were each given a blank postcard and a pencil, and told to write home of their wonderfully positive treatment.

"Good food, and plenty of it!" yelled a young German officer, strutting about in front of the tables. "Warm, comfortable accommodations. A friendly welcome with music and festivities. You will write of this!"

If only. Hanne turned her card over to see a pretty picture of an alpine peak, then looked up to see the officer squinting directly at her. She swallowed hard and began writing, but could not find the words.

Dear Steffen, she wrote, but her tear fell directly on the "dear."

We have arrived at the town of Terezin, which the Germans call Theresienstadt, and I am well . . . enough. There will be much to do here. Please don't forget me.

She thought about crossing out the last line, which in retrospect seemed a bit melodramatic, but it was too late for that. The officer now paced from table to table, collecting their letters.

"These will be delivered to the Red Cross," he told them. "You may address them to whomever you wish."

But the dark-eyed young man next to Hanne had ideas of his own, and she overheard his grumblings.

"Transport unbearable," he said as he wrote, "and the food will make us sick. But at least we've been allowed to keep our belongings. And they say we'll be staying in old military barracks around the city."

"Let me see that," said the officer, snapping away the young man's card. After scanning it quickly he crumpled it in his fist and tossed it aside.

"That was my letter!" protested the young man, but the officer shoved another card at him.

"I said good food, and plenty of it!" he barked. "A friendly welcome. Good music. This you will write!"

The young man accepted the card but did not pick up his pencil. This time he simply ripped the blank card into tiny pieces—which of course was the wrong thing to do. Without hesitation the young officer grabbed him by the arm and pulled him away into a nearby storefront, leaving the others to glance nervously at each other. Who would be next? Hanne finished her note, but as several guards herded them away from the tables she looked back to see her card—and the alpine peaks—flutter to the pavement.

For a moment she thought about turning to try and rescue it, but perhaps it was just as well. Steffen would be better not knowing she was well enough, when in reality she had never felt worse. She clutched her stomach, feeling as if she might lose the potato soup in the midst of all this yelling and shoving.

"All luggage!" The big gendarme now bellowed, over and over, in accented German. "Baggage inspection!"

Apparently he knew the language no better than did they, but well enough to get his point across. Hanne looked nervously at Bela's mother, whose bag was suddenly ripped from her arms and torn open, like lions attacking helpless prey. So much for the warm welcome. But no one objected, or only feebly. Now Hanne had no choice but to add the woman's other bag to the "inspection," as well as her own little travel purse, which several of the gendarmes eagerly rifled through for anything of value.

Several meters away one of the men laughed when he found and claimed a gold pocket watch, then held it up to his ear. An older woman raised her hand to protest the theft, then apparently thought better of it. What could they do? Another gendarme discovered a small engraved music box, which he tossed to a friend. Fortunately there would be nothing of value in Hanne's bag, at least not to these men.

"They can't do this!" whispered Bela's mother, but obviously they could and they did. Hanne just stood by with her hands curled into fists, waiting for this cruel storm to pass as the men shoved the bags back towards them.

"Thank you," she whispered, because her lips betrayed her in their automatic response. Perhaps the gendarme did not hear her, but she thought he hesitated for just a moment before releasing her bag.

And it went on. Five minutes later shouting guards separated the women from the men—with considerable shouting on their part, and renewed crying and wailing on the part of the Jews. Hanne could not even look at the young couples being pried apart. Instead she tried to reassure a young teen girl whose father was dragged away with the men.

"It's only for the time being, I'm sure. You'll see him again."

Perhaps yes. Perhaps no. The girl watched with exhausted resignation as her father disappeared with the other men. Then several other guards escorted the women away from the processing area in groups of ten or fifteen, parading them through narrow cobblestone streets glistening with rain. This time Bela stumbled alongside, holding Hanne's hand. Only the occasional movement in an upper story window told them anyone else was alive. More phantoms, she supposed.

"Just a minute, now," Bela's mother told her daughter, her voice barely above a whisper, "and we'll be sleeping in our own comfy bed. You wait and see."

Around the next corner they came upon a row of ancient two-story buildings, each one leaning upon its neighbor to remain standing. The lower floors had perhaps once been shops, with small windows facing the street and signs with Czech writing, full of strange accent marks and even stranger-looking words. Most of the windows were broken; some crudely boarded over. But when one of the gendarmes shone his light inside, all Hanne could see was row after row of crude bunk beds. The guard pushed open one of the doors and pointed.

"In here?" Hanne asked, pausing to peek inside.

"Ja, ja," replied the guard, sweeping his hand impatiently at their group. "Barracks tomorrow. Tonight you sleep in here. Plenty of room."

There would be no arguing, despite the fact that at least thirty or forty women and girls had already been crammed into the small shop for the night. Perhaps more. In the dark it was difficult to tell how many. At least half huddled under blankets, two or three to a bunk, with hardly enough room even to sit up. The others had curled up with their blankets around the floor, leaving nowhere to walk. But the door slammed behind them so that Hanne and the others were left standing, suitcases in hand. An angry voice berated them from across the room, probably saying something like "Get out!" or "Be quiet!"

"I'm sorry," said Hanne, "but I don't understand your language."

The woman repeated herself, a little more loudly. But it would do no good. The woman knew no Danish, or German, and Hanne knew no Czech. Hanne could only stand in the darkness, tears flowing down her cheeks.

"Mor," came Bela's small voice. "Where is my bed? I'm so tired. I don't feel so well."

28

Who takes the child by the hand takes the mother by the heart.
—Danish Proverb

The next morning Hanne knew she could have done something for Bela, if she'd only had the right medicines. She mopped the little girl's forehead with a rag torn from the sleeve of her own blouse and dipped in a bucket of cold water of questionable clarity. She grabbed the arm of an official-looking woman who came hurrying through their overcrowded sleeping room. Wearing a yellow armband of some sort, surely this woman would be able to help.

"Pardon me." Hanne used her best German, which the woman was sure to understand. "This little girl needs something for her . . . I'm sorry, I don't know what the word is in German, but you can see, can't you? She needs medication."

The woman frowned but did stop for a moment to glance at Bela's little body, shaking with a fever that had attacked with a vengeance overnight. By now poor Bela would not even respond to her name.

"You may take her to the dispensary, if you like," replied the woman, as if they were talking about an inconvenience she would rather not deal with at the moment.

"They'll have medicines there?"

"No."

"What do you mean *no?*" Hanne snapped. "Don't you understand? We need medicines! Where are the medicines in this horrible place?"

The woman just shrugged and walked away.

"I asked you a question!" Hanne nearly screamed, but the woman wouldn't stop. So Hanne fumed and tried not to look at Bela's mother, who still had her hands full with a crying baby.

With permission from an outside guard Hanne took Bela to the dispensary anyway, a building five blocks away, crowded with dying people who sat as they did all around this city of Jews. So many sat in the hallways with the pitiful, lost look Hanne was coming to recognize. How long had they been here? So many simply waited to die.

But not this one, Hanne promised herself. *Not yet.*

Gritting her teeth, she carried Bela in her arms through the crowds, stepping over anyone who would not or could not move. A gray-haired man in a dirty white coat appeared to be treating some of his patients at a table near the center of the room. With what, Hanne could not be sure. In any case, she would bring Bela as close as she could, to find whatever care she could. Surely she could do something.

Bela looked up at her with wide, red-rimmed eyes, lucid again for a moment. She could barely speak for the chattering of her teeth, but she pulled Hanne closer and whispered in her ear.

"Is this what Jerusalem is going to be like, Hanne?"

"Oh, honey, no." Hanne looked around at the patients in that crowded room with the peeling wallpaper of faded flowers. It smelled to Hanne of urine and death, and certainly not the way a real clinic ought to smell. "Jerusalem is going to be so much better. You'll see."

Hanne felt her cheeks flame the way they had when she was six, when she had stolen a cookie from her mother's kitchen and had made up a preposterous story about her imaginary friend Sofie taking it instead. Her mother had instantly recognized the fantastic lie, just as surely as Bela would now recognize the more hopeful lie Hanne let slip from her lips. But the little girl closed her eyes and nodded, allowing Hanne to help her up on what she thought to be an examining table.

"Why are you bringing her here?" asked the bespectacled older man, the one Hanne assumed was a doctor. He looked to be perhaps her father's age, wiry and spry, no taller than she herself. He looked over his glasses at her from the other side of the table, where he was bandaging a man who had obviously been beaten. He spoke in heavily accented German, obviously a Czech.

"I'm a nurse," she told him, steeling herself for a battle—or whatever it took. "This girl has influenza symptoms. Or perhaps meningitis. A high fever. Headache. Sore limbs. Fatigue. She needs help."

"We have no medicine to speak of." He frowned and lifted his hands. "Today not even an aspirin. Haven't they told you?"

"Yes they told me, only I wasn't prepared to believe it."

"You're new. Try to get her to drink something and put her in the isolation ward over there." He pointed with his chin in the direction of a nearby door. "Do you understand? *Isolationen.* And then you can come back here and give me a hand."

"No, but you don't understand. She needs—"

"I *do* understand, nurse. I only wish I did not. Now take her to isolation. If she really does have the influenza or—heaven help us—meningitis, we don't want to be introducing her illness to the entire city. But yes, as a matter of fact, I could use the help."

She looked down at the quivering bundle in her arms and prayed for something she could do—anything—to help Bela. Getting angry didn't seem to help, did it? As the little girl shook with fever and convulsions, Hanne could only stroke her burning forehead and follow the doctor's orders. Bela groaned now, probably no longer conscious.

"Shh, it's okay." Hanne thought of what she might have to tell Bela's mother, waiting outside. "You're going to be okay."

But by this time she didn't even believe her own words.

"So. What do you think of the Paradise Ghetto so far?"

The little doctor grunted as they carried an older woman from the exam table to a cot on the far side of the clinic. The woman, who had collapsed earlier that day and who perhaps had some kind of kidney problems, tried her best to walk, but could not, so Hanne took the woman's other side and did what she could.

After just an hour at the clinic with no medicines and no modern medical equipment, Hanne wasn't sure how to answer politely.

"Some paradise. Is that what they call it?"

"Paradise Ghetto, yes. Hitler's gift to the Jews. You'll see more of it, I'm sure. The parks, the lovely boulevards, the flowers, the happy children playing in the quaint cobblestone streets. It's quite lovely. Oh, wait. That was the propaganda movie version I had in mind. It's so easy to confuse the two, if one isn't careful."

She wasn't sure how to respond to his dark humor, other than to flash a confused smile. But he kept his voice low and always seemed aware of every time a German guard or Czech gendarme might be entering the building. In fact, it wasn't long before she could tell without turning around, just by the way Dr. Aleksander Janecek brightened up and began saying cheery things like "This one will be up and back to work in no time!" or "That's going very well now, isn't it?"

But then as soon as the soldier left the clinic, he would return to the controlled desperation she had seen of him from the start. And it wasn't long before she had to ask.

"Why do you say such things?"

He paused to wipe his brow with the back of his hand and looked at her with red-rimmed eyes. Did this fellow never sleep?

"I have tried it both ways, Nurse Hanne Abrahamsen. In the past I have allowed myself to be surly and demanding, yelling and screaming at anyone who would listen that we need this and that medicine, or this and that supply. Much like yourself when you first stepped in. I thought it made me feel better. But do you know what it brought me?"

She shook her head, waiting for him to go on. He put his thumb and forefinger together in a zero.

"It brought me absolutely nothing. Worse than nothing. I found that when I complained the loudest, my patients would simply be transported from the dispensary, never to be seen again."

"To where?"

He shrugged. "They say there is a death camp, more than one death camp, to which they are transporting our people, and that this is just a transfer station. But you and I know this is the end for all too many, do we not?"

Hanne had to nod. She had already seen more than she cared to see.

"So now I put on a friendly face," he said. "I do what I can, and every once in a while they throw me a bone. Perhaps a few bottles of aspirin here, a few bandages there."

"And you're satisfied to work like that?"

"Satisfied? Ha!" He snorted and shook his head, as if the concept had never occurred to him. "We don't use that word to describe anything or anyone in this place. Satisfied, indeed. You're new here and you're Danish. Danes have never dealt with hardship. But you'll learn, my dear. You'll learn."

Hanne spent the rest of the day learning, doing what she could, following the doctor, holding the hands of desperately ill patients for whom they could do little or nothing, changing bandages, emptying bed pans, smiling at little children with a wide variety of ailments brought on or made desperate by a lack of nutrition and seriously overcrowded, unsanitary living conditions. She checked in on little Bela every few minutes, changing the washrag on her forehead, praying for help. And she caught the doctor watching her once, shaking his head with an expression of pity on his face—or was it exasperation?—and she wondered if he thought her still too naïve. Perhaps more time in this nightmare might change her.

During the afternoon she tried to press a wet sponge to the little girl's lips, but the fever had taken so much from her, and she didn't even open her eyes. Now her mother waited outside, asking questions and looking hopeful, holding her baby.

"We're doing all we can for her," said Hanne, which was the horrible, shameful truth. And the feeling of helplessness overwhelmed Hanne like nothing ever had before. Could she tell her anything else? There would be no hiding from it. Minutes later Hanne knelt by the little cot where they'd laid

Bela and whispered the only thing that came to mind, lines from one of the poems in the book Steffen had given her. A poem about a flower, but she thought perhaps much more than that.

"So I bend down to the ground, and gently kiss your fragile bloom, a hint of mercy's throne, thou little anemone, how great is our Creator!"

The words seemed strange coming from her mouth, rhyming and musical, almost like a prayer or perhaps of the same stuff. In any case, it was the best she could do. In fact little Bela actually did seem to stop shivering for a time, while a more peaceful look replaced the tortured one she'd been wearing since the night before. Hanne could not help but kiss the fragile little girl's feverish forehead—and she gasped in surprise as she did.

"Doctor Janecek!" she cried. "This one's fever has broken, I think!"

She felt Bela's forehead once again and smiled in her excitement—but only for a brief moment, until she realized what had actually happened. It took the doctor only a glance to see for himself, and he sadly shook his head.

"I'm sorry, Hanne," he said. "I will tell the mother."

Hanne could only bury her face in the doctor's shoulder, sobbing in a manner contrary to her professional training. But she could not help it.

"No, please," she said, finally pulling up straight and looking him in the eye. "I will tell her. This is something I need to do."

He looked as if he might use his authority to insist, but instead nodded quietly. And five minutes later she almost wished she hadn't, as she stood with Bela's mother on the sidewalk outside the clinic.

"Please," she took the woman gently by the hand. "Perhaps we should find someplace where it's more quiet."

"That's just it!" Bela's mother shook with frustration, causing the baby in her arms to begin fussing again. "There's nowhere in this forsaken prison city where there aren't people upon people upon people. But just tell me now: How is Bela doing?"

Hanne breathed hard, feeling lightheaded. Nothing in nursing school had ever prepared her for this kind of conversation.

"I'm so sorry, but Bela died. There was nothing we could do."

The woman looked at Hanne with a kind of indescribable horror and rage.

"You're lying!" Her voice rose to a panic. "She was fine just yesterday!"

"Sometimes these things happen quickly. And you know I cared for her too, like a little sister."

"You didn't care for her. If you cared for her, you would have saved her!"

The words cut deep.

"I'm telling you we did everything we could." Hanne tried to give the other woman a hug. "I'm sorry. I'm so sorry."

Still Bela's mother would not be consoled; she pushed Hanne away.

"No! I trusted you with her life," she told Hanne, the grief twisting her voice. "And you failed me. Get away from me. *Væk!* Get out of my sight!"

By this time the little baby in the woman's arms screamed and fussed with nearly as much fury as its mother. Hanne had no choice but to turn away, wishing they could have grieved together, wishing she had never told anyone she was a nurse.

29

Danmark, defiled and bound, here we've sworn an oath:
That we will never rest until we have won your freedom.
—KAJ MUNK, IN "DANMARK, OUR LIFE"

Steffen nodded at the receptionist in the Danish Red Cross office and tried to look patient. Perhaps he should have worn his clerical collar, after all, if it would have gotten him in to see Herr Madsen a little more quickly.

"Yes, he'll be expecting me," Steffen assured the efficient young lady behind the desk.

"Hmm." She consulted the calendar on her desk once more. "I don't see your name here, Herr Petersen. However, Herr Madsen usually arrives at nine, so if you'd like to take a seat for a couple of minutes, I'll see what—oh!"

Steffen turned to see Poul Madsen walk in through the office door just then, briefcase in hand and the wind at his back. He paused for a moment to grab some messages, then had to set down his briefcase before he could accept Steffen's outstretched hand. Steffen thought the man telegraphed his confusion rather effectively.

"Steffen Petersen." Steffen hoped the man would remember. "My father is Mikkel Petersen?"

It took a moment, but finally Herr Madsen's face lit up in recognition. "Mikkel! Of course! I knew there was something about your face. Although the last time I saw you, you were probably not ten years old, but you had a little pair of binoculars and you kept an eye on the birds. I do remember that. Do you still?"

"Well, in the city, you know. I have a feeder outside my office window, nothing more."

"Ja, ja. I know what you say. But please come in. Have a seat. What brings you here?"

Steffen smiled as the pleasant, round-looking man brought him into his cozy office, decorated mainly with pictures of African children and lovely Danish scenery. He would be the same age as *Far*, Steffen's father, since they had been school buddies. Steffen found a place in a worn leather chair, but couldn't get comfortable.

"I appreciate your seeing me, Herr Madsen. My father—"

"You know Mikkel and I were best friends all through our school years, don't you? How in the world is he?"

"He's doing well, as far as I know. Haven't seen him in several years."

"I see."

"Perhaps you remember he was chief engineer on one of the *Mærsk* ships, at sea when the war started. So now that most Danish merchant ships are reflagged, he's based out of New York. That's all I know."

"Ah, this war is crazy, isn't it? I'm glad they got our ships out, but now—what can I do for you?"

This time Herr Madsen looked at him and waited. Steffen took a deep breath. This is what he came for, after all.

"I'd like to be included in a Red Cross inspection team to wherever the Jews have been taken."

"Pardon me?" Herr Madsen lifted his eyebrows in surprise, then wasted no time getting up to close the door before returning to his chair. He lowered his voice. "What makes you think there's going to *be* an inspection team?"

"I'm assuming, of course, but it's very important. A matter of life or death. You might say it's a calling."

Herr Madsen tapped a pencil on his desk. "But you're a pastor, correct?

"If necessary I'll take a leave of absence. Whatever is necessary."

For a moment a flash of doubt crossed Steffen's mind. Surely his father's old friend would not betray him to the Nazis. Would he?

But Herr Madsen's voice softened even more.

"Well, your request shouldn't surprise me, I suppose. After all, it's no secret where our clergy stands on the issue of deporting Jewish citizens. I might have assumed you shared those sentiments."

"Yes, but to tell the truth, I hadn't actually given the matter much thought, until . . ." Steffen chose his words deliberately. "Until several, er, rather personal experiences brought it into focus."

Now Herr Madsen studied Steffen as he leaned in closer.

"A *calling*, hmm. Sounds like Moses and the burning tree."

"Yes, well," Steffen rubbed his forehead and looked away, and he didn't have the heart to correct the man. Bushes, trees, close enough. "I wouldn't compare myself to Moses, but I do feel compelled. Perhaps that's a better way to describe it. I feel compelled to help in any way I can."

"Hmm. And you think you could do some good?"

"I don't know. I wouldn't expect any pay. I would do this purely as a volunteer. And I hope you don't feel it presumptuous of me to say so, but I simply must do this. I must go to . . . wherever it is."

"Theresienstadt." Herr Madsen stood and pointed to a map of Europe on the far wall. He walked over and planted his finger on northern Czechoslovakia, not far south of the German border. "They've been taken to a fortress city called Theresienstadt. Or Terezin, as the Czechs call it."

"Terezin." Steffen came to see the little dot on the map for himself.

"I hear it's a sort of model community. One of my German contacts calls it a 'paradise ghetto.' Apparently they have recreation facilities, parks, good jobs, a music hall, a café— one could almost wish to be Jewish, eh?"

When he laughed it sounded weak, for he could not believe it anymore than did Steffen. Even so he continued, as if thinking it over.

"I must admit, I don't have many people asking me for jobs who can get away with saying that God wants them hired. And I suppose . . ."

Steffen bit his lip until Herr Madsen let a small smile escape as he went on.

"And I suppose as a pastor you would have a degree of expertise in dealing with people, as well as a good deal of stature in the community. It's not a bad resumé."

"So you'll include me in the inspection team?"

Herr Madsen held up his hand.

"I can make no promises—not even as a favor to an old friend. We haven't even received permission to visit Theresienstadt, yet—though we're in daily contact with German authorities about it. Between you and me, though, I believe it's going to happen."

Again he paused, and once again smiled.

"Actually, assuming that plans do come together, I would in fact need an assistant. Normally I would prefer to bring Marie along on such a trip." He winked at Steffen, who didn't care for the implication. "But I have a feeling conditions might be a little more rustic than she's used to. More to the point, she's due to have a baby in a couple of months, and she's in no shape to travel."

Speaking of Marie, a soft but persistent knock at the door interrupted them, and when Herr Madsen stood Steffen took his cue.

"Herr Madsen," came the receptionist's voice, "Untersturmführer Schneider here to see you."

"Send him in, please." Herr Madsen gave Steffen an apologetic shrug and walked him to the door. "You just leave your phone number with Marie at the front desk. We'll give you a call as soon as we know anything new, all right? I'll do what I can. And if you hear from your father— "

"I'll be sure to greet him for you." Steffen shook Herr Madsen's hand. "And thank you. I can't ask for anything more."

"Yes, well, I can't say I understand your motivation, Pastor, but I do admire your determination. Reminds me of your *far*. Speaking of which, did he ever tell you the story of how he saved my life once?"

"I don't think so."

"So we were on a bicycle trip together in Norway, and this is the summer before my final year at the university, before he ships out with the Merchant Marine, and—"

His voice fell away as he opened the door to reveal a younger Gestapo officer standing not a meter away, arms crossed. Herr Madsen didn't even hesitate.

"Aha," he said, smiling broadly and putting out his hand. "Untersturmführer Schneider. So good to see you. Hope I didn't keep you waiting."

In a stage whisper he told Steffen he would finish the story some other time, and Steffen was only too glad to slip away with a quiet "tak." While Steffen jotted down his name and telephone number, Herr Madsen chatted with the German officer like they were old friends, laughing at an inside joke until the door was closed once again.

What did I just get myself into? Steffen asked himself.

"You're doing *what?*" Pastor Viggo nearly chewed off the end of his cigar as he paced alongside a line of garbage cans behind the church while Steffen explained about his possible leave of absence. "This is most unusual. Highly unusual."

"I know it is." Steffen followed his mentor through the smoke screen, holding his breath as he did. "But I feel compelled."

"You *feel* compelled?" Pastor Viggo interrupted as he wheeled around to face Steffen. When the older man looked like this, it reminded Steffen of Winston Churchill, the British bulldog. "You would make this big of a decision based on *feelings?*"

"No, that's not what I meant to say. It's just a figure of speech. I am compelled, and it really has nothing to do with feelings. I simply must do this."

Pastor Viggo didn't take his eyes off Steffen, just ripped the cigar stub out of his mouth and threw it to the alley pavement. A moment later he realized what he'd done, however, and retrieved what was left of the smoldering stogie.

"In any case, your church needs you above all else." Viggo dusted off his treasure. "I can't believe you would set all that aside."

"It would only be temporary. Perhaps you wouldn't mind filling the pulpit for a couple of weeks in my absence, if it came to that. And if the bishop approves, that is."

Viggo only shook his head.

"That's not the point. Of course he would approve. But for a pastor to get involved with prison camp inspections—I just don't think it's proper."

"You're the one who taught me about *hupakouo*, remember? I obey."

"All very good to throw a little Greek into the equation. But I would ask whom you're obeying? God or your own desires?"

This was getting a bit more personal than Steffen had anticipated. But he had an answer for that, no matter how impertinent it might sound.

"You think I would actually want to go to a dirty German prison camp instead of staying here in my safe church? That I would want to take a leave of absence when it might endanger my career or my future? How can you call that my own desires?"

"It's the Jewish girl, then, isn't it?"

Steffen flinched as the older man let the words sink in for an awkward moment. Finally Steffen had to say something in his own defense.

"I don't know if it is or not." That was as honest as it got, even with himself. "All I know is that everything is all jumbled up right now. My ministry, my faith, my anger at what's going on around me, my sense of justice—and I suppose yes, my attraction to Hanne."

Viggo nodded at this, even allowing a slight smile.

"There's the first honest words I've heard from you. Good. So now I know how to pray—that you'll start to sort things out." He blew a large puff of cigar smoke into the air above their heads. "Instead of seeing everything through a dark gray cloud."

"Then you do approve, after all."

"No, you don't understand, Steffen. There's a big difference between speaking your mind from the pulpit and stepping out beyond the walls of this place."

He motioned to the building they both knew and loved. Steffen knew every bit of it, from the altar and its lovely ship model hanging from the soaring ceiling, to the catacombs and hallways below. This they shared.

"You can preach all you want from our pulpit up there," said Pastor Viggo, "and you know the kinds of things the Germans won't like. But what's the worst thing that can happen? They complain; you apologize. Nothing more."

Steffen thought it was probably a good thing he hadn't told Pastor Viggo about his visit to Vestre Prison, or how Wolfschmidt had threatened Hanne. Perhaps later.

"But once you leave this place behind and step out there, Steffen, you're stepping into their world. Are you sure that's what you want to do?"

"You talk as if I'm leaving the ministry. I remain a pastor. That doesn't change. It's just a leave of absence."

"So you say. When would it start?"

"I don't know, yet. Madsen at the Red Cross office is already working on the details for a visit to the camp. It may happen tomorrow, or it may not happen for months. But when it happens, I intend to go along."

"For how long? Days? Weeks? Months?"

"I, I don't know." Steffen looked away. Too many questions. He couldn't stand Viggo's piercing, blue-eyed interrogation any longer. "Perhaps not that long."

"Fine. You do what you think is right. As I told you, I will pray."

And with that the older man turned and shuffled to the rear entry, replacing what was left of his cigar in a vest pocket. He seemed slower than usual, as if his legs had stiffened or the conversation itself had aged him. As Steffen watched him go, though, he wished for—what? A blessing? Perhaps.

"I'd hoped you would support me in this decision." He regretted the words as soon as they left his mouth. Viggo halted and steadied himself with an arm against the door-jamb, and glanced over his shoulder.

"My dear Steffen, of course I support you. The question is, are you making a huge mistake which you will later regret? I think perhaps yes."

And with that he closed the back door behind him, leaving Steffen to stand alone in the remnants of Viggo's advice—and his cigar smoke. Steffen wasn't entirely sure which one now made his eyes water, but a cold breeze had picked up and now blew a swirling couple of papers down the alley. Steffen stopped them with his shoe and looked down.

One appeared to be yet another crudely worded warning from the German authorities, the likes of which had littered city streets for the past four years. Like all the others, this one warned of curfews and other security measures "for the safety of the residents of greater København." The usual trash.

The other, however, was a fragment of an obviously home-printed newspaper, *Den Frie Danske. The Free Dane.* He folded it carefully to read later. And after another moment of staring up at the Sankt Stefan's cross he shoved his fists into the pockets of his trousers and followed the old man inside.

His decision had been made.

30

I have found the paradox, that if you love until it hurts,
there can be no more hurt, only more love.
—Mother Teresa

Steffen doodled on his desk calendar with a pencil stub as he waited for Herr Madsen to answer the phone, or perhaps Marie at the front desk. Four, five, six rings: how many days had it been since the man had said they'd be back in touch with him "shortly"? It seemed some people had different definitions of the word.

"Come on," he mumbled, "answer the phone."

Finally Marie answered, Steffen was connected to Herr Madsen, and they exchanged the usual polite greetings. But Steffen didn't bother to bring up the dreary fall weather, or how dark it was getting so early in the evenings, or any of the small talk one would normally endure. He really only wanted to know one thing.

"So what do we hear about Theresienstadt, Herr Madsen?"

Herr Madsen sighed audibly. "As I told you last week, still nothing yet. These things take time."

"Yes, but our people have been gone for several weeks now. Some of them might be needing medical attention. We need to make sure they're getting mail. For all we know, they could be starving to death."

"No one is starving to death, Pastor. Of that I assure you."

"How can you assure me? All we know is what the Germans deign to tell us."

"More than that. We've just received a package full of postcards indicating that they've been received well at Theresienstadt, and that all four hundred and sixty-six have made it safely. They say they will accept mail to and from Denmark."

"Wait a minute." Steffen nearly pulled the telephone out of the wall in his pastor's study. "Postcards? From whom? And to whom?"

"I have no idea of the specifics, Pastor. All I know is that we've received the correspondence, and that it's being processed as quickly as possible. Meanwhile, although we have not yet received medical reports, we're reasonably certain everyone is all right, so far."

"Perhaps they are." Steffen did his best to keep his voice level. "But isn't that what we need to find out for ourselves?"

Don't push, Steffen reminded himself, biting his pencil. *Don't put him on the defensive.*

"Look, Pastor, they have already agreed to consider our request for an on-site inspection, and apparently it's going through the usual channels in Berlin. That could take a while."

"How long?"

"Perhaps a few days, perhaps a few weeks. You'll be the first to know, I promise."

Steffen didn't answer right away.

"Are you still there?" asked Herr Madsen.

"Still here. Just wondering what else I can do."

"We're doing all we can, as you know. But in the meantime, if you want to make yourself useful, perhaps you can help us put together a few packages."

"Packages? Of?"

"Medical supplies, foodstuffs, chewing gum, reading material—anything that would be of use to the people there. We have some of the supplies on hand, but if you could assemble donations from your parish, that would be helpful as well."

"I'll gather a few things and drop them by your office this afternoon," he promised. "Thank you."

Twenty minutes later Steffen knocked at the locked door of the Ibsen Boghandel, pressing his face to the glass. Inside the lights were off, though it was only three in the afternoon.

Odd.

He knocked again, louder this time, until he caught a movement in the back.

"Henning!" He tried to shout through the glass. "Open up. It's me."

He had to pound just a little more to prove to his brother that he wasn't going away. And Henning did not look pleased to open up the door, even a crack.

"What are you doing here?" Henning asked as Steffen slipped by him. His voice sounded hoarse and distant.

"That's not the question. The question is, why in the world are you closed on a Thursday afternoon?"

His voice trailed off as his eyes adjusted to the dim light and he finally made out his brother's bruises. A dark ring framed Henning's sunken left eye, while his right eye squinted through a puffy, swollen eyelid. An angry gash across his cheek looked even more painful. Henning held up a hand after he closed and locked the door behind them.

"Don't say it, all right?" When he took a deep breath, it rattled in his chest. "I have a mirror. I know how bad I look."

"What happened to you?"

Henning paused, as if he was debating whether to answer.

"Let's just say we ran into a little trouble last night."

"That looks like more than just a little trouble. Your face looks like it's been through a sausage grinder."

"Thank you. What a lovely way to describe it. *Morsomt.*"

"Of all the ways to describe your face right now, the word *lovely* does not come to mind."

"Anything else?" Henning crossed his arms now and waited.

"Actually, I did come to ask you something." Steffen decided to change the subject for now. "I'm putting together some packages for the Red Cross, and we'd like to include a few books for the people in Theresienstadt. We assume they don't have anything in Danish to read. Do you have any you'd like to donate? Damaged goods, perhaps? Anything would help."

"For the Red Cross, eh? Why didn't you say so? You going to deliver them personally?"

Henning rummaged around behind the counter for a minute, pulling out several books with covers that had been torn partly off, then several more. A few novels, even a thick stack of popular news and gossip magazines, *Billed Bladet* (*The Illustrated Magazine*) and *Alt for Damerne* (*Everything for Women*). He piled everything into a cardboard box and shoved it across the counter, then looked up at his older brother.

"There you go. But I wasn't serious. Please don't tell me you're actually thinking you can go to the camp by yourself. Are you?"

"Thanks." Steffen pulled the box across the counter.

But Henning reached over and held on to a corner of the box, not releasing his brother just yet.

"You didn't answer me."

Steffen sighed before explaining about the leave of absence and his new connection with the Red Cross, while Henning's expression clouded over, darker and darker.

"Well?" asked Steffen. "Don't just stare at me like that. What do you think?"

"I think you have no business getting involved this way. The Red Cross? Since when did pastors join the Red Cross? I thought you had sermons to preach."

"Again you confuse me. Once I was the big brother who was too cautious. The one you said was too scared to get involved and do the right thing. Remember?"

"This is different. You probably don't want to hear this, but there's a new Gestapo sturmbannführer in town, and word is that he's even tougher than Wolfschmidt."

Steffen gulped. Worse than Wolfschmidt? He pushed back the thought.

"It doesn't matter. For once in my life, I think I am doing the right thing."

Now Henning paced behind the counter, and it was a good thing the sign on the doorway read "lukket." Closed.

"In fact," Steffen continued, "ever since the rescues, I know I've been doing the right thing. I think I—"

"Would you stop it?" Henning nearly shouted. "Just because you helped a few Jews escape to Sweden, doesn't mean you're a card-carrying member of the Underground."

"I didn't help them all escape, now, did I?"

"Oh, so now you're going to act all guilty. That's what it is. One escape goes wrong, and now you think you have to do penance to make up for it. That's a stupid idea, if you ask me."

Steffen studied his brother, wondering.

"I can't figure you out," he finally told Henning. "No matter what I do, it's not right. In your eyes I can't win."

"Well, I'm sorry if you feel that way. So let me just say I'm proud of my big brother for finally stepping out and putting his high ideals into practice. Bully for you. But that's as far as it goes, okay?"

"You just want me to run back to the church building and hide behind my pulpit. That's what you're saying, isn't it?"

"Worked pretty well for you before."

"Oh, come on." Steffen groaned. "First you tell me to get involved, and now when I do, you tell me not to. Make up your mind, will you? What am I supposed to do?"

Henning just stared at his brother, then finally shook his head and pointed to his eye.

"All right. You see this? We were working on a section of railroad tracks last night. You know, modifying them."

"You mean tearing them apart. Sabotage."

"But my point is, it was supposed to be a low-risk operation. There weren't supposed to be any guards along that section."

Steffen felt his eyes grow wide. He couldn't help asking.

"Just like at the beach? What happened?"

"You don't want to know." Henning shook his head. "See, that's what I'm trying to tell you, but you're not listening. It's getting rougher by the day. You have no idea."

"I do have an idea. You forget where I spent some time."

"Spent some time, sure! You were in and out in a matter of hours. Most people I know only come out of Vestre Prison to be buried in a shallow grave."

Steffen said nothing in reply. After the shame of his release, what could he say? Instead, Henning's voice softened a notch.

"Listen, brother, I'm not going to ask what they made you promise or what they made you say. It doesn't matter. I can guess. But Steffen, don't you see? If they catch you again, you're not going to be released with a slap on the wrist, no matter who you are."

Steffen actually nodded. Henning went on.

"Just this past weekend a friend of mine went to do a job, and Germans were waiting for him."

"What does that mean?"

"It means my friend is probably dead."

"I'm sorry."

"Not as much as I am. And it also means there's a stikker inside our organization somewhere, and he's going to betray everybody if we don't find him soon."

"A Judas."

"You would call him that. But no matter what, please don't get any high-minded ideas. I was wrong. This isn't for you, Steffen. It's just too dangerous."

"Looks as if it might be a little dangerous for you, too."

For a moment they stared at each other, neither backing down. But this time Henning finally cracked a grin and allowed his brother to take a closer look.

"You look ridiculous," Steffen told him. "Although, I remember the time when you were twelve, and that fellow down the street did about the same thing to your face. You remember his name?"

"Ulrik Andersen. He wanted me to share my piece of licorice, and I wasn't giving in. But this isn't about my black eye or Ulrik Andersen. This is about you."

"Oh? I didn't think so."

"Well, it is. And I'm telling you now that you need to forget about this leave of absence thing. Go back to the church and do what you do best. Let the Red Cross do their job and stay out of their way."

"Too late for that, Henning. I can't stay out of the way. I'm going to the camp as soon as they'll let me."

Henning paced some more, pulling a handkerchief from his pocket to mop his forehead. It wasn't that warm.

"All right, fine. You don't listen to me anyway. Just stay away from the bookstore for a while. We're being watched, more and more. I don't want you swept up with the rest of us if the new Gestapo fellow decides they've had enough."

"You sure it wouldn't be safer if you left for Sweden, too?"

"That's it! Out!"

"No, wait. I'm serious."

But now Henning just pushed him toward the back door, past tall shelves of dusty books that needed sorting and straightening.

"So am I," replied Henning. "And I am not going to Sweden, although if you don't settle down, it might be a good idea for you. Think you can row yourself there? Now get out of here and don't come back unless it's an actual emergency. Don't ever call me on the phone, either."

"But what about those books?" Steffen dug in his heels, then waited by the back door until Henning returned with the box.

"Here you go." Henning plopped the books and magazines into Steffen's arms. "But let the Red Cross deliver this stuff, all right? You keep your head down and stay out of trouble, and I'll give you a call sometime."

"Thanks." Steffen nearly stumbled out the back door, clutching his books. "I think."

31

When I came to power, I did not want the concentration camps to
become old-age pensioners' homes but instruments of terror.
—ADOLF HITLER

As the cool, crisp days of autumn gave way to the cold dreariness of Danmark's long, dark winter, Steffen's life consisted of waiting for his chance to visit the camp. On those days when overcast eased its grip on København—which was indeed rare—a feeble splinter of pale sunshine might peek over the southern horizon around nine or nine-thirty, causing the sea of red tile roofs to glitter, and the city's tired residents to peer out of their windows, entertaining their own glimmer of hope that perhaps winter would loosen its grip. But then the slim bronze sun would only slip back out of sight, just after four in the afternoon, as if it had somewhere else to go and was in a hurry to leave. The only antidote was to light yet another candle and try to create an evening of *hygge*, that famous Danish coziness where people could enjoy each other's company inside a warmly decorated home.

Being a bachelor, however, Steffen knew little of hygge, and his tiny apartment proved it. Perhaps his version didn't warm the room quite as well. For him, the shortest days

reflected his dark mood and the distant hope rising and setting in his soul.

Even so, it helped that he could count the weeks on his
church calendar, and the weeks of Advent seemed to help
the most. From here he could look forward to the day when
this dark tide of waiting would indeed turn once more, bringing with it the lengthening days.

And as he prepared his sermons, his carefully veiled protests against the Nazi threat, he could look forward to Hanne's
brief but welcome letters.

From his sermon, December 19: "This snow will melt, and
the fog will lift." Steffen could not remember ever using the
word *Nazi* in the actual sermon. He would not dare, remembering Wolfschmidt's blunt threats and the dark shadow that
man once cast over Hanne's fate. Could Wolfschmidt's suc-
cessor do worse?

But as Steffen nearly shouted the words, his people
seemed to lean forward that much more, as if they understood his meaning almost better than he himself. "It's winter,
but spring is on its way. The green will return to the land
we love. Because this is the land of Bishop Absalon, and we
all remember from our school lessons how he defeated the
Wendish pirates, destroyed their idols, and brought faith to
their lands. But my question is this: What would our friend
Absalon have done today?"

Steffen had a fairly good idea how the legendary bishop
and founder of København might have reacted to the Nazi

occupiers had he been alive today instead of the twelfth century. But in his case, Steffen clung to his routine like a drowning man to a lifeline, in between sermons punctuated by increasing heat and fervent heart.

On Sunday mornings he would collect donations for the captive Danish Jews, usually small five or ten kroner notes slipped to him with a wink as his parish left the building after the Sunday service. He would nod and quietly thank each donor, then gladly discuss the latest weather report or the scripture of the day. Anything other than the heavy-handed, thinly veiled tirade he had just shoveled at his congregation from behind the safety of his pulpit.

These days the messages seemed to spring out of nowhere, as if he hadn't given them a thought and they simply leaked out from tortured corners of his mind, too filled with worries to hold anymore.

It did encourage him that people seemed to care enough to keep up their donations to the ongoing cause. And as Pastor Viggo noted wryly on his way out on Second Christmas Day, December 26, "The pews are filling up, my friend. Only watch what you say. There are Germans in the audience. Watch what you say."

❦

Steffen did watch what he said, and he never forgot his conversation with Sturmbannführer Wolfschmidt. But on January 9 of the new year he asked, "Generations from now, what will our children remember from this day?" Steffen gazed out over the congregation, pews overflowing with expectant faces. Whose German toes would he step on this morning? Steffen was as curious as the next person to see. "Will they look at the cross in our flag and realize what inspired us and kept us alive through this long winter? What will we tell them? What kind of land will we leave to those who will follow?"

Perhaps there was more of God in his "new" sermons, and certainly more raw emotion; Pastor Viggo thought so, and told Steffen as much. But Steffen explained to him that he simply wrote and spoke what he now saw in the weekly Gospel reading, and prayed that God might inspire the words— if not the exact word choice, then perhaps the general idea.

He could point to one clear difference, however. By this time he'd had more than enough of his old notes from years past, which he no longer bothered to consult and which sat tucked away in several file drawers. Now every week took on a life of its own. And although he still customarily wrote out every word in advance, after the service he honestly wasn't sure what he had really said, or how he'd said it, or even how closely he'd followed his own script. It was just done, come what may. So he could only smile and nod when congregant after congregant came up to him afterward, looked him in the eye, squeezed his hand, and told him to please keep saying what he was saying. And that they were praying for his safety.

"I admire your courage," one older man said to him after a service in January; he forgot which one. "No one else is telling the truth these days."

Steffen had to stop himself from laughing.

"Courage?" he asked. "Is that what you think it is? Thank you, my friend, but I never thought of it that way. To tell you the truth, I'm actually afraid."

"Pardon me?" said the man.

"Afraid of what would happen to me if I didn't say what I say."

———∞———

From his sermon of January 30: "And now we're faced with another choice. Who do we trust in? Our king? He stands for freedom. For our fatherland, *fædrelandet*. We all look for him when he rides his horse through the streets of the city, and our hearts are all warmed. But let's not forget he's only a man. Then what else can we trust in? In our famous social security? At our peril! We trade our souls, and in the end it slips through our fingers. No, there is only one worth trusting."

———∞———

Did his congregation really believe his words sounded that dangerous? That part actually scared him the most, since he wasn't always sure what prompted their concern. But he cared little for his own safety in those early days of 1944 and thought much less about it than he had in what he considered his "previous life." Only for the safety of Hanne.

So on one particularly chilly Sunday night in early February, he lay awake once more thinking of what might be happening to her at Theresienstadt, or how soon they might receive word of the visit. It had been months since he'd first spoken to Poul Madsen, after all! And this was the way he spent most of his nights, if not all. His weekly collection sat in an envelope next to his bed, carefully counted and, like most weeks, fairly substantial. In the morning he would deliver it to the Red Cross office on *Blegdamsgade Street*, and he would ask again if there was any news. He was afraid he was becoming quite the pest.

———∞———

Meanwhile his mind kept circling back to ugly imaginings of Jewish families huddled in dark corners, pursued by Nazis, while he himself traipsed on the fragile ice between waking and dreaming. And whether awake or dreaming he saw her face in the middle of the ragged crowd, blue and drawn and shivering, her hazel eyes pleading for help while he remained trapped in his ornate, carved pulpit, hurling rocks at the guards but still completely unable to help.

He sat up and snapped on his bedside lamp, heart thumping, to check the time.

Three a.m., and his pillow was soaked with the outpouring of his nightmare.

Certain he could not sleep now, he crawled out of bed and pulled on a sweater, then his faded brown house robe and slippers, and found his way to the little desk in the opposite corner of his bedroom. Still he shivered. And he stared at the piece of paper he'd left there earlier that day, his thoughts unfinished.

Actually the hardest part of his days was not the church work or the sermons, the visitations or offering communion or the baptisms. It was not collecting money or books or other supplies for the care packages, or volunteering at the Red Cross office every other day, putting together packages and preparing them for delivery. The hardest part was not hearing all the depressing war news, which was all around but which Steffen avoided as much as possible.

No. The hardest part came every evening, when Steffen sat at his little desk and pulled out pen and paper to write Hanne a few lines in the letter he would send every week. He knew the German censors would probably sift through every word before passing the note along to its intended destination, if they could be bothered even to do that much. So he chose his words carefully, and often—like tonight, like sleep—those words simply would not come. Chin in hand, he stared at what he had written earlier that evening, and the words danced before his eyes in the tiny pool of pale light from his desk lamp.

Though it's still only February, this will be the longest winter I've ever lived through, by far. But you certainly don't want to hear me complaining about the gloomy weather. Shall I complain of something else? As of today we are still waiting for word on whether our delegation will be granted permission to visit. Once more Herr Madsen told me "Perhaps next week." If I hear that again, I'm going to scream. But I read and re-read your letters, grateful for your encouragement.

There his partially written letter left off, and he wondered anew if the German censors would have a problem with him mentioning the delegation and their so-far unsuccessful efforts to visit Theresienstadt. Perhaps not. Did it matter?

"Let them take it out, if they want."

But since he still could not think of anything else to add, he simply added his "warmest greetings" and signed his name before folding it up and sealing the envelope for tomorrow's package.

And now he could sleep. Perhaps.

On the way to the Red Cross office the next morning, Steffen stopped by the back door of his brother's bookstore, careful to look both ways before picking up the box that would be left on the back step.

"Thanks again, my *bror*," he said to the back door, and he blew off a dusting of powdery snow as he hunched his shoulders against the cold and hurried the box of cast-off and damaged books back down the alley. Perhaps by now they might have word from the German authorities about their request to visit Theresienstadt. And if not, they would keep sending package after package, letter after letter, request after request. If nothing else, the Germans would know that they were not giving up on these people.

He wondered again if there really might not be some way to mail himself in one of the packages, and that would give the person on the other end quite a fright, would it not? He smiled weakly as he walked down Nørrebrogade, keeping his eyes on the sidewalk to keep from slipping on a patch of ice. He didn't bother this time to check which books his brother had donated, but he was sure they would be welcomed. A travel book, perhaps, or a lighthearted novel.

He wondered if she liked the poetry.

Hanne did her best to escape the cold by burrowing deeper underneath her blanket, curled up on her hard bunk in the women's unheated bunkhouse. If there had been more tears, she might have cried them. And if there had been other books, she might have read them. But the Jewish theology books in German didn't interest her. Hardly anything did. So once again she read through the book of poetry by Kaj Munk. Judging by the portions underlined in pencil, it had apparently been a favorite of Steffen's. She kept it down low, in case anyone else should notice, but it also served as a place to keep the letters she'd received from him, courtesy of the Red Cross.

The weather was growing even colder, he told her, and she nodded.

Same here, Steffen.

A sweetness shone through even his most cautious words—and she wasn't sure how much of the caution came from anticipating the German censors who would read the letter, or . . . just caution. Still, "I miss you" in any language helped keep her warm on those awful, dark nights, when she tried to block out the groans around her as she read his letters over and over, along with his poetry.

When he mentioned once in his December letter about preparing for the Christmas season, and the coming of the Messiah, she wondered more about what kind of faith would make a man risk his own life for hers, or if it was something else. She would reply in the morning, perhaps in between patients, but in the meantime she composed a note in her head.

Dear Steffen, she began in her mind. Or perhaps, *Dearest Steffen*. Better.

I read your latest letter four, no five times tonight, and it gave me hope that there is someone waiting for me, after all this is over and I am released. But there is one thing I was hoping you would explain, because I have thought about it every day since I was captured.

Your kiss.

Did it mean what I thought it to mean, or did it mean something else? Did you kiss me as you would a sister, or perhaps in a more romantic context?

"Romantic context?" She made a mental note not to use that phrase. Far too clinical. But still she had to ask.

Because if you have feelings for me, then I would like to inform you that I, too—

"Lights out!" roared a gendarme from the floor below as he slammed doors and stomped about. That would be his five-second warning before all lights in the women's barracks were abruptly cut for the evening. A few of the other women scurried for their bunks. But Hanne didn't mind; she snuggled a little deeper into her threadbare blanket, holding her book, her letters, and her hopes close to her chest.

She would figure out the rest of the letter in the morning, if she even dared broach the subject. Perhaps she might use more discreet language. But she would sign it—

Love, Hanne.

And so Steffen marked off the days—slowly, daily, one at a time, but with a distinct red pencil that eventually formed a crisscross fence across the face of his calendar and the days of his life since he had last seen Hanne. December into January and February into March. Days and then weeks, weeks and then months. Winter and ice into early spring and thaw, and he told Hanne about everything he could think of in his letters, week after week.

I hope you don't tire of all the details, he wrote one day in early March. *It's just that I've grown so accustomed to telling you everything. It wouldn't seem right if I didn't. Of course, it would be better if I could tell you in person. Much better.*

In the first several letters he'd signed off with the usual "With Friendly Greetings," but that had changed to "Warm Greetings" and finally just "Love, Steffen."

Because . . . did she see?

As a joke, he even once tried signing his name "Rabbi Petersen," which she thought was funny. At the same time, he struggled with the emotions that escaped his fountain pen, emotions whose course he could not quite predict, like an explorer headed down an uncharted stream. In Danmark, however, there were no uncharted streams. And just like anywhere else, they flowed inevitably and predictably to the sea.

So he unfolded his struggle on paper, and told her of his own Jewish Messiah, as gently as he knew how, so as not to offend. She wrote back with more questions, with what appeared to be genuine interest.

How is it that the Messiah didn't bring peace, if he came as you said? she asked. *Would a Jewish person still be Jewish, if she accepted your view of the Messiah? And Lutherans really don't believe in three gods, do they?*

He had to chuckle when he read that last question. He would have a good answer for her. At the same time, the German censors did not seem to mind such a romantic, theological exchange, since they left each word intact for them both to read.

But no matter how much Steffen wrote to Hanne, and no matter how much she wrote back, the correspondence only fueled his growing desire to see her in person once again. And perhaps out of his frustration, or perhaps out of a growing realization of what he really believed, his sermons grew even more fiery as time went on and they still had not heard from the Germans about their request to visit Theresienstadt.

How long could such a thing take?

Steffen had long since run out of patience for the process and knew full well how his impatience threatened his precarious standing with Poul Madsen. The only response he could think of was to work that much harder in the back room at Red Cross headquarters, filling boxes and covering them with brown kraft paper, taping them over and filling out labels. On one of those spring workdays, his pair of long-handled scissors flew across the paper, nipping his finger and drawing blood. He noticed too late that he had decorated one of the labels with tiny spatters of red, but he popped his thumb in his mouth to stem the bleeding as much as he could—just as Herr Madsen filled the doorway to the supply room behind him. Steffen pulled his thumb out of his mouth as quickly as he could.

"It's June 18." Herr Madsen waved a paper at Steffen. "I thought you'd want to know."

Well, no, actually it was still May. Even Steffen could have told him that, though he frequently lost track of the exact date. But seldom the month. Herr Madsen waved the paper again and smiled.

"Don't you understand? We finally have approval to visit Theresienstadt. This is what you've been waiting for, no?"

"We?" Steffen dropped the package on the floor. "That includes me—is that what you're saying?"

"Of course it does. Right here." He pointed to his paper. "Herr Poul Madsen and his assistant. You're the assistant, are you not?"

"Yes, of course. I mean, I suppose I am." Now Steffen couldn't help smiling, though he wasn't quite sure if that was the correct response. Would Herr Madsen mind him screaming or dancing a jig in the middle of the floor? Instead he fixed his tie and cleared his throat. "But that's just three weeks from now. I'll need to get ready."

As if he hadn't been preparing every day of this longest winter.

32
Northern Czechoslovakia
Friday Morning, 23 Juni 1944

My life in the camp was one of desperation,
hard work, hunger, disease, [and] being eaten alive by vermin.
Instead of plush toys, small children played with live rats.
—Charlotte Guthmann Opfermann,
Theresienstadt survivor

Normally the northern Czech countryside might have looked quite cheery in June, as the hillsides rolled out vast carpets of snow-white and golden wildflowers, and fields of lush green hay rediscovered new life in the first glittering rays of a morning sun. Little towns along the rail line appeared freshly scrubbed, and there even might be several birds he had not seen before. But as Steffen stared out the window of their southbound train, he saw none of that. He simply rested his head back against the seat and listened to the rhythm of wheels beneath their feet, imagining what lay ahead but afraid to anticipate the horror that must be waiting.

He did allow himself to imagine her face, however, and the memory of a smile he had kept with him over these long months, through winter and spring. Despite everything that had happened, would she have held on to that, at least? Perhaps. If God answered prayer, perhaps.

In his pocket he clutched the dozen treasured letters he'd received from Hanne while she was in Theresienstadt, and he might have read them all over yet again if he didn't already have them memorized. She worked in the clinic and found it a challenge. She missed her friends at Bispebjerg, of course, but there was nothing to be done about that. She wanted to know more of what he believed, wanted to know more about his Messiah. And she missed Steffen most of all. He smiled at that part. Perhaps she might have said more, but they both labored under the constant assumption that others would be reading each letter before it reached its intended recipient.

In the seat next to him Herr Madsen shuffled papers on the little briefcase desk he'd balanced on his lap since they'd departed København the evening before. The man seemed never to sleep, rarely left the first-class sleeper compartment they occupied, and never stopped working. If he wasn't reading thick, bound reports, he was apparently writing them—despite the constant rocking of the train. The motion seemed to do little to make the man's illegible handwriting any worse.

The only diversion Herr Madsen allowed himself was the hourly cigarette, lit precisely at the top of the hour and smoked for precisely three minutes, then extinguished. As a result Steffen could set his own watch by the regularity of Herr Madsen's personal habits, and frequently he did.

Finally, upon the lighting of the morning's second cigarette, Herr Madsen turned for a moment to his assistant and peered at him over his glasses.

"We'll be there shortly, you know."

Steffen adjusted his tie and nodded as he consulted his watch, though he knew the time without looking.

"Another hour?"

Herr Madsen nodded. "Let's go over again exactly what I'd like you to do. I'm unsure how much of our tour will be on foot. I assume they'll allow us to tour the camp in some kind of vehicle, given the size of the place."

"Approximately five city blocks by nine city blocks. Streets are laid out in a grid pattern. Completely walled on all sides. I have a map for you, when you're ready."

Herr Madsen smiled at Steffen's efficient answer.

"You've done your homework. In any case, please be sure to have several of your notebooks on hand, as I'll be calling on you to take notes as we go."

Steffen patted his small case, full of writing supplies and extra pencils. Given Herr Madsen's penchant for efficiency, it would not do to run out. Next to these he'd packed a small camera case with the Kodak Retina camera and several rolls of 35 millimeter film. A fine little camera, actually. He would not come up short.

"Also," added Herr Madsen, "you will take photographs of whatever I indicate—but only what I indicate. Nothing more and nothing less. They will probably also have official military photographers on hand, but it will be convenient to have our own resources, as well."

"I understand."

Yes, but the butterflies in his stomach obviously did not arise from the complexity of his task. Anyone could take notes and snap a few directed pictures. But the farther south they traveled, the more his stomach knotted into a tight ball. So when a white-jacketed porter stopped by the compartment a few minutes later offering coffee and small German cookies, Steffen could only hold up a hand and decline. Herr Madsen looked at him quizzically.

"Better take advantage of the offer, Steffen." He took a cup as the porter poured steaming black coffee, and several small round cookies besides. "You won't get this kind of treatment back home."

Very true. Steffen was sorely tempted to take a few cookies and save them in his pocket. But that was just the start of their VIP treatment; when they finally pulled into the *Bogosovice* station later that morning, one would have thought der Führer himself had paid the little Czech town a visit. Colorful red and black banners decorated the station, along with large signs shouting their "*Velkommen Dänuschen Roten Kreutze!*"

Welcome to the Danish Red Cross, indeed. A brass band of perhaps ten or twelve lederhosen-clad musicians played a lively German dance tune from the moment Herr Madsen and Steffen stepped off the train. Smiling uniformed Germans lined the platform, some of them clapping their polite, orchestrated welcomes. All that was missing, thought Steffen, was a champagne reception. Perhaps that would come later. For now, a little blond girl, perhaps six or seven years old and as cute as they came, stepped up with bouquets of daisies for each of them. Steffen smiled his thanks, though he wasn't sure what to do with his bouquet and tucked it under the flap of his portfolio case.

Close behind the girl a smiling SS officer in polished boots stepped up, nodded his head, and clicked his heels in Teutonic fashion.

"A very warm welcome to Theresienstadt," he told them, offering his hand. "I am Obersturmführer Karl Rahm, the camp kommandant, and I will be accompanying your delegation today. If there is anything you require in the course of your tour, you can be assured that I will see to it."

Herr Madsen made the introductions from their side, and they were hurried off the platform to a waiting black Mercedes. German efficiency and all that. But when Steffen held back just a moment to tie his shoe, he noticed the band had already stopped playing, and with their machine guns, two gray-suited German guards immediately poked and prodded the unfortunate musicians toward the back of a waiting

troop transport. The poor man with the tuba had the worst
time of it, and he was harried most mercilessly.

Late for another concert? Steffen didn't think so. But when
he finished tying his shoe and caught up with the others, the
meaning behind Rahm's sharp glare could not be mistaken,
even when masked by a smile.

"For your safety," he said, "I must ask you to stay with the
group at all times. This is imperative. And now, the city is
only a short drive away."

Without further discussion they were guided into the
idling car. And almost before the doors slammed they were
hurtling down a gravel lane toward the distant walled city.
Herr Madsen pulled out a neatly typed list from his briefcase
and extended it to the obersturmführer in the front seat.

"Here's a list of the places we'd like to see," he told their
host. "Although if you have additional suggestions, we would
consider that, as well."

"Of course." Rahm gave the list a cursory glance before
folding it neatly and slipping it into his own vest pocket. But
when Steffen craned his neck he could see the clipboard on
Rahm's lap. A carefully drawn city map indicated a route
marked in red, along with x's and times penciled in. He had
a feeling their route, and their schedule, had already been
determined.

And so it had. For the next two hours they kept to Rahm's
plan—to the minute. First the welcome center, nearly as
festive as the train station. Then the day care center, filled
with happy children painting lovely pictures and enjoying
a mid-morning snack. Their center seemed freshly painted
and newly decorated with child-sized tables and chairs.
Everything one might expect in a similar center back home.
Rahm beamed and patted a youngster on the head.

"You like it here very much," he said, "don't you?"

The little boy nodded and returned to his painting, a castle with clouds and a fire-breathing dragon. He looked freshly scrubbed and his hair was cut short, and he pulled at the collar of his little shirt as if he had never before worn one. Steffen bent down to ask a question of his own, and the rosy-cheeked little fellow looked up at him with a hint of fear in his eyes.

"Did anyone tell you what to say to visitors like me?" Steffen asked in a quiet voice. But the boy would only press his lips together and look toward the nearest soldier. The entourage was already leaving.

"A photograph over here, Petersen." Herr Madsen had already located another photogenic view, this time out the window and down the street toward the central plaza.

"Excuse me." Steffen thought he would try asking one of the well-dressed women attendants. "But do you happen to know a Danish nurse? Her name is—"

"Herr Petersen!" This time Rahm called his name, and motioned him to follow. "I believe your assistance is required."

The woman backed away with a moment of palpable fear in her eyes, shaking her head and muttering something in Czech that Steffen obviously did not understand. Well, he could try again with someone else.

Back in their entourage, they hurried down one of the main streets to a nicely decorated central park—a grassy area with fountains and flowers and a gazebo where another brass band played. So much music in this place! And though they wore different clothes this time, Steffen was almost certain the tuba player was the same one who had greeted them at the train station. Perhaps some of the other instrumentalists, as well. Steffen paused to listen, trying to discern what about this visit bothered him so much, when everything looked so . . . perfect.

Perhaps that was it. The concert appeared so perfect, as if they had been rehearsing many weeks for this day. Not that there was anything sinister in that. But the way the well-dressed couples strolled from bench to bench, smiling and chatting with each other under a canopy of lovely linden trees, just coming into leaf—had that been rehearsed the same way? Yet it made Steffen all the more determined to make contact with someone—anyone—outside Obersturmführer Rahm's tightly choreographed boundaries.

"Another photo, Petersen." Herr Madsen pointed to the gazebo, where several young families were enjoying the mid-day sunshine. Steffen stepped off the path, looking for a better angle, yet still keeping his eye on a young couple approaching him from the other direction with a baby stroller. He fiddled with the camera for a moment until they nearly bumped into him from the rear and he turned to smile at their baby—only to see an empty carriage.

"Pardon me," the young father told Steffen in hushed but accented German. "We were just taking our baby out for some fresh air."

Steffen took another quick look, just to be sure, since by this time Rahm was quickly approaching to intercept. But the couple's point had been made, and Steffen nodded as they hurried off without another word.

"Very handsome baby," he said, and turned to frame Rahm in his photo.

"Hold it right there, Herr Obersturmführer," he called out, holding his hand up. "I'd like you in this shot, as well!"

Rahm paused several meters in front of the camera, mugging for the photo.

"Perfect!" Rahm clapped his hands together and motioned them on to the car. "And now I'd like you to see something we're very proud of. The dispensary. It's quite well-equipped, we think. Almost makes me want to get sick here in the city, the care is so good. In fact . . ."

Steffen scribbled the best notes he could as they neared a neat, whitewashed building on one of the street corners. Red crosses painted on two of the front windows identified it as their next stop.

"In fact, some of the staff here are your Danish nationals," Rahm went on as they followed him inside and into a small but clean waiting room, then into what appeared to be a well-equipped exam room, with exam tables and bright lights, cabinets along the wall filled with supplies, and several doctors and nurses in white coats watching over their patients.

Steffen most surely couldn't hear what Rahm told them now, his heart was beating so loudly in his ears. He hid behind his notebook, pretending to be writing, as he nervously scanned the rooms for any sign of her. For she had to be here, did she not?

"A photo here, please, Petersen." Herr Madsen waved at the examination room, but despite all the bright lights, in here Steffen knew he would have to use his flash attachment. His hands shook as he assembled the unit, found a flashbulb, and plugged it in. Perhaps no one would notice his nervousness. Finally ready, he looked through the viewfinder to see a neat row of beds in the distance, a doctor in the foreground, and . . .

Steffen choked when he realized the nurse standing in the corner, holding back, was . . .

Hanne.

"Is there something wrong with the camera?" asked Herr Madsen.

"No, no," mumbled Steffen. "Perfectly fine."

He clamped down on the shutter to fire the flash, though with all his shaking this picture would most certainly turn out blurry. Still he stared through his viewfinder, hardly able to believe what he saw. But it *was* her.

"Shall we continue?" asked Rahm, already moving for the door.

Steffen could not make his legs move. He could only stare toward the corner of the exam room, where Hanne stood staring as well. He had to do something.

"Er, Herr Obersturmführer?" Steffen smiled apologetically. "I really need to find a WC. You have one in this building, I assume?"

"Er, yes." The officer didn't look so sure. "Perhaps it would be more convenient down at the recreation center, which is next on our tour."

"No!" Steffen didn't need to act for the desperation to show through his raised voice. "I really need to find a WC now! I'm very sorry."

"Yes, of course." Now the *obersturmführer* looked more understanding as he pointed to the far side of the room, a door opening into a hall. "No need to panic. I believe it's down there, and to the left. I'll have one of my men show you."

Rahm pointed to one of the guards standing by, but Steffen stepped up to the young man and patted him on the shoulder.

"Thank you, *Oberschütz*, but I think I'm perfectly capable of going to the WC without your help. You just stay here. I'll be right back."

The two-stripe corporal looked over at Rahm, who hesitated only a moment before nodding his okay. Breathing a sigh of relief, Steffen tried not to look again across the room. By this time Hanne must have already slipped out through another door. She had heard his little speech, had she not?

He hurried across the room and down the hall, making sure he ducked out of sight around a quiet corner just beyond the restroom door. Where was she?

"Hanne?" he whispered, hoping no one else would come down the hall from the other direction. Here empty wooden crates lined the walls, some of them labeled with the names of medical equipment. Curious. When he heard footsteps approaching, he slipped between two of the crates and held his breath.

"Hanne, are you there?" he whispered once more, and he nearly reached out to grab the sleeve . . . of a passing German guard. No! He bit his tongue, praying the guard had not heard him, and pressed himself up between the crates as the footsteps receded once more.

She's not coming, he told himself, and was about to step back out when he heard footsteps approaching once again. Only this time they paused for a moment, long enough for him to peek out around the corner, to see Hanne standing in the hallway, peering around the corner in the direction of the washroom. She must have seen him step out of the shadows, though, and wheeled to meet his embrace.

"Steffen!" She held on and did not let go, and neither would Steffen. After all these long weeks and months!

Several moments later she finally backed away to look him in the face. "How in the world did you get here? You said nothing in your letters about coming!"

"I couldn't. You understand."

"No, I mean, yes, I do." She nodded, and the tears filled her eyes. "I understand. And you understand why I haven't told the whole truth in my letters, either."

He smiled at her.

"It's all right. I could read between the lines, here and there. Did you know what I was trying to tell you, only I couldn't?"

A noise out in the hallway made them both jump. Perhaps it was nothing. He couldn't let her go.

"But this place," he said, looking around. "It's not real, is it? I mean, this isn't how it normally is?"

She shook her head.

"We've never seen all this equipment before. It hasn't even been installed, just rolled into place to look as if it's been there. The supplies were unloaded last night, before you came. They'll be gone the minute you leave."

"And outside? The scrubbed streets?"

"Everything is a show. There's nothing in the stores to buy. The theater and the community hall were put together for this tour, and for any others that come. I hear they're going to make a propaganda film. The playgrounds, the children's home, the bank, the café . . ."

"All a show?"

She nodded. "To make you think it's so pleasant and nice, and so to leave the Nazis alone to do their evil—here and in all the other camps. Steffen, it's not as it seems! If they were to let you go just a few meters off your approved route, you would see the real Terezin, where people are sick and starving and dying. But you won't see those people. I see them in here every day. Today they've all been ordered to stay away, out of sight."

"What about the park, with the young families?"

"Ha! The park. None of us have ever been allowed in there—only a few slave workers in a factory tent. It was fenced off with barbed wire until just the other day, when they brought in loads of flowers. The meals, the swimming area, the happy people—it's all a horrible lie."

The weight of her words hung heavy between them. But still he had to know.

"I understand the why, Hanne. But how? How did they get everyone to smile and just go along with it?"

"Don't you see? If anyone doesn't do just as they're told, they know they'll be the next ones transported to the death camps. The Nazis have already transported several thousands, we think to make it look less crowded here. We've heard rumors, Steffen. Are they true?"

Steffen bit his lip, not sure what to say. He'd heard the same rumors. But who could say? Most sounded far too incredible to believe.

"I don't know. But enough of the camp. I don't care about the camp. I care about you. What about you?"

She turned away. He noticed her cheeks looked sunken, and so much thinner. And she had been slender to begin with, back home in Danmark.

"I'm fine. They treat us Danes a bit differently than they do the Czechs or the Germans and the Poles, you know. Perhaps it's because of the pressure from home. From people like you. Oh, Steffen, there's so much I need to tell you, but—"

"Petersen!" Herr Madsen's voice floated down the hallway and around the corner. Fortunately he would not be able to see them unless he ventured closer. Steffen held a hand over his own mouth, hoping it might sound like he was answering from behind the washroom door.

"In a minute!" he called back.

"We're on a schedule, you know," Herr Madsen answered back. "Let's hurry!"

"Be right there."

But the last thing Steffen wanted to do was release Hanne from his grip, and Hanne wasn't letting go, either.

"I don't know how you talked your way into this camp, Steffen Petersen, but—"

She gave him another hug, but now he had to find his way back.

"Listen to me," he told her, gripping her thin shoulders. He could feel her shoulder blades. "I'll do everything I can to get back here, again. And meanwhile we'll send more packages. What do you need most, more medicine? Food?"

"Of course." She smiled at him. "The problem is, will it get past the gendarmes? They go through everything, you know."

"The packages we've sent?"

She nodded. "Everything. They skim off what they like."

"Then I'll just have to bring it personally."

He wanted to say so much more, but now he tore himself away from the exquisite torture—hearing her voice, feeling her close—but only for a few short moments! Perhaps he shouldn't have come.

"You must go now," she told him. "They're probably wondering what happened to me, as well."

He stroked a lock of her hair with his hand and slipped quietly to the corner, just to make sure no one was watching him come out from where he should have been. Then he turned back and kissed her softly on the lips.

"I pray for you every day, Hanne Abrahamsen."

He glanced at her one more time, and she let her fingertips touch his before he slipped back around the corner. And as quickly as he could he slipped straight into the washroom for a moment, not even bothering to find a light. He simply leaned back against the door in the darkness, his head spinning, catching his breath in wild gasps.

And then someone pounded on the door once more.

"Petersen! For goodness sake, are you sick in there or something?"

Steffen wasted no more time, just pulled open the door and stepped back out into the hallway with a sheepish smile, hopefully not overdone.

"So sorry, Herr Madsen." He straightened out his shirt and tie for good measure. "I didn't mean to hold you up. I'm feeling fine. Really."

"All right, good." Herr Madsen looked him over as if trying to decide whether to believe him or not. "Let's get back on the tour, then. The obersturmführer is getting quite nervous, and there's much more on his schedule."

33

NORTHERN CZECHOSLOVAKIA
SATURDAY, 24 JUNI 1944

*I remember my affliction and my wandering, / the bitterness and
the gall . . . / Yet this I call to mind / and therefore I have hope: /
Because of the LORD's great love we are not consumed.*
—LAMENTATIONS 3:19, 21-22 NIV

Steffen had not expected the dark cloud of his depression
to descend so quickly and heavily, even before they'd left
the Bogosovice station on their way back north, back home.
As Herr Madsen resumed his work in the seat beside him,
Steffen could not possibly pull his thoughts together.

"I said, number of beds in the dispensary?" Herr Madsen
paused from his writing and looked over expectantly at
Steffen. In a delayed reaction, Steffen shuffled through his
own hastily scrawled notes.

"Oh, yes. I'm sorry. I wrote it down here somewhere."

Steffen finally found the figures, but Herr Madsen wrinkled his brow and frowned as he wrote.

"What's your opinion of what we saw? Quite impressive,
don't you think? I was pleasantly surprised."

"Pardon?" Steffen wasn't sure if he meant the dispensary,
or Theresienstadt in general.

"I mean, for example, the dispensary seemed to have all
the latest equipment and very clean conditions. Honestly,

I had been expecting far worse, but I thought it all rather impressive, don't you think?"

Steffen paused before he responded. How could he pass along what he knew without endangering the source?

"Pardon, but did we actually see any of the equipment in use?"

"What are you saying? That we should have waited there and observed patients being treated? You know we didn't have time for that. Besides, that would have served no purpose."

"Yes, I know. It's just that everything there may have been set up to impress us, yet it might not have actually been used there. It might be gone even now, for all we know."

Again Herr Madsen wrinkled his brow.

"Gone? Why would someone go to such lengths? As far as I could tell, everything in all the other areas of the city was of adequate quality and in good repair, as well. The schools. The recreational facilities. The café and the dining areas. The performing arts center. The library. Even the central park. Did you notice all the flowers?"

"I heard the park had been barricaded until just hours before our arrival. Off limits to all residents."

"Who told you that?"

"Just . . . chatting with people along the way. One hears things."

"I'm sorry, but that sounds rather conspiratorial. I'm much more willing to take things at their face value."

Herr Madsen returned to his report, which would apparently include glowing praise for the situation and administration of Theresienstadt. Steffen wondered how he could bring light to the lies.

"Please, Herr Madsen. Just think about it for a moment. The kommandant had us on such a tight schedule, and on such a carefully planned route. We weren't allowed to go out on our own. What if things were different in the rest of the camp?

"I wouldn't call it a camp, Steffen. Besides, we could have been days exploring every last corner of the city, and for what purpose? I believe we saw a reasonable cross section."

"I believe we were shown a façade. A false front. I don't think that conditions beyond our view were anything like what we were led to believe they were. I suspect that as soon as we left, those nice facilities were all taken away."

"Steffen, please. You're making strong accusations here that cannot be backed up with fact. This is wild speculation only. I would expect a much more levelheaded assessment from you."

"Perhaps, but don't you think we could include some of those . . . reservations in your report? At least we could raise the questions."

"I'll do nothing of the sort. All I can report on is what I observed. And all that I observed was encouraging. I cannot go spreading rumors based on things you may or may not have heard from someone on the street. Can't you see how irresponsible that would be? Unethical, even."

"Wait, wait." Steffen raised his hand as he felt his own temperature rising. "I think if we're going to be talking about unethical and irresponsible, the only unethical or irresponsible course of action right now would be to allow ourselves to be used by the Nazis, and not to report on the whole truth. That's unethical and irresponsible."

By this time Herr Madsen studied Steffen through narrowed eyes. When he finally spoke his words sounded guarded and measured, doled out for maximum effect.

"Listen, Steffen. I'm sorry if you feel I'm missing something. But you begged me to be able to come along on this inspection. You said you wanted to see things for yourself, and we accommodated you to that end. Now you were able to see for yourself, and I'm just a bit puzzled at your reaction."

"No, let me explain. I—"

Herr Madsen held up a hand to cut him off.

"I believe you have explained yourself adequately and well, and you know I have valued your opinion. Frankly, however, I'm not sure what else you can expect, because there's really very little else you can do to change this situation, one way or the other. Unfortunately these people will remain in Theresienstadt, but now we've seen the conditions, and they are apparently adequate. This is what I will detail in my report."

"And you won't even—"

This time Herr Madsen silenced the objection just by lifting his eyebrow, and he went on.

"If you feel you've accomplished your goal and you'd like to focus all of your efforts once again on your work at the *kirke*, I would fully understand. Or if you'd like to continue helping with efforts to send supplemental medical and food supplies into Theresienstadt, you're more than welcome to do that, as well. The German authorities have pledged their continued cooperation in that regard. Although quite frankly, after seeing the place for myself today, I'm much less apprehensive about the condition of our people or the critical need to send them these things."

Steffen nodded. Herr Madsen just didn't understand, and it did not appear that he would entertain any further objections. What else could Steffen do to convince the outside world something was not right in Theresienstadt?

"I'd like to continue volunteering, if I may." Steffen wasn't sure if Herr Madsen would hear the whispered words, but apparently he did.

"Good. Then I assume your representation of what we saw and experienced today will align closely with mine. It would be most confusing to our public if they received mixed messages. Do we agree?"

"I understand." Steffen understood that Herr Madsen did not want to embarrass himself or lose footing with German officials. After all, he depended on those same officials for the goodwill necessary to conduct inspections such as the one today. He had much to lose.

But then again, so did Steffen.

After the Red Cross visit Hanne stood at the door of the dispensary, watching transport after transport rumble by on the main street, rattling the windows. She choked on the exhaust fumes but willed herself not to back away. A young man caught her eye from the rear of the fifth or sixth truck, and he still wore the bandage she had wrapped on his elbow last week after a minor work accident. She caught her breath and waved.

"Jakub!" She couldn't help calling out his name, and for a brief moment their eyes met. He raised his hand in a sad goodbye, with the awful look of one who knew he was being taken to a place from which he would never return. What was he, barely fifteen years old?

"So many," she whispered, and she made no attempt to stop the tears now running down her face.

If only she could turn away from this death parade. And she would have, except that she knew she must stand as a witness. Who else would do it? No one else walked the streets and no one even dared peer out from nearby windows—as if looking at these poor souls might bring misfortune.

So by default Hanne stood like a soldier, her stomach churning at the sight of each truck in the long line. And she hated the fact that she recognized so many, like Jakub or his aunt and uncle, who had worked with him in the gardens just outside the city walls, pulling weeds, hauling manure, and tending vegetable starts for twelve hours a day.

But they had played their roles for the Red Cross visitors, perhaps all too well. They had done what the Nazis had demanded, thinking their cooperation might buy them a greater measure of safety. Instead for their complaisance they had received a one-way ride to a death camp in occupied Poland, if rumors could be believed. Wherever they were going, most surely they would not be coming back.

Finally the last truck rumbled past and disappeared in a cloud of smoke, on its way out of the same city gate through which Hanne and the other Danish Jews had once entered. The gendarmes shut the chain-link gates, their dogs straining and snapping at the air from the end of their short leashes. After a minute or two a large rat scurried across the street and after a look around disappeared into a sewer drain. After that two small children peeked out of a street-level door, then chased each other around the corner. Finally a mother followed them outside, keeping a wary eye on the gate and the dogs. One by one this weary cast of survivors took to the streets again.

Now Hanne could finally turn back to the empty clinic, though her head throbbed with the awful truth of what was happening there—as if she needed yet another reminder. At the same time, yet another reminder stared her in the face: All the nice new equipment that had been set up around the clinic for yesterday's visits had already been pulled out and shipped away to its intended destination. Probably a German field hospital, or perhaps an actual clinic in Berlin—one that

did not treat Jews. She could make out the marks on the lino-
leum floor where they had been parked for their short display.
Dr. Janecek stood staring at the empty room, as if mourning
the loss, as well.

"They waste no time," he declared, hands on his hips. "Do
they?"

"Did you hear the trucks?" She motioned toward the door.
He nodded.

"I heard."

"All those people we worked so hard to help," she said, rolling up a stray bit of gauze and tossing it on the exam counter.
"And they're just taken away to die. What's the . . ."

Her voice faded away. She could not finish her question,
so Doctor Janecek kindly filled in the words for her.

"What's the use? What's the point? Hanne, you know the
answer. We all die. Some sooner. Some later. You and I, we
just do what we can today, and we leave the rest to *HaShem*.
He has brought us here for a reason, you and I."

She nodded absently as he went on. Like other observant
Jews, Dr. Janecek used the respectful term for God, *HaShem*,
to avoid misusing the Lord's name. Thus *HaShem*, or "The
Name."

"You remember it is written? '*HaShem* is a refuge for the
oppressed, a stronghold in times of trouble. Those who know
your name will trust in you, for you, *HaShem*, have never
forsaken those who seek you.' "

Hanne thought she recognized the words of a familiar
Psalm, but still she had no answer. He rested a hand on her
shoulder.

"I'm sorry, Hanne. You've seen much more than you want
to see, I'm sure. It's all *meshugge*, you know. Insane. So if
you'd like to take a break, I would understand. Even if you'd
try to find something else to do, I would understand that, too.

Like it, no. Understand, maybe. But you do such good work, and you have such heart. You're like a wildflower that has bloomed here in Terezin. We still need you here."

A wildflower. How sweet of him to say such a thing. She nodded as a mother came into the clinic with a crying child in tow. What else could she say? Perhaps he was right: *HaShem* had brought her here for a reason. In her mind there really was no choice.

"I'd like to continue working here, if I may." She nodded at their new patients. "The children. They need someone."

"I had a feeling you'd say that."

He smiled crookedly, despite what they'd been through the past couple of days, and helped her clear off the nearest exam table. They might not have the latest equipment, and they might not have many supplies. But they could do what they could, with what they had.

34

God creates out of nothing. Wonderful you say.
Yes, to be sure, but he does what is still more wonderful:
he makes saints out of sinners.

—Søren Kierkegaard

S o glad you made it home safely." Pastor Viggo was the first to greet Steffen on Sunday before the service as they both stepped into Sankt Stefan's foyer. Steffen smiled and sighed as he looked up to see morning sunlight streaming in through stained-glass windows.

Home!

"So am I." He shook Pastor Viggo's hand. "So am I. And you know I'm grateful to you for filling in last week."

"It was nothing." Pastor Viggo casually waved off the thanks. "I could preach that week's sermon in my sleep. And I probably have, several times."

They laughed at that, but Steffen had to rub a bit of soreness in his throat and in the glands below his jaw.

"You're feeling all right?" asked Pastor Viggo.

Steffen rolled the stiffness from his shoulders and cleared his throat. "Maybe just a little something I picked up along the way. *Ingenting.* Nothing serious."

Or so he thought. But by the time he stood up in front of the congregation that morning, he knew that the "little something" was perhaps more than just a little.

"Pardon me." He took an extra sip from a glass of water under his podium and tried to work through his hoarse voice. That only made it worse, and he had to pause several times before getting through the lackluster sermon. Afterward Pastor Viggo patted him on the back and told him they could certainly postpone the lunch gathering they'd planned.

"No, no. I'm fine, really." Steffen had always thought that he could talk a sore throat out of existence, and that denial carried with it nearly as much power as prayer. He put on a brave face. "Besides, they've all been waiting to hear about the trip. I don't want to disappoint them."

So he didn't, and he met with seven couples in the small overflow room they used for a modest library. Pastor Viggo's wife had brought extra pickled herring for him along with a rare loaf of excellent pumpernickel, which made it all worthwhile.

"I haven't eaten this well in months," he admitted to the little group, and it was the truth.

"But you have to tell us what you saw on your trip," said an older gentleman named Jens Lund. He was one of those who sat in the second pew every week without fail, intent on the sermon and singing off-key. "Was it as pleasant as we've heard?"

Steffen suddenly felt a little too hot around his collar, and he thought perhaps someone should open a window. He mopped his forehead with a handkerchief. He thought about what Herr Madsen had told him about not spreading rumors, and he thought about what Hanne had told him, and what he knew to be true. And Pastor Viggo stood up for him.

"The pastor is still a little tired from his travels," he said. "Perhaps he would prefer to bring us a full report a little later."

"No." Steffen held up his hand. "I've been home two days, now, and I'm as rested as I'm ever going to be. Just a little warm, perhaps. Is it just me, or is anyone else warm?"

The rest of the small group looked at each other and shook their heads. Viggo's wife still kept a knitted shawl wrapped around her shoulders. All right, then; it was just him. He sighed and went on. These people deserved to hear the truth, not a whitewashed official rumor, especially after all their faithful giving. He mopped his forehead again and cleared his mind.

"Herr Lund, you asked if Theresienstadt is as pleasant as you've heard, and I must tell you the truth: What we were shown was clean and nice."

The little group seemed to relax at his announcement. Obviously they'd been waiting for some good news, hadn't they? But as he looked from face to face, he knew without exception he could trust each one.

"But that's not the whole story," Steffen went on. "Because we were deceived. Deliberately and systematically deceived."

He made sure to emphasize the "deceived" part, as if he were delivering a pointed sermon. And everyone in the group seemed to hold their collective breath as Steffen explained.

"The Red Cross officials and I were only allowed access to a narrow section of Theresienstadt. They made certain we never veered from their predetermined route. It was decorated and painted and made to look pleasant. Beyond that there's a much darker side, where people are starving and where they live in constant fear of being transported to death camps in other places. Living conditions are harsh and medical treatment is poor at best."

He mopped his forehead once again, wishing he could shrink away. But he had more to say, and they deserved to hear it. He even noticed Margrethe standing in the hallway, as well, holding a mop and listening. Well, perhaps she should hear his report, as well.

"Perhaps Theresienstadt isn't the hell we feared. But to borrow an analogy from our Catholic friends, it is the worst kind of purgatory. It's the doorstep to the worst kind of evil you can imagine, and in Christian conscience we must continue to do everything we can to help those who are unjustly enslaved there by their Nazi captors. Jens, since you asked, we are being deceived. And I was sickened by what I witnessed there."

Perhaps literally, as well. He looked around at the wide-eyed little group of faithful people. Poor Jens Lund sat with an uneaten bite of pickled herring still on his fork, hoisted halfway to his gaping mouth.

"I'm sorry." Steffen held the side of his head to keep it from throbbing, but he couldn't help now feeling as if he had stepped into a furnace. "I didn't mean to overwhelm you all with such a grim report. And thank you, everyone, but I'm afraid I do need to excuse myself. Perhaps I do need a little nap, after all."

With that he dropped his napkin and pulled himself to his feet, a little unsteadily at first, then made his way to the door. Pastor Viggo intercepted him with an arm slipped around his shoulders.

"I'll walk back to your apartment with you," he offered, but Steffen shook his head no.

"There's no need. It's just—"

"Your face looks flushed, my boy. I think it's a touch of something serious."

"I'll be fine in the morning. But thank you for your concern."

He smiled and waved again at the others as if everything was as fine as he made it out to be, then felt a touch of conscience as the fever shook him in cold shivers. His head and shoulders ached.

Perhaps I shouldn't have been so stubborn, he told himself. Perhaps it would have been better to have Pastor Viggo walk him home, after all.

He paused at the street corner just outside the church to lean against a building as a wave of nausea swept over him. By this time his throat had nearly clamped shut in pain and he gasped for breath. A passing bicyclist slowed and stared but did not stop, but Steffen did not notice as someone else came up behind him and took him by the arm.

"You're not as well as you say," said Margrethe, nearly pulling his arm loose as she guided him down the sidewalk. "You should be home in bed."

"Yes," he agreed without question this time. Good thing he lived so close.

Now he looked over at her and saw something different in her face, something anxious—almost the way his mother might have looked at him when he was a little boy and sick with a stomach flu. But by this time he was having trouble keeping focused as his mind spun and his body shook. So cold, and yet so hot. He thought he remembered her asking for the keys to his apartment door, and he thought he remembered fishing them out of his trousers pocket.

But then?

Steffen would have written Hanne again much earlier than he did, but two weeks flat on his back in bed weakened him more than he expected. After that, all he could manage was to crawl out of bed and scribble a few lines.

Please forgive the delay, he told her. *But my brother says I needed to rest. It's too bad I could not have asked your medical opinion, as I'm not so sure about his. I am, however, much better than I was.*

So much could be said. She wrote back that he most surely should follow Henning's advice, that he should rest and drink plenty of fluids, and that such an illness—whatever it was—would be nothing to trifle with.

Trifle? Not at all. He grinned as he wrote the next letter, sitting next to the open window of his study and enjoying the warmth of July. *It's just that I have a favorite nurse who attended me before. It would have been nice if she could have been here this time, as well.*

Naturally she agreed. And so it went through the rest of that troubled year, week after week, as Steffen struggled to meet the needs of his parish, perhaps never quite recovered but avoiding the subject of his failing health in letter after letter. And as they shared their hearts more and more deeply, Steffen fought harder and more desperately against the darkness all around him, using the sharpest and best weapons at his disposal—carefully veiled but ultimately fiery anti-Nazi sermons from the pulpit at Sankt Stefan's.

35

*Never cease loving a person, and never give up hope for him,
for even the prodigal son who had fallen most low,
could still be saved.*

—SØREN KIERKEGAARD

Steffen hadn't meant to be prophetic, at least not in a personal sense. He simply thought the verse made sense in his talk that morning, though it wasn't the "official" text for that week.

From his sermon of 19 November: "For it was the apostle Poul who said he was 'already being poured out like a drink offering,' and I fear we all know his meaning here, and today. Who do you know in our city who has poured his or her own life out for the rest of us? We are near the end, you and I. And the occupiers must know this, as well."

As he delivered the final lines of that sermon he gripped the sides of his pulpit, fighting to remain conscious as stars filled his eyesight. He paused to catch his breath and found himself sweating profusely, just as he had some months earlier. Had the fever returned?

Now the entire congregation swam before his eyes. The ship model hanging from the ceiling seemed to have hit rough water, as well. He hoped the good ship Sankt Stefan was equipped with lifeboats.

"And now," he managed, "You'll please excuse me, as I'm feeling a bit faint. Perhaps it's the heat."

Yes, but in November? He must have managed to climb down off the elevated pulpit, and he must have made his way home safely. Those details remained somewhat hazy in his recollection. He must even have made it to his den, where he collapsed on his sofa. The next thing he remembered, however, was someone lifting a glass of cool water to his lips.

"*Tak*, Hanne," he told his nurse, smiling up at her. She'd finally come!

"Now you're hallucinating, too." Hanne turned into Henning, which to Steffen was not a pretty sight as he choked on the water. "Here, drink some more."

"How did you get here?" asked Steffen, recovering his breath.

"Your Pastor Viggo called me, sounding quite concerned. Said you didn't look well, just like before. But I was on my way over, anyway. Listen, can you hear me clearly?"

Steffen shook his head to clear his thoughts, then nodded.

"All right, then we're going to get you out of here, Steffen."

"What do you mean, out of here? Out of my apartment? To where?"

"Sweden. Across the Sound."

"Henning, that's crazy. You know I can't do that." He tried to focus. "There's no reason. And there's too much here for me to do."

"I'll drag you out of here myself, if I have to." Henning set his jaw. "I just found out you're next on the Nazi hit list."

Steffen paused as the words sunk in, though he didn't want to hear them.

"How would you know this?"

Henning didn't answer, just shook his head.

"Please, Henning. I can't deal with puzzles right now. My head hurts. My brain hurts. I can hardly think. Just tell me straight out: Was it Margrethe?"

This time Henning averted his eyes, giving Steffen reason to assume he was right about the church cleaning woman.

"I assume she needed the money," Henning finally explained as he stood up next to the sofa. "Germans pay well for information, you know. But maybe she was also concerned about you. In any case, she came to me with what she knew."

"That's good."

"Yes, but I want you to know I'm sorry. I didn't have anything to do with the decision to—"

"Decision to what? What decision? What are you talking about?"

"Don't ask me anymore. Believe me; you don't want to hear it."

"Henning!" Steffen forced himself to sit up, which made his head swim even more and his world go blurry. But he had to know. "You have to tell me."

Henning crossed his arms and sighed.

"Come on, Steffen. You know that people like her are in danger of . . . not waking up in the morning."

Steffen groaned when he finally understood his brother's meaning. It just seemed impossible the cleaning woman could have been a stikker—that she could have betrayed them, after all this time. Or that the Underground could have liquidated her.

"No." He laid his head back against the sofa, feeling as if he might faint. "Not Margrethe."

"Yes, Margrethe," his brother told him. "And if you stay here in København, you'll be as dead as her before tomorrow. The Nazis aren't going away, brother. We can't protect you anymore."

"They don't need to bother." Steffen grimaced in pain as he coughed and it rattled his chest. "Don't they know this darn recurring fever is going to take me out, anyway? All they have to do is wait a couple of days. Save themselves the trouble."

A moment later he gasped at the splash of ice-cold water to his face, and the shock snapped open his eyes.

"Don't you ever say that again, Steffen!" Henning shouted at him as he held an empty water glass. "I know you're sick. I know you've had a relapse or something of this scarlet fever thing. But you are not going to die, and you are not going to have that attitude. Do you understand me?"

Steffen gulped and nodded. If this was a nightmare, it was easily the most vivid he'd ever experienced. And if he didn't agree, Henning would surely strangle him, or worse.

"I hear you," he croaked, drying his face with the sleeve of his pajamas. Henning had certainly gotten his attention.

"Well, you'd better. Because I am not going to waste my time on anyone who has already given up on life. In fact I'm going to write your girlfriend, and she's not going to want to hear about your death wish. Because you, my brother, are going to live—whether you want to or not."

By this time Steffen could see clearly every bulging vein in Henning's neck, every broken blood vessel in his red eyes. Henning wasn't joking.

"Yes," Steffen replied, "but if I'm dead, too, they'll stop worrying about me."

"What did you say?"

"I said, if I'm dead, the Nazis won't care about me anymore."

But now the fog began to descend on his mind again, and all he could do was mumble.

"I could just hide under the bed, and . . ."

He couldn't finish his thought. But he thought he felt Henning's strong grip on his shoulder, and his help as he got dressed. Everything else faded into a dream, bits and fragments of remembering, blended with half-remembered fantasies, and there was no telling the two apart. He lost all track of time—minutes and hours, or days and weeks? He could not say, except he did recall something about riding in the ambulance. Later the cry of gulls and a salty tang in the air told him they were by the sea, then the rocking of waves and the feeling of being surrounded by fish told him he was even closer. Perhaps on a boat of some kind?

He begged God for forgiveness, for allowing Margrethe to be killed, as if he could have done something to prevent it. He called for Henning, and for Hanne, but neither of them could help him. Neither of them could hear.

And then he fell into a long, feverish sleep.

<hr>

"Another Red Cross package from your friend in København." Dr. Janecek pulled the parcel up on the table. It did not take much to tear it open, since it had obviously been inspected at least once before. He reached into the top of the package to pull out a card, and handed it over to Hanne without even checking.

"How did you know it was for me?" she asked, and tried not to blush as he teased her.

"You mean, like all the other notes? They're all for you, of course. And I assume they're still from the same gentleman. Rabbi Petersen, is it?"

He winked when he said the name. Rabbi, indeed. He knew who it was.

"Well, yes." But instead of saving it for later, as she'd intended, she frowned and looked more closely this time. Whose handwriting was this?

"Something wrong?" asked Dr. Janecek, and she quickly scanned the note for clues.

"It's written by Steffen's brother, Henning."

"Another interested party?"

"No, no. Steffen apparently wasn't able to write himself. He's very ill. Henning says he's been getting worse for the past several days."

"Hmm. Not good," said Dr. Janecek, craning his neck just a little to see. "And what else does the brother say?"

"He says he's taking care of him, but that Steffen had a terrible rash across his face and neck, and down his chest and back. He's doing everything he can, but . . ." The words had blurred and she turned away as she handed him the letter. Dr. Janecek scanned the rest of the letter and frowned.

"Fever, rash, unaffected area around the mouth . . . Sounds like he's describing scarlet fever. I've lost people to scarlet fever, but mostly young people." He read on to the end of the letter, then set it aside. "He should have taken him to the hospital for treatment. There's a very promising new treatment in the United States, I hear. Something called penicillin. They say it's an antibiotic, something they've been working on for decades. What I wouldn't give for some of that."

"They wouldn't have it at Bispebjerg," she whispered, and it was sadly true. What could they do for him at the hospital, that Henning couldn't do himself at home? Still she wished Henning had taken Steffen to the hospital, as well.

"But this is written nearly two weeks ago." Dr. Janecek handed her back the letter. "I'm sure he's fine by now. It usually takes its course in a week or two."

Usually, yes. But she also knew the potential deadly effects of scarlet fever. She nodded, but Henning's words played over and over in her head.

"I'm sorry," he'd written. "He's very sick this time. Worse even than before."

36

The tyrant dies and his rule is over,
the martyr dies and his rule begins.
—SØREN KIERKEGAARD

H anne thought he might have written her by now, but
nearly three months had gone by. And as she went
about trying to stay alive during what everyone knew was
the last days of a dying regime, she couldn't help wondering.

What's wrong with you, Steffen? Why don't you write?

"Hanne, are you with us?" The doctor's words brought her
back to the present, and he nodded at the arm they were
stitching. "Then please apply some gauze there to the wound."

"Of course, doctor." She would have done it automatically,
had she not been lost in her own world. And afterward she
would have apologized to Dr. Janecek, had he not mentioned
it first.

"We all have a lot on our minds," he said, washing in a
simple basin. "I take it you haven't heard from him?"

She shook her head, thinking at first that she didn't want
to talk about it. But who else would understand?

"Not since the note from his brother about his illness," she
finally told him as she cleaned up some of the instruments
they'd been using. "And that's been weeks, now."

"That doesn't necessarily mean what you think," he replied as he lowered his voice. "Everyone knows it's chaos out there as the Americans and the Russians advance. You expect a letter to reach you under these circumstances?"

"Well . . ."

"Of course you don't. We haven't had a Red Cross package for a long time. And you see now they're cleaning up the camp once again."

"I hadn't noticed."

He chuckled. "You don't notice anything outside the walls of this little clinic, these days. I invite you to take a look around and tell me what you see. The cleanup, for instance, can only mean one thing."

"Not another Red Cross inspection?"

"Yes, another Red Cross inspection. Let me tell you a secret. You know that strutting SS man who visited here last week? That *macher*, the big shot? Do you know who that was?"

Hanne shook her head no.

"His name was Adolph Eichmann. A very important official, by the way everyone acted around him. It was "Herr Obersturmbannführer this, and Herr Obersturmbannführer that. You see how he was making some kind of inspection? Then I heard one of his assistants say that everything is nearly ready for April 6."

"How do you hear all this?"

"I keep my eyes and my ears open, my dear Nurse Hanne, which is something you do not do. But here's what I think: Your Danish rabbi friend is going to find a way to be on that inspection team."

"I'm not so sure."

"I am." He clapped his hands dry in the air. "You just remember my words. You'll see him again in just a few weeks."

Hanne didn't officially allow herself to believe the doctor's prediction. But she couldn't help counting the days to April 6, especially after they were told by the gendarmes to clean up the clinic and make sure that it smelled especially good by that date.

"Look at this place!" The doctor held up his hands before the gendarme could leave. "Does it look to you as if it needs any more cleaning?"

"I'm just telling you." The young gendarme shrugged and headed for the door.

"Well, kindly tell your commander that the clinic will be spotless as always, and that we'll be looking forward to the Red Cross visiting here on the sixth."

The gendarme stopped in his tracks, obviously trying to recall when he'd mentioned anything about the Red Cross or their expected arrival time. He shook his head momentarily, said nothing in return, and pushed through the door. Dr. Janecek glanced over at Hanne with a grin and a wink.

"What did I tell you? Three more days."

Which happened to be three of the longest days in Hanne's life, as she helped clean the clinic while also helping Dr. Janecek and tending to their usual variety of patients. Most were older, these days, since the younger and more able-bodied had already been transported to death camps in Poland and elsewhere. But somehow April 6 arrived as promised, and with it the expected flurry of advance SS guards, German officers, and Red Cross officials in civilian dress. Hanne stood next to Dr. Janecek, presiding over a scrubbed exam table and a newly stocked supply cabinet. As the inspection team entered she scanned the crowd—

and recognized no one other than the camp's Kommandant Karl Rahm.

"The clinic, ja?" He swept his hand around as if it might be self-explanatory. "You are of course welcome to examine anything you like. Otherwise we will proceed."

One of the Red Cross men did seem curious, running his finger along the edge of a counter as if looking for dust. With his trimmed black beard and serious expression, he seemed to Hanne just like a government inspector. And when he approached a little closer, Dr. Janecek extended his hand.

"Dr. LaPorte," he told the visitor, "we're glad you're here."

"I wish under better circumstances." The man shook Dr. Janecek's hand and looked quizzically at Dr. Janecek. "But do I know you, sir?"

"We met at a medical conference in Geneva," answered Dr. Janecek. "Before the war. I'm sure you don't remember."

"I'm sorry, no."

"Well, that doesn't matter. Actually, I wonder if I might ask you a brief question."

The other doctor glanced around the room as if he might be found out, but he needn't have worried. The others—including the kommandant—seemed quite unconcerned. And Dr. Janecek didn't wait for the Red Cross man to respond.

"We're wondering about one of your Red Cross colleagues," he said, "a Dane named Petersen. Steffen Petersen. We assumed he might be with you this trip, as he was here on the first inspection last June."

Pierre shook his head, and Hanne's heart fell.

"I never met the man, but I was sorry to hear the news recently."

"The news?" asked Hanne. She did not want to hear this. She wanted to run away from what she feared would be his next words. He looked from the doctor's face to hers with pained surprise, then bit his lip.

"Yes, of course. How would you know? I only heard through Red Cross channels. I'm very sorry to tell you that Herr Petersen died last month. He was actually on the list of delegates to be included on this trip, since from his earlier experience he could offer a valuable frame of reference. I believe it was complications from scarlet fever."

He must have recognized Hanne's shock, though she turned away with her head in her hand. She escaped into a storage room.

"No, no, no!" she sobbed quietly and slid down the door to sit in the darkness. Why this, and why now? She had witnessed more death in the past year than in all her professional career combined. But she had survived. She should have been able to deal with it as a nurse.

She should have learned how to deal with watching innocent children suffering from typhus or being mowed down by viruses they could not treat. Yet a part of her had died every time a child had died in her arms.

And now this. Nothing had prepared her for this unseen horror, which wasn't even here where she could see it. As she sat on the cold tile floor she literally felt her soul deflate into darkness. Whatever small hope God had given her in this walled prison, He had just taken away. And whatever future she had hoped for now lay shattered in the wake of a casual meeting with a complete stranger.

A soft knock on the door she leaned upon made her sit up straight, but she made no other move.

"Hanne?" Dr. Janecek called her from the other side. "Hanne, are you in there?"

But Hanne didn't answer, just sat still when he tried the doorknob but did not force the door open. He must have known she was sitting there.

"They're gone, Hanne. But I'll be here if you want to talk."

The doctor was kind, beyond sweet. But at the moment talking was the last thing she wanted. After he finally left her alone she just curled up into a ball in the darkness of the closet, broken and desolate, feeling more alone than she had ever known was possible.

And she wept.

37

Don't cry because it's over, smile because it happened.
—THEODOR GEISEL

H anne knew only one way to stay alive after the blow she'd been dealt. Though it was actually more like a sedative—like morphine for the emotional pain. Not an actual drug, of course. But for Hanne, plunging back into her work during the weeks after she heard of Steffen's death and caring for the remaining children of Terezin was really the only way she knew to cope. It was either that or remain curled up in the closet.

"There, good as new." She patted a little girl on the head as she finished cleaning a nasty scrape on the chin. Funny how kids always fell chin-first. The girl looked up at her with puppy-dog eyes and nodded seriously as Dr. Janecek came sweeping through the clinic. He paused next to them, clipboard in hand.

"I know some young children who are going to miss you," he said. "Not to mention the rest of us."

"I'm not going," she said quietly as she helped the little girl down from the table.

"What? That's absurd. Of course you're going. You heard the announcement. The Red Cross will be bringing in buses to evacuate all Danish Jews, and that includes you. There can be no exceptions. You're required to go."

Hanne straightened up and looked Dr. Janecek in the eye. Dear, sweet Dr. Janecek. She did not mean to defy him, but her mind had been made up the moment she heard the announcement this morning.

"You said yourself I was brought here for a reason, doctor. Do you remember you said that? I still may not understand the reason fully, but I do know my place is here for as long as there are children here. So I am staying. I am not going with the others. That is my choice."

She parked her hands on her hips, waiting for him to respond. Finally he rubbed his chin and nodded.

"You're a stubborn young woman, Hanne Abrahamsen. I don't know anyone else who would choose to stay in a prison camp when she was offered freedom. But you offer a good *mitzvah*, and I will bring the matter before the Jewish Council. Perhaps they can make arrangements for you to stay."

She smiled her thanks, but he raised a finger of warning.

"But let me say this. It's going to get worse before it gets better. Do you hear me? The rumor is that before this war is over, we're going to see thousands of Jews come here from some of the other camps. And if they do, they're not going to be in good health, let me tell you that. We can expect all kinds of diseases. Typhus, too, perhaps. So I still think you should go now, while you have the chance. You may regret this decision."

"Thank you for your concern. How could I regret staying here with you? You've been like a father to me."

He smiled sadly and patted her on the cheek.

"I'm afraid you don't need a father, my dear."

She squeezed his arm for a moment, wishing he wasn't right.

"But come, then," he said, serious once again. "Perhaps I can still convince you to change your mind and get on one of those buses. In the meantime, we have a patient over here who needs our help."

⸎

As it turned out, Hanne did experience a moment of doubt as she stood in the shadows between two buildings and watched the last Red Cross bus fill with excited Danish Jews, just nine days after the Red Cross inspection.

There was a time when I would have been first in line to get on that bus, she thought. *But now?*

She dabbed at her eye with a handkerchief while some of the people sang the old folksong *"I Danmark er Jeg Født"* as they climbed aboard, "In Danmark I Am Born," while others waved to the onlookers who had gathered around the white-painted buses with the red cross on the side. And she couldn't help singing along, quietly.

"In Danmark I am born, that's where my home is. It's there I have my roots, from where my world begins. You Danish tongue, you are my mother's voice—so sweetly blessing, as you touch my heart."

Naturally she knew the words by heart; didn't every Danish schoolchild? Though she had not sung them for years, perhaps, they tugged now at her own broken heart as she watched Bela's mother climb aboard, her toddler in tow. For a moment the other woman noticed Hanne where she stood, and she paused for a moment before waving. Hanne returned the wave as the rest of the line pushed aboard and the door closed.

⸎

A minute later the bus pulled away, turning toward home. And the last words to the song drifted back through the city gates as the bus disappeared from view:

"I love you, I love you—Danmark, my homeland!"

Hanne didn't notice at first when a couple of the usual gendarmes passed by on the sidewalk in front of her. But then she recognized the younger one who pulled his partner to a stop.

"Say, you!" He looked up the street where the bus had just disappeared, then over at her. "Aren't you Danish, as well?"

"Danish?" She hesitated a moment, the words of the song still on her lips, before finally answering back in German. "I'm a nurse."

———

Henning paused in the shade at the *Assistens* Cemetery, scanning the surrounding park to make sure no one saw him standing with a bouquet of flowers next to his brother's grave marker. Though he would not have admitted it in public, he wished he didn't have to spend quite so much money on the flowers. Twelve kroner; what were they thinking? He could have enjoyed several beers for that amount.

Somehow it seemed quite appropriate, though—the prominent København pastor laid to rest in the same cemetery as Hans Christian Andersen and Søren Kierkegaard. Yes, it was appropriate. And so was the simple inscription he'd ordered, which he paused for a moment to read once more:

Steffen Arne Petersen, 1910–1945.

He read the rest of the plaque, a short Bible verse he had heard his brother quote more than once. So even on a gravestone, Steffen had something to say, did he not? Henning allowed himself a little smile and, with one last look around, he set his flowers on the side of the freshly placed marker.

———

38
SOUTHERN GERMANY
MONDAY MORNING, 14 MAJ 1945

Just living is not enough . . .
one must have sunshine, freedom and a small flower.
—HANS CHRISTIAN ANDERSEN

In some ways, the chaos that had spread across Germany after the official surrender 7 May made it almost easier to travel. Well, in some ways. Steffen found that by simply flashing his official Red Cross identity card, he could usually board any train he wanted. The trick was finding a train that was actually going somewhere, and that would continue on schedule toward its destination. Because with Russian and American troops scrambling for position all across the German countryside, as well as the defeated and dispirited German soldiers trying to get home, there was no telling how the chessboard had been scrambled. Not to mention all the bombed-out rail lines that made travel all the more difficult.

None of the celebrations back in Sweden mattered to him. None of the cheers or the spontaneous parties at the end of the war, none of the parades or flag waving. The only thing that mattered to him lay to the south. Or so he hoped. So he continued on as best he could, from Magdeburg to Leipzig, with a stopover in Zwickau, where he slept on the hard wooden bench in the waiting area of the *hauptbahnhof* for a couple of hours before catching another train to *Chemnitz*, almost to the Czech border.

Will she still be there? Is she still alive?

In all the confusion he had no way to know. All he knew for certain was that she had probably not received the last four or five letters he'd tried to send with the Red Cross packages, since all indications were that the packages had never made it to their intended destination. More than likely they'd been pilfered or stolen along the way.

Henning! His fists tightened and he wished all over again that he could strangle his younger brother. Yes, the elaborate ruse had worked, just as he'd said it would. For that he was grateful, though he'd wondered why they'd had to go to such lengths. Could they not just have brought him to Sweden, and left it at that? But Henning knew what he was doing, and at the time Steffen had been in no condition to argue. The Germans would not pursue an enemy of the Reich whom they thought had died. And in truth, he nearly had, there in a Swedish clinic. Even so, Steffen thought they could have done without all the drama.

My parish, they all think I've died! And Pastor Viggo, even!

He would set things right as soon as he returned home. Though he might still be a little weak after his last bout with the fever, he would make it home. But he had another, more important task to tend to first. And in this he took a small measure of comfort: At least the news of his so-called death would not have reached Hanne in Theresienstadt. Just think if it had!

Only, why had she not been on the Red Cross bus? That's the part he still couldn't understand. Her name had been on the roster, of course, but she was one of only two who had not reported for their seat, and the other had apparently died months earlier.

Hanne, where are you? He stared out the window at the vaguely familiar Czech countryside at sunset, trying to get his bearings. Seventy kilometers to go, perhaps? Fifty? He wondered as the train screeched to yet another stop, and he got up to investigate.

"What's happened?" he called out to a conductor, who rushed by him on the way forward. By that time other curious passengers had stepped outside into the warm early evening, as well, only to see a collection of trucks clustered on the tracks ahead.

"It's another broken stretch of track," said an older man, and Steffen feared he was right. They might be here all night. But when a headlight flashed on the adjacent road, he wasted no time jumping back inside and grabbing his bag. A moment later he had flagged down the farmer's truck and jumped into the back.

"Red Cross!" he told the farmer, who smiled back at him with a toothless grin. "Are you going anywhere near Theresienstadt? Terezin?"

"Terezin. *Ano! Bude to napravo.*"

Except for "Terezin" Steffen had no idea what any of the Czech words meant, but the old man said them with such warmth that he let it go at that and settled in between a roll of wire fencing and a pile of obviously salvaged spare parts, perhaps off a German vehicle, as it seemed anything German was being stripped to the bone, like vultures picking carrion.

Never mind. If the junk man was going in the direction of Theresienstadt, he would make it, too. A bit jostled and scratched up, but he would make it. So he held on, tried to keep his teeth from chattering, and prayed Hanne would still be there when—and if—he arrived.

By ten that evening Hanne was ready to collapse, and her legs throbbed after being on her feet for the past, well, perhaps fifteen or sixteen hours. She looked over at Dr. Janecek, who was still examining one of the newcomers streaming in from the eastern camps ahead of the advancing Russians. Many of them looked barely alive, shrunken skin on bones, walking ghosts. She rubbed her forehead with the back of her arm, trying to focus.

"You must be exhausted," the doctor told her. "Please. Why don't you quit for the night?"

"Not until you do."

"As I have said many times, Hanne Abrahamsen. You are Terezin's wildflower, and you are one stubborn Danish woman."

"And aren't you glad of that?"

They both managed tired smiles. But she shook her head as she looked around the room where several patients still huddled, waiting. Children from the camp had also found their way into the clinic, as they had the past few days.

"What did I tell you about staying here?" She walked over to where a small group of younger orphans had curled up in the far corner of the room, under one of the exam tables. "You need to be staying in your own barracks."

"But there's no room." A small girl of perhaps eight years looked up at her. The sadness in her eyes made her look eighty. "All the new people need a bed. The hungry ones. So we thought perhaps if we came here, you might tell us a story."

"A story?" Hanne sat down on the floor beside them. "I told you this morning, I don't know any stories. And it's late, don't you know?"

"Then how about your poem?" The little girl persisted. "The one about the flowers!"

Speaking of stubborn . . . The others chimed in, and they would not stop until she held up her hand and nodded.

"All right, then," she agreed. "But then we'll find you blankets, and you're all going to bed."

They seemed satisfied enough with that, so she recited for them the lovely poem from Steffen's book, telling it like a bedtime story. Though from Danish to German it lost a bit of its rhythm and rhyme, the kids didn't seem to mind, and would not recognize the difference.

"What is this, that's happening?" she recited for them, snuggling in and slipping her arms around their shoulders. "My stony winter-heart melts, this first day of spring."

They smiled at her words as she leaned a little closer.

"It poked its head through dark black earth, an azure blossom now gave forth . . . the hint of Heaven's call. That tiny blue anemone, I planted it last fall."

She paused at a tap on her shoulder, and turned to see yet another little one, holding out a small but beautiful bouquet of wildflowers and dandelions. A little wilted, perhaps, but still lovely.

"For me? You are so sweet," she said, smiling broadly. Perhaps in all the ugliness and sickness and death of this place, this *HaShem*—Steffen's God—had a touch of consolation for her, after all. But the little boy shook his head.

"It's not from me," he told her, pointing at a slip of paper tucked between two delicate purple blooms. "He said to read the note."

"He?" Now Hanne had no idea what was going on, but she unfolded the note… and nearly fainted.

"Thou little anemone," it read, "how great is our Creator! Love from Steffen."

Her confused mind spun until she looked up toward the clinic entrance, where a wonderful apparition stood framed in the sunlight, leaning against the doorway and smiling in the most pleasant sort of way. But it couldn't be.

It absolutely could not be.

"You, you . . ." She wasn't sure the words would come. "You're not dead!"

"Dead?" He looked startled as he hurried toward her. "Oh, no. Then you did hear. Oh, no! I can explain. Truly. That was Henning's idea; I had nothing whatever to do with my death. But Hanne! You're here!"

He looked wonderful—absolutely wonderful. A bit gaunt, perhaps, and nearly as pale as her latest patients. But she was certainly used to that. All she saw now were those wonderful gleaming eyes and the smile that she'd remembered each day for the past 581 days. Right now, though, it didn't seem to matter.

"I'm here?" she replied, allowing the children to help her to her feet and Steffen to scoop her up in his arms. "Ja, I suppose I am."

"Look," she said, pointing at the grave marker. "Someone actually left flowers on your grave."

"Henning thought of everything, didn't he?"

Sure enough, they could still make out the remnants of a bouquet, left there some weeks ago, by the looks of it. Steffen laughed and kept his arm around her shoulder. Now that the war was truly over, and Hanne was back in København, he wanted to be sure she didn't get away again.

"I'm glad he did," she said. A tiny black-headed sparrow flitted past, alighting for a moment on the marker before moving on.

"Well, yes. Though I have to say it's a little unnerving to look at one's own gravestone."

"As long as there's really no one underneath."

"Henning promised there wasn't, although now he wants me to help pay for the plaque, if you can believe that. He said I could use it later."

"But not yet!" she protested.

"I do rather like the verse, though."

They stood just a little longer, enjoying the late summer breeze through Assistens Cemetery and the smell of late summer green. Steffen had to admit his brother had done a wonderful job on the inscription, right down to choosing the scripture verse.

Og enhver, som lever og tror på mig...

"And whosoever liveth and believeth in me," he read aloud.

. . . skal i al evighed ikke dø.

". . . shall never die."

He looked over to see tears in her eyes as she left her own memorial—three of the small dried flowers she'd brought home with her from Terezin. She set them down carefully next to the marker, and even took a moment to run her hand across the inscribed verse.

"Ready?" He helped her to her feet as she nodded her yes. And hand in hand, they left the empty grave behind them.

AFTERWORD

A lthough this is a work of fiction, many of the scenes are inspired by actual events.

The overall timing of the events is as accurate as I could make it, particularly the days leading up to the attempted roundup of the Danish Jews and the final days of the war. I wrote these scenes with one eye on my history books, mindful of my responsibility to portray well both the agony and the hope.

The incident in which the Jewish directory was stolen actually happened, though it is dramatized in our story. Bispebjerg Hospital is a real place and figured prominently as a hiding place for Jews. Sankt Stefan's Kirke is real as well. Georg Duckwitz was an actual German shipping agent, and he did warn his Danish friends of what he knew to be coming, just as described in the story. His conversations and thoughts here are dramatized, though I believe them to be consistent with what we know of this man's integrity.

Many Danes did actually help in ways described here— from trading apartments to hiding their friends anywhere they could. The scene in which money was raised for the rescue operation was based on an actual event, as was the escape using a casket. The Danish Underground did actually use an ambulance—an account one of my father's friends, Court Nielsen, told me personally. He had been the driver and a member of the Resistance, until he had to flee to Sweden. And of course Danish Jews were actually taken to Sweden much as described. The way that ordinary Danes helped their Jewish neighbors—despite the danger—continues to inspire the world today.

Conditions at the Terezin camp are based on eyewitness accounts, and the Danish Red Cross inspection occurred much as the book describes it. There was no assistant along for the inspection, however. In the final days of the war, the Red Cross evacuated Danish Jews from the camp just as described. I remain full of respect and admiration for the courage of those Jews—both in Denmark and beyond—who endured the nightmare of those difficult days.

I've also attempted to blend smaller, actual details in my narrative. For example, the Danish bishop's letter of protest is word-for-word accurate, and some of the radio broadcast wording is borrowed from actual sources, as well. There are too many others to list.

In all of this, I am indebted to the support of so many people. To fellow writer Bill Myers, who first suggested this book years ago. To my Danish parents, Knud and Evy Elmer, whose stories from their childhood years inspired me to write the "Young Underground" series for children, and eventually this book. To my editor Barbara Scott, who caught the vision early on and who championed *Wildflowers of Terezin* from the start. To Tricia Goyer, who gladly loaned me many books on the Terezin camp from her collection. To my wife, Ronda, who tirelessly read through first drafts and who always kept me going. And to my Danish friend Mogens Maagaard, whose unwavering enthusiasm and support inspired me as we brought characters to life. Mogens gladly provided Danish research materials, insight into the Danish church, excellent ideas and encouragement.

To all of you, *tusind tak*. A thousand thanks.

—Robert Elmer

Discussion Questions

1. As a nurse, Hanne wrestles with her sense of duty and compassion on one hand, and her instinct for survival on the other. Is she able to balance the two, and if so, how?

2. At first, Steffen calls resistance workers "troublemakers" who "shouldn't rush their own funerals." Yet just a few chapters later, he finds himself deeply involved in the Resistance movement. How does he switch sides? What brings about his change? Is it really, as Henning suggests in chapter 12, all about "the girl"? Describe how his outlook shifts from the beginning to the end of the book.

3. Describe a time when you have found yourself switching sides, like Steffen. What caused you to change?

4. This jumps ahead to chapter 31, but again relates to change: What's the difference between Steffen's "old" sermons and his "new" ones?

5. The epigram (quote) that opens chapter 3 says that for the Danish people, "our form of heroism is cheerful defiance with the least possible show." Describe a place in the story where Hanne or Steffen demonstrates this kind of attitude.

6. At one point Henning criticizes his brother for being too cautious. Later, he worries that Steffen is being reckless and tells him to stay in his church. What makes him give such contradictory advice? Is he being consistent in his concerns?

7. Who do you think takes the greatest risks—Steffen, Hanne, or Henning? Why?

8. Georg Duckwitz was an actual historical figure. In the story, what do you think prompts him to warn his Danish friends? Do you think you could have done the same if you were in his position? Why or why not?

9. In chapter 4, Henning warns Steffen about his association with Hanne—a woman who does not share the same faith. He asks, "Isn't there some kind of church law against pastors dating Jewish nurses?" How would you have responded if you were Steffen?

10. In chapter 6, we learn of Hanne's younger sister Marianne, who had died years before. In what ways did Marianne affect Hanne's Jewish faith? Has a family member ever affected your faith, even without knowing it? Describe what happened.

11. In chapter 7, Hanne faces discouragement after assisting in an operation on a young member of the Resistance. (He was, by the way, the same one who helped Steffen in an earlier scene.) After the boy dies on the operating table, she thinks "If she could just lock the door and keep it locked until this was all over . . . perhaps she could better survive the nightmare." Do you think she was justified in feeling this way? When have you ever felt like that? Share some of the circumstances. How well does it work to hide?

12. At the end of chapter 15, Steffen "rowed away from the scent of freedom and back to the terror before he could change his mind." Why do you think he returns? If you've

ever faced an opportunity to escape trouble, but didn't, explain what made you stay.

13. In chapter 9, Hanne refuses Aron's demand that she come with him into hiding. What gives her the courage to say no? Do you think she makes the right decision? Why or why not?

14. In chapter 11, Hanne readily admits to Steffen that she is Jewish. But in chapter 37, when guards ask if she's Danish, she simply says she is a nurse. What is she? Jewish, Danish, or a nurse? How do you know? What factors contribute to her conflicted self-identity? Have you have experienced anything like that? Describe your situation.

15. Steffen reads aloud a letter from the Danish bishops (chapter 16) in which they assert that "we should obey God rather than man." How does Hanne or Steffen follow this advice? Give a modern-day example where the same principle might apply in your own life.

16. After the "outrageous fundraising" scene (chapter 17), Hanne and Steffen seem closer than ever. What really happens to cause this?

17. In chapter 22, Pastor Viggo discusses his way of dealing with and serving church families after his retirement. Do you think he takes the correct approach? Why or why not? Describe a time in your life when holding back worked better than charging ahead.

18. Margrethe, the church janitor, is a tragic figure in this story. Do you think the Resistance is right to do what they did?

What would you have done if you were a Resistance leader faced with her betrayal? Can you think of other times where the momentum of consequences outweighs a change of heart?

19. When Steffen is jailed (chapter 26), he tells his German captors what he thinks they want to hear. Is he justified in doing so? Why or why not? What would you have done in a similar situation?

20. In chapter 37, Bela's mother waves to Hanne as she is boarding the bus for home. What changes between the two women and how? What makes the difference?

21. Describe Hanne's attitude toward imprisonment. What does Doctor Janecek call her in chapter 33, and what kind of example is that for us?

Want to learn more about author
Robert Elmer and check out other great
fiction from Abingdon Press?

Sign up for our fiction newsletter at
www.AbingdonPress.com
to read interviews with your favorite authors, find tips
for starting a reading group, and stay posted on what
new titles are on the horizon. It's a place to connect
with other fiction readers or post a
comment about this book.

Be sure to visit Robert online!

www.robertelmerbooks.com